A NEW DAWN

REGINALD ANDAH

ISBN 978-1-63961-470-7 (hardcover)
ISBN 978-1-63961-471-4 (digital)

Christian Faith Publishing, Inc.
832 Park Avenue
Meadville, PA 16335
www.christianfaithpublishing.com

Printed in the United States of America

NEW

DAWN

CHAPTER 1

I WONDERED SOMETIMES *when we knew our race would fall. Scientists may say it was when our folly got the best of us. Theologists may argue that we were doomed as soon as Eve disobeyed. I got a much simpler theory. I think it's just when we gave up faith.*

A soft yet distinctive hum peered my eyes open. "I can tell you're still buried in your thoughts," Leona whispered after she stopped the melody, caressing my shoulder.

A white haze surrounded my vision as I woke up from bed. I never got tired of looking at her. Before I met Leona, I thought loyalty was dead. However, trying times make a good catalyst, allowing people to see what's truly important. When I look into her eyes, all I see is pain. But when they look back at mine, I see a faint flicker of hope. All it takes is that instant of our pupils locking onto each other to give me the strength to wake up. Her touch is electric. As her forest-green irises console my thoughts, every nerve in my body yearns to feel more. The fair skin she has that's been tested rugged by battles, leaving scars in its wake, still radiates beautifully to me. I'd like nothing more than to run my tired fingers through her brunette hair and stay in bed, consoling each other. But every time I woke up, I knew I'd have to prepare myself for another fight.

"What time is it?" I asked as she stood up from my makeshift bed. She had on a stitched-up shirt with cargo pants that had a hole in the knee.

"Does it really matter? It's not like we have control of our lives anymore anyway."

As she said this, I stared at the sea of people sleeping on the cold, manufactured floor like I was. After getting that euphoric feeling seeing Leona, I'd be brought right back down to reality as I saw the people lie there. Though we were alive, when I saw the bodies of strangers, malnourished on the floor, I couldn't help but feel as if we were already dead—at least on the inside.

"Good point."

"Take a bath. You know you got to wake up super early to avoid a long line."

"Yeah. Thanks for looking out."

"Don't mention it. You got my back. I got yours."

"I meant...for always looking out," I said as I briefly stared into her eyes again. She stared back into mine, lost in a momentary trance. We quickly averted our gaze.

I walked away, trying to avoid the awkward tension between us. I tiptoed around the warm bodies lying and snoring on the floor. The sleeping area was huge, along with the rest of the ship. The amount of people it could house was unreal to me.

"Pssst," I heard her call as I headed away. "I'll save the usual spot for you at breakfast," she whispered.

I nodded.

As I made my way across the room, trying not to wake people, the overwhelming site before me always took me for a loop. The world used to be filled with oceans. The view was a lively blue hue with natural earth colors of green and brown in large areas. But as I looked out the window of the huge spacecraft we were in, I saw more shades of brown, displaying barren wasteland from space. All of it, our beautiful planet, had been shot to hell.

I sighed, depressed as I made my way to the bathroom stalls. It had a strange aroma of soap mixed with stench. Water was a luxury. We did everything we could to save what little we had. Expeditions helped us slightly as we found fresh water to bring back aboard the ship. However, it's never easy to transport. With the blueprints for the water renewal system we had on earth, engineers were able to build a new type of water infiltration integrated with the ship. But that was also a luxury since it ran on power. Due to the electricity we had to preserve, fresh water was only given by the half cup to drink during mealtimes. Like the past ages in our history, most of us didn't shower with clean bathwater unless the ones in the tubs became murky. In fact, not bathing for a couple of days was encouraged to ration water supply.

Smack!

I jumped back, startled. A man came from around the corner of the entrance to the men's facilities. He smacked the side of a wall for leverage as he made his way out of the bathing area. I saw a few more guys in the stalls glance at me before returning to their business. The guy who was still grasping onto the wall used a walking chair in front of him to move. One of his legs were gone from the knee down, tightly wrapped with bandages. It looked wet from a shower, and spots of red were visibly clear.

"Ah! Sorry. Didn't mean to scare you," he said in a tired voice. The pain reflected in his movement and the way he spoke. "Still getting used to this thing. Gotta keep fighting the good fight, right?"

"Yeah. I'm just wondering if it'll ever end."

"Heh. I heard that," he replied as he made his way back to the sleeping area.

I looked to my right and saw spots of blood on the steel floor from a shower. A sign read, "Showers for Injured Only to Prevent the Spread of Bloodborne Pathogens." As I made my way to the mirror with a sink below it, I saw another man to the next sink over. He caught my attention a little, using his finger to brush his teeth. Some of the squeaky-like sounds it made as he rubbed vigorously made me cringe a little on the inside. I pulled out my brush from my pocket. It was inside a plastic bag I made sure to keep on me at all times, along with soap and toothpaste. A lot of people stole on this ship as you slept. Even while unconscious, you had to fight tooth and nail just to keep what you had. People never let you forget for a second that we were all fighting for our lives.

"That's smart," the man next to me said, spitting in the sink. He glanced over at my little bag. "I kept mine next to my pillow, thinking no one would dare take it while it's next to me, even if I was sleeping. Bad move on my part."

"That sucks, man," I said, squeezing my paste on the tip of the brush's bristles.

"Yeah, but what doesn't suck about this place?" he said. "The plastic bag does keep your stuff in an enclosed space, causing bacteria to fester. But heck, it's not like anything around here is hygienic either."

"I'm guessing you were a doctor before this?" I asked as I paused between brushing. My voice sounded funny as I tried to talk without saliva and paste dripping from my mouth.

"Dentist, actually."

He noticed me glance at his finger he just used to rub his dingy teeth.

"Oh, yeah…" He chortled as he wagged the same finger in a playful gesture. "Ironic, isn't it? But I suppose none of us are the same people we were before."

"Heh, you can say that again," I said after I spat out in the sink.

"Who were you before all this if you don't mind me asking?"

"I—"

Bzzzzz!

The sound of an intercom blasted over the speakers placed throughout the ship.

The man banged his hand on the side of the sink. "Damn it! It's been seven months, and they still haven't fixed this thing? How many times do we have to hear that the world is ending?!"

"I think they purposely repeat this broadcast every morning."

"For what?"

"To remind us why and what we're fighting for."

He let out a huge sigh as I said this. I saw him take a moment to reflect the weight of the situation. As he turned to walk away from the bathroom, I saw him in the reflection of my mirror pass me a quick wave. I nodded back in response. For a moment, I was alone, listening to the words of the broadcast. It was always that female voice with the Thai accent.

"A lot of you may be confused as you wake up from your cryostasis and understandably so. During your stasis, your bodies have been acclimated to a state similar to that of a coma to make your transition more manageable. Due to your suspended state, your brain needs time to adjust. Do not panic. Amnesia is a common side effect to the stasis program you volunteered for. After time passes, the memories you had will return. However, we must divulge information to keep you fully aware of the situation that has been set before us. Before continuing, there is a high chance that what you're about to hear may cause traumatic stress and rapidly shift your confusion to a more heightened, anxious frame of mind. We have armed military personnel stationed in key positions around the craft, instructed to subdue you should you become a danger to yourself and the people around you. After hearing the plight of the world, if you seek psychiatric help, we have professionals on board we can direct you to."

As I listened to the rest of the broadcast, I took a good look in the mirror. Worry lines plastered my face. I grew a rough, rugged beard for the last seven months after I woke up from my stasis. My eyes were a deep, dark brown. When I looked at myself, I didn't even realize who was looking back at me anymore. I got thinner, my hair was scraggly, and my body ached from labor. I was slightly giddy when I saw a little muscle tone on my arms and chest. From what I can remember, I didn't have any type of muscle definition back on Earth. I was a little chubby. I always dreamed of losing weight and getting the killer body I've seen portrayed in media. But as I saw my skin start to hug the outer frame of my rib cage, begging for more nutrients, my giddiness faded. I swear, you have to laugh at the irony of life sometimes, or you'll make yourself crazy thinking about how cruel fate can be. I thought about my responsibility as the broadcast continued.

"Our world's scientific and religious beliefs have been at odds for centuries. However, in the year 2022, it was revealed that government facilitated projects have been conducted with taxpayers' money to finally find the answer to our existence. No authority was given by the branches of government nor the people to proceed with such projects. However, different sects within the government became privately institutionalized and funded scientific ventures to find this answer on their own. These groups of people had great influence and acted in their own self-interests. As a result, they stumbled upon a breakthrough too great to conceal. In the year 2024, an entirely new species was introduced to the world as extraterrestrial lifeforms. However, these lifeforms did not seek peace with us. In fact, they were something else entirely that was void of life."

As I continued to listen, I made my way to a bathtub and looked at the murky water inside. The rim was filled with brown residue. There were towels and rags beside it for men to dry themselves off. I dreaded going in there. In many ways, I actually felt dirtier taking a bath than not taking one.

"I think I'll just sleep in tomorrow even if Leona does wake me up," I mumbled as I reluctantly stepped into the tub.

"No one could have anticipated," the broadcast continued, "World War III. Unlike past wars where we fought for freedom or territory, this time, we fought for our souls and are still fighting. Strange occurrences were continuously reported by eyewitnesses in the latter months of 2024. Citizens experienced dramatic changes in behaviors, others vanished without a trace, and supernatural phenomena, previously categorized as myth and speculation, suddenly ran rampant throughout our society. Reports of people achieving great feats of strength, using telekinesis, and able to withstand inhuman amounts of pain and still live took the public by storm. As unbelievable and unlikely as the scenario was, ranking military officials suspected foul play within the government and its relationship to these 'extraterrestrial beings.' The revelation of these beings and these unprecedented scales of cases were too coincidental to ignore."

Another guy went in and out of a stall to relieve himself as I got out of the dirty water and wrapped myself with a towel while the broadcast paused. I wasn't sure which military official had the misfortune to announce this at the time, but I could tell by the woman's voice she didn't want to. By her tone, I got a sense of just how difficult it was for her to relay this information. Heck, I didn't believe it myself at first. All of it sounded made-up. Two military personnel had to restrain me while a therapist instructed me to breathe. I was hyperventilating once I saw the state the Earth was in from the ship. At that moment, it dawned on me that our reality would never be the same again.

"Military officials found that the beings thought to be extraterrestrials didn't come from another planet at all. It was later discovered that the breakthrough scientists made in 2023 was actually a huge incident the government tried to hide. By utilizing a particle accelerator, a gateway was opened to a different world entirely. These beings could inhabit your body as a vessel and wanted nothing more than our destruction. Once it was discovered that high officials of our government had been working with these beings all along, our military took over. Ever since, we have been fighting this threat for six years. During this time, breakthroughs were made by highly respected experts in their field and everyday people alike. We found that ancient relics buried beneath the Earth's crust had the power to fight these beings. By combining scientific discovery with religious doctrine, we've made exo-suits capable of harnessing the power of the relics we find. Unfortunately, the discovery came too late. In the year 2030, the human race dwindled down to the hundreds. The stasis program was initiated to save the humans who were left until we could fight another day. This decision wasn't forced. Those who lost hope and wanted to die peacefully were brought to rest by lethal injection. If you are currently on our ship, you have volunteered to stay and fight when the day arose. Though food, water, and power are scarce, you've been awakened because we have finally found a fighting chance."

Her voice cracked before she relayed the final piece of information. I put my previous clothes back on. There weren't many chances to do laundry. My stomach was growling as I made my way toward the cafeteria area. The ceiling of the craft reached tons of feet well above my head. A vast area with dining tables sat ahead of me. I looked to see if I could spot Leona in the distance. She usually did a slight wave if she spotted me from afar, but I was still too far away from the dining area to see. Fortunately, the line to the serving area wasn't too bad. The smell of powdered eggs, sizzling pancake batter, and meat substitutes tickled my nose. I knew the food was crap, but my stomach growled louder the closer I got.

I recognized an old man at the tail of the line. Somehow his dark complexion highlighted how pale he actually was. His patches of gray hair among his black strands stood out too. He unenthusiastically smirked in my direction. As people were inching their way to the food, I could tell he was doing his best to keep his balance. He walked with a cane. By the amount of pressure he put on his hand that was holding the handle, I could tell he strained more to walk than he was letting on. The broadcast entered its final statement as I half-heartedly smirked back at him.

"We know how overwhelming and surreal this information may be to you. However, unlike our government who swore to protect the interest of the people, we will not lie to you. Every personnel you see here has been working tirelessly to find new discoveries on Earth we could use to end this war once and for all. Therefore, we are in the same position as you. Now, we need your help. Together, we will reclaim our world. Further details will be relayed to you once you have adjusted to this revelation. Thank you, and may God bless us all."

I chuckled as I stood directly behind the old man. "God, huh?" I said sarcastically. "From what I recall, so many people deterred from Him in 2020."

He snickered at my remark. "I know that's right. Funny how heretics form at the peak of civilization and conformists start to believe in a higher power during times of strife." He paused to clear his throat. "Hell, they were even trying to write God out of the constitution."

"Heh. You've been reading books, Burrel?" I replied sarcastically.

Burrel laughed as he grabbed a dish and a tray from the plate holder. "Naw, just been thinking a lot lately. Didn't mean to catch you off guard. I know I'm not usually the poetic type."

"It's okay. I was just teasing," I said as I grabbed my tray. "So what's going on with you?"

"Oh, same old, same old, another day. They did find a use for me, though, even with my bum leg and all." He tapped his right leg with his right hand, holding his cane as he stepped with his left leg.

"That's great! Where are you?"

"Excavation, which is way more interesting than I thought, by the way."

"Really?" I asked as we inched further to the servers. I could tell by their solemn expressions that they weren't in the greeting mood. They just wanted something in their bellies too.

"I swear there's more buried beneath the Earth than just relics. Yesterday we discovered the top part of huge humanoid like fossil remains dating back to ancient Greece, perhaps even further."

"Woah... No kidding."

"Yeah. Judging by the sheer size picked up from the video feed of the excavation site, our machines may prove that giants actually did exist at one point in time."

"You make that sound way better than the training I've been having to go through."

I watched as the server plopped a gooey substance on his plate while behind a glass partition. I think it was supposed to be grits, or at least I hope it was. They designated a server, of course, to ration the food. Without them, I knew people would horde all the food themselves. I'd be one of them. A military official was behind us with a weapon in his holster the whole time to remind us to behave. He was also strapped with a baton and armed Kevlar. We had some riots in the past, so I understood why it was necessary, but I couldn't help but feel like a child sometimes.

"Dishwasher said he caught something this morning. I didn't have a chance to clean the bowls," the server said depressingly.

Burrel nodded to the server in response. "Well," he said as he continued his conversation with me, "it looks like you're making progress. I see you toning up a little."

"I guess... Everything is still so surreal. I saw a guy this morning with his leg cut clean off from the knee. He had two legs before he was called up for an expedition a week ago."

"Damn!" Burrel said. His eyes widened a little in disbelief. "Lord, have mercy. It looks like he's in the same boat as me then." He slightly lost his balance as he inched closer with his cane to get pancakes and eggs from another server. I put my hand on his shoulder to keep him steady, but he gestured with his hand to leave it alone. This wasn't the first time this happened. I wasn't sure if it was pride or stubbornness, but he liked doing everything alone. Useless was the one thing he didn't want to be. I respected that about him. "Anyway, don't let it get you down, though. If you let negative thoughts get in your head while you're out there, you may end up worse than he was."

I teasingly scoffed. "Easier said than done. Have you seen this place?"

He smiled. "That's why I like talking to you—no bull. You're just...*real*, unlike some people around here. Others talk to me like they're still in a dream, waiting for the other shoe to drop so they can wake up. But this is reality now..." I saw him look down, reflecting a bit. A server gave me a small portion of pancakes and eggs. Both were runny, but I didn't care anymore. I just wanted to devour it whole. "I'm sure that's why Leona sticks around you. You seal the deal yet, by the way?"

I blushed a little as we made our way to the end of the line and toward the dining area, which was basically a cafeteria. "It's... complicated."

"Relationships usually are, son."

We both spotted Leona in the middle of the many tables wave at us. Though it was early, there were still quite a few people sitting at the tables spread throughout the cafeteria.

"Well, we met before being put in stasis, and we're both slowly getting our memories back. I like to know more about a person before getting into a serious commitment." I paused briefly to reminisce. "During the war—heck, even before—people did all kinds of messed-up things. I need to know what I'm getting myself into."

"Smart. I get it. Just don't wait too long. It's not like we're promised tomorrow these days."

"When were we ever?"

"Heh… Good one. Don't get too wise on me. Then there *really* wouldn't be a reason for us old folks to stick around."

We smiled as we parted ways. I watched him for a bit as he hobbled to the other side of the cafeteria. He headed toward a table where no one sat. It saddened me a little, but I understood why he did it. Trust is hard to come by and verify. I wondered if I'd become like him if I let myself be alone.

As I walked over to where Leona was sitting, I squeezed in between the little walkway of the tables. Due to the high volume of people, they made the tables close as possible to where you could still walk in between them. Luckily, it was still pretty early and few people were sitting at each table. Getting through the small space was usually another task in and of itself. My shoes squeaked on the spotless floor. I nearly tripped due to the difference in friction.

"At least they make an effort to clean the cafeteria before everyone wakes up in the morning," I said as I set my tray down in front of Leona. Another woman was at the far end of the table where we sat. She had the same dead look others had around here.

"I suppose," Leona said.

It's like her forest-green eyes penetrated my very core. I felt my heart speed up a little as I sat across from her. I looked down at her plate, and there was no scrap of food left. If I didn't know any better, I'd say she licked the plate clean. She was probably trying to hide the fact she was more hungry than she was leading me to believe most days. After all, I was still training how to use these "exo-suits." She learned how to use the new technology quickly and started on expeditions a couple of months back. Unlike me, she was actually in the military before all this happened from what I could remember. It would make sense why she's a quick study. The scars were adding up, though. She caught me staring at her plate and started talking.

"Is Burrel sitting alone again?"

"Yup," I said.

She sighed.

"Leona, he's—"

"I know… I know. He's been through a lot. I shouldn't push it. But he's actually one of the few people other than you and some other soldiers I actually trust here."

"I know what you mean," I said as I began to dig into my eggs.

"What were you thinking about this morning, by the way?" she asked out of nowhere.

"What are you talking about?"

"I don't know… You were kind of mumbling in your sleep. You looked peaceful, yet worried at the same time. There was a sort of calm about it."

"You watching me sleep now?"

Her cheeks immediately became hot and flustered. "Shut up," she said playfully. "I know you do the same thing."

I smiled. "Sometimes."

We stared at each other in silence for a moment.

Suddenly, she grabbed my free hand and took it into hers. "About this morning, I—"

"Don't worry about it," I interjected. "I know this thing between us is at an awkward stage. Neither of us fully remember who we are except that we were seeing each other before being put under in stasis."

"Yeah, I can't help but feel anxious and nervous. To be honest, whatever this is, it's scaring me a little more than being out on the field." Sincerity filled her eyes. In that instantaneous moment, I forgot everything again, and it was just me and her. "When we do remember everything, will that break us apart, or will it strengthen what we already have? You're the only constant I have in my life so far that I've been able to depend on for all these months." Her voice broke slightly as she tried to regain some composure. "I… I don't want to lose you."

"You won't. Believe me, Leona."

"You're going on faith, huh?"

"After everything going on in this world, are you really going to tell me you're still a skeptic?"

She drew her hands away from mine. "I don't know… I still haven't seen a 'second coming.' Have you?"

I sighed, looking down at my food, not responding. I continued eating while delving into the gooey substance I prayed was edible.

She noticed how she incidentally brought the mood down and changed the subject. "Did you hear that vessel 8 is rapidly running out of supplies?"

"Oh no… Are they going to try to transport the people on this one?" I asked in between chewing.

"Nothing's official yet."

"I hope they don't come to this one. We're on our last legs as it is."

"You do know the other vessels are in similar situations, right?"

"I know… I try to forget that our entire existence has turned into a screw-up by our own government," I replied sarcastically.

Bzzzzz!

Leona and I passed each other worried expressions as we heard the intercom again.

"Another broadcast *this* early? I don't ever remember this happening before," Leona said, distressed.

I sat silently as I heard a military official make the statement.

"Attention! We have stumbled upon a relic, perhaps ancient treasure that could turn the tide of the war in our favor. The radiation emanating from it is astounding. Not even our instruments can fully measure it. We must act to use this energy to our advantage. To avoid suspicion from the 'beings' that have infested Earth, we will need a small platoon of three. This platoon will consist of Henry Rosenburg, Joselyn Fairbanks, and Xander Williams. Please report to the dock to receive the rest of the debriefing. That is all. Thank you."

Leona stared at me wide-eyed, petrified. I caught a glimpse of Burrel from a distance looking at me with his mouth open. My heart sank to the pit of my stomach.

"They called your name, Xander…"

"I… I…heard."

"They called your name… They called your *freaking* name! This doesn't make sense!"

I slowly got up from my seat and made my way to her on the other side of the table.

"*I'm* the soldier. You're still in training! What is Command thinking? I will—"

I placed my hand on her shoulder. She instantly stopped talking as the reality of the situation synced in. A tear grazed her face. She looked up to me as I was standing by her. She saw the residue of the fallen tear stream down my cheek, realizing it was mine and not hers. As she placed her hand on mine, we both felt each other, shaking in fear.

"It…it's not fair," she managed to utter.

She stood up next to me. I saw her eyes start to water. I leaned in and gently kissed her on the forehead.

"Since when has life ever been fair?" I managed to say.

And just like that, what started out as a normal day by our standards turned into a moment I'd never forget. After I walked away from Leona, everything was a blur. I don't even remember how I got to the deck. I guess my body knew no matter how much I didn't want to go, I still had to take those steps.

CHAPTER 2

So THERE I was staring at our commanding officer as he relayed the information. The place was huge. The sides of the room were integrated with complicated wiring and technology I couldn't begin to explain. My nostrils were filled with a rusty-iron smell. Cold steel and other metals made up the bridge we were standing on at the upper deck. At the deck below, I saw the three suits we were supposed to pilot. The material inside the suit was expandable so that it could fit people of all sizes. However, the exterior was different. One suit was heavily armed with rare Earth metals with extra protection to the helmet for the pilot's head. The power lied in its heavy hits for close combat and bomb-rushing enemies. It was basically a walking tank. The second had internal weapons integrated into the suit as well as firearms connected to the suit's power core. The suits were powered by a combination of electricity, along with the energy the relics exuded. Somehow, they found a way to harness the radiation coming from the ancient items we found and incorporate it into the suit. A combination of old alchemy practices and modern science helped achieve this amazing feat. I always found it amazing that science actually derived from alchemy. When alchemy practices were first initiated, churches labeled it as magic.

However, my stomach turned in knots when I saw the third exo-suit. The deck's overall heavily fortified structure highlighted how all the more risky it was to be in this suit. It had the least amount of armor and only one weapon. I saw the hilt of it. The power from the relic was supposed to power the saber sword formed by pure energy. As bleak as things looked, something told me it was going to get worse.

"In the case of enemy fire," the commanding officer proceeded. I missed the introduction speech and found myself refocusing while he was in the middle of the mission debriefing. The commanding officer had a dingy, wrinkled uniform. A badge he sported read "Brauns." Bags were clearly visible under his eyes. Plus, they were bloodshot red. I could tell sleep was a stranger to him.

"We need two experienced soldiers. One will pilot a fortified suit to draw fire. If overwhelmed, the other soldier will pilot the suit made for artillery to do enough cover fire within the vicinity to allow for escape." Brauns took a second to pinch the bridge of his nose. I assumed he was stressed and trying to stay awake. His apparent lack of sleep could've even caused him to experience headaches or migraines from time to time. "A third pilot will proceed into the suit for stealth. Since exo-suits designed for stealth are exponentially faster, it will be that pilot's job to enter the location of the excavation site. Rosenburg, you have the fortified suit. The artillery one goes to Fairbanks." My heart dropped as soon as he said, "Stealth goes to Williams."

I knew I was going to get the least protected suit as soon as I saw it. I also knew the world was at stake and my life was on the line, but the only thing I could think about was making it back to Leona. The odds of doing that were slim to none on a suicide mission.

"The role you play, Williams, is vital. You'll face two main obstacles—the enemy and the excavation machine. There may be a few beings already in the area. Eliminate them quickly without drawing attention. The excavation machine is also running low on power. You'll have to resupply it with some of the energy from your suit, so it can finish digging. If the beings get a whiff of the machine, they'll most likely destroy it." He took a moment to eye each of us. I think he wanted us to understand exactly how dangerous this was if we didn't already know. "Rosenburg, Fairbanks, and you"—he stared directly at me—"will have to defend your position until it can completely dig out the relic. Any questions?"

"Yeah, I have a few." Everyone in the room looked directly at me. "I'm still in training. Why did you choose *me* for this expedition?"

"You have the highest score on your PT test for stamina and sprinting. We need those skills to retrieve the treasure hidden beneath Earth's crust."

"There are other more qualified soldiers for this mission, and I'm getting the suit with the least amount of protection. As I see it, anyone performing this role has the least chance of surviving." At that moment, I knew I was speaking out of line, but I felt my blood pumping in my ears. Maybe it was stress, anxiety, fear, or a combination of them. I just kept going. "You didn't want to risk good soldiers being unprotected out there, so you send someone who is… expendable. In the case of my death after retrieving it, you still have two qualified pilots with fortified suits to grab it from me and take it back. Am I right, Commander?"

Brauns smirked. "It's good to see you got a head on your shoulders, son, but watch your step." He passed me a menacing glare. "I'm not going to lie to you. Your chances of surviving are low. However, you technically knew what you signed up for when you accepted the stasis program."

Henry and Joselyn glanced back at me sympathetically after Brauns uttered those words. At that moment, we all knew what we were in for. If the slightest mistake occurred, we'd have a horde of those *things* out there surrounding us. We made our way to the elevator shaft to get us to the suits below. Brauns stayed on the platform, watching as he was potentially sending me to my doom.

"I'll make sure you get back to her," Joselyn said as we entered the elevator.

I didn't bother to take a close look at her before, but she was pale. It looked as if the life drained from her face.

"Excuse me?" I replied, confused.

"I'm sorry, but I've seen you around the ship sometimes. Whenever I do, I see Leona and you, nearly attached to the hip." She tittered. I was slightly embarrassed as she said this. It made us seem clingy. "She's a good soldier. I've been on a couple supply runs with her."

As the elevator shaft descended to the floor below, I noticed a sense of longing in her voice, perhaps even envy. Goosebumps formed on my skin. The difference in temperature was getting significantly lower.

"Why worry about me? Don't you have family to get back to?" I asked.

Joselyn sighed. "I remember fragments, but I'm pretty sure the people I cared about died during the battles on Earth. I'm the only one who made it."

"I'm sorry."

"Enough of the pity party. Focus, you two," Henry interrupted. I incidentally got a hint of his morning breath as he was talking in a confined space right next to me. He must've not even had time to brush his teeth when the broadcast aired. "We got one chance to pull this off. All of our lives are on the line too, rook. If we manage to get this, we won't have to be on this stupid ship anymore!"

"I hate this ship too, but you're getting a little ahead of yourself, aren't you?" I said.

Unlike us, Henry's eyes were wide open, anxious, in fact. I saw his hands shake a little in anticipation. His light-brown buzzsaw haircut stood out. It faded slightly down from the top. He was toned from the neck down. He must've been a hotshot on the field. The military gives quality soldiers slightly more food so they could perform at optimal efficiency. It wasn't really a secret. Everyone could tell, but it's not like the higher-ups were exactly announcing it either.

"Don't you get it?" Henry continued. "The tide would rise in our favor. We could permanently return to our planet again and breathe fresh air! *This* is why we're still alive."

"He's right. Let's all do the best we can so others can see tomorrow," Joselyn said.

If I wasn't nervous before, I sure was now. I knew how much was riding on our shoulders, but I actually *felt it* this time. The gravity of the situation hit me once we were at the bottom deck in front of our suits. There was a hatch in the back of each suit we could climb in. The inner lining was laced with fabric for comfortable mobility. The lights overhead made the exterior shine brilliantly. As I looked around, I saw storage of coolants on the sides of the room. They must've been for the suits to prevent overheating. It explains why it was so cold down here too. I saw a pod ahead where teams would enter with their suits. The pod's structure was built with heavy metals and heat shields like used in early NASA to withstand the impact upon entering the Earth's atmosphere. If we tried to enter with our suits alone, we'd burn to a crisp even before getting to see the clouds. That is, if we didn't die from running out of air in our suits while we were in space first. Even with the pod, it had to be shot toward earth at a specific angle to not burn as well. Some lost their lives due to half-baked calculations. Everything we did was a risk.

"Look alive, people!" Brauns shouted atop the bridge of the upper deck. Henry, Joselyn, and I looked up as he instructed us what to do next. "Brace yourselves to deploy in five minutes. Enter your suit quickly and strap yourself into the pod. We'll try to direct you to a landing zone not too far from the excavation site. Retain radio contact with each other and Command at all times, so we're all aware of each individual's situation. Good luck. We're counting on you!"

"Yes, sir!" We shouted in unison as we were trained to do.

As I hopped into my suit, the hatch closed behind me. The mechanisms in the inner casings started to make noises and move around. I felt the inner fabric tighten around my body, hugging it. Though it looked rough on the outside, it felt as if I was wearing another skin on the inside. First, there was a warm sensation rising as I had it on, and then, it stabilized as the coolant kicked in. The visor on my helmet made it seem like I was peering out from a movie frame. I saw Joselyn and Henry signaling me to hurry up while they were in their suits.

"Come on, Williams. We don't have time to warm up. This is time-sensitive," Henry stated.

"Right. On my way!"

There were magnets and latches inside the pod that strapped our suits in securely. We were all looking at one another with our faceplates retracted in the confined space of the metal entrapment.

"Don't worry," Joselyn said. The terror in my eyes must've been more obvious than I thought. "I'm nervous too. I don't do well with heights."

"Deployment starts in 5…4…3…2…" As the automated voice began the countdown for launch, the pod shook vigorously. My stomach felt like it wanted to exit my mouth.

"1… Beep!"

I heard the hatch to the ship open as our pod dropped to space. I felt the pressure of the launch propel us to Earth. I clammed up once I realized there wasn't any ground beneath us. It's as if my body was suspended in limbo, and I had no control over it. I gripped on the handlebars beside us with the suit for dear life. The sensation of Earth's gravity pulling the pod was like no other experience. As the pod shook violently again once we entered the atmosphere, I opened my eyes a little. Henry had a determined look on his face, concentrating on the mission ahead. Joselyn, on the other hand, still had her eyes closed. I caught a glimpse of her mumbling something. I figured it was a prayer. The vibration of the rocket at the bottom of the pod initiated. It softened the landing of the descent once we were close to the surface. I heard the pod make a small impact with the ground as we landed. The door slid open. To my surprise, Joselyn was immediately the first one to get out. It was a good thing the faceplate to her helmet was open because she heaved out on the sandy surface. I wanted to throw up too, but I held it in. She was doing enough for the both of us.

"Command, this is Rosenburg. We've touched down," Henry said as he made his way out of the pod. He pressed two fingers to the side of his helmet to access his communicator.

"Roger that, patrol. We'll now be streaming your audio feed," a woman's voice said through my communicator on the side of my helmet. It sounded like the same one from the morning broadcast we heard every day. This must've been her full-time position now. "Since you're the most experienced, you'll take point on this, Rosenburg. Survey the layout and converge on the location."

"Understood," Henry replied.

"You all right?" I went over to Joselyn who was trying to regain her composure. I thought the suit would weigh a ton walking over to her, but I moved with ease.

"I'm good. Let's just get this over with," she said as she wiped her mouth with the forearm of her suit.

"My thoughts exactly," Henry chimed in. He sounded a bit irritated. I couldn't say I blamed him. After all, he was stuck with a rookie and a soldier who was barely keeping it together.

"I thought you ran missions before," I said, trying to put her at ease with conversation.

"Yeah, but I never get used to that descent." She pushed the button for her faceplate to go back on.

Debris from the sand blew in front of my visor as we followed Henry atop the sand dune. I saw the sun in the background. I kind of wanted to take off my suit, but I knew it was too dangerous to. I couldn't remember the last time I've felt the sun's rays caress my skin. All of my training occurred in the ship in space. Even when I practiced in a suit, it was always in a cold, controlled room made up of hypothetical scenarios. Nothing really prepares you for actual combat other than real-world experience.

"Hey, uh, Henry," I said.

"Yeah?"

"Have all the places become like this? Like a desert?"

"No. There are some areas with overgrown wildlife. Others are barren with destroyed buildings. Well, at least the ones I've been deployed to so far." Henry examined the environment in front of us. "You'd be surprised how much a landscape changes without human interference."

"I can only imagine," Joselyn commented.

We grew silent again for a moment. As we hiked up the sand dune, I saw things that used to be part of our world poke up from beneath the sand. A phone with a cracked screen, one of the wooden legs of a broken table, and even the hardcover and torn pages of a book were now things part of our past. I took a moment to examine the book closer. It appeared to be an old Bible. Perhaps the most disturbing thing I saw was what lied by it. Part of the head of a teddy bear was planted in the sand. I saw part of the stuffing where its neck was supposed to be. I couldn't even imagine what children had to go through during this time.

"There! That's our objective," Henry shouted over the wind, grabbing my attention.

Joselyn and I stood beside him and spotted the excavation machine. Even at this distance, we could tell the drill stopped. There was also an outline of what appeared to be a person. I activated the magnification setting on my visor to zoom in. It looked to be a man, but his movements were inhuman. The tattered clothes he had on flowed amidst the sand and wind. My eyes widened. I could've sworn Command told us there were no survivors left on Earth.

"What are we going to do about that man lingering in the area?" I stupidly asked.

"Are you serious?" Henry said in a patronizing tone. "That's one of the beings."

"Are you sure?"

"I'm sure. I know it still somewhat looks human, but trust me, it's far from it."

I glanced over to Joselyn who nodded with her helmet on in agreement.

"Okay," I said hesitantly. "So what's the plan?"

Henry took a minute to contemplate. "Have you learned combat yet with a saber sword during your training?"

I gestured with my suit's hand in a side to side motion to say "so-so."

He sighed. "Well, you're going to have to learn quickly. Haul ass and strike him from behind without being detected." He pointed to Joselyn. "Since you have the most weapons, Fairbanks, lay down cover fire for him just in case you see any more coming his way."

"Roger. I'll equip my sniper laser once I activate the relic energy on my suit. That way, I'll get a sure shot even at this distance."

"Good idea. I'll pace myself behind you, Williams, but remain hidden behind smaller dunes. Just in case this goes south, I'll be near you to draw enemy fire." He looked over to Joselyn again. "However, since I can't scope the area while behind dunes, it'll be your job to alert us if there are too many coming our way."

"I understand. No pressure," she added sarcastically, trying to lighten the mood. I think more than anything, she was trying to calm herself down.

"We'll be fine, you guys, okay?" Henry looked over to me and saw how nervous I was too. "We just need to do our roles and get out. That's it. All right?"

We both nodded.

"Good. Okay, Williams. As you know, our suits run on two types of energy—one source is from the Earth that powers the suit and the other is from the relics that powers our weapons. In training, they should've taught you that you need relic energy to do any damage to these beings. I can't explain the science or magic behind this technology, but there's a tiny push switch on the side of your suit." He showed me the tiny button by demonstrating on his suit. "Equip the hilt of your saber sword on the back of your suit's hand. The current will run through your suit and toward the hilt. Then, a large saber will eject from the back of your hand. It slices through these things like butter."

I equipped the hilt to the back of my hand and activated the relic energy with the button like he said. Suddenly, a long, glowing saber emitted from my hand. It was a thin, elongated triangle with the sides meeting at the tip of the blade, formed by the energy.

"Woah… Am I really harnessing some type of mystical energy through this suit?" I asked.

"Like I said, I'm not sure how to explain it. The higher-ups don't know what to call it either. But the treasures we find that have this type of mysterious energy can put an end to these things. There are still skeptics among us, though."

Henry and Joselyn saw me admiring the invention. Joselyn came from behind and turned the switch off.

"You need to conserve power, remember?" Joselyn said.

"Agreed. Only use your weapon when you see a clean strike. You also need to use some of your suit's energy to power that drill. Needless to say, time isn't a luxury."

"Roger that. I'm ready," I said half-heartedly. "Let's do this."

I saw Joselyn equip what looked like a scope on the back of her hand. From the look of it, I guessed she could aim and fire with the same mechanism on her hand once she activated the relic energy from her suit. She then planted herself in the sand, lying down on her stomach to minimize detection. I stretched my legs a bit before getting prepared to run.

"After you," Henry directed.

I took a deep breath and charged forward, sprinting as fast as I could across the sand. To avoid being spotted by that mysterious figure, I was sprinting from sand dune to sand dune while his back was turned. Henry trotted behind at a distance. As I was running, I felt the mechanics of the suit propelling my body forward to compensate for the slightly extra weight of the material. It was no wonder I didn't feel difficulty moving. It was designed to promote movement for stealth missions. My heart was pounding. The thumps sounded as if they were next to my ear.

Could I really kill someone? I thought. *I know they said that wasn't a man, but he looks so human. What is going on here?*

I managed to get behind a sand dune that was close to the figure. It moved in an awkward motion from side to side. It was almost like some type of ritualistic dance. I looked over at Henry who was behind a sand dune at a distance. He poked his head out and gave me a thumbs-up. I looked back at my target and saw that he had his back turned.

"I'm looking around and you're all clear," Joselyn said through the communicator in our helmets. "I'm a good shot, but it's less risky if you silently eliminate him with your saber. On the off chance I could miss, he'll alert more to come."

"I agree. If there was any chance, it would be now," Henry added.

"Understood," I said.

My mouth became dry. Sweat trickled down the side of my face, although I wasn't hot. I kept my eyes on the target, bracing myself of what was to come. I breathed in deeply. As I breathed out, I sprinted toward him using the balls of my feet like I learned in training for stealth. Using your whole foot while running makes slightly more impact with the surface, causing more of a sound and leaves obvious tracks.

As I was inches away from him, I activated the button for my relic energy. I felt the energy surge through the lining of my suit. As the energy from my saber retracted from the hilt of my hand, it made a low humming noise. The man was alerted by it at the last second and turned around. But before he could act, I dashed harder and sliced the saber through his torso. I looked down at the corpse before me and saw blood gushing and oozing from the wound I caused. The red liquid mixed in with the sand, causing an unholy site with the Earth. The man's eyes stared at the sun above in shock. I froze in fear, thinking I just committed the worst type of action a person could.

Does that mean this thing was alive? Was this really a man I had just slain? I thought.

"Rook! What are you doing? Get to the excavation machine now!" Henry shouted through the communicator.

I pushed the thoughts to the back of my mind and followed orders like I was programmed to ever since I came out of stasis. The rest happened so fast. When I got to the drill, I remembered there was a port on the side, designated for a power connection. There was a compartment integrated into my suit to link with external power sources. I jacked into the machine. A message popped up on a small screen that read, "Remaining time: 1 minute 24 seconds." To our luck, the drill began functioning again. I was breathing hard.

"Yes! Both obstacles out of the way. Now to get that relic," Joselyn said through the communicator.

At that moment, as if fate was mocking us, I heard the most inhumane shriek known to mankind.

EEEKKK!

The hairs on the back of my neck stood up. I looked behind me and saw a black figure towering over me. It was surreal. Its form was literally just a black silhouette. It was floating above the sand instead of standing. If it were a person, glowing circles is where its eyes would be and the outline of what I assume was a mouth, deviously grinned at me. It launched toward me, ready to strike. I attempted to shield myself by putting up a free hand.

The dark figure instantly vanished as I saw Henry punch it with his fortified suit from behind. The fists of his suit were lined with relic energy, emanating from the knuckles.

"Are you okay?" Henry asked.

I nodded. "Thanks."

"Uhm, guys. Look around. The worst possible scenario is happening," Joselyn said through the communicator.

Henry was beside me. We looked around atop the sand dunes and saw more of those monsters surrounding us. A laser shot one of them and made it disappear.

"I'll get rid of as many targets as possible with my weapons from afar to try to thin out the herd converging on your location." Judging from Joselyn's hard breaths, she already sounded overwhelmed on her end.

"Command, are you hearing this?" Henry asked.

"Unfortunately, yes. I'm sorry, patrol, but the commander is telling me that the relic is top priority. You can't retreat. In other words—"

"Defend it with our lives," I said, finishing her sentence. My heart was about to explode out of my chest.

Her voice cracked before replying. "I'm sorry." Her communication line cut off abruptly.

"Well, rook," Henry said, "hold onto that connection with your life. I'll draw their attention."

I looked at the screen as it now read, "Remaining time: 46 seconds."

"Shit!" I said under my breath.

"I knew you had the look on your face after you struck it by the way."

I peered through my helmet visor at him, startled.

"It's what they do. They possess people and feed on their negative energy. Even without a vessel, if they feed enough, they turn into these things." He equipped a mechanism on each of his hands that looked like mini turrets. "I had the same look when I eliminated my first one. But I realized, they're not human anymore." He pushed the button on the side of his suit and the mechanism on his hands lit up. "So don't worry about getting your hands dirty. Our government made sure there was plenty of filth to go around."

I saw the determination in his eyes as he ran toward the dark silhouettes. He activated the mini turrets as he fought at a distance. His suit moved around in a circle to shoot all the enemies surrounding him. When they overwhelmed him, he bashed his fist into the sand. It created a shockwave with the relic energy and blasted the dark silhouettes away in a brilliant flash of light. As determined as he was, I knew he couldn't hold out.

I looked at the small screen again. It read, "Remaining time: 17 seconds."

"Come on! Just a little more. Hang on just a little more," I mumbled.

When I looked up again, I couldn't believe my eyes. Amidst the crowd, another man possessed by one of those things came up behind Henry and punched through his armor with uncanny strength. I saw his fist drenched in blood through Henry's chest cavity.

"Henry!"

His suit dropped to its knees and fell lifeless on the sand's surface. The dark silhouettes and possessed people gazed back in my direction. My blood ran cold with dread.

"Joselyn! Do you read? Henry's down!"

She didn't respond.

"Josclyn, do you copy? Multiple targets are converging on my position!"

No response.

"Fuck!"

All of a sudden, I heard, *Beep!*

I looked at the screen as it read, "Remaining time: 0."

I saw a latch deploy from the machine as it reeled in the relic from below. The drill retracted back to its original position. The enemies were just a few feet away from me now. I broke the connection of my suit as I waited for the latch to ascend with the treasure we came for. The only weapon I had on my suit was the saber. I pushed the button and the energy retracted from my hand. I don't know what got into me, but seeing what just happened sparked a fire I didn't know I had. Seeing someone die for others made me finally realize why we were still fighting in the first place. I seethed angrily.

"Henry put his life on the line for the mission and for me," I said, unaware I was talking to myself. "I was never thrilled about fighting, but there is no way in hell I can let him nor Joselyn down. I can't. I won't…" *Especially seeing how hard they fought for me—for everyone*, I thought. I couldn't let Leona down either. No way!

A couple of silhouettes lunged for me. My technique was sloppy, but I swiped my energy saber at them. They disappeared. I saw the possessed man who killed Henry walk slowly toward me. I was blinded with rage. I swiped at those dark things left and right. At that moment, I didn't care if I died anymore as long as I retrieved that relic.

Suddenly, the possessed man put his hand up. The enemies stopped attacking me. Several possessed bodies were bleeding out at my feet. The silhouettes and other possessed people watched as the man walked closer to my position. He stopped a few feet in front of me with a devious grin.

Is this thing actually enjoying watching me struggle? I thought, trying desperately to catch my breath.

Before I could realize what was happening, the man charged at me. I put my hands up to block his punch. I should've known better after seeing what his strength did to Henry.

Crack!

"Ahhh!" I yelped in pain as the force of the blow knocked me back. I managed to land on my feet, but my right arm, holding my energy saber, dangled at my side. I was pretty sure it was broken. The tip of the saber made a small crackling sound on the sand's surface. It's like the man's grin grew even wider when he saw me in pain.

I looked to my right and saw the latch retract all the way up. At the end of it appeared to be an antique box. The carvings on it were strange, nothing like I've ever seen before. To my dismay, the being saw me spot it too.

EEEKKK!

That terrible sound blasted my eardrums again. I don't know how I was going to do it, but I had to get to it before they did. I bent my knees and sprinted to the excavation machine. The man ran at an abnormal speed. I lunged my body toward the box and grasped it with my functional hand just in time. The man tried to swipe it from my grasp but missed. As I landed on my feet, I heard the possessed man's feet lunge at me, even amidst the sand and wind. The force he was running at must've been insane. I pivoted my foot and used the momentum of my body to fling my right arm, protruding with the energy saber. I had the box clasped under my left arm. In one fell swoop, I manage to slash my energy blade behind me. The man's head toppled to the floor, along with his body.

Once the beings surrounding me saw the man fall, they lunged at me. I tried to run with the little strength I had, but I tripped in the sand. The box escaped my grasp and rolled a few feet away from me. I thought I was done. My saber started to slowly dissipate as my suit was running out of relic energy. I didn't even realize how long I had it active. To my surprise, fortune was on my side. As I looked at our last hope dwindle away beneath the sand as the enemies were about to strike me, I saw that the box was open from the fall. A strange light emitted from it. I watched as the dark silhouettes vanished and the possessed people fell to their knees.

I hesitantly stood up, staring at the sight before me. However, I knew I had to quickly snap out of my momentary trance of disbelief. Panic still rose in my chest because I was bewildered and didn't know if more would come. I gathered the strength I could and retrieved the box from the sand. I peered at its contents, unsure of what I was looking at. I thought I was going to witness something divine, but it appeared to be an ordinary piece of wood.

I closed the box and jogged back to the pod while my right arm was still dangling at my side. The taste of iron filled my lungs. Sand and wind hit my suit as I was running, causing some resistance. It made it harder to press on. Possessed bodies of people were scattered across the sand. I eventually saw the pod in the distance as well as a large object buried beneath. I stopped. It was Joselyn's suit. I set down the box and strained to turn her over with my one arm.

"Joselyn! Are you okay? Can you hear me?" I asked through the communicator.

I heard her struggle to say something. "I'm...coughing up... blood." I scanned her and saw that her torso was punctured.

"How did you survive that onslaught?"

"I could ask you the same thing." She coughed. "Right when I found myself cornered, I saw some kind of light and everything just stopped."

"You were actually fighting that long?"

"I said I'd make sure you get back to Leona, didn't I?"

I paused for a moment, shocked. *What's her deal?* I thought.

That one promise was the only thing keeping her going. She didn't even know me that well. I was lucky to get two comrades who gave it their all, although we were complete strangers to each other. I realized if our fighting spirit was any less today, we all would've died.

"Can you walk?"

"A little."

"Here," I said. "Get your arm around my neck. I'll support you with my good one."

She noticed my right arm dangling at my side. "It looks like we're both pretty banged up."

My left hand held the case while my arm supported her as we made our way to the pod. I closed the door and strapped both of us in.

"Command. This is Williams," I said, pushing the buttons to launch.

"You survived! Do you have the relic?" the woman asked.

"I have it. I'm emitting a signal from my suit so you can find us in space as the pod leaves the atmosphere." The pod rumbled. I saw Joselyn across from me losing consciousness.

"Good. We'll send the vessel to your signal's location for extract. What's in the content of the box?"

"I don't have the capability to explain. It's something you have to see to believe."

The communication cut off. Joselyn kept herself awake, staring at the box.

"Is that the thing responsible for that light?" she asked as we propelled through the sky.

I pushed the button to detach the faceplate from my helmet and smirked. "This has been *the* strangest day. Leona asked for a second coming this morning. I think we've finally found it."

CHAPTER 3

JOSELYN SMIRKED WITH her faceplate open too. "That's good to hear," she said as her eyes began to close. I could barely hear her through the violent shaking of the pod as we left the Earth's atmosphere.

"Joselyn! Stay with me!" I yelled. "We're almost there. Don't lose consciousness! You've lost too much blood."

The turbulence stopped as I saw her struggle to keep her eyelids open. *Sssss!* I heard the oxygen storage system kick in from the pod.

"We must be in space," I said. At this point, I was saying anything to keep her awake and talking. "They should come for us at any time now."

She was panting at an uncomfortably slow pace.

"Can I ask you a question?"

She nodded slowly while putting pressure on her abdomen.

"Why would you fight so hard for someone you barely know?"

"Heh... Heh..." She tried to muster a smile as she chuckled. "I'd like to say it was for the cause and humanity's survival, but I never liked spouting bullcrap."

I looked at her, surprised. "So you don't believe in what we're doing?"

"I believe," she said as she coughed. "Don't get me wrong, I see the logic in it. After all, we're not only fighting for ourselves but for the generations after—if we live that long." I heard her heavy breathing between sentences as she spoke. "I just don't like people."

I stared at her, perplexed. "Then, why—"

"My late husband loved that about me," she continued, cutting me off. "People have come and gone in my life that manipulated me, lied, and betrayed my trust…that much I remember. But he was different. He didn't like bullcrap either. It's how we found each other. The way you spoke to the commander reminded me of him."

As she said that, I thought back to what Burrel told me about myself at the cafeteria. He could also see what Leona saw in me.

"What happened to your husband, if you don't mind me asking?"

"Most people on the ships have difficulty remembering their final moments on Earth before stasis. My husband acted as a shield to save me and our kids from those beings' attacks." She shifted in her contraption as she continued putting pressure on the wound. I could see blood trickling down the material of her suit. "Despite his efforts, I'm the only one who survived." Joselyn's voice cracked as I saw her reminiscing the moment. Her eyes became watery. "I remember… I remember that just fine."

I didn't respond. There were no words to comfort her. I felt like even the usual "I'm sorry for your loss" schtick would've been inappropriate to say.

"I thought I had nothing keeping me going, but when I see you and Leona from time to time together on the ship…it reminds me of the bond I once had."

"It gives you hope…"

"Eh…yeah. I guess you can say that, not to get sappy on you or anything."

We both passed a half-hearted smile.

"Williams! This is Command. Do you copy?"

I accessed the communicator on my suit, startled and flustered by the sudden audio.

"Yes! We're here."

"Standby. Vessel 7 is above you. Initiating extraction now."

Joselyn let out a sigh of relief. "Thank goodness." Suddenly, her eyes rolled back to her head as she fell unconscious.

"No! Joselyn, come on! Stay with me. We're at the home stretch."

As I shouted at her, the empty contraption to my right caught my attention. Mixed feelings came over me.

Thank you, Henry. We're almost home, I thought.

Things became hazy as I began to feel dizzy. The last thing I remember is our pod opening at the deck. Personnel rushed over to us immediately. I think I caught a glimpse of Leona and other people fighting with guards, as well as Brauns, at the upper level before I collapsed to the floor. I guess I was more beat up from that battle than I realized because I just blacked out.

CHAPTER 4

"Aiiiii!" An intense pain shot down the right side of my arm, jolting me awake.

"Easy, easy!" Leona's worried expression greeted me back to reality.

I tried to put on a smile while wincing in pain.

"What's with the grin?" Leona asked while caressing my head gently back onto a pillow. Judging by the lumpy surface and sound of old springs creaking while lying down, I ventured to guess I was on a cot. "Is the pain making you delusional?" she teased, smirking.

"No. I'm just glad the first thing I saw waking up is you again and not the commander. I was expecting to be probed for an immediate debrief," I said, chuckling.

Leona looked away awkwardly, flushed with embarrassment. "Well, about that..."

"Enough, Leona Madigan. You have made quite the commotion already for this man." The figure was standing below a fluorescent light, blurring my vision at the angle I tried to sit up in. I saw the figure pass Leona a menacing glare. She looked away, ashamed. "If I could discipline you for insubordination, I would. But we're going to need every capable person for what comes next. And just for the record, Williams, seeing a disrespectful rook isn't exactly the highlight of my day either."

I recognized that voice, that man—the same man who sent me to die.

"Surprised that I'm alive, Commander?" I said smugly.

"Save the sarcasm and drama, Williams," Brauns replied.

A female in a nurse's gown stood beside him, along with another woman. Her uniform was pressed from head to toe, and she was poised with self-confidence. She had a dark complexion, too, that looked to be of Hispanic or Native American in origin. But who knows? With the melting pot the world fell in before the war, I could've been wrong on both fronts. Leona had no choice but to step to the side, observing the situation unfold.

"My job is to ensure humanity's survival by organizing strategic operations with the highest probability of success. Our very existence depends on it. So if you're expecting an apology, then you're in the wrong field." Brauns got closer to me. "I know military-like training is new to you, considering that your files show you haven't had any experience in it from your life before this, but you signed that document. What did you think being a soldier meant?"

"Tch... Ahhh!" I cringed in pain right after I sucked my teeth, aggravated by his response. Leona sympathetically looked away as it was hard for her to see me in such a position. I could tell she felt bad since there was nothing she could do for me in this situation.

"Apologies for the agony you're feeling," the nurse said as she approached my side to tend to my arm. "You were also dehydrated, and due to your physical state, you may have exerted yourself more than you could. I think that was the cause of your blackout."

At that moment, I realized my arm was tightly wrapped in a makeshift cast. I was so happy to make it back to Leona when I woke up that I didn't bother to take a look at myself to see just how bad my injuries were.

"As you can imagine," the nurse continued, "we deal with a lot of wounded every day due to supply runs and excavation missions back on Earth. So naturally, we've run out of antiseptics some time ago. Some even die in this infirmary due to the extent of the affliction caused by those beings. Look around. Even if people are lucky to find some more and bring it back, we end up using it immediately."

I scanned the room and saw that I was on the ship's makeshift infirmary. I was so focused on myself for a bit that I neglected to take a step back to see the bigger picture. The ship's steel walls made the cries of the injured echo throughout the room. People filled the cots that were spread throughout. Everyone was struggling with their own mortality. I even spotted Joselyn on a cot bearing an unbelievable amount of pain as they stitched her wound. A sealed plastic bag beside her, which I assumed was our less sophisticated version of an IV, dripped down the tube to the injected vein to replenish the fluids she lost. My mouth dropped in awe at the sheer sight.

"As I said, what did you think being a soldier meant?" Brauns repeated.

I let out a sigh as I looked away from their gaze. As I did this, I spotted the nurse and the woman with the uniform giving each other uneasy glances.

"What did you mean before by needing every capable person for what comes next?" I asked, breaking the silence.

"Well—"

"Hold on, Commander Brauns," the female in the uniform interjected. "I think I can answer this one more effectively."

Brauns nodded his head for her to proceed.

"You see, ummm… I'm sorry what was your name again?"

"Xander Williams," I said, trying to ignore the jolting sensations of my broken arm.

For a person in a pressed uniform, her demeanor was opposite of her attire. Upon closer inspection, her hair was unkempt, her eyes were bloodshot red, and she spoke frantically.

"Yes, Mr. Williams. My name is Imala. I'm an informant from our R&A department—"

"R&A?" Leona and I asked at the same time. The nurse and Brauns were startled for a second.

Brauns passed Leona an annoyed look for interrupting.

"Sorry," Leona replied in a low voice.

Hmph. Great minds, I thought.

"It stands for *Research and Analysts*," Imala resumed. "It was R&D, but we stopped getting material for months to really develop anything, so we changed it."

"To the point," Brauns said.

"Right! So that relic you found is unlike *any* we've encountered before." As she was talking, the nurse came to tend to my IV drip next to my cot. "Can you explain your experience with it?"

"Sure..." I said. Imala and Brauns listened intently. Leona was behind them, focusing on me with both curiosity and concern. "Henry—I mean, uhm, Platoon Leader Rosenburg used himself as bait to draw the beings to his position." I choked up a bit.

"It's all right. We understand how traumatic experiences on the field can be. Take your time. Any facts you present will aid us greatly in the long run," Imala said.

Brauns nodded in agreement. The nurse's interest was piqued, and she stood beside the party to hear the information as well.

"Private Fairbanks was designated by Rosenburg to be our cover fire." I motioned my head toward her across the room. Everyone by my bedside glanced over to her. She was groaning in pain. I couldn't imagine being awake through any type of invasive procedure. I guess in a way I was lucky I blacked out before they put a cast on me. "I attempted communicating to get her location twice, but there wasn't a response." They turned back to me. I could tell Leona was slightly concerned about Joselyn now, too. After all, they were deployed on past missions together, although I didn't know if they were particularly close.

"You can be less formal with the titles, Williams," Brauns said. "Just get to the details. Besides, due to the amount of casualties we have every time we try to retrieve something from Earth, rank seems trivial at this point."

"Understood, Brauns." I intentionally said his name without "commander" in front, trying to get a rise out of him for his comment from earlier. A vein protruded from his head, but I swear I saw an instant where he smirked before returning back to his solemn expression. Maybe he secretly admired my passive resistance to authority. Who knows? "Anyway, since Joselyn wasn't responding, I assumed I was the only member left in the platoon. I came face-to-face with this...possessed man who tried to kill me. But there was something strange about it."

"Strange how?" Imala asked. Medical staff came rushing down the walkway between the cots in the middle of the room. Leona stepped out of the way and inched closer to our conversation.

The nurse propped the pillow behind me as she saw me squirming, trying to get comfortable while keeping my arm elevated. "He raised his hand among the crowd of beings, and they appeared to stop at his signal."

"Stopped? As if they were following a command?"

I nodded. I spotted Leona, looking on in confusion.

"Huh... Just as I thought our ranking system was becoming meaningless now, it looks like the enemy could have one of their own," Brauns said. "In all of our deployments, this is the first time I'm hearing of something like this. It's also too much of a coincidence that a being with that kind of authority arrived when we were excavating a relic with so much energy."

"Are you implying that these *things* could have intelligence now?" the nurse asked nervously.

"Is something like that even possible?" Leona added, peering her head over Imala's shoulder.

Imala glanced at Leona and the commander with concern before turning back to me. "When the exo-suits were invented, people assumed that scientists and engineers were the sole contributors to its mechanics and functionality. That was true, in a sense, when dealing with the suits' main components to operate. However, its weapon systems would be useless against those things without theologists and religious parties. They somehow figured out how to utilize relic energy through old scriptures and practices used as doctrines for churches long ago."

"The public was made to believe that religious sects only helped scientific discovery by providing history of the relics," I said. "But now you're telling us they actually contributed to converting those relics into energy for the war? Why keep it a secret?" I felt anger rise in my chest. Leona mouthed the words "calm down" while the rest of the party was focused on me. She knew my beliefs and how upset this would make me. At this point, I was questioning if the military was any better than the government.

"Let me explain this one," Brauns said as he saw tension build in me too. "When the military told the public of the government's schemes, people were divided. Even some people who questioned our governing body had a dependence on their structure in society. Though the facts of their betrayal to the people were obvious, denial was becoming our segregation. Sects started to form, calling the military corrupt and how we just wanted power for ourselves. Others claimed it was just a ridiculous conspiracy to enact martial law on citizens to better control them." He sighed, reminiscing the times. "Needless to say, at the time, the truth was more dangerous than the lie. Can you imagine telling people that texts from the Quran and other ancient writings had tangible truth behind them? Younger generations in 2020 were already migrating their belief systems away from religion. Giving it merit would've only thrown fuel to the fire."

"I get it," Leona said. "Saying the breakthrough solely came from science, a study of our world through practical applications, was the safest bet."

"Exactly."

I sighed. I disagreed with keeping such a thing from the public, but I couldn't really argue with it. The reason behind it was sound.

"With that said," Imala added, trying to break the tension and refocus the topic back to the matter at hand, "science and religion became one to stop this new threat without a huge commotion from society. Though we made breakthroughs in a lot of areas, there is still so much more in the dark we don't know about. For example"—she pulled out the antique box holding the familiar piece of wood from her uniform's pocket. I was amazed she was holding something so powerful so casually—"this small item's readings were off the charts and doesn't appear to run out of energy. Can you continue telling us what you've witnessed so we can get a better idea about it?"

"After the possessed man signaled the others to stop, he charged at me and gave me this broken arm." I motioned my head to the cast. "I knew I had no other option other than to run for the relic case that was attached to the excavation machine. After retrieving it and taking the man down by the skin of my teeth, I stumbled on the sand. I thought I was dead…" I glanced at Leona and she cringed at the very thought of how close she was to losing me. "But before I knew it, the relic fell out of the case and a brilliant light blanketed the entire area. I'm not sure of the magnitude of it, but every single one of those things were gone from sight. That's when I found Joselyn still conscious and made it back to the pod for extraction."

"It wiped out every single one of them just after touching the sand?" Imala questioned in disbelief.

I nodded.

"If you're right, this could be our chance! With its effect and unlimited energy, we could make somewhat of a force field of this thing."

Brauns smiled as Imala exuded excitement from her eyes.

"For what, exactly?" I asked.

"For our foothold back to Earth," Brauns said. "We can build a base from within the magnitude of this relic's energy. Since the energy is unlimited, it will create a safe haven where those things can't penetrate." He coughed to clear his throat. "But as I was saying before, we're going to need every capable person for what comes next."

"What do you mean?"

I caught Leona looking down as if a new weight was put on her shoulders. "We need capable soldiers to clear the area first before we can set this force field down," she managed to say.

"Correct," Brauns replied. "We got lucky that the relic reacted the way it did in Williams's possession, but it didn't continue to output energy after its initial release, did it?"

I shook my head.

"The generator we build will have to sustain the constant energy output of this thing, not to mention the materials we need to build it," Imala said. "So after we send out smaller platoons to retrieve the material we need, we'll need a massive squad to hold the position down where we're going to deploy the generator to give it enough time to work."

"Isn't that just going to create more wounded and KIAs? I can't imagine what that'll do to the other ships' morales. This infirmary is already filled to the brim with the injured as it is!" the nurse exclaimed.

Imala passed the nurse an uneasy glance again. She must've known before what Brauns's plan was asking of the remaining people on board of all the ships. An invisible pressure pushed down on my heart as I knew what that meant for Leona. After all, she was one of the most adept fighters we had. No doubt Brauns was going to use her as one of the soldiers to defend the generator.

"If I may speak plainly, Commander," Leona said.

Brauns nodded. Imala and the nurse turned their attention toward her.

"What if this is all for nothing? You saw the lengths those monsters went through just to make sure Xander didn't get his hands on that relic." Her voice broke up a little. She took a moment to regain her composure. "We've just learned that they could quite possibly possess intelligence and you want us to embark on a mission *this* risky? I know we're running low on everything, but is there not a better plan? Maybe we could observe their movements a bit more before acting rashly." This is the first time I've heard Leona concerned this much about a mission. She's a very capable soldier. For her to have shown this much concern, made me believe we were in for more than we bargained for.

"Though my mission is to ensure our very existence, I'm not unsympathetic. I know what I'm asking of all of you," Brauns replied. He relaxed his rigid posture to show he was speaking candidly. "Think about it. With our one foothold, we could grow vegetation, analyze the planet, and study these things in closer habitats to better know how to combat them. Perhaps we could find more relics with unlimited energy or even manipulate this one to acquire better resources to create more bases around Earth. We can finally get back home! If we prolong our stay on these ships further, we will likely die of other causes. The risk is great, but the sacrifice is necessary."

The nurse sighed. "I understand, Commander." She wrote down notes on my chart, placed it at the foot of my cot on some type of attachment, and walked away, clearly aggravated. The rest of the party stared at her for a second as her actions resembled the situation we were in—frustrated but had to keep moving.

"Right then," Imala added. "I'll go back to R&A to get our team working on this right away."

"I'll relay this information to the other ships to prepare us for the battle ahead." Brauns walked behind her.

"Actually, Commander, you might want to walk the other way to avoid the commotion Private Madigan caused. They're still in the mess hall protesting—mainly Rosenburg's family and friends. Guards are trying to get the situation under control."

"Good point. I'm also going to have to relay the information of Rosenburg's death to his loved ones." He sighed. "The man was a natural leader. This is a huge loss." He then daggered his eyes toward Leona. Leona looked away regrettably. "By the way, Williams, despite how you feel about me, I'm grateful you were out there. We'll continue your training as soon as that arm heals up. The contribution your efforts gave us is invaluable to the cause."

"I didn't do it for you," I replied as I looked at Leona and glanced over to Joselyn across the room. Her stitches appeared to be done as I saw her resting. The last image of Henry's death and Burrel's surprised expression popped in my mind too. "But I understand the weight your title comes with, Commander Brauns."

He smirked and walked out of the infirmary the other way with more weight than he carried before.

CHAPTER 5

"**PHEW... THAT WAS** intense," Leona said as she sat on the edge of my cot.

"Yeah. It was a lot to take in at once," I said, smiling. "What exactly did you do to piss the commander off anyway?"

She couldn't help but give an innocent, nervous smile and chuckle a little. Sometimes she would do that when she was embarrassed to admit things she would do that showed how much she cared for me. It could be awkward at times, but at this moment, it was cute.

"Once I got word you left the dock and were sent to the Earth's surface, I don't know what came over me. It was like a feeling, you know."

She grabbed my hand on the other side of the bed while leaning part of her athletic frame onto my abdomen. The sounds surrounding us of other patients in the infirmary was like white noise to us. When we locked eyes, it was like we were in another world. I listened intently.

"When you were gone too long, Burrel kept me company. It was even his idea to cause a protest in the mess hall."

"Burrel? The same old man who doesn't like getting in people's business?" I asked sarcastically.

"Yep," Leona said as she fiddled with my hand. "I was surprised myself."

"What was the endgame?"

"We figured the more commotion we caused, the quicker they'd try to get help for you through the mission. Or at least give us an update on what was happening."

I gave her a scolding look.

"It was stupid and silly. I know. But for some reason, at the time, it seemed like a good idea to…" She let her train of thought drift midsentence.

"To what?" I studied her eyes as she tried to avert them.

"To… I don't know…retrieve back a piece of you—a semblance of what was left." I could tell it was difficult for her to admit it.

I felt her squeeze my hand hard as I glanced at it and then back to her. She was looking right at me as her eyes started to water.

"I really thought you were going to die, especially the way you teared up before you went."

"Heh… And to think you doubted your faith in us this morning," I said jokingly.

She gave me a playful hit on my chest. "Seriously! I'm not that close to anyone else here. Losing you would be like…"

"Losing hope—your last reason to live, right?"

"Exactly! A-and I know how crazy that sounds since we both don't have our memories fully restored, but I feel like I know you on a deeper level already since these past few months have slid by."

Burrel's words echoed in my head. *Just don't wait too long. It's not like we're promised tomorrow.* After what happened to me, now more than ever was a good time to heed that advice.

I gripped her hand now as she gripped mine. "Don't worry." I brought her hand up to my lips and kissed it. "I feel the same way."

She passed me a smile and blushed. "How did you know what I was trying to say by the way? Do we already have that thing where we're finishing each other's sentences?" she teased.

I smirked. "No, nothing cliché like that. When Joselyn and I"—I motioned my head over to her bed as Leona took a quick look—"were drifting in space waiting for extraction, I asked her what kept her fighting to not lose consciousness before boarding the ship. It was us."

"Us?" Leona said, confused.

"Yeah. Turns out seeing us together was her motivation. Her late husband died sacrificing himself so their family could live, but she was the only survivor after those beings attacked them on Earth."

"My gosh…so seeing us reminds her of her husband and family she lost?"

I solemnly nodded.

"I don't know how I feel about that." Leona looked over to her direction again as Joselyn had her eyes closed, resting. "I'll have to make sure to thank her for doing her best to keep you alive. I've been on a few runs with her, but do you think she's another person we can trust?"

"Considering she gave it her all just so a stranger like me could survive and live out the life she once had, I'd say yes. We can trust her."

Leona looked back to me and looked down, almost shamefully.

"Hey!" I said, lifting her chin with my free hand. Her green irises met my eyes again. "If you're thinking the state she's in now is somehow your fault, it isn't. Okay?"

"It's not that. Hearing you talk about your mission reminded me of Rosenburg's family."

"What about them?"

"They caught wind of the ruckus Burrel and I were causing in the mess hall and joined us. I didn't mean for them to get in trouble. Now, I'm pretty sure they figured out he died in action, considering only two of the three members of your platoon made it back."

"I figure his death is going to haunt me for a while."

"You saw how it happened?"

"Unfortunately. It was an inhuman punch straight through his chest."

"Damn. Now I really feel guilty," she said, averting my gaze.

"Don't stress out about it. You couldn't have foreseen the future. How did you escape any disciplinary action by the way?"

"Like the commander said, he needs all the soldiers he can get right now. Although, knowing him, I'm still going to get punished in one way or another." She smirked as she adjusted herself on the edge of my cot.

We stared into each other's eyes for a moment without a care in the world. I think we were both just relieved to be in each other's company again. She placed my free hand gently on her face as I caressed her cheek. You always wish these moments could last forever before life hits you again. After all, it's the little things that keep you going, allowing you to take larger strides to something bigger. I hoped whatever big thing was coming for us next would be a good one.

"I'm sorry by the way," she said out of the blue.

"For?"

"You remember when we first came out of stasis?"

"Yeah. We found each other after our mental breakdowns and coming to terms with the new world. Both of us recalled having something on Earth but didn't know how to approach one another. It made for an awkward icebreaker," I said, grinning.

"You tried to open casually with the fact how you saw me deployed for supply runs and how dangerous it was. It was so weird and out of nowhere. You didn't even like *know me*—know me. You know what I mean?" she said teasingly.

"And you immediately got defensive and thought I was playing the gender card." I chuckled as I air quoted "gender card" with my free hand. "It took me forever to convince you that I wasn't fussing because I thought the field was dangerous for a woman, but because—"

"You cared," she said, completing my thought.

A smile slowly spread across my face. "I guess we *are* finishing each other's sentences now."

She rolled her eyes, trying to keep from laughing. "Oh my gosh! Do you have to be corny while I'm trying to be serious?"

"*You're* the one who brought it up before!"

We laughed. I felt our little social bubble pop as eyes were on us. I almost forgot we were in a depressing infirmary. Our positive laughter contrasted the setting and drew attention on us a bit. We spoke in low voices again. The constant pain on my right arm flared up again as well. I barely felt it while talking to Leona this whole time. It's amazing what you can cope with when you allow your mind to focus on something else.

The head nurse from before came beside us. "I don't mean to be rude but more injured are coming soon to occupy the cots next to Mr. Williams. They were only vacant due to some important information Commander Brauns chose to share with you. He wanted to keep the discussion within earshot and only discuss it with those present around him. I'll give you five more minutes, but I'm going to have to ask you to leave after that. We need the space so doctors can tend to the wounded."

"We understand," Leona replied.

I nodded in response while she walked away.

"Anyways..." Leona turned back to me, trying to recollect her thoughts. "What I was trying to say is that I get it now." She held my hand in hers. "Hearing your name over the speaker and knowing you were out there risking your life scared me to death. I get what you feel every time I go out there. I promise I'll be more careful."

"I appreciate it, but I don't think that's an option now after the commander revealed their next move to us."

"What are you thinking?"

"What am I not thinking?" I replied, worried. "They have to risk more lives just to get supplies for the generator. We are admittedly in the dark about how these relics and beings are connected. You will most likely have to defend a vast open area until the generator functions. I was training to fight, but now I'm sidelined due to this cast. Need I go on?" I said sarcastically.

"I agree. This sucks all the way around. But we could focus on the positive instead of the negative."

"Okay. You lost me. What is possibly good about the enormous shit storm we're in right now?"

She smiled coyly and walked her fingers toward my chest, whispering, "We'd have our own room."

Suddenly, everything was a blur. I saw myself in some type of bedroom with Leona. We were under the covers, intimately looking into each other's eyes.

Hummm...

She was humming that same tune again when I woke up this morning. "We have our own room now," she said smiling.

Then, just as quick as that daydream happened, I was right back with her in the infirmary.

"What?" I said, confused. Her words stunned me. It came out of the blue.

"You okay?" she asked, still at the edge of my bed. "Do you have a minor concussion or something? You had this blank look on your face."

"No, I'm fine," I said. "Just got lost in thought, I guess."

What was that just now? I thought. *Was it really a daydream? It felt so real.*

"I get it... I know it might seem unrealistic of me to say that right now, but think about it," she continued. "If that relic was able to blanket the entire area in just that instant it released its power, there's no telling what the size of its magnitude could be. The force field they make could have an insane reach. It would give us more space and possibly rooms to ourselves if we can pull this off."

I was flushed with embarrassment, trying to hide how excited I was by avoiding her gaze.

"Oh, come on," she said, resting her head on my chest. "Do we really need to hide this anymore? I know we've been cautious about one another due to our suppressed memories, but after today, all of that seems trivial. Don't you think? I don't care what we find out anymore." She sat up and looked at me directly in my eyes, as if penetrating my very soul. "I think it's worth the risk."

I passed her a playful, suspicious look. "Why are you being so bold all of a sudden? I like to think it's because my life was on the line, but you acted kind of weird this morning too, and I think I've figured it out. What else did you hear in my sleep before I woke up this morning?"

She bit her lower lip to try to keep from laughing. "I may have gotten an idea of how you really felt about us by hearing you moan my name once or twice."

I felt my face becoming hot. I was utterly speechless. The pain in my right arm momentarily dissolved again too.

She smiled and leaned in to kiss me. Her lips were slightly cracked, but honestly, it still felt like one of the tenderest kisses I've ever had because of the feeling and emotion behind it. Plus, it was the first time we ever did anything this intimate before. Since this was new territory for both of us, we took things very slow and tried to get to know each other. But after today, I felt like a barrier we had left between us, came shattering down, allowing our bond to grow.

"If we can pull off this force field thing, what would you say about having our own place if possible?"

"I don't know." I pointed to my ring finger on my left hand. "I'm pretty traditional when it comes to that type of stuff."

"Hmm…okay. I'll keep that in mind." She grinned from ear to ear. "I'll come see you when I can. I got to prepare for the battles ahead, okay?"

I was in a trance while nodding obediently. Any word she said afterward was my command. As she got up to leave, I stopped her, remembering the empty tray in front of her before I sat down to eat my breakfast in the morning. "By the way, I've been meaning to ask you…"

"Ask me what?"

"You skipped brushing this morning to be the first one in line for food, huh?"

Her cheeks grew bright red. "Shut up!" She couldn't keep from grinning. "I'll see you later, Xander." She waved one more time before leaving.

Before Leona left, I thought I noticed a faint change in her expression as she tucked her hair behind her ear. But maybe I was overthinking it or imagining it. I had a feeling she was struggling more internally than she was letting on, both physically and mentally. I looked around and saw all of the injured, including Joselyn. The pain in my arm increased as soon as Leona left the infirmary. Everyone's struggles, including my own, made me realize just how much we needed Command's plan to work for all of our sakes.

CHAPTER 6

"BESIDES THE BROKEN arm, everything looks good," the doctor said the next day as he was standing beside my cot, reading my chart. Judging from his dark complexion and heavy accent, he definitely had an Indian background. The doctors in the infirmary still had white lab coats, but they were made out of synthetic material instead of the regular polyester and cotton. Needless to say, without animals, everyday material we previously used became pretty scarce. There was an idea to transport some of the animals still on Earth back to the ship, but most needed regular game and vegetation for food that required sunlight and water—resources we simply didn't have a lot of. I heard some medical personnel from various healthcare facilities were quick enough to take old lab coats before boarding the ships years ago. However, the fabric from any nonessential clothing was recycled for making other materials such as for the lining of the exo-suits or other necessary purposes.

"Vitals are normal and some of the cuts and lacerations from your mission didn't affect any major arteries," the doctor continued. He lowered the chart from his face and looked at me sincerely. I spotted his name tag. "Dr. Pranav Ravi" was written legibly in ink. Printing devices seemed like a thing in the past too. I'm sure we could scrounge up some undamaged ones on Earth or make some with materials we'd pick up, but running the device at least took batteries and paper as well. Plus, it didn't make sense to risk people's lives for nonessential items. It's like almost everything I looked at was a reminder of how much we've regressed as people. "Considering the amount of force you told me that thing hit you with, you got pretty lucky. It could've been much worse."

"Be straight with me," I replied sternly. "How much time am I looking at for the arm?"

"Like I said, you were lucky," Dr. Ravi said in a serious tone. "The military still allows the infirmary to use power for our medical machines. We were just going to go with the X-ray, but after you told me you used your arm as a shield and were knocked back several feet from the force, I took a CT scan too."

"And?"

"Though rare, you showed signs of fat embolism syndrome where the fat tissue from your bone marrow leaks into your bloodstream. FES is uncommon but causes lung complications and seizures."

I began to panic a little from what he said.

"Not to worry. We caught it before anything serious happened and also stopped any potential infection," he said, noticing my worried expression.

"Then why are you trying to scare me? I appreciate you fixin' me up, Doc, but just tell me how long this will take to heal." His suspense was irritating me.

He sighed. "It's hard telling soldiers this information. Your records show you are still a trainee and yet, you already have that look."

"What look?"

"The look of a man who wants to get back out there by any means. This will take a couple of months' time, maybe more to fully heal. For your sake, do not rush recovery. We don't have the supplies of most modern medicine." He leaned in closer to me. "I'm not going to pretend like I know your situation, Mr. Williams, but what or whomever you're fighting for or protecting, make sure it doesn't kill you in the process. We have enough casualties as it is."

I sighed and nodded. "Sorry for snapping at you."

He waved it off. "You're discharged and free to roam around the ship again. Just don't do anything to aggravate the arm."

"Understood," I said, slowly getting up from the cot.

Dr. Ravi briskly walked to the other side of the room to take care of another patient. The pain and not getting to train to better myself in the field must've been bothering me more than I thought. The cast felt cumbersome and uncomfortable. It didn't help either that I suddenly had an uncanny urge to scratch my arm wrapped in it. As I made my way toward the exit, a sea of injured people were moaning and groaning. Doctors and nurses worked tirelessly to keep their pain under control. Without anesthetics, medical areas became a horde of people crying out in pain. I've never seen so much misery in one place. I wondered if this is what hell was like.

As I was passing by Joselyn's cot, I noticed that she still had her eyes closed, resting. How anyone could sleep through all this noise was beyond me. I was given earplugs yesterday to dull the sounds, but it still kept me up. I barely got a wink of sleep

Just as I was leaving, I heard a low voice say, "Hey…"

I turned back around to Joselyn's cot and saw her eyelids half open. Life was even more drained from her face. Her eyes were red too.

"I'm guessing you couldn't sleep either, huh?" I said as I stepped closer to her cot.

"I tried closing my eyes, thinking it would help…but nope," she said, talking slowly in between breaths.

"It's like going to see a movie in peace but having loud ass people ruin the scene for you, right?" I joked, trying to make her feel better.

"Heh… Heh…" she coughed while attempting to laugh. The sound of her cough was similar to how phlegm gets caught in the respiratory system. But I saw blood coming from her mouth when I picked her up from the sand during our mission. I knew it wasn't that. "Strange analogy…but yeah…it's like that."

"Don't talk. You still need more rest, okay?"

She studied my worried expression. I think she was trying to gauge how serious her condition was by judging my reaction. "Okay, but were you able to at least see Leona again?"

"Yeah. She's the first person I saw, in fact, after waking up. She'd like to thank you personally once you're out of here. *I* can't thank you enough."

"For what? You're the one…who got us…out of there. I got… my ass handed to me," she said, smirking.

I contemplated for a bit, trying to figure out how to word what I was about to say next without making her sound like a coward or me pretentious. "I know you didn't want to freak me out, considering it was my first deployment, but I saw how scared you were. Henry was calm like he did it a thousand times. But you, even though you were experienced as well, you were still terrified. Seeing you get yourself together and fight confidently anyway, despite that fact, gave me strength."

She listened intently as I took a moment to gather my thoughts.

"I saw your injuries before I got you from the sand. I would've been dead long before retrieving the relic, alongside Henry, if you didn't hold out for as long as you did. The sheer stones it took to pull something like that off makes you one hell of a person in my book."

I saw a tear stream down her cheek. "You sure…you weren't a politician…before all this? Because that was…one hell of a speech."

I smiled. "Politician? I thought you didn't like bullshit."

She burst out in laughter, causing her to cough again. "Get out of here…before you make me go into a coma," she said, grinning while wincing in pain.

"Will do."

"Oh, and, Xander," she called while I was walking away.

"Yeah?"

"I'm glad I could help."

I waved with my free hand as I made my way toward the exit. I pressed my hand against the biometric scanner to open the automatic doors. It was a safety precaution to prevent theft of medical supplies, or God forbid, we experience a biohazard that would require a quarantine lockdown. We're still advanced in some areas while primitive in others. The contradiction of this ship is comical, even bizarre at times. I had a feeling there were still concepts that took the contrast deeper than I could've imagined. Right before I left, I caught a glimpse of a teenager. His skin was pickled with freckles. He looked about sixteen, maybe a bit younger. I really hoped he was just sick because if we were deploying people that young on missions, then we deserved this hell.

The corridor was dimly lit as I made my way toward the huge mess hall where most of us usually were. It was the biggest space on the ship. Naturally, people would congregate there and converse even if no food was being served. I was silently praying for the Rosenburg family. The last time someone acted up in the mess hall, the guards put the guy in an isolated room for several weeks with only one hot meal a day and a cot. Being on this ship is already like a prison. I imagine taking away the little amenities we had was like torture to some, even if it was just a few weeks.

As I walked through the opening frame of the mess hall, one person sitting on a table spotted me and immediately pointed. Before I knew it, all eyes were on me. It felt like minutes had passed, although it was only seconds. In that instant, I felt like I was in the twilight zone with so many people staring at me at once. I was speechless and didn't know what to do.

"He's the guy that brought back the relic," I heard one person say in the crowd.

"It's him! He was part of the platoon that's given us a chance!" another person shouted.

Clap! Clap! Clap!

I gazed in amazement as a thunderous applause boomed and echoed throughout the mess hall. The guards had to calm some of them down as it was beginning to become rowdy. People came up to me and kept thanking me for my contribution to the cause. I even had a couple of kids sign my cast. Although my arm was still throbbing in pain, I grinned and bore it. I remember being told that everyone who volunteered to aid the cause had their children in stasis along with them. However, if a child was below a certain age, stasis was too dangerous for them since their mind was at too early of a stage in development. Tampering with their growth could lead to disabilities. Shock was the only reaction I could give as their eyes gleamed at me. After all, I was just trying to survive while getting the relic back. I wasn't trying to be some kind of war hero.

"Attention!" one of the guards yelled at the top of his lungs while standing on one of the tables. "Calm down and back away from this gentleman! Entrances and doorways have to be cleared at all times for authorized personnel to get through. Huge crowds are also not permitted so that we, as authorized militant enforcers, can monitor any suspicious or potentially dangerous situation that can occur between occupants on the ship. If we have to repeat these standard policies again, disciplinary action will be enforced. Last warning! Spread out and settle down!"

People reluctantly did as the guard said. Just like that, the crowd dissipated. I spotted Leona and Burrel emerge from the sea of people.

"Hey! You okay? Sorry for the unwanted attention. It's kind of my fault," Leona said as she walked up to me.

"No need to take all the blame, Leona. I coerced you into this. It's my fault too," Burrel said as he hobbled with his cane toward me.

"What's going on?" I asked, confused. I motioned with my hand for us to step to the side from the entrance to the mess hall so people could get through.

"The people from the commotion we caused yesterday saw Command acting anxiously once your platoon came back from deployment," Burrel replied.

"Yep. I just got some news myself about training with top soldiers from the other seven vessels orbiting Earth," Leona chimed in. "They want us to strategize tactics once it comes time to guard the generator."

"That soon? I know the commander was speculating, but we just came back yesterday with the relic," I replied.

"And the R&A department have been working tirelessly around the clock, studying it. The data they're receiving makes it look more and more promising that we can use it in our favor."

"For sure," Burrel added. Some people were walking by. He waited for them to pass and looked around. Once he saw the coast was clear, he began speaking in a lower tone. "There are people here who are friends with some of the guards. They have rotating shifts that station them in other areas of the ship, including the R&A department. Some of R&A's discussions can be overheard, and you know how fast word can get around here."

"Ah," I replied. "And that's how people know what's going on before anything has been officially said."

"Well, that and the deployments for supply runs have been increased to get more material," Leona said. "They've been deploying soldiers in areas with the least amount of enemy activity to prevent more casualties. We're going to need a lot of able bodies to defend the generator. No more unnecessary risks are being taken until that time comes."

"Wow! A lot has happened in such a short amount of time."

"What you and your platoon did was critical in turning the tide of this war. Nobody wants to waste time with the chance you all gave us."

"I see..."

I looked down at the tiled floor beneath my feet, riddled with shoe marks. I guess everyone was so busy and anxious that cleaning seemed like a minuscule task too. Everything was happening so fast. I felt an unspeakable weight on my heart as I knew it was Leona's turn to share the weight of the world. Even now as people saw me as this important figure, I couldn't help but feel useless. I looked up at Burrel and Leona again. Burrel passed me a worried glance. Judging by Leona's expression, I think she could tell the concern I had for her.

"Now that you know what's going on, it's time for me to rendezvous with Command at headquarters to discuss future plans. I was on my way there but saw you walk into the mess hall. There was no way I was letting you face this crowd alone," she said, grinning at me.

Suddenly, to my surprise, she reached out and hugged Burrel. They've spoken before, but I never knew him to be a hugger. He wasn't shy about conversation, but he still distanced himself from getting too close with people. I guess the thought of me dying struck a chord in him not even he knew he had. Burrel awkwardly patted her on the back. I don't think he was expecting that either.

"Thanks again for being there, Burrel. I appreciate it. I'll let you two catch up."

Burrel nodded.

Leona then leaned in close to my ear and whispered, "Don't worry about me too much. Our own room is all I'll be thinking about to get me through this," she teased to make me feel better.

I shook my head and couldn't keep from smirking. It was also awkward for us being that familiar around each other right in front of Burrel. He has seen us interact but never intimately. Hence, it got even a tad weirder when she gave me a peck on the lips.

"I'll see you later," she said. She tucked part of her hair behind her ear in a shy, dorky way after she saw Burrel look away uncomfortably. I could tell us being this close now in our relationship was new territory for her, and she didn't quite know how to act around me yet. Her brisk walk out of the mess hall made it all the more obvious. She was usually pretty stoic.

Burrel passed me a coy look. "Leona has been in high spirits ever since you got back."

"Yeah… I was lying on the cot in the infirmary that could have easily been my deathbed. I thought I'd follow your advice."

"Then why do you still look down? It's like someone killed your puppy or something."

I chuckled. "I know I should be grateful I'm even alive right now. The doctor told me I'm lucky to even be moving, but I still can't help but feel stuck."

Burrel studied my solemn expression. "Walk with me," he said, touching my shoulder. "Tell me what's on your mind."

He limped with his cane, walking beside me as I spoke. "This right arm is going to take at least a couple of months to heal, and I was just getting the knack of training." I was maneuvering past the people walking around us. Some stared at me like I was some kind of celebrity. Ironically, I still felt like the rest of them. "I pushed myself through exercises before to not be dead weight on this ship. I also wanted to be able to fight alongside Leona if the time came. But now…"

"But now you feel like life has pushed you two steps back after you did your best to take a step forward."

"Exactly."

Burrel sighed. "I know what you mean all too well."

We took a moment to stare outside the huge window toward Earth. If you focused enough, you could actually see other vessels orbiting the Earth in the darkness of space. It was beautiful and depressing at the same time. All the potential creation of life had become squandered by our instruments of destruction. We couldn't help but succumb to our curiosity and take a peek into another dimension. Now that world's darkness has entered ours.

"You seem to be getting pretty chummy with Leona by the way," I said, breaking the silence.

"She was broken up about your departure. The thought of you not coming back was getting to her harder than she thought. So I gave her a shoulder to lean on for you."

"Only she was broken up, huh?" I said suspiciously with a smile.

He smiled back. "Yeah, only her." He knew what I was getting at.

"Well… You got any wise words for me?" I asked as I stared out the window again.

There was no response. I looked his way again and saw him scanning my cast. His demeanor was concerning me. I even started scanning my cast too to see if something was wrong. The only thing I spotted was writing the kids put on it from before. One perked me up as it read, "Thanks for being awesome, mister!" I bet the kids didn't even know what was going on. They were probably just happy because their parents were happy.

"Is there a problem?" I finally asked.

He contemplated for a bit. "If I showed you something, how much can I count on your discretion?"

I studied his serious expression. "After being there for Leona while you both thought I was most likely heading toward my death, I'd say wholeheartedly."

He smirked. "You still have that blunt sarcasm. I guess you're not completely down. Follow me."

I followed him through droves of people on the ship. I never really did take a personalized tour through other areas here. After hearing the state the world was in after being awakened from stasis, I slept, used the bathroom, ate, and trained for months. Any room that didn't involve any of those activities didn't really interest me. I found myself now following him down through a dimly lit metal staircase.

"Uhm, Burrel. Where are you taking us?"

"You'll see once we get there. In the meantime, tell me about your deployment in detail. Leona kind of generalized it when she told me."

As I was explaining my time on Earth, I noticed that we were getting further away from most of the occupants on the ship. We were so far deep in the recesses of this ship's corridors that I didn't even see a guard stationed anywhere. I'm surprised we didn't get stopped by one for straying too far. I was slightly concerned, but it's not like I was panicking. Besides, if Burrel tried something, all I'd have to do is kick his cane from beneath him. As bad as that sounds, it's a logical tactic to go for an enemy's weakness first to get out of a dangerous situation.

"Interesting," he said as I finished telling him my story. "Well, here we are."

I examined around me and found that we were in a secluded area in the lower deck of the ship. I'm not sure what they used this room for before, but it was dusty.

"Okay. I'm stumped. What is this place?"

"Believe it or not, it was meant to be a place for the UN leader and his family. The blueprints for the interior design were never finished. The military turned it into a potential storage place if they ever needed it."

"Wait a minute. UN? As in the United Nations? I thought the ships—the orbital vessels were only meant for the people and essential departments from the start?"

Burrel smirked. "So does everyone else. There's so much you don't know...like how these ships were only intended for the rich before."

Before I could even process what he said to me, he attacked me with his cane out of nowhere. As he took a swipe down at me with it, I raised my right hand, forgetting the cast was on it. He stopped the cane right before it hit the cast. Not knowing what was going on, I quickly tried to back away, but he lunged at me with a punch toward my midsection. I noticed he leapt off of his supposedly injured foot. I was able to step aside and evade it with my left arm that was free. However, I suddenly felt my feet get swept from under me when I was attempting to recover. Right when I thought my head was going to land on the solid floor hard, I felt Burrel's hand pull mine with force. I stopped before my head collided with the hard surface below. He helped me get back up. I pushed him away from me.

"Burrel! What the hell, man?" I shouted, trying to catch my breath.

"It's as I thought. You're a natural."

"What are you talk—"

"You told me you lost count of how many of those things you swiped at with your saber once Henry fell, defending you."

"Yeah? And?"

"Any other inexperienced soldier would've died, son. It was more than dumb luck that you survived. You got a knack for this."

"You got all that after bringing me down to the shadiest place you could've brought me and attacking me for no reason?!"

"I got that from the way you reacted to my attacks. Although you only have a few months of training, your reaction time is close to top-notch," he said, picking up his cane from the floor. "After realizing the initial attack with my cane was a fake, you didn't freeze. You tried to get distance. When I tried to close in on you again with a punch, you evaded it well."

"Then how come I almost fell on my ass?" I was furious and confused at the same time. I didn't know how to take his words or act toward his calm demeanor.

"That's due to your lack of experience. You don't know your strengths and weaknesses yet." He took a second to clear his throat. "For example, you told me you blocked that being's attack with your right arm, which is your dominant arm. If anything, you should've blocked with your left. At least if that arm was broken, you would've had more options to consider in a fight besides holding the relic."

"Hold on, Burrel! Rewind for a second," I said, trying to make sense of what was going on. "I thought we were down an arm and leg between us, but you can walk? Do you even need that cane? Is the limp real?"

"First of all, keep your voice down. The metal walls throughout these corridors echo. Second, yes, I can walk. I have pain in my leg. I just exaggerated a little."

"A little?" I said, passing him a scolding look.

"I have my reasons for keeping this quiet, kid. I'm not looking to be a martyr because of others' mistakes. This whole war is their fault."

"But even with the pain in your leg, you could pilot an exo-suit that does cover fire at least. Your skills are invaluable!"

"I said no." He exhaled, resting his hands on the top of his cane. "Even at my age, I was one of the first ones to pilot those suits. The first war I was in with it wasn't even one where we fought for our world. It was a civil war before those beings took over."

"A civil war before the world war? You remember that much already after coming out of stasis months ago?"

"Yeah, why? How much do you recall?"

"I'm getting snippets of random years and other moments, but they're coming in pieces so far."

"Hmmm…" He looked perplexed as if the way my memory was coming back was odd. "Then it's best to tell you this information after you've retrieved your memories. No point in risking a mental breakdown right now."

"You got me curious, but I get it. I've had one mental breakdown already."

"Yes. The mind can be fragile if it doesn't have the support of other experiences to receive new information. Even then, certain concepts can be too overwhelming to bear."

"Okay, but can you at least tell me why you're revealing your secret to me?"

"You have promise and someone you care for. I could tell you're trying to get stronger so neither you nor Leona are out there fighting those things without each other. That's all the reason I need to help you."

The anxiety I once had was swept by relief. I was starting to think he was a psychopath. It just turns out he cares, although he shows it in a very different way than I was expecting. Though Burrel had his secrets, something told me I could still trust him. I ignored the past doubts in my head and was just thankful he was showing his amazing skills to me of all people.

"All right, Burrel. I hear you. But are you sure you want to waste time on me? I am still recovering."

"What will you do if you lose use of your arm again in a fight? Are you going to stop fighting? No. The enemy won't give you a choice."

I nodded.

"This is a perfect chance for you to learn how to overcome your weaknesses even if you can't get the full training of the military right now." He dropped back into a stance. "Now, enough talk. Come at me!"

CHAPTER 7

MONTHS PASSED. THINGS were picking up more smoothly than intended. All eight vessels were able to collect materials R&A used to construct the generator. We even surprisingly had a surplus and used it to repair the damaged exo-suits from the many deployments from before. Due to our lack of supplies, we had limited units of those suits, and they kept getting damaged. Even the one I used to retrieve the relic had a few tears in the inner lining and small chips of lost armor that were never tended to. Building more exo-suits would be one of the first priorities if we were able to activate the force field the generator would cause. Some of the department's engineers even volunteered to make drones from some of the surplus to monitor the battles on Earth for loved ones. They were actually more like mini robots that could hover and had a camouflage feature to avoid getting spotted by the enemy. But we called them drones for short.

Command was against people peering in on battles as it might cause them to act out, seeing the ones closest to them hurt. Some commanders of the vessels allowed this, however. If this mission didn't go well, there was no hope of the remaining vessels surviving in space with the limited reserves we had. Luckily, Commander Brauns of our vessel caved in to the idea to let occupants on the ship view the battle too on big screens in the mess hall. The last time they brought those out was to keep kids distracted with old DVD movies while we had to bear with one meal a day due to the shortage of food for a time. Whenever they brought out unnecessary amenities for us, we knew the situation was severe. After all, it could be the last time any of us saw the people we cared about as they fought on the battlefield. Brauns understood the situation. This was literally do or die.

Pant... Pant...

The room echoed with my heavy breathing as Burrel continued to train me.

"Out there you need to be able to seamlessly take out one enemy and go to the next without depleting your stamina," Burrel said as he watched me bent over, placing my hands on my knees. "You can only do that if you get control of your breathing."

The sessions with Burrel in the isolated room had been going well. I got the cast off and was able to move my right hand again. Though, it was still kind of weak. So I had to take it slow to build up muscle and resistance in it again. On a positive note, I learned how to fight with one hand. Plus, I figured out how no guard spotted us down here. It turns out Burrel knows one of them positioned at the front of the location before entering the area. They were old war buddies back when we were still on Earth. Whenever he saw us coming through, he just let us pass without a word. I found out no one is allowed back here anyways because the cameras don't reach that far. I didn't even know they were monitoring us until Burrel told me. The only time we had privacy was when we were supposedly in the bathrooms. After finding out, I'm even skeptical about that. There's more to what Burrel knows than he was letting on, but I let it be. I didn't want to push him. Besides, it took this long for us to even get to this point in our friendship. I didn't want to lose my footing with him, especially if he had more information that could help.

"Don't get me wrong, Burrel," I said, raising my head. Tricklets of sweat were plopping onto the cold, hard floor. I didn't notice how tired I was until I saw a tiny puddle at my feet. "I'm grateful you've been teaching me hand-to-hand combat, but when I get back in the exo-suit again, it has weapons. And I need those weapons to take them down, especially the ones that resemble dark silhouettes." I started to slow my breathing back to normal. "A punch isn't going to do squat against that. It's basic exo-suit training that the suit is nothing without relic energy."

"Besides that relic you found, all relic energy runs on borrowed time. What will you do when you face one of those things in a human body again?"

"I see your point, but their uncanny strength would just blow me away too like last time, right?"

"No matter how strong, human bodies still have weaknesses. The military still isn't sure those things can feel pain, but they are still weak at the joints." He dropped into a ready stance. "Come! Punch me. You'll see what I mean."

I squared up with him into a fighting stance and threw a straight right. He dodged and clasped my arm at the wrist. He used his other hand as a palm strike to put slight pressure on the back of my elbow.

"Ahhh," I cried out in a low tone as I felt how easily he could've hyperextended my elbow. I also felt him hit the back of my knee as it buckled. Before I knew it, I was already kneeling on the ground at his mercy. I had no idea how he could still be so agile, but I sure was glad I was never on his bad side.

"As you can see, joints are an easy target if you know where to hit and you time it properly. It'll buy you some time until you can figure out your next move."

"Cool. I'll just have to hope they don't break my leg like my arm, so I can still evade."

Burrel smirked. "Yeah, there's that too." He snapped his finger as if remembering something. "Oh, and thanks for keeping my... *condition* between us by the way. I'm not making you keep this from Leona. I'll tell her in my own time. I know you don't like keeping things from her."

"Don't worry. To be honest, it is *your* business after all. Keeping it quiet is the least I can do after you've been doing this for me between your excavation assignments."

He nodded.

Bzzzzz!

The signal to the speakers activated. I was surprised there was one in this room too, but if this ship was built for the rich like Burrel mentioned, then the main construction of the ship's design was made long before the military took control over it. In that regard, it made

70

sense considering all the rooms needed to be privy to announce-ments. Hearing the speaker overhead reminded me of how relieved I was that they finally did away with the "end of the world" announce-ment. I agreed with the dentist I met that time ago. Though I under-stood the reasoning behind it, it did get quite annoying.

"Attention to the occupants on all eight vessels. The selected individuals chosen to embark on the mission to defend our last hope are ready to deploy. The ships whose commanders have agreed to broadcast the battle to the remainder occupants not supporting the fight directly, please proceed to your designated viewing stations at this time. For the ships whose commanders have not agreed to broadcast the battle, we ask you to wait patiently until we're able to deliver the final results of the mission."

"Man… I can't imagine the anxiety friends and families are feeling on the other vessels who don't have the broadcast," Burrel commented.

"Yeah," I replied, thinking about Leona. I'd be climbing the walls if I couldn't at least see how she was doing at a time like this. "We should start heading back before people start wondering where we are."

"Good call."

I noticed the voice from the speaker was now a man's. The woman must've permanently been part of communication for the battlefield now. Burrel and I made our way back to the mess hall as the broadcast continued, passing by the familiar guard on the way. I thought I'd at least wave to him so that it didn't feel so awkward. He gave a slight nod and continued to look forward while maintaining his rigid stance. It must've been a pain to exhibit the same disciplined demeanor in one spot until your shift ended.

"Though these are trying times, we ask that you exercise patience and remain calm. We understand how anxious you must feel as our very survival depends on the outcome of this venture. However, giving in to your panic and distress will only cause disar-ray, making everyone's situation even more difficult. Command has worked tirelessly with the top soldiers of each vessel to formulate the best strategy, so the outcome works in our favor. We may seem pushed to the brink of extinction against insurmountable odds, but we implore you to have faith."

"Wow," Burrel said as we made our way to the mess hall. He walked with his cane beside him and exaggerated his limp again. I had to try to keep from rolling my eyes. "That almost sounded like they cared."

"You know, one day, I'm going to hold you to telling me why you have a prejudice against the military so much."

"It's not prejudice if their past actions actually warrant my ill will."

I studied his face to see if he was just teasing or being stubborn like always. His expression was stern. I could see a deep contemplation in his eyes. It's like what he saw in the past is something he couldn't unsee or let go even in the present. At that moment, for some reason, I had a bad feeling that once I completely got my memory back, how I viewed everything would change.

Several crowds of people were already in front of big screens spread out in the mess hall. And when I say big, I mean like IMAX big. They rolled down giant projection screens. It was all the more surreal how big the mess hall actually was. You get used to it after a while. They put most of the tables where people ate to the side. I'm not a technician or anything, but I assumed they programmed the drones on the battlefield to sync up its video feed with the projectors that were going to display the content. The more older amenities I saw that came with the ship, the more I realized that the vessel's structure *was* made for elite individuals of our past society. To think that there were people so greedy in the world that they would've hogged all this to themselves was baffling to me. The extent of their selfishness was unfathomable.

As soon as we approached, people immediately recognized us. After the mess hall commotion Burrel started, people started making small talk with me, trying to get to know me better. No matter how much I told them that I didn't need special treatment nor attention, they liked my modesty and respected me all the more for it. I couldn't win. After all, I didn't feel like I deserved anything more after countless people risked their lives so that we could keep having a tomorrow. However, my contribution still preceded me and raised my reputation. Leona, who was already well-known for being an adept soldier, received more attention too when it was found out that she would be leading one of the squads formed for this mission. Whenever she had breaks from combat routines and strategizing sessions with Command, she'd come see me when she could. In those moments, we felt like all eyes were on us whenever we were around people. We had to find spots on the ship that had less foot traffic just to talk and catch up.

"Don't be shy!" a person exclaimed. "We saved a spot for you two right by an old friend."

Old friend? I thought as Burrel and I were trying to make headway through all the people. I was trying to make sure not to step on anyone as I tiptoed around. It reminded me of the struggle I had to go through in the morning when everyone was asleep. Some people were really scrunched up together just to make room for others. I saw a piece of paper with the words "Southern Squad" written on the side of the projector screen. It was the squad Leona told me she was leading. Other projectors indicated which drones would be broadcasting which teams as well.

"I know what you're thinking," Burrel said to me in a low voice as we made our way to the front. "It's uncomfortable, yeah. But it could be much worse. You could've been in the back trying to see over people."

I chuckled. "True."

"He's got that right," I heard a familiar voice say as we were finally to the spot in front of the screen.

"That's some good ears she has," Burrel chimed in.

"Joselyn?" I asked. She was one of the few people actually sitting in a chair. Last time I saw her, she was pale. Some color came back to her face. Although, she was still slightly hunched over in pain. I caught the glimpse of some bandages acting as support around her torso. She must've had some broken ribs as well during that time.

"In the flesh, Xander. Long time no see."

"Wow. I'm glad to see you're well. Were you dismissed from the infirmary today? And I'm guessing you received the same ovation as I did from everyone?"

They saved Burrel a chair too for his "hurt leg." I sat on the floor between them. I was kind of self-conscious about how Burrel and I smelled after training but forgot that everyone was naturally musty already.

"No. I'm only out for today. You know…for the mission that could make us or break us and all…" She paused, staring down at the floor as I saw the severity of the situation weighing down on her.

Come to think of it, everyone was doing a good job at keeping their wits about them. Maybe we were all in denial of what was to come next if we failed. Facing that reality was too much to handle right now.

"They said I need more time to recover," she continued. "The damage to my abdomen was more extensive than they thought. Honestly, if our soldiers didn't work as hard as they did on supply runs after our mission, I would've died on that cot in the infirmary already."

"Is that so?"

"Yeah. During the mass supply runs for materials these past months, vessel 4 stumbled upon a heap of medical equipment. They found a horde of medicine, including anesthetics and shared it with us, vessel 7, and the other ships. It must've been the spot of a hospital before it got destroyed."

"Wow… I guess we did inspire the cause in more ways than we thought, huh?" I was beginning to understand the impact people felt we made.

"I guess. I could do without the standing ovation like you said before. It's…weird."

"Especially for you since you don't particularly like people."

She nodded in agreement.

"Don't say that," a random woman chimed in. She poked her head out the front row. I noticed her holding her child's hand so as not to lose him in the crowd. "Both of you are survivors that have given us the opportunity for this mission. We'd be stuck without you."

Joselyn passed me an irritating look. "You see what I mean?"

I smirked.

Burrel chortled, which reminded me how I haven't introduced him yet.

"Oh! I almost forgot. This is my friend, Burrel." I leaned back so she could get a better view of him.

"Hey," she said.

Burrel waved.

It was surreal sitting next to a veteran of the cause without people knowing about it.

"You'll have to thank Leona for coming by and checking on me these past months once she makes it back," Joselyn said, keeping up the conversation. She adjusted herself to get more comfortable in the chair. "I don't really talk to anyone else here... Anyways, I appreciate it."

"Don't mention it," I replied.

I looked over to Burrel who glanced her way after she said that. Knowing how he was a loner himself, I could tell how he sympathized with her. During the months that have passed by, Leona made it a point to check in on Joselyn, after seeing me, when she could during breaks from training. She was more grateful toward Joselyn than I thought. I guess after hearing about her deceased husband, it scared her to think that it could've easily happened to me too. She'd be going through the same as Joselyn.

I haven't seen Joselyn since our discussion in the hospital when I got discharged. I wanted to visit, but due to the increase in the wounded at the time for supply runs, the infirmary wasn't accepting any visitors. Thankfully, there were more injured than fatalities. The only ones allowed were soldiers designated to protect the generator. They were authorized to collect any new intel they could from soldiers who fought the enemy during supply runs. Leona was able to sneak in under that guise. Plus, my increase in reputation at the time inadvertently caused a commotion everywhere I went. I'd probably be a distraction from medical procedures as a visitor. Seeing how people still reacted toward me, I say I'd be right. I mean they let me sit in the front row of one of the projectors while they have loved ones on the battlefield they wanted to see too. I hope Joselyn would be fine going back to the infirmary after this since people now knew she was in good health as well.

"By the way, it may be just me but seeing Leona show so much... how should I say...*compassion* is off-putting to me," Joselyn said.

"Nope," Burrel interjected. "It's not just you. I know what you mean." He was probably thinking back to the time Leona kissed me in front of him.

"See? I'm not the only one."

"What's strange about it?" I asked.

"Well, you're used to it because you two are...you know...a *thing*. You get to see her soft side all the time. But seeing her empathetic is a new experience for me, considering how she is on the field. She's usually so focused and stern."

The lights dimmed. Everyone started to calm down and focus more on the projectors starting up. I quickly examined the room and saw others' anxiety begin to surface. I even saw some praying. Murmurs of conversations in the background started to fade too. I stretched out my legs and leaned back on my elbows. My body ached from training with Burrel earlier.

"I know she's built up a reputation of being tough in a fight, but the fact she went out of her way to see you should show you how good of a person you are. She rarely trusts anyone."

Joselyn grinned, flattered.

"Damn, Xander. Are you trying to hog all the women here for yourself?" Burrel said. He tried to hide it, but I could tell he was flattered too, since Leona also trusted him.

"Huh? It's not like that," I said nervously.

Oh, gosh. I hope I didn't give the wrong impression, I thought.

"He wishes," Joselyn responded, ignoring my comment.

I glanced at the both of them and could tell they were just teasing me.

"Man, forget you two."

They both laughed.

"Well, either way, I won't give her a hard time about it. She's at least trying to open up to people unlike some of us," she said.

It was good to see Joselyn in good spirits, although she was still recovering. Plus, I noticed that Burrel was less tense and more relaxed. *Were Leona and I actually able to trust other people besides each other?* I thought. If so, we needed all the help we could get. If we didn't pull this off, the ships really would have to start merging occupants just to ration. I couldn't explain it then, but for some reason, this brief moment of reprieve felt like a calm before the storm.

CHAPTER 8

Bzzzzz!

Every crowd stared at their designated projector as it started displaying video feed. The voice from the speaker informed us of the immense battle that was about to commence.

"The soldiers' pods have now landed. Drones for each vessel who has chosen to relay the video feed to occupants have been assigned to follow each Alpha or Beta team, corresponding to the soldiers' occupying vessel. Due to Delta's numbers and position on the battlefield, we could not designate a lot of drones for those soldiers. Command has their own drones to coordinate the battle on their end. Also, only audio output from the vessel's corresponding team and part of Command's can be heard through relay drones to cause less confusion. For those who are not participating, please stand by for further details of the battle. We appreciate your cooperation."

Parties over radio communications were usually referred to by the NATO phonetic alphabet code starting from A to Z to avoid miscommunication. However, a lot has changed apparently in the years these things came to be. The military had to alter some of their strategies and coordinations to accommodate the changes with their ranks and people.

"They sound like a damn infomercial," Burrel blurted out.

"Shhh." I heard some people in the back hush him. I surveyed the room behind me and saw people huddled together, worried.

They were nonchalant a few seconds ago, but now they were intently staring at the screen as reality hit them.

Burrel loved playing to his stereotype—the cranky old man. His cane was in his lap, crossing his arms in protest. I glanced over to Joselyn who was covering her mouth, trying not to laugh. It was like being in the theater between two obnoxious people you regrettably know. Yet, it was somewhat comforting to have them both beside me while Leona was fighting.

The picture came into focus. I saw a team equipped with exo-suits. Behind them was the tip of the sun beginning to peak out from the horizon while they stood in an open, grassy plain with some old one-story buildings in the background.

"Why did they choose an area so open to enemy fire?" Joselyn asked in a low voice. "They'll get picked off by the enemy faster exposed like that."

I was about to answer, but Burel cut in before I could get a word out.

"None of us have been familiar with any of Earth's territory for quite some time. These things have been roaming it since then. Plus, the landscape has changed quite a bit." He took a pause as if reflecting. "Anywhere obscuring our view from the enemy like a forest would only favor them and put us in more jeopardy. Though risky, I bet Command thought choosing this terrain was the best play to see all of the enemy's movements."

"That's unexpectedly insightful, Burrel," Joselyn said suspiciously.

I felt a sudden rise in my chest. I realized it was panic as Joselyn could question Burrel about how he knew so much about battle layout.

"It *is* the job of an excavator to know these things," Burrel replied confidently in a low tone without looking at her. "Surveying the land with our instruments on the ship allows our soldiers to retrieve objects of significance with the least amount of enemy threat in the area."

"Ah, you're right. I didn't even think of that."

Phew, I thought. I guess I shouldn't be surprised since Burrel was this good at hiding his secret this long.

I focused on the screen again, displaying the team in their gear. From the looks of their pocketed hilts and what looked to be very similar to the barrel of a gun at their sides, they were most likely inside the Equalizer.

"Alpha, Beta, and Delta, confirm your positions," I heard the female voice of the communication relay to the teams. It was the same voice from the "end of the world" announcement and during my mission. I heard through the grapevine that her name was Arinya.

Our feed became silent again as I saw the soldiers in the exo-suits wait to confirm their status. Gazing at them reminded me of these past months. I learned there were four types of model suits in total left. We had more, but they kept getting destroyed left and right. The Equalizer had one close-quarters weapon and a long-range weapon, making it the most balanced model in combat. The Juggernaut, the one Henry wore before he passed, was equipped with lining for relic energy to emanate from the knuckles. Impacts with objects or surfaces created shockwaves. Mini turrets could also be equipped for crowd control and to get the enemy's attention. If the Beta team all had Equalizers, then I assumed Alpha had the Juggernauts due to their position. It had the most armor, and they needed to last longer since they were the final line of defense. By process of elimination, Delta must've had Cavalry. The Cavalry was equipped with weapons for sniping and cover fire to thin out enemy numbers from a distance. This was the same model Joselyn fought with in our mission together. The stealth model I used, Infiltrator, wouldn't provide any benefit since this was a straightforward fight. Though our suits had their strengths, our enemies tended to exploit their weaknesses.

"This is South Squadron from Beta," I heard a familiar voice say through the feed. "We're in position."

Some people around me cheered as they knew who it was, even if she was behind a helmet. Others still stood with anxiety and worry. The same was for the other screens as different squads also confirmed their location. Joselyn glanced around and then to me with a smirk. Burrel briefly touched my shoulder almost as if gesturing, "Try not to worry. It's going to be okay." A huge room of mixed feelings caused this unusual density of anticipation in the air.

"Roger that, Squad Leader Madigan!" Arinya said.

I couldn't help but feel kind of proud that Leona was chosen as a squad leader for this mission. Though our very existence stood in the balance, it felt good to know how acknowledged she was. Through our visits, Leona informed me that they dropped formal military rankings since there weren't a lot of soldiers left for rank to hold merit in missions besides the commanders of the vessels. The people who exhibited leadership or exceled in certain types of missions were promoted to squad leader for that deployment only. Seniority no longer played a factor unless your experience showed your qualifications during battle. It ruffled some feathers, but Command was solely organizing platoons on the best chance of survival at this point.

I saw Leona's visor of her helmet look directly into the drone while her team was waiting for Command to confirm Delta's position before proceeding. It was as if she was saying "hey" to me from the other side. I smiled as if she could see me. It was faint, but I think the communicator picked up her low humming again. Though a bit odd at a time like this, the tune was kind of soothing.

It seemed tedious to check their locations, but it was crucial. Their strategy depended on it. Leona also informed me of their plan. It consisted of three rings of defense. If you were to look at the soldiers from a bird eye's view on the battlefield, you would see three main positions consisting of Alpha, Beta, and Delta. Alpha was the smallest, closest circle defending the generator. Usually, the best were among the frontlines. In this case, saving the best soldiers for the last line still gave us a chance to buy time for the generator to activate if Beta and Delta failed to hold their positions. Apparently, Alpha was that good.

Beta was the frontline split into four sub teams of five. There were the north, south, west, and east squads that guarded each direction as their labels suggested. We were low on soldiers, so Command thought it was best to have the frontlines consist of a few adept ones. Delta, the soldiers who act as the circle in between the first and last lines of defense, would assist and provide support between the two if either needed it. Delta were capable soldiers, although their combat prowess wasn't as polished as Beta's, and their skill level didn't come close to Alpha's. Though Delta had the lowest-quality soldiers, their numbers were the most. The idea was for them to spread out and plug the holes of either circle's defense to keep the enemy from getting to the generator.

Vwip!

The low sound effect of the Equalizer's relic energy activating on the suit snapped me from my train of thought. Leona shot a dark silhouette that was close to their proximity. Her long-range weapon attached to her wrist for the current of relic energy as she pointed it like a firearm.

"Looks like we already have some enemies in the area," Leona said. "They don't seem to notice us yet, though. If you have a sure shot and they get close, take it. Otherwise, they can alert more. If not, conserve your relic energy. We don't want an all-out fight until Command has confirmed all positions."

Two of the teammates nodded but not all responded. Everyone didn't seem to be on the same page. They pressed the trigger on the side of their helmet to engage their face plate. I could see all of their faces now.

"Well, at least we're dying for a good cause," one of Leona's teammates said through the communicator in their suit. It sounded like a young man. With his wrinkle-free skin and inexperienced look in his eyes, I'd place him around seventeen, twenty at most. I couldn't tell if he was nervous or trying to awkwardly break the tension.

I saw Leona's helmet turn toward him. She had an insignia on it, indicating to others that she was a squad leader. The expression around her deep, forest-green eyes were neutral. Every time she went into combat, you could tell she's seen some crap. "You're from vessel 3, right? What's your name?"

"Hunter," he replied. He was standing slightly hunched in the suit, timid even.

"All right, Hunter," she first said in a neutral tone. "Cut the shit!" Her tone changed to serious like a switch. "We're all going to make it out alive. That's the only thought that should be in your head. You start thinking that way, the enemy's already won."

"Y-yes, ma'am!" Hunter quickly fixed his posture.

Burrel leaned over to me while we were watching the feed and said, "Joselyn was right about her being stern on the field, huh?"

"I know right," I replied.

"Great… We have a hard-ass optimist as a squad leader," another teammate said through the video feed. This one sounded like a woman. Part of her hair tucked in the helmet peaked out a bit. It looked to be blond with pink highlights. A nose ring shined on her face too as it reflected part of the rising sun.

Leona looked irritated but didn't respond and let her vent.

"Leona is just doing her job, Christine," the fourth teammate cut in. "Knock it off." He was an older gentleman with dark brown hair. The way he pronounced his vowels had traces of an English accent. Trickles of sweat showed on his forehead, and he kept tapping a finger against his relic weapon. Even from here I could see his anxiety.

"Ugh! You know I go by Chrissy. My parents can go to hell with the Christian name they gave me. They never gave a crap anyway," Chrissy said. "And we're from vessel 5, Evan. Just because vessel 7 found *that* relic doesn't mean I'm going to praise Leona. I'm more experienced. I should be lead."

After the first month of occupants were awakened from stasis, we were all depressed and virtually had little to no will to fight. Command came up with the idea of giving 2 to 5 percent more nonessential supplies like snacks and knickknacks found to the vessel who contributed the most. Such minor supplies didn't seem like much in our past everyday lives. But now, even having something like paper and pencil to play a pointless game of tic-tac-toe kept people from depression. It was made to be an incentive program to work harder so we could rebuild. Needless to say, it caused competition and unnecessary bickering between vessels instead. Some people like Chrissy were more passionate about it than others. Why anyone thought that was a good plan was beyond me.

"Now, now, now." The fifth teammate sauntered over to the rest of the group. His accent sounded Australian. He sported a goatee. Heavy bags sagged under his eyes. His face seemed even a bit depraved of color. It definitely didn't look like he had much sleep. "We're all on the same side. And speaking of sides, it looks like I got the best view of you and *hard ass* over there. Thank God they don't put much on the fanny if you know what I mean."

Although there are exo-suits that have more armor than others, there are common areas with less sturdy material to allow for flexibility. The buttocks just happen to be one of them. He was clearly trying to undress Leona and Chrissy with his eyes. His behavior in a time like this was irritating me.

"Shut it, you vessel 6 *Aussie*! Y'all have done the least to help the cause. Besides, I don't like sausages, you dick."

"Ah, you're *that* type," he arrogantly teased. "I take it that's why your sanctimonious parents didn't give a crap about you?"

"Shut up!" she said, coming face-to-face with him. "It's none of your damn business!"

Evan took Chrissy by the arm and pulled her back. "Just ignore him. Focus on the mission."

"Dude. Do you not realize we're most likely about to face a horde of those things?" Hunter chimed in, looking behind him at the Australian guy, bewildered. He was beside Leona, studying the perimeter. "What's wrong with you?"

"I'm just trying to appreciate life's sweet pleasures before we '*die for a good cause*' as you put it, kid."

The team took a breath from engaging with each other. Leona continued to survey the land for any enemies approaching. I saw the Australian guy's gaze switch toward her. He was leering her way. I clenched my teeth in frustration. Everyone in the mess hall was quiet as our respective feeds continued to broadcast.

"It looks like Leona got a crappy team," Joselyn said. She must've noticed how antsy I was getting.

I sucked my teeth. "You can say that again."

Suddenly, an audio feed from Command briefly interrupted the output from the video feed. It was a bit staticky.

"Commander Heisen from vessel 6, do you copy?" Arinya asked.

"Yes. This is Heisen," a male voice answered.

"Command is monitoring the situation and shows concern for one of your soldiers currently teamed with Beta South. Do you have any intel on his usual demeanor during missions?"

Demeanor? I thought. *What does that have to do with anything?*

"Ah yes, you must be referring to Harper Walker." Heisen sounded as if he was used to vouching for his actions. "He becomes a bit…ostentatious when he's nervous. As unconventional as it may sound, it helps him cope with the situation and finish the mission."

"So would you say his flirtatious behavior toward the female members of the team is normal?"

"Yes. He excels in self-control and discipline once the situation calls for it. Nothing to worry about."

"Thank you, Commander."

The audio feed from the two ended and the one on the battlefield was being broadcasted again. *Why is Command so interested in his behavior at a time like this?* I thought. I looked over to Burrel who also looked skeptical.

"What about you, love?" Harper asked Leona while inching toward her and Hunter. Hunter got in between them when he thought he was getting a little too close for comfort. If by some miracle they all got out of this unscathed, I wanted to personally thank him. "Come on, kid. I'm just asking her to relax with me after this. She's *so* tense. A little fun would do her some good."

Leona didn't bother to entertain him with a response and maintained her focus. She continued to observe the battlefield. Evan and Chrissy joined her, shooting a couple of unsuspecting silhouettes that got close to their proximity in the process.

"Could you stop disrespecting our team members?" Hunter said. "You could at least pretend to acknowledge our situation and give a damn!"

"I second that," Evan added, briefly glancing Harper's way. "Even if you are a pig, appreciate the fact that there are people risking their lives here for you and everyone else."

"All right, guys. Calm down. I'm just messing around," Harper said, putting his hands in front of him in a defensive manner. He started to back up. "But I couldn't help but notice that the lady still hasn't responded." He paused, contemplating. "Ah, I see…the stoic type. You must be holding out for someone for you to be this loyal for a mission that's a suicide run."

Leona reacted and broke her concentration by moving her head slightly before immediately staring forward again.

"Aha!" he said triumphantly. "You *do* have someone. Well, let me tell you something. None of us were meant to be monogamous. We're polyamorous creatures by nature."

I clenched my fist as I was boiling at the seams. Burrel and Joselyn noticed. I wanted to punch this guy so bad.

"Calm down, Xander," Burrel said. "You told me yourself that Leona is a soldier through and through. If that's true, you should know that she's more than capable of handling herself."

"I agree," Joselyn added. "She's dealt with way tougher things than this guy. Being the jealous boyfriend isn't going to help matters right now."

"That's not what's getting at me," I responded.

Burrel and Joselyn glanced at each other, confused.

"It's like Evan said. They're risking their lives for us, these people here, and the ones on the other vessels. Everyone could very well witness their loved ones die for them at this very moment." I clenched my pants in frustration. "Tell me. Out of all the times in the world, why on Earth does he think it's a good idea to act this way now? Does he not realize the shit hole we're in?"

They became silent, sympathizing with my words. They studied the situation on the feed more intently as I did.

"I'm starting to agree with the kid," Chrissy exclaimed. "I'm not fond of you, broad." She looked toward Leona's direction. "But just give me the word." She pulled out her weapon and pointed it at Harper. "I'd love to shut this bastard up."

He started making demeaning kissing sounds. "Come on, love. I'm just being honest. I bet that guy of hers thinks the same way. After all, why choose one huss when there's plenty of fish in the sea?"

Leona immediately jerked her head back and shouted, "Enough!"

Chrissy, Hunter, and Evan were stunned. A moment of silence passed. Even Harper was thrown back some by the sudden outburst.

"Command, this is Squad Leader Madigan. Permission to alter squad formation."

"Yes, we read you loud and clear. What do you propose, Madigan?"

"Harper Walker will join Delta squad for the remainder of the mission."

Her teammates and everyone staring at our feed on the vessel were shocked by her decision.

"Are you sure about this, squad leader? South Squadron will be more vulnerable to attack with a four-man group rather than the original five-man one. I must remind you that making brash decisions due to personal emotions will not grant you permission to change formation."

"I believe Harper Walker's priorities as a soldier have been compromised due to his own self-indulgence and would render him ineffective on the frontlines. By falling back to Delta's position, he can still support our unit without interrupting our main objective."

Nice come back, I thought.

"Understood. Formation change approved."

"Are you sure about this, Leona?" Evan asked. "He's an ass, but he's still a skilled soldier. Our odds are low as it is and—"

"If I wanted to follow your lead, then you'd be calling the shots and not me," Leona interrupted, agitated. "Now all of you shape up and listen or you can join Harper. I'll hold this line by my *damn* self if I have to! I'm holding onto something real and fighting for it. If you're not here for the same reason, then get the hell off my squad!"

All four of them immediately kept quiet. Leona's passion allowed the team to feel the gravity of the situation and how serious their fight was. The weight of her words resonated with the chill in the air. Her determination to see the mission through was felt by them along with the people viewing the video feed. I heard someone behind me say under their breath, "God bless Leona. She's one of the few with any damn sense in her head out there."

I was giddy inside as I knew the *something* she was fighting for was a life with me. However, I didn't show it. Feeling proud for Leona at a time like this felt wrong.

"Fine. I'll go," Harper said through the feed, cutting through the uncomfortable silence. "But you might regret it." And with that, he finally jogged to Delta's location that was a bit of a distance away. I could see the outlines of the Delta squad behind them but just barely.

"I understand," Evan replied after Harper was out of earshot. "The more I think about it, the more of a wildcard he was. I meant no disrespect. I'll follow your command." He stood in front of her, waiting for orders.

"I second that," Hunter said. "I apologize for what I said before. I have someone I'm fighting for too. She doesn't know I'm here right now. She talks about how much of a hero her brother is, and here I am talking like we've already lost. I guess it's easy to lose hope when staring hell in the face." I saw Hunter reflect on those words as he kept his eye on some of the silhouettes that were at a distance. "Anyways, we've got your six."

Chrissy chuckled. "Well, well...look at the stones on you," she teased while kneeling and aiming at potential targets with her weapon. "I guess you are lead if you can whip the boys into shape like that."

Leona looked her way, surprised to have heard that compliment from her. I was too.

"I still don't like you, though," she added bluntly.

Leona ignored her and focused back on the fight ahead.

"Now that's the woman I'm familiar with," Joselyn said, interrupting my focus on the video feed.

"I gotta hand it to your girl, son," Burrel added. "She can lay down the law when she has to."

I refocused on the screen, concerned. "I want to be happy that she's found her ground, but I'm just hoping she makes it out of this in one piece," I said, clasping my hands in a prayer next to my face.

"Alpha, Beta, and Delta, we're all set," Arinya said through the audio. "Commencing with the generator's descent."

A large object in a metal container could be seen overhead. Thrusters deploying from the metal entrapment were slowing its descent.

"Leona, look," Hunter said. He pointed at the few dark silhouettes mindlessly roaming the area. They suddenly retreated into the horizon.

"Did one of you accidentally miss and alert it with our presence?" Leona asked.

"Negative," Evan replied. "There was no sign of them reacting to our movements."

Chrissy nodded in agreement.

"Command, are you getting this?" Leona said with a hint of fear in her voice.

"Yes!" Arinya confirmed. "What's happening at your position is happening to the other three Beta teams as well. Enemy stragglers are retreating for an unknown reason."

I glanced at the other screens in the room, and Arinya was right. Other squads were as confused as Beta South was.

Almost on cue, the all-too-familiar sound echoed through the sky on the feed.

EEEKKK!

Leona and the rest of the South Squadron had their mouths open in awe as they saw droves of those silhouettes converging on their location. Dread crept into my veins. There were so many that it was blocking out the sun peeking from the horizon.

CHAPTER 9

THE SQUAD INSTINCTIVELY put their face plates back on, almost in unison.

"These things just happen to all come at once when the generator is descending?" I heard Leona say. "That can't be a coincidence." She and her team equipped the long-range weapons to their suits, preparing for the onslaught.

"My thoughts exactly," I said, not realizing I was talking out loud.

Joselyn turned to me wearily. "You think those things possibly set this up to be some type of trap?"

"All the capable skilled soldiers we have left are all down there. You tell me."

"One thing is for certain," Burrel said unexpectedly, narrowing his eyes at the screen. "These beings have intelligence for sure."

"Engage!" Leona shouted through the video feed. "Holding this line until the generator is active is our priority!"

"Roger that!" Hunter said enthusiastically. He seemed to really be putting her words to heart.

The South Squadron was shooting silhouette after silhouette, trying to not let any through. I saw sniper lasers from Delta shoot enemies at a distance. All the relic energy shots put on one heck of a light show. Those things were getting showered with our attacks as they disintegrated immediately when our fire made contact. It reminded me of a time before all this.

I have little snippets of my memory where I remember the silhouettes were actually harder to take down than possessed people before the discovery of relic energy. The negative energy wasn't that potent in people who had it yet, and they would go down like a normal person. Silhouettes were literally like transparent shadows who couldn't take physical damage. But now the possessed people were the ones to watch out for after the invention of exo-suits. I suppose if negative energy festers in someone too long, it turns them into something else entirely. It was like our previous lives before these beings crossed over into our dimension, except our negative energy is now a weapon they could use against us—kind of poetic really.

"Leona, we can't keep firing at this pace," Evan said. "We'll tire ourselves out before our suits run out of relic energy."

"Speak for yourself, Evan!" Chrissy exclaimed. "I'm having the time of my life taking these shits down. Wooh!" She let out a hysterical laugh.

"Great...you've already gone mad," Evan replied as he kept firing.

"Command!" Leona had one hand on her helmet to access the communicator for Command, and the other held her weapon as she kept shooting. "It looks like we're going to need some of Delta to approach the frontlines sooner than expected."

A silhouette charged at her. She quickly switched from her long-range weapon to her short range. Relic energy in the form of a small blade released from the hilt. As the silhouette attempted to slice her with its eerie, shadow-like claws, she instinctively dodged by flipping out of the way and slashing it while in midair at the same time. When she landed, she quickly switched back to her long-range weapon and kept firing as if nothing happened. The whole sequence took less than three seconds.

Amazing, I thought.

"Hhm. Impressive," I heard Burrel say under his breath while his eyes were locked on the screen.

I saw Leona put her hand back on the communicator. "There's a lot more of these things bombarding us than we thought," she continued.

"Understood, Squad Leader Madigan. However, north, east, and west Beta squadrons are already spread thin with Delta soldiers as it is. Not many can assist you on the frontlines."

"How is that possible? I thought Delta had the most soldiers, more than Alpha and Beta combined."

There was no response.

"Command? Do you copy?"

No response.

"Arinya!"

"My apologies, squad leader. We're getting word from other teams on the battlefield of a situation occurring at Alpha's location. Delta soldiers are en route to your position. I will get back to you."

"A situation?" Hunter said as he backed up Leona with rapid cover fire. "What's more important than *this*?"

"Good question," Leona replied.

"Well, Delta better come soon," Evan was shooting in every direction next to Chrissy as they stood back-to-back now. The silhouettes were starting to surround the whole squad. "I need a breather." I heard his pants through his communicator while watching the feed.

"Stop acting like an old man," Chrissy said excitedly. "Where's your fighting spirit? You're only thirty-eight."

"See, when you're like this, I can't tell if you're being sarcastic or whether to take that as a compliment or insult."

They chuckled amidst the danger they were in. Considering the way they spoke to each other, they must've been good friends at vessel 5. It made me realize why having friends especially during these times were so important. They make you forget the world is falling sometimes, even if it's just for a moment, and share the burden of that weight. I glanced at Joselyn and Burrel as they intently focused on the screen. Leona and I had trouble trusting anyone besides each other due to everything that's happened. But I do admit it felt good to have these two by my side when she wasn't here. I didn't want to think about it, but the rational part of my mind was telling me that the situation might get worse. I still had to believe Leona would pull through and if by some miracle she did, we would definitely need allies to keep surviving in this world.

More relic fire rained down on the silhouettes beginning to surround Leona and her squad. The feed showed three Delta soldiers rushing over to their position.

"We're here to back you up, South Squadron," I heard one of them say.

"The shit? Why are there only three of you?" Chrissy so "aptly" asked.

The Delta soldiers looked over to Leona's squad leader insignia to know who to reply to. She nodded with her helmet to answer.

"We were all that was available," the Delta soldier said, still doing cover fire.

"You surely can't be serious," Evan replied.

"Uh, guys," Hunter interjected. He was now a little ways up continuing to shoot any near his proximity. "I see more coming on the horizon."

They all looked while continuing to defend their position. Not only were there more silhouettes, but there were possessed people among the crowd now also approaching. It's as if the enemy was waiting until they were exhausted to bring out more heavy hitters.

"Is Walker not among you three?" Leona asked, almost as if trying to peer through their helmets.

"No, ma'am. No one named Walker is here with us," the Delta soldier replied. The other two shook their head with their helmets, not knowing who that was.

"I'm surprised that asshole isn't here to run his perverted mouth again," Chrissy said.

"I agree. If he was here, he doesn't seem like the type to miss out on a chance to degrade you two with his incessant behavior," Evan added, pointing at Leona and Chrissy. "Perhaps he went to aid Alpha or another Beta team?"

Leona shot a silhouette that was about to attack Hunter from the side. Hunter thanked her by giving her a thumbs-up. "Maybe, but why? We would be the closest squad to him. He would encounter more enemies trying to go to other positions." I saw Leona contemplate for a second. "Hunter! Regroup with us," she said, motioning her hand for him to come. Chrissy, Evan, and the three Delta soldiers covered him as he ran back. "Command," Leona said in an angry tone, "what the hell is going on? We need answers!"

I heard Arinya let out a sigh on the other end of communication. "I'll be frank, Leona. That is all the support you can get. We are losing soldiers rapidly. We started out with fifty Delta soldiers."

My heart sank. I looked around and also saw the color fade among the people beside me and behind me, including Burrel and Joselyn. I was so focused on the screen that I didn't realize just how dire the situation was around me. Other projectors showed soldiers from our vessel and others injured or dead. People began to cry uncontrollably. I guess I inadvertently tuned out everything around me like white noise.

"Fifty? Fifty?!" Leona exclaimed. The rest of the squad stood there holding their positions warily, except for Chrissy who kept fighting eagerly despite the news. "We only started with fifty Delta soldiers for this mission? Then how much of Alpha did we start out with?"

"Eight," Arinya solemnly replied.

"Eight? But there were five of Beta in each direction. Are you telling me that we only had seventy-eight soldiers here to begin with?"

"I'm sorry," I heard Arinya's voice crack. "This is new information for me too. Command thought it would be best to keep certain positions in the dark about the actual number of soldiers to prevent further decrease of morale."

"Holy crap… Harper was right," Hunter said. "This *is* a suicide run." I saw the enthusiasm Hunter gained slowly diminish to its original state when the mission began. The people around me resonated with him.

All the supply runs and excavations from before must've taken a greater toll than we all foresaw. We knew there were injured or recovering soldiers that weren't available to take on this mission, as well as soldiers still in training who would only be in the way in a big operation like this. I knew the number of skilled fighters we had left were low, but for it to be *this* low was a tragedy in and of itself.

"What do we do now, squad leader?" Chrissy said in a patronizing tone.

I couldn't see Leona's expression since her face plate was on, but I'd imagine she was in shock right now.

"Give me a sec." Leona frantically scanned the area for a place to rethink their strategy. "There!" She pointed at an abandoned lower-story building in the distance. "We'll retreat in that building and hold our ground until the generator activates."

They ran to the building. Chrissy was still straggling behind, taking as many enemies out as she could.

"Chrissy, come on!" Leona shouted.

"Don't worry about me. I'm right behind you. I'll hold them off while you take cover."

"Is she always this erratic during missions, Evan?" Leona asked as they ran to the building.

"If I said no, would that make her seem less crazy?"

They both looked back and saw Chrissy laughing hysterically as she continued to fight.

"No," Leona replied.

"Then, yes."

"What's the plan once we make it there?" Hunter asked frantically. "It's not like that building will prevent them from coming to us."

"Once inside, we'll deploy one of our relic flares one after another." She pulled out a small device from the side of her exo-suit. "Each of them stays active for about two minutes."

"Uhm, we don't have those," a Delta soldier said.

"R&A didn't have enough material to make it for every soldier here," Evan shouted among the shrieks and cover fire. "Between the exo-suit repairs and drone inventions, only Alpha and Beta are equipped with them!"

"I see."

"As I was saying," Leona said between breaths. "That will give us about eight minutes of time without those things trying to claw us to death. The flares keep them at bay as long as we're within the area of its light." They were almost within reach.

"I get it. Being in the building will also obscure the silhouettes' view of us, causing less to come."

"Heh, you show promise Hunter," Leona said, almost as if sounding proud. She put her hand to her communicator again. "Command, we're falling back to part of an abandoned building in our area. How long until the generator is up and running?"

"That's the thing. It should've been activated already. We never planned for the mission to last longer than the time it took the generator to function."

"Then what's the delay?"

"One of our own defected and is screwing up our entire formation!" I heard a man yell at another screen, temporarily distracting me from the feed.

Defected? I thought.

"The trigger that activates after the timer for the relic to output energy has been jammed," Arinya said through the feed, replying to Leona's question.

"How did it get jammed? The enemy would have to go through Delta, not to mention Alpha to even get near the generator," Leona responded.

"There are only three Alpha members left. East and West Beta have been eliminated and there are only a couple left at Beta North. Delta is now in the single digits."

The team stopped at the entrance of the building. I felt the hopelessness between them.

"Well, what in the world do we do now?" Evan asked, panicking. "Is the mission over? Did we fail?"

More of the silhouettes were closing in on them. Everyone had their heads down in defeat, except for Hunter.

"No!" Hunter exclaimed, shooting more silhouettes. "All they need to do is get that trigger functioning. I say we go in, guns blazing."

"Are you crazy, kid?" Evan asked. "We only have three Delta soldiers and three of us. Hell, I don't even know if Chrissy is alive right now." He took a minute to digest the thought of his friend being dead. "It's too risky."

"I'd have to agree," a Delta soldier said. If five Alpha members succumbed to the enemy, who knows what's going on near the generator."

"Don't you get it?!" Hunter exclaimed. "It's all the more reason we need to go! That's our main objective. We don't have to fight every enemy. We just need to trigger the generator, and all those *things* spanning the area will vanish. This is the reason we're here! Remember?"

The team looked toward Leona to decide. She stood silent for a bit, trying to consider their options.

Her helmet glanced toward the drone and then back to the team. I could tell she was thinking about me and others on vessel 7. She nodded. "We're fighting for something real. The generator is why we're here in the first place. That's our mission!"

The team agreed and nodded.

Just as they started toward the generator's direction, a silhouette swiped at Leona. It scratched her armor. More silhouettes came for the team. They ran the opposite direction, trying to fend them off. The drone followed Leona. She quickly got into the entrance of the building and shut the old doors behind her. Metal rods were scattered on the floor. She used one to shove through the handles of the door to prevent them from coming in. To her dismay, the silhouettes just phased through the solid door.

"Damn it. I guess I have no choice but to use this now," she said.

She grabbed a device from the side of her suit and threw it on the ground. The impact made a burst of light stream throughout the room. The silhouettes vanished.

"Leona! Are you okay?" Evan asked through the communicator.

"I'm good," Leona said, out of breath.

"We'll come as soon as we can. Just hold on!"

She raised her faceplate, checking the relic energy indicated on her forearm. It was significantly low.

"Shit!" she said.

Suddenly, the entrance doors began to shake violently. The metal rod actually snapped from the force. When Leona looked back toward the entrance, the inside of my stomach turned knots in horror, watching from the video feed.

The door swung open to a familiar face inside of an exo-suit. His helmet was off. Grotesque black lines around his face jutted out like veins against his skin. His color was even more pale than before. His smile grew, taunting her as she stared back in utter disgust.

"Come on, love. You let me go. I did say you might regret it," he said. As he spoke, it sounded like there was another deeper voice talking alongside him, although he was the only other person in the area. It was as if there was a reverb to his vocals.

He walked toward the light the relic flare was emitting. The light seemed to burn his face a bit, but he didn't react to the pain.

"Harper?" Leona managed to utter.

CHAPTER 10

"DAMN! HE'S POSSESSED," Burrel said, staring at the feed, gritting his teeth. "Is he the traitor people around here are talking about?"

Possessed? I thought. Then I remembered what Henry said about these things.

It's what they do. They possess people and feed on their negative energy.

"But how is that possible?" Joselyn asked in disbelief. "The military told us in our training sessions that wearing the suit should make us immune to their influence. It's the reason we have it on at all times during deployments!"

"It looks like it was just another lie," Burrel replied.

"Oh my God! It's him!" a woman said, peering over at our screen from across the mess hall. "He's killed so many."

"Then he *is* the traitor," I said. "But how come he's still able to talk? I thought the possessed weren't capable of intelligible speech."

"Sometimes a victim who succumbs to possession echoes the repeated phrases or final words of an individual when they were alive," Joselyn said. I saw her hands shaking. She must've been terrified for Leona. I was too. "I've encountered some do it on missions before."

Some people viewing other screens started to gather around our feed now, showing Leona attempting to talk to the possessed Harper again. The building should've had light peer in through the old, cracked windows since it was dawn. However, only beams of light would break through for moments at a time due to the hordes of silhouettes passing by. The only thing keeping her safe from their onslaught was the relic flare that was beginning to dim.

"Harper, answer me," Leona repeated in shock. "What the hell did you do?"

"This one no longer answers for himself," Possessed Harper said in the same reverb voice. "We thought it would please you to hear something familiar this waste of life said." He deviously grinned at Leona while speaking.

Leona stared back in pure disgust.

"That's definitely not an echo," Burrel said. Joselyn was more worried for Leona now as was I.

I heard static come through the other end of the video feed the drone displayed.

"Commander Heisen, report," I heard Arinya say. Static wasn't heard the last time Command patched through to communication. I wonder if the drone's audio system was partly damaged during these fights.

Suddenly, I heard inaudible sounds coming from the communication line. It sounded like someone else was trying to talk.

"Heisen! This is Captain Commander Voorhees. Get your ass on the line now!"

Everyone around me grew silent. Captain Commander Voorhees was the commander in charge of all of the other seven vessels that he oversaw in vessel 1. Vessel 1 consisted of Command, himself, and other important officials who delegated our missions and analyzed our situation. He rarely spoke through communication. Whenever he did, it enforced just how vital our task was.

"Y-yes, Captain Commander. I'm here." His confidence from before sounded shot to hell.

"You told us there was nothing to worry about! Now we're knee deep in this crap you put us in. How did his vulnerability to the enemy slip past you?"

I saw Leona cringe away from her communicator as Captain Commander Voorhees shouted through it. Command must've not cared if their line was private or not anymore. Possessed Harper was staring at her hopelessness with an odd sense of bliss. He was genuinely happy observing our misery. His eyes rolled back, and the part that was once white turned pitch black. I didn't even have to be close to this thing to know that it was pure evil.

"I-I honestly don't know how this is possible. Background checks were performed on all potential soldiers before they entered the stasis program years ago. Besides a few misdemeanors, his records were clean. I swear it!" It sounded like he was confirming something with another person. "My personnel even informed me we double-checked everyone before we boarded their stasis capsules they were in."

"You better pray that the generator goes up, Heisen. If not, you answer to me!" The line cut out.

"We know your feeble mind attempts to find out how we got to him," Possessed Harper said to Leona as the audio cut back to the video feed.

I saw drops of sweat trickle down Leona's face while her faceplate was up. She gritted her teeth, trying to show no sign of fear. But I knew her. She was scared. If you looked closely enough, you could see her hands slightly quivering.

"This one's gotten away with a lot. Ahhh... We can see it through his mind and feel it through his actions." He whisked his head up with a sense of euphoria. "Murders, assaults, abuse...all covered up due to his allegiance to a covert military organization ran by the government."

I didn't need to look around to feel what everyone was feeling. Our blood ran cold with every word he was saying.

"As long as he did as they said, his records were scrubbed clean of filth." He looked toward Leona again, tapping his index and middle finger toward the temple of his head. "But they stay in here and fill our very core. His negativity was enough for us to infiltrate his flesh even with this hunk of metal." He stared at his arm equipped with the exo-suit in fascination.

Is this why Command was questioning Commander Heisen about Harper's behavior earlier? I realized. *If so, that would imply they knew something like this was possible from the start.*

I glanced over to Burrel who was seething in anger. He tried to calm down, but he had his hand curled up to a fist so tight I could see the natural color of his thumbnail turn white in his chair. I was beginning to understand his prejudice toward the military.

Leona exhaled. While trying to calm herself down, she braced herself into a ready stance. She still had a look of defiance and determination on her face even after being backed into a corner. It was one of the things I admired most about her—her will to keep going. But I'd be lying if I said I wasn't terrified for her right now. My heart grew heavy with sadness, too, as it finally sunk in that she very well may die. The way she was trying to force her body to stop trembling while taking a fighting stance made me see that she thought the same thing.

"Oh, please," Possessed Harper mocked as he noticed her getting ready to fight. "There's no meaning to your bravery. You can train, gain pointless achievements, and defy all you want. You're all still helpless children that know nothing about the world you're in, except for the inevitable death waiting for you."

"Save your shitty speech for someone who gives a damn! If you took over Harper after he went to Delta, then it makes sense why five Alpha members fell along with East and West Beta." Leona equipped her short-range weapon as the saber emitted a low hum. Anger was the one thing she had left to find the strength to face him. "You caught our allies off guard, giving the chance for those silhouettes to strike. I bet you're responsible for jamming the generator, too, aren't you? I'm going to slash that grin right off your face!"

He let out a sinister laugh. "Go ahead. We have his skills, his exo-suit, and our power. We will enjoy indulging ourselves in all of the malicious thoughts he had for you before you die."

My heart felt like it was about to thump out of my chest. I shouted at the screen as if she could hear me. "Leona!" I didn't care if everyone was looking at me as if I was insane. I was probably witnessing her last moments.

By some miracle, as I thought all hope was lost, I heard the craziest war cry that became music to my ears.

"Haaa!"

All I saw at first was the leg of an exo-suit knock Possessed Harper away from the building entrance and across the room. His neck had to have snapped from the impact. The relic flare emitting light on the floor was on its last legs. However, there was a relic flare on this person's exo-suit to deter the silhouettes from attacking. The light was supernatural as it seeped through her body and illuminated the room. Normal light couldn't shine through solid objects, let alone human bodies, but I guess light from relics was different. Upon closer inspection, Leona's dimming relic flare on the floor shined through solid matter as well. The suit was torn apart at random parts of the armor. Scratches from claw marks littered the surface.

Leona looked on, bewildered as she uttered the name, "Chrissy?"

Chrissy activated her face plate to detach. Part of her pink highlights were now red as blood streamed down part of her face. She had her saber ready in hand and her relic gun in the other. "When I saw Evan and the rest split from you, I fought my way over here. I saw this piece of crap infiltrate the building." She pointed at Possessed Harper who was trying to get up from the ground. "What did I miss?" She smiled maniacally.

CHAPTER 11

POSSESSED HARPER STOOD up. Leona looked on in horror at his grotesque and unnatural movements. He snapped his head back in place with just the neck muscles alone. Chrissy jumped back in surprise, standing closer to where Leona was.

"Ah!" Chrissy yelped. "What the fuck? What kind of freak show did I just step into?"

"Wait. You didn't know he was possessed before you nearly kicked his head off?" Leona asked, perplexed.

"Nope. I just saw my chance to hit this asshole."

Leona smirked. The subtle shaking of her body also dissipated. Chrissy's obnoxious behavior was annoying at first, but I could tell Leona was a little relieved by her sudden appearance. So was I. After all, she probably just saved her life. As I sat back down on the floor, I saw everyone hooked on the feed and disregarded my outburst. I think everyone was just hoping—praying that they could still pull this off.

"I thought we couldn't be possessed as long as we had these suits on," Chrissy continued.

"Apparently, Harper had so much negative energy inside of him, these *things* were able to inhabit his body anyway."

"Heh, I guess there is a god. I get another crack at this guy while taking down a monster in the process." A grin spread across her face. "A win-win if you ask me."

"Your pride will be your downfall, girl," Possessed Harper said in his reverb voice again.

"Uhm, okay. That's new," Chrissy replied, creeped out.

"Yeah, he can talk," Leona said. "I don't know how powerful he is, but he's partly responsible for the death of over half of the Alpha squad as well as East and West Beta."

"He admitted to it?"

"He didn't deny it."

"Enough! We'll be happy to show you what we're capable of up close and personal." He got into a ready stance while smiling from ear to ear.

He then charged with his exo-suit's short saber weapon. Chrissy met him head on and clashed her saber with his. His saber was getting closer and closer to her suit, overpowering her.

"Shit, he's strong," Chrissy said.

"I'll communicate with Evan and Hunter. They said they were on their way anyway. They can back us up with Delta," Leona replied.

"Wait!" Chrissy shouted, kicking Possessed Harper away. "Why don't you let us gals settle the score with this dick? The boys can focus on the generator."

Possessed Harper charged at Chrissy again while her back was turned. Leona quickly equipped her long-range weapon and shot him. He staggered a bit, taking a knee to the ground. He stared at Leona and Chrissy menacingly. Leona contemplated a bit on what to do. Chrissy locked eyes on him, prepared to strike as soon as he moved.

Leona accessed her communicator. "Evan, this is Leona. Do you copy?"

"Leona! You're still alive." I heard him say through the other end of the line, relieved. "We were coming back for you, but there are so many of these things. One Delta backup already fell. Hunter wants us to rally the rest of the North squad and help Alpha with the generator. I said we weren't leaving you behind."

"Listen to Hunter," Leona replied.

"What?" Evan said, shocked.

"Chrissy is here with me engaging with Harper. He's possessed and the reason why our formations failed. We'll hold out on our end. You need to do the same."

"Hold on! You're telling me Harper is possessed, and Chrissy is okay?! We need to come and assist—"

"Evan, I'm fine!" Chrissy shouted through the communicator. She prepared herself as Possessed Harper was ready to pounce. "We don't have much time. You need to go."

"But—"

"Evan!" Leona shouted, losing her patience. "What is your mission?"

There was a pause before he spoke. "To get the generator running. I understand your command." I heard him getting choked up. "Just…please don't die, you two."

Possessed Harper did a downward strike with his short saber. Chrissy blocked using hers. Leona jumped in and used her short saber to push against him to assist Chrissy. Even with the two of them, the force of his strength was still bearing down on them.

"Even though this was made to kill us, it still cuts through human skin like butter," Possessed Harper said in delight. "We will enjoy cutting both of you to pieces. The clash between all three sabers created an intense sound like buzzsaws.

"Leona!" I could hear the distress in Arinya's voice as she patched through from Command. It didn't sound like she was talking as a command official but more as a person genuinely concerned for her well-being—a friend even. "What exactly are you planning? Why aren't you trying to regroup with the remaining soldiers?"

Chrissy let her back fall to the ground, releasing her saber clash with Possessed Harper's. Leona bore the extra force coming down on her for a moment. Then, Chrissy did a kip up from the ground and used the momentum to propel her feet into Possessed Harper's torso. He staggered back a little. Leona followed up with a punch to his face, knocking him back more.

"We've been fighting these things in the dark for years, not knowing how they really operate. We have a specimen right in front of us who is strong enough to even withstand a relic flare up close.

If we manage to pin him down, we can learn a lot more about the enemy."

Chrissy glanced over to Leona in shock. I was just as surprised. Who knew she was still thinking ahead even at a time like this? "I think I'm starting to like you," Chrissy uttered.

"But if our soldiers are successful in activating the generator," Arinya stated, "all the enemies in the vicinity and further will be wiped out. There's no guarantee he would be immune to the effect even if he is as strong as you say. The entities inside Harper could vanish anyway. The capture would have been for nothing."

"That's a risk we're going to have to take. Not knowing the enemy's full capabilities is what got us into this mess in the first place." I saw Leona stare back into the drone as she said, "I know it seems reckless, but you're going to have to trust me."

I felt a tear stream down the side of my face as she said those words. Burrel and Joselyn looked at me sympathetically. As she looked directly into the drone, I knew those words were meant for me. Her plan *was* reckless, but it would help all of us in the long run if she pulled it off. I didn't want to lose her, but I had to accept that this was bigger than the both of us. After losing so many in this battle, she most likely realized it early on. It was the same feeling I had after Henry gave his life, so I could retrieve the relic. I didn't care what happened to me either as long as I retrieved it. At least Leona and the others would get to see more tomorrows. If we could get even a shred more information about the enemy, it would be the same for me and the others. I knew exactly what she was thinking. Whether we wanted it or not, we knew it was the right thing to do.

"How much time does that flare on you have?" Leona asked Chrissy.

"After all this shit that went down, my count is fifty-two seconds."

"Heh, you were still keeping track while fighting? Nice." Leona smiled. "And here I thought you were just crazy."

"That's the first smile you cracked since you've been out here. I just thought you had a stick up your ass."

They both chuckled in the face of death as Possessed Harper recovered.

"Touching," he mocked. "We wanted to take things nice and slow with you two, but your antics give us no choice."

He put his hands up. Suddenly, Leona's and Chrissy's bodies were moving toward him against their will.

"Fuck! He has telekinesis too?!" Chrissy shouted as her body rapidly floated toward him.

Leona took a metal rod beside her and tried to dig it into the scattering debris on the floor. It scraped against the floor and various objects, delaying her body from coming close to his reach.

Chrissy's head covered by her helmet was now grasped by his palm as the rest of her body followed. His expression changed in an instant, exuding anger and pure hatred.

"It's time to kill you."

Chrissy's helmet caved in. Her body moved unnaturally and shook violently from the neck down. Leona looked on in horror as her comrade succumbed to his grip.

Leona's eyes must've nearly bulged out of her sockets in disbelief while shouting, "Chrissy!"

"Your turn!" Possessed Harper shouted.

His telekinetic ability appeared to grow stronger as Leona lost her grip of the metal rod. He swung her against a wall. Her shoulder made a sickening impact. Her body swiftly moved toward his grip. He was choking the life out of her. She desperately hit his hand with one arm, trying to break free. My mouth gaped in awe as I saw how helpless she was. One of her arms was dangling at her side, unable to move. Leona tried to use her relic weapon but glanced at her arm as she realized she had no energy left. Possessed Harper took note of the metal rod jutting out of the floor from before.

"Impaling you through this rod will have to satiate Harper's malice."

"Nooo!" I yelled out, watching the feed in desperation.

Just as he was about to slam Leona's body through the rod, a familiar voice struck like a ray of light through the darkness.

"Take this," Chrissy said.

Possessed Harper looked back in astonishment.

"You piece of shit." Her body was lifeless on the ground. One of her arms was outstretched in an unnatural fashion, aimed at him. It looked like the last of her will was the only thing keeping her breathing. She had her long-range barrel equipped and used the last ounce of her energy to shoot him in the leg.

His leg flinched with the shot. It loosened his grip on Leona. She wrapped her arms and legs around his arm and used the momentum of her body to twist it. It forced him to let go completely. However, he outstretched his other hand and moved it slightly to the right.

Snap!

Chrissy's neck contorted, followed by the gut-wrenching sound of bone snapping. Her lifeless eyes stared back at both of them in shock.

"Nooo!" Leona shouted. She slammed the same shoulder that hit the wall earlier into Possessed Harper. "Ahhh!" She yelped in pain, but she was surprisingly able to move her arm again.

"Did she just snap her dislocated arm back into place while knocking him down?" Burrel uttered in disbelief. "Even while psyched up on adrenaline, she's still making calculated moves."

"Unbelievable," Joselyn added as her jaw dropped.

She lifted the metal rod from its jutted position. Possessed Harper was attempting to twist his arm back into place. "You son of a bitch!" she screamed. The rod connected to Possessed Harper's face as she swung it with full force. He fell to the floor from the impact.

"Hahaha," he laughed. "This one still feels all the pain. We're the only thing keeping this body alive. *He* feels all while *we* feel nothing!"

Leona, with a metal rod still in hand, walked over to Possessed Harper, who was trying to get up from the floor. "No skin off my bones." She jutted the metal rod into the back of his knee, which was one of the spots where the exo-suit had less material for protection. "A win-win if you ask me," she said, repeating what Chrissy said before.

Squish!

The sound metal made piercing flesh was disturbing. With the metal rod jutted through his knee and stuck between debris on the floor, he couldn't move. She picked up a couple of more metal rods and did the same to his other leg and an arm. He tried to use his telekinetic powers with his free hand, but she whacked it with a rod before he attempted it. Before sticking the last rod into his other arm, she looked over to Chrissy, whose flare was dimming. It was as if it represented her death as the last remnants of light from her soul was leaving her body. As soon as that light faded, Leona's life may end too, as she would be overrun by silhouettes and possessed people who were still rapidly passing by the building.

Rumble! Rumble! Rumble!

"What now?" a guy behind me said, staring at the feed.

All of a sudden, what sounded like large footsteps echoed throughout the battlefield.

"Eh-heh-heh," Possessed Harper chuckled while all of his limbs were pinned by rods. "You're in for quite the treat."

"What exactly *are* all of you?" Leona asked. I could tell her blood ran cold with dread.

"You refuse to admit it, but deep inside your bones to your very core...you already know the answer."

Leona disregarded him and dragged her beat up body to peer out one of the window sockets. The drone followed closely behind. At a distance, there was a dark shadow as huge as a giant. The outline of its form was the same as a human's, only a lot bigger. As the drone panned out, we could see more of them, surrounding the battlefield.

"What...on Earth...is that?" Joselyn shook in fear.

I saw Burrel tense up in rage. He seemed to have some idea of what they were to feel such animosity toward them.

More possessed people came from the horizon. One of the shadowy giants outstretched their arms. A tremor violently shook the battlefield.

Leona nearly fell over from the quake. "Evan... Hunter... Talk to me. Any luck on the generator?" Leona spoke with grief and hopelessness in her voice while accessing her communicator.

"Leona! We got it. Alpha's on its last legs!" We could hear fighting on the other end of the line as Evan replied.

"I'll cover you! Just hit it!" I heard Hunter shout to another soldier.

We could hear the activation of the generator through the audio as it echoed through the air. A force field of light blanketed the area and dissipated the darkness surrounding the battlefield. The drone followed Leona as she stepped out of the building. Lifeless possessed bodies were at her feet, spanning for miles in all directions. At a distance, there were some exo-suits on the ground, containing the bodies of dead soldiers. We could finally see the sun and heavenly clouds shine on the hellish landscape. Leona dropped to her knees in exhaustion.

CHAPTER 12

DAWN FINALLY BROKE freely. Leona took a moment to soak in the sun's rays. I'm guessing she was relieved for the nightmare to be over even if it was just temporary. After all, having a place on Earth to call home again was just the first step. The next was trying to get the rest of our territory back. The idea seemed ludicrous right now, considering how much we lost just to get to this point.

Heavy breathing could be heard not too far from her. Leona looked behind her to see Evan rush toward the doorway of the building, no doubt staring at Chrissy's corpse. She must've been so out of it that she didn't notice him approaching. We could all see him through the feed slowly stumbling in and breaking down emotionally before he was out of view. Leona stood up and walked back toward the entrance of the building. The drone continued to follow behind. As she got closer, we could hear quiet sobs through the audio. I took a look behind me and saw everyone empathizing with the sounds of Evan's grief. Parents held their children close. Men and women were drowning in tears. I even caught a glimpse of guards in the back, looking down, depressed.

"I'd be dead right now if it wasn't for her," Leona said through the video feed, breaking the silence.

Evan took a moment to respond, trying to gather himself. His helmet was off. Leona's faceplate was still up. "We first met on the ship. Our past lives were vastly different. In fact, if it weren't for this"—he looked around and directed his hand to the situation they were going through—"we would've never crossed paths. I was a schoolteacher, believe it or not. She joined the army." He took a moment and sighed. While sitting on the floor, he was staring at her corpse, reminiscing as tears streamed down his face. Leona listened intently. "My parents couldn't understand why I would choose something with a middle wage salary when I was smart enough to be a doctor or a lawyer. Her folks couldn't understand their daughter's sexual orientation."

"I see," Leona replied.

"We became friends because of our disapproving families. Both of us were a rebellious pair, I suppose." He tried to let out a laugh but was choked up by tears.

Leona looked on with empathy.

Evan looked up at Leona who was standing over him. "Did you know she was a candidate for becoming an Alpha soldier?"

Leona shook her head. "I wasn't aware, but it does make sense how she was able to fight so many of these things for so long, even without our help for a short time."

He chuckled while more tears came forth. "Yeah, she was stubborn as hell. Command was aware of her eccentric behavior on the field. They were trying to gauge if she was able to follow orders as well as give them." He wiped his face with the forearm of his suit. "She pretended not to care about her parents scolding her decisions, but that's why she fought so hard. Though her parents have been dead even before she joined the stasis program from what she could remember, she still fought for their approval."

Leona stared at him, startled. She took off her helmet. Her brunette hair flowed in the wind. I saw the dried sweat and marks from the battle envelop her face. She placed her hand on Evan's shoulder.

"I saw how tough she was. She fought tooth and nail with me. I'm sure her parents would've at least been proud of the strong woman she became."

"One can only hope, right?" he said, passing her a half-hearted smile. His eyes began to wander to the other corpse in the building. "Harper," he uttered in an angry, low, menacing tone.

The black lines protruding from Harper's face were still apparent, but his eyes appeared to be glazed over in some kind of white, hazy color. Metal rods still jutted out from his joints that Leona jammed in. The Possessed Harper could no longer move. It was as if the body was frozen in time.

"He's going to pay," Evan got to his feet and walked over to where he was. He brought one of his legs back, attempting to kick his face. Leona quickly grabbed him and dragged him away.

"I assure you, he's already paid. I made sure of it."

He shrugged off her grip. "Why is he like that?"

"He wouldn't stop coming after us, so I pinned him with those rods."

"No, I mean why is his eyes glazing over in some type of white shade?" Evan started to calm down. "He also still has signs of possession. Usually, the possessed look like a normal dead person after those dark creatures vanish from the body."

Leona studied Harper's dead expression. "I don't know. Maybe it's something I can give to R&A for them to study. I was trying to capture whatever this was alive."

"Huh? Why?"

"Please, another time."

Suddenly, they heard footsteps near the entrance of the building. Leona got into a fighting stance, although she didn't have any relic energy left. Evan put her hand on her shoulder, signaling her to calm down.

"Don't worry. The force field holds. I ran over here as soon as it was active to see if you two were okay."

They went back outside. The rest of the soldiers who survived were looking for them. There were two Juggernauts, eight Cavalries, and four Equalizers left, including Leona's and Evan's. Judging by all the scrapes, scratches, and dents in their suits, they fought with everything they had as well to stay alive. The mission started out with a measly seventy-eight soldiers and now we were down to fourteen.

"There they are," a soldier said, spotting Leona and Evan.

I saw Leona stare at the remaining soldiers with concern. "I only see two Equalizer suits from Beta North." She stared at the strangers' faces of the Equalizers who had their face plates up. "Where's Hunter?"

Evan avoided Leona's gaze as he uttered, "The kid's gone."

Leona gaped her mouth open in shock.

A Delta soldier near them came up to Leona. "The trigger to the generator was jammed due to a traitorous Beta soldier tampering with it. He even took out some Alpha soldiers while they were fighting hordes of those monsters before spreading more havoc throughout the battlefield. It took us by surprise. No one expected one of our own to succumb to possession." Leona and Evan glanced back at Harper's corpse, infuriated. "Hunter thought hitting the trigger would activate its sequence to release the relic energy."

"Hitting it?" a Beta North soldier interjected. "Are you saying we won this battle by dumb luck?"

The Delta soldier shrugged, not knowing what to say.

"Maybe it was more than luck," I said in a low voice, staring at the screen. I was clasping my hands in a prayer-like fashion.

Burrel and Joselyn took notice. I saw that they also wanted to believe there was more at play here.

"Anyway," the Delta soldier continued through the feed. "He... he shielded me from a possessed guy, trying to attack me while I hit the trigger."

"Oh, God..." Leona uttered. She plopped down on the ground, trying to process everything that happened.

What Hunter shouted over communication makes sense now, I thought.

Evan studied Leona's saddened state, not knowing what to say. "If it makes you feel any better, the kid was determined in following your command to a tee. The generator was his main focus like you said."

"That actually makes me feel worse, Evan," Leona replied. "He died because of my command."

"You're wrong," Evan said.

Leona stared back at him.

"He died because he had something real he wanted to protect, a lot like you. He told me it was all worth it if the girl he was fighting for survived. Apparently, he thought she's been through too much pain not to have a chance to live her life."

Leona continued to listen. An Alpha soldier was attempting to contact Command.

"I don't know who you're fighting for, Leona, and I know this was a crappy victory." He started to choke up again. "But thanks to us, a small band of ingrates following your command, we were able to help get the generator running. Even when I wanted to go back and save you and Chrissy, you put the mission first. At least take solace in knowing you and others have more time with their loved ones if nothing else." He looked over to Chrissy. "Life is too short nowadays not to appreciate what we still have."

Leona stared at the ground, contemplating his words.

"Command, this is Alpha. Mission is complete. Are you sending for evac?"

"Not yet. Wait there. A pod from vessel 1 is touching down. Command wants to see the progress of the generator itself," Arinya said. "Oh, and I know none of you want to hear this, but it needs to be said."

The remaining fourteen soldiers listened intently.

"Thank you."

I saw Leona look up before the video feed cut out.

Bzzzz!

The speaker signaled overhead.

"Attention! The mission to establish a base on Earth was a success. Officials from vessel 1 are touching down to ensure the capability of the generator's force field. Once we confirm the diameter the perimeter expands and how it holds against enemy forces, we will deliberate in which manner vessels should be brought to our newly established base on Earth. Please be patient as we assess the status of all those who gave their lives to ensure our survival as well. Details will be available soon. Remain calm. For those of you who witnessed the battle through the drones' video feed, we have therapists on site ready to consult with you during this time. Please seek help if you are experiencing an emotional breakdown."

"Don't the therapists have loved ones too? Who consoles them?" Joselyn asked.

"They don't care. As long as the mission's done," I heard a woman say. It was the same one who poked her head out from before with her kid. She was in a less pleasant mood after seeing what happened. Who could blame her?

I stood up. My legs fell asleep and my behind was sore. All I saw was a crowd of people trying to console each other after witnessing such a bloodbath. I looked down, ashamed. I was sad for all of those who died, but deep inside, I was still relieved that one of those people wasn't Leona.

Should I really feel even an ounce of happiness right now? I thought.

Burrel got up with his cane and looked over to me. "I was wrong before. The ones who were exempt from seeing this were the fortunate ones, not us." He began to walk away.

"Wait, Burrel!" I shouted. "Where are you going?"

"Don't worry about me right now, Xander. After all, you have someone out there who needs you right now." He walked through the crowd of people and left.

I looked on in concern. He was going into his shell again after he was doing so well, beginning to open up. This small yet vital victory was still nothing to celebrate. The casualties were unforgettable, and there was a mountain of questions needing answers.

"He just needs some time." Joselyn poked my arm, standing up. She winced, holding her torso. We continued to stare at the sad expressions that filled the mess hall. "We all do."

CHAPTER 13

IT FELT LIKE hours passed since the last announcement on the speaker. Joselyn was instructed by personnel and guards to return to the infirmary. I told her I'd give my regards to Leona. Maybe Burrel wanted to give me time alone with her too once I saw her, considering I was so close to losing her. Having them both by my side while viewing the feed was something I needed, even if I didn't realize it. There are moments in life where someone's presence is enough to get you through a hard time. I was thankful they were there. I wondered what Leona and the remaining soldiers were doing with officials from vessel 1 as I stared out the window of the ship, looking down at the barren wasteland of Earth. I could hear everyone behind me still grieving or quiet while locked in a state of depression. It could've easily been me too. I didn't take their emotions lightly. I felt the pressure of their loss, pushing down on me.

Bzzzzz!

Heh. Speak of the devil, I thought.

"We are pleased to announce that the force field is functioning continuously as intended."

I saw some people's reflection from the window. The expressions that were full of gloom and misery started shifting away from it. It was hopeful but not quite hope, at least not yet.

"Also, the span of the field is several hundred acres, capable of fitting the remainder of our population with extra space for other purposes. However, we still want to exercise caution and run diagnostics for the generator. There is always a chance the enemy could be leading us to a false sense of security. Therefore, only one or two vessels will be instructed to land on Earth at a time. Part of Command will stay at base to monitor the situation on the ground while most of our HQ will still hold positions in vessel 1, orbiting space. After all other vessels are safe and secure on Earth, the rest of Command will descend. To determine the order of landing, it was unanimously agreed upon that vessels who contributed the most so far to the cause will be first. We are aware it isn't a favorable decision, but we do believe it is a fair one."

I noticed some people stirring and getting antsy from the news.

"With that said, we will allow the following two vessels to descend first. Vessel 3 can descend who has the least amount of soldiers due to continuously volunteering to take on difficult missions."

Wow. They have the least amount of soldiers? I thought. About a little over half of every vessel is occupied by soldiers. For them to have the least must mean they didn't have many people left either. No wonder a kid like Hunter was among the Beta squads. They must've not had many others to choose from.

"The second and final one for now will be vessel 7 due to their involvement in getting us key victories to turn the tide of war in our favor."

Some people gave a half-hearted smile from what I could see in the reflection of the glass. Others glanced at me, knowing I was one of the soldiers involved in some of those key victories. Getting to smell fresh air and feel the sun kiss your skin after all this time, without worrying about monsters trying to kill you, had to bring some type of relief to this misery. I was beginning to get a little anxious myself.

"Oiga, joven, por favor," I heard someone say behind me in a Spanish accent.

I turned around to see an elderly woman. She was hunched over and wrinkles hung from her skin like bags. Blemishes were also apparent on her face, and she stood as if everything ached. I could tell she had quite the life so far.

"I'm sorry, could you repeat that?" I asked.

"Que?" She squinted her eyes and leaned in closer with her ear.

"Oh…" I said, realizing what was going on. "I don't speak much Spanish."

"No Español?"

"Uhm…" I tried to recall the little Spanish I could remember. "Piquito."

"Ah… I'm sorry. My English…not so good," she said, slightly embarrassed.

I nodded.

"Did you know, eh…my grandson?"

"What was his name?"

She looked at me confused.

"Uhhh… Como se llama?"

"Ai. Yes. Si! Henry Rosenburg."

My eyes grew wide. "Si!" I anxiously nodded.

Her eyes lit up like she just won the lottery. As soon as she looked like she was about to ask a follow-up question, a little boy came rushing from the crowd in the background. His complexion was tanned and smooth, with a head full of black hair. He looked like a preteen.

"There you are, Grandma!" he said. "I thought I lost you in the crowd."

"Mijo!" she said excitedly.

Before she could get another word out, he took her by the hand, attempting to walk away from me. "We're sorry for bothering you, mister. My abuela is old and can't read situations anymore—like trying to talk to random people when they're clearly sad."

"Wait," I replied.

He continued walking, thinking his grandma was being a pest. It made me laugh a little on the inside. It's usually the other way around with adults and children, but I guess once you get to a certain age, even children treat you like a kid again.

She yanked her hand from his grip and shouted, "Chico! Escucha!" The boy was startled. Some people nearby glanced over, wondering what was going on.

They started whispering to each other to not draw anymore unwanted attention. I stood there, curiously trying to make out what they were saying. However, my effort was fruitless. Not only did they speak very low, but it was in Spanish.

The boy looked at me and asked, "You knew Henry, mister?"

"Uhhh…yeah. Kind of, sort of," I said. "Call me Xander."

"Xander? As in Xander Williams?" He came closer to me, excited. His grandmother followed behind. "You were on the last mission mi hermano—I mean my brother was…" His voice drifted off, not wanting to think about the loss. "Anyways, we never got to see your face since they punished us along with the others who made noise in the mess hall as soon as your team came back to the ship. We were released like a month ago."

"That long?"

The military must not want to lose their control on these ships even for a bit, I thought. I guess they thought even one uproar or protest could cause a rebellion, sprouting more issues when it was crucial for us to be united.

His grandmother leaned in closer to him, muttering something.

"She said they did it to de…uhm…*detour* others from making a fuss in the mess hall."

"Do you mean *deter*?" I asked, raising an eyebrow.

"Yeah, that!" he said, as if he was the one who pronounced it correctly. "It wasn't *that* bad. They gave us three meals and a bed. Others had two or one. We were together too since I'm eleven. We were just isolated from everyone else, especially other kids. I was really bored."

I guess they had sympathy for a little boy and an old woman, I thought.

"Did your grandmother tell you to say most of that? I thought she didn't know much English."

"A little," she replied, gesturing with her hand as her index finger and thumb almost touched. Her smile made me realize she was mimicking me earlier when I said "Piquito."

"I'm bilingual. I've taught her some words, so she could pick up on some things when people talk to her. This place is filled with strangers, after all. My abuela always told me strangers can be dangerous and take advantage of you."

I smirked. "You both take care of each other, don't you? What's your name?"

"Miguel Rosenburg."

"Nice to meet you, Miguel. Rosenburg doesn't sound Hispanic in origin. Is it safe to say your father had different roots?" I asked, trying to get to know more about Henry's family. His death still played on repeat in my head. I felt bad that I couldn't honor him in some way.

"Yeah, but we don't talk about him much." Miguel looked down at the dirty floor, littered with shoe marks. Due to all that's been going on, no one has been able to clean it lately. "He wasn't a good man." His grandmother patted his head, comforting him.

An uncomfortable silence filled the air for a moment. "So why was your grandmother asking about Henry?" I asked, trying to break some of the tension. "Does she not know that he's—"

"Oh, no! It's not that." He shook his head. "My abuela, Maria, is not *seenil.*"

"*Seenil?*" I was confused. "Oh! You mean *senile.*"

"Yeah, that!" he said with the same proud demeanor again. "The lessons kids are taught here are mostly about the basics we need to know. There's hardly time for extra stuff. I found a dictionary in the station for nonessential items discovered in supply runs and excavations. I've been trying to use new words I learn while talking."

"Huh… You're pretty bright for your age."

"Thanks!" he said gleefully. "But my abuela has been asking soldiers if they knew Henry because we're trying to see if he had connections with any of them about my sister and how she's doing."

"You have a sister?"

"Yeah, not all families woke up on the same vessel. My sister is older than me. Henry managed to hear that she was on vessel 3, but he never got the chance to see if she was okay."

"Your grandmother took care of all three of you before stasis? Where's your mother, if you don't mind me asking?"

Suddenly, an expression of sadness was plastered on his face almost in an instant. He turned around and buried his face in his grandmother's shirt. She had him in an embrace, consoling him.

"Uhm, Maria usted," I said, not knowing what to do or say. I'm pretty sure I used "usted" incorrectly. "Did I say something wrong? Was she taken by those monsters?"

She sighed. "It's okay, mijo. Tell him."

His face was red, turning back around. I could tell he was doing his best not to cry. "When Henry, me, and my sister, Valeria, lived with my parents, there were always fights. I think I was like six. From what I can remember, Madre—my mama was sweet to us, but she always seemed anxious and timid around Papa. When he'd get angry, he'd punish us for the smallest things." He took a moment to collect his thoughts.

"It's okay, Miguel. Take your time," I said.

"We were very poor. My big brother, Henry, was the oldest and had to get a job to support us. I didn't get it at the time, I still kinda don't, but Mama, Papa, and Henry were always fussing about money."

He paused while Maria rubbed his shoulders to encourage him to get through with it.

"I don't know any details, but one day, Mama was taken away from us by Papa. My sister told me Henry came home from work one day to find Mama on the floor in the living room, not moving. He searched the house and found Papa standing over my sister with a hammer."

I noticed Maria's bottom lip quiver as he told the story. The bits and pieces of English she understood must've been enough for her to get an idea of what he was saying.

"My brother knocked him out and called the cops. If he was a second late from coming home that day, my sister wouldn't be here, and I'm pretty sure Papa was coming for me next."

My heart wrenched in pain. "I'm sorry that happened…" I said.

"Yeah…we all are." He and his grandma glanced at each other, reflecting. "Well, afterward Abuela took us in, and Henry worked to be a police officer. When I was younger, he told me he joined the force to make a difference in the community. I think he felt responsible for Mom…" His voice trailed off a bit. "Either way, he was a hero to us, especially to big sis—I mean Valeria. Ever since, my big brother was tough for all of us, no matter how hard it got. He helped Abuela with money and went out to help other people after being recruited for the war, even before we were in stasis."

"I can tell you for a fact that your brother is everything you say he is after being deployed with him," I said with a smile.

Miguel smiled back.

Heroes still exist, I thought. Henry's personality made so much sense to me now. I thought back to my deployment with him. He was headstrong and remained that way for Joselyn and me so that we could get through the mission. Even faced with impossible odds, he didn't use that as an excuse to not do the right thing. I was beginning to get inspired by his ambition, even though he was no longer with us. I studied Miguel's face as Maria stood beside him. I didn't even know Henry that well, but I could tell he had a big impact on people's lives. I wondered what type of person I was compared to him.

Suddenly, my head was reeling in agony. "Ahhh!"

"Xander! Estas bien?" I heard Maria say.

"Hey! Do you need help?" Miguel said before their voices faded away.

* * * * *

At first, everything went black. Then, I found myself sitting on a Ferris wheel. A combination of salt and butter marinated on my tongue as I held a package of popcorn in my hand. I felt different. It's like I was still in my body and seeing through my eyes but somehow in a different perspective of time. Kids and parents on the upper and lower pods were giggling, having a good time.

"Thanks for this, Xanny," a guy sitting beside me said. He startled me. His hair was short and mostly black. He had a few short strands of gray hair poke out, but his skin was clear of wrinkles and blemishes. I'd say he was in his midtwenties. Maybe the strands of gray hair at his age were caused by stress or genetics. There was a little depth to his cheeks, but it was rounded out nicely by his jaw line. Upon closer inspection, his facial features resembled mine.

"First of all, you know I hate when you call me, Xanny," I replied. I felt my lips move and words come out, but I gave no intent to my nerves to say them. "It's a horrible nickname. And second, what are big brothers for? You always liked this place as a kid."

"Yeah… I miss being one. Exploring without a care in the world while your parents support you… Now, it's all about jobs," he said, reflecting. I caught a hint of depression in his eyes. "Reporter work is never ending in Los Angeles. There's always stories to cover on celebs, politicians, movies…that sorta thing. My boss can be a real ass about pushing that shit out."

I chuckled.

He sighed and leaned back in the Ferris wheel seat. "I'm surprised you didn't take a job like that. You like investigating stuff. Heck, you could even crash with me in LA, and I could put in a good word for you."

"If I was to become a reporter, that wouldn't be the type of investigative work I'd be into. I like looking into *real* things, not some glamor pieces to stroke famous people's egos. They get enough attention."

He playfully jabbed me in the arm and smiled. "You still got some of the old Xander in you. The one that doesn't take bullshit." He laughed. "You used to give mom and dad such a hard time. Then you found religion and got all boring."

"Hey, don't blame me for being boring on my faith. Adults just *are* in this economy—always working and barely having time for anything else…" I sighed. "Sometimes I feel trapped."

"Eh… True. I know what you mean. It's been a while since we've seen each other. What are you, forty?" A sly smile spread across his face.

I punched him hard in the shoulder. The Ferris wheel seat shook a bit.

"Owww!" he laughed, rubbing his arm. "Okay, your hit was much harder."

"I'm twenty-nine, you dick! We're only five years apart, Samuel."

"No need to say my full first name. You sound like mom when she's mad," Sam said. We both started laughing, almost hysterically. Maybe it was nostalgia.

"Anyways, Sam," I said, calming down. "Anything new you're reporting on?"

"Well..." He looked up at the sky, pondering for a bit. The sound of the wheel support made creaking noises as we went around. "There are conspiracy theorists going on about particle accelerators and beings from other dimensions."

I raised an eyebrow and looked at him crazy.

"I know. I made the same face when I heard it."

"How do they even relate to each other? People are nuts."

"Yep. Oh! There is this new type of tech people are investing in—well, people that can afford it. It's something called cryostasis, almost like something you'd see in a movie." He leaned forward, looking down at the people below while continuing to talk to me. "Apparently, they freeze your body to preserve it so that you can wake up in a different time. Your physical appearance doesn't even change. Although years could pass, you'd look the same age as you did before stepping into 'cryosleep' as they call it."

"Sounds like science fiction to me."

"You're probably right, but tech like cars, airplanes, and so many others seemed fictional too. Now, look at the world."

"Hmmm..." I observed the environment around me. A plane passed in the sky. Cars sped by on the freeway at a distance from us. I even looked at my phone and realized I was carrying a device capable of sorting various data exchanges. "You got a point. The very things we thought were impossible in the past are now real."

Sam broke his attention from the ground below and smirked at me deviously. "Speaking of *real*, it seems like you finally found that in Leona, huh?"

My cheeks flushed as I turned away from him.

"Ahhh..." he said as if he caught me in some type of act. "Don't be coy. You and GI Jane have been clicking ever since you met at the conference."

"You have the worst nicknames for people."

"C'mon! At least admit that she's a step up from some of those broads you used to date."

"Leona's actually something else," I said gleefully. "She's strong, compassionate, understanding, and above all else, loyal."

"But?" he replied. He could tell something was eating at me.

"Like you said, we click. But there's just something I can't put my finger on. It's as if there's a tiny side of her my intuition is telling me to be cautious about."

"You and that intuition of yours. I don't know how you do it. I envy you sometimes." He studied my face, staring at me intently. "Making life decisions on instinct alone isn't something I can do. Why can't you settle for good enough like the rest of us?"

"I don't know... It's gotten me this far, though."

* * * * *

Abruptly, like a dream, everything faded. I opened my eyes to a floor riddled with shoe marks. I felt myself kneeling on it while holding my head. The pain started to fade away too. I must've been shot back to reality on the ship.

"Senior Xander! Abuela is about to get help," I heard Miguel say.

I immediately shook my head. "No need. I'm back from... whatever that was."

I saw Maria turn around from where she was walking to. She started walking back as I stood up. I saw some worried expressions on others' faces as I came to.

"How long was I like that?"

"A minute, I think," Miguel said.

"Que paso?" Maria asked.

"She said—"

I immediately put my hand up. "I got that one." I took a second to regain my composure. "I think I got caught up in a memory with my younger brother."

"Oh, Abuela! Memory flare," he said, conversing with his grandma and pointing to me.

"Ahhh." She nodded.

"Huh?" I said.

"Lots of people on the ship get it when remembering the past. Memory flare is what those guys in uniforms have been calling it," Miguel said to me enthusiastically. "When I get mine, there's a tiny tingling sensation, and I start remembering more things. I heard from others you feel it the more signifi…" He took a moment to pronounce the word correctly. "Significant! You feel it the more significant the memory is in your life. Although, I've never seen someone hold their head in pain before." He scratched his head, gawking at me oddly.

Only a minute passed? I thought. *It felt kind of longer. Did seeing this kid and hearing his story about his brother trigger this?*

I wondered what was so significant about that conversation with my brother. At any rate, more pieces to this puzzle were locked in my mind. No need to dwell on the details now. My head needed time to recover the other scattered fragments of my memory.

"Is everything…okay?" Maria nearly struggled in saying those English words.

"Yeah, I'm fine. No need to stress over something I can't do anything about right now."

Miguel and Maria glanced at each other. Miguel turned back to me and shrugged. "If you say so."

"I don't want to sidetrack you with my family. Let's get back to yours. I know you've said you and your grandma have been trying to track down your sister, Valeria, for a month now."

Miguel nodded.

"But you must've heard the announcement. We're about to meet up with vessel 3 occupants when we land on the new base on Earth. You can see her for yourself."

"Well…" Miguel looked down. His grandma studied him. "We don't want to get our hopes up. The last time we heard any news about her, we were told she was training to be a soldier like Henry. We don't want to search for her and find that she's…"

"Also gone."

Miguel nodded. "It'd be…too much."

"Well, the supply runs and excavations have been run mostly by experienced soldiers from what I heard. And you must've seen the broadcast of the fight earlier too. Did either of you see her on any of the screens?"

Miguel translated some of what I said to Maria. They both shook their heads.

"I'd say it's okay to have hope then." I smiled, trying to reassure them.

Maria breathed out a sigh of relief. She then took my hand and said, "Gracias, Xander."

Bzzzzz!

Everyone in the mess hall looked up toward the speaker.

"Attention, vessel 7! Vessel 3 has landed safely at our new base on Earth. You can now safely pilot to the base's coordinates. We wish you a safe landing as well. Commander Brauns, please be on standby as Central Command will coordinate with you in case there are any unexpected developments interrupting your arrival."

Just as the broadcast cut out, I saw Commander Brauns at a distance passing through the mess hall with some officials behind him. I gritted my teeth at the very sight of him, thinking what Leona and others had to go through due to Command's decision to leave out tidbits of information. Imala was among them as well.

"Excuse me for a sec," I said to Maria and Miguel.

They looked back at me, bewildered.

I hurriedly made my way over to Brauns, attempting to block his path. I nudged some people out of my way to get there. However, as soon as one of the guards saw me coming toward them unexpectedly, one of them hit me in the nose with the butt of his weapon. I felt a little warm liquid run from my nose.

Brauns glanced over to see what was going on. "Williams?" He pulled the guard's shoulder to gesture him to be at ease. "What are you doing? Can't you see we're on the verge of a breakthrough for humanity here?"

"Answer me, Commander!" I picked myself up from the floor. Miguel and Maria inched closer to see what the commotion was about. "Did you know about the possibility of us still being possessed while in the suit?" My eyes pointed daggers at him.

"First of all, don't start ordering me around, son. I give the commands around here!" he said, getting in my face nose to nose. Some people stared in anticipation at our confrontation. He stayed in my face for a second and then backed off when I calmed down. "Second, yes we did know, but it was for the soldiers' own good. Everything else was new information to me too."

"Bullshit!" I uttered in disdain.

"Hey!" Brauns shouted in a boastful tone.

"Tápate los oídos, chico," I heard Maria say to Miguel in the background.

"Why do I have to cover my ears?" Miguel asked. "You swear all the time, Abuela."

"Shhh," she hushed.

Silence began to fill the air. Everyone could feel the tension rising between Brauns and me. I even caught a glimpse of Imala, looking worried while she stood by the guards.

"You need to watch your tone with me," he said menacingly while pushing his index finger to my chest. "The only reason I don't have you confined for insubordination right now is because of the contribution you and your platoon gave us to get this base on Earth. But one more outburst like that, and you'll find I'm not so lenient. Do I make myself clear?"

I reluctantly said without breaking eye contact, "Yes, sir... crystal!"

"Good." He backed up a bit. I noticed him ponder for a second to decide whether or not to say what he was about to say. "Those things feed off of negative energy. And yes, the suit protects a soldier against that ability but to an extent. Can you imagine the panic and fallout if that information was divulged? If we were to let our men and women on the field know that there was still a possibility of it happening, their anxiety would leave them open for those entities to possess them. Now the cat's out of the bag."

I sighed. "I understand, sir. But what about the other mess that happened out there? With all due respect, sir, the mission was a massacre! Squad leaders weren't privy to our force's actual numbers until the battle commenced. They paid for it dearly."

"Damn it!" He banged his hand on a nearby wall. It startled most people. It made me kind of on edge, too. "Don't you think I know that? What's the point of this? You lookin' for someone to blame, huh? You think there's some type of conspiracy happening like with the government?" He narrowed his eyes at me. "You people seem to forget that we thwarted that—the military. You don't need to tell me we lost good people. I know that. We all do!" He made a gesture by waving his arm and directing me to all the people grieving.

Though not everyone knew a soldier that was fighting on the battlefield, I could tell they felt the pain all the same. After all, those soldiers were the best we had at the moment. If even they could fall so easily to the enemy, then hope seemed dim, though we just clutched a victory by the skin of our teeth.

"He's right, Xander," Imala interjected. I was a bit surprised she remembered my name. "My department, R&A, was actually the ones who decided against telling soldiers about the full extent of possession. They have to battle with enough emotions as it is while fighting in the suits. We didn't want to put that stress on them while they fought. Plus, only a select few knew of the soldier's actual numbers—not even I knew."

I looked down at the floor, not knowing what to say. A small pool of blood stood out among the tile pattern. I almost forgot I still had a nose bleed. I could make out some murmuring from Miguel. He was most likely translating everything for Maria.

"I'm not your enemy, Williams," Brauns added. "We're on the same side."

Just as Brauns turned to walk away with the guards behind him, Imala stopped them.

"What is it?" he asked.

"Perhaps we could let Xander and other soldiers in training get in on some of our discoveries so far. R&A from all ships are having a meeting to trade and study information tomorrow. It wouldn't hurt for trainees to learn more about our situation, right? It'll better prepare them for the enemy once they get out there."

I could tell Imala was coming up with this all on the spot as she barely took breaths in between words. Brauns looked back and studied me for a bit. The guards stood still behind him like robots, following his every command.

"Do you swear to bring that same fire you just displayed to the enemy once you fully recover?"

His question startled me. I saw a glint in his eyes. I couldn't be sure, but maybe he wanted this nightmare to be over just as much as any of us.

I nodded. "Yes, sir!"

"Then I'll consider bringing it to Command's attention once we meet up with them."

"Sounds good, sir," Imala replied.

They continued walking out of the mess hall and toward the helm of the ship. Imala glanced back at me quickly and gave me a friendly smile.

I mouthed the words, "thank you" and nodded.

"Here." A teenage girl approached me and gave me a cloth to wipe my nose. "I know it isn't much, but thank you. We all needed to hear those words from the commander himself." She awkwardly looked around at others and then pointed her eyes to the floor. I could see she felt a bit ashamed. "We wanted to do what you did, but honestly, most of us were too scared to do it ourselves with the repercussions and all."

I gazed at the crowd of people staring at me in admiration. I sensed my reputation solidifying, receiving more respect.

"You're loco," Miguel said, coming up to me with Maria. He pointed at me and made a circling gesture with his finger next to his temple, indicating I was crazy. "If any of us did that, we'd be confined for sure."

"I'm sure he was just being lenient because everyone was watching," I replied.

"No. He likes you. If it were any of us, we would be punished."

I panned the room and most people solemnly nodded.

Was what I did really that big of a deal? I thought.

"Do you…think…he tell truth?" Maria said in broken English.

I shrugged and said, "Yo no se. We'll see."

"Do you mind if we stick by you until we see my sister?" Miguel asked. "You're good with authority and might give us a better chance asking around about her once we meet up with vessel 3, since you're a soldier and all. Our isolation before wasn't as bad as we thought, but we'd rather not do it again." He empathetically glanced toward Maria and back to me. "Not everyone who is a soldier or works in another field talks to us. I'm a kid and my abuela is old. We can hardly help the cause. Sometimes people walk by like we're not here." He stared at the floor, depressed.

I smiled and said, "Then I guess it's a good thing not everyone thinks that way."

He looked up at me and grinned reassuringly.

Maria saw how Miguel's giddiness returned and grinned too.

"Just don't attract too much attention once we meet up with others down there," I said. "All three of us are on thin ice as it is. No need to make unnecessary cracks, understand?"

"I think I understand. Just play it cool, right?"

"Right."

Maria walked closer to the ship's window and observed as the ship moved. We stepped up beside her, pondering the view too as the vessel got closer and closer to a planet we once called home.

CHAPTER 14

ENTERING EARTH'S ATMOSPHERE was a spectacle in itself. Once the vessel felt slight turbulence, people knew the only thing between us and fresh air was the metal container that sheltered us from our very home all this time. To step on grass, dirt—the very ground—was a gift alone. Not everyone appreciates the simple things in life until it's gone. It's another flaw we have alongside many that's probably gotten us to this point in the first place.

The sky looked amazing as ever. If it wasn't for this pressure pane reinforcing this glass window, such a beautiful experience could turn awful in a heartbeat. Though we were flawed, some of our inventions were near perfection. To my understanding, the funds put into building these vessels in the past were monumental. Engineers even figured out the science for the ship to maintain its own gravitational force inside the interior. This principal made sure that our weight and center of gravity wasn't altered going in or out of our planet. According to the information relayed to us in the first couple of months we were out of stasis, it's what prevented us from floating within the ship or crashing into things and losing balance in its structure as the ships orbited Earth. Plus, we didn't need passenger seats whenever we had to move. It saved room for other necessities, freeing up space.

Everyone around me got closer to windows stationed around the ship now. We could see the dome of the force field cast its light among a wide range in the area.

"My God… This is real. It really worked!" I heard a man exclaim not too far from me.

Maria and Miguel glanced at me and smiled in relief. In fact, I could tell most of the vessel's inhabitants were relieved as I scanned the mess hall. After watching the onslaught it took to make this happen, we could finally be a little hopeful seeing that it wasn't all for nothing. Families and friends stood close, comforting each other. Kids clenched their parents in anticipation. Couples held hands or stayed in each other's embrace as we descended into the safety zone of the force field. It made me even more anxious to see Leona.

I unexpectedly felt a warm touch on my shoulder.

"Don't worry," Maria said.

"Excuse me?" I asked.

"You see chica soon."

"How do you…"

"As soon as you said your name, I knew you were one of the same soldiers people around here were fussing about," Miguel interjected. "We watched the battle on a different screen, trying to spot Valeria if she was out there. Abuela saw people making spots for you at another one. I never saw your face, but once the crowd died down, Abuela got a better look. She rushed over to ask you about Valeria, nearly forgetting about me."

"Ah… That connects some dots. But how do you two know about Leona and me?"

Maria's face was flushed, avoiding my gaze. I guess she understood most of what I said.

"Are you serious?" Miguel rhetorically asked. "Everyone pretty much saw you as 'the two who are like glue' already. After the stunt she pulled getting us and others in on the commotion after you deployed, there's hardly anyone who doesn't know about you two now."

My cheeks grew hot with embarrassment. "Right. I nearly forgot about that. Dumb question. I guess my head is somewhere else…" I continued to stare at him and Maria awkwardly.

"Por que?" Maria asked.

"What?" Miguel said alongside her, nearly in unison.

"'The two who are like glue'…is that really a thing people say about us around here?" I scratched my head. "I mean, I've seen some other couples around here too. We're not the only ones, and we're not always together, you know…"

"Yeah, but I've seen some that break up or separate for a while. You two never seem to mind each other."

I smirked. "Thanks, I guess."

"De nada," he said, smiling, completely oblivious to how embarrassing this was for me. "Plus, grown-ups love gossip around here. They practically don't do anything else after working in the different departments."

"Si!" Maria added. "People…nosy!"

"Says the ones commenting on my love life," I muttered.

"Que?"

"Nada," I replied.

Bzzzzz!

"We have successfully descended on the Earth's surface. Please standby and await further instruction. Central Command will signal us when to depart from our vessel. We implore you to exercise patience during this critical time. Thank you."

Kind of anticlimactic, I thought. For some reason, I expected the announcement to our landing to be more dramatic or at least have some flare.

As we continued to peer out the window, I spotted tents and equipment outside on the ground floor. Across from us was vessel 3. It stood tall like a tower. I got a glimpse of other vessels orbiting Earth from afar sometimes. However, to be this close to it was surreal. Gray metallic material reflected the sun's light on its surface. The engineering it took to make the steel contraptions, interior wiring, and other various compartments must've been incredible. We were told that developers in the past were able to work out the kinks for the ship's main functions for engines, stability, and movement through solar energy. If you looked close enough, you could see solar panels integrated into the ship's outer structure. Huge, reinforced glass windows were on the sides too. I couldn't be sure, but I think I could faintly make out people staring back at us as well.

Debris from old buildings stood out like a sore thumb among the grassy plain that now had burned patches. Seeing this from the video feed compared to up close was quite the difference. Though the picture was clear, it still felt more real now that we were right in front of it. Only the vessel's window was a partition between us and it. Though anxious, I couldn't help but notice the absence of bodies that were on the battlefield that was on the video feed.

I see part of the reason why it took so long to signal the vessels to land, I thought. *They had to cremate the bodies while recovering the exo-suits too, no doubt.*

"There's nothing left of him to bury!" someone cried out next to their family.

I could only imagine what they were going through.

"Why did they do that?" Miguel asked.

I looked over to him and saw Maria shielding his face with her hand.

I sighed. "I'm not sure I should be telling this to a kid, but after what you've been through already, it'd be stupid of me to try to treat you like one. I could tell you the truth if you want."

He translated what I said to Maria. She nodded in approval and muttered something back to him.

"She said better to hear the truth now than question lies later."

"Wise words," I said, smirking to her and then focusing back on him. "We're low on supplies and manpower as it is. As inhumane as it may sound, digging graves for every single person, including the possessed, would waste those resources and time we need to combat the enemy."

"So are we all just bodies to whoever's in charge until this is over?"

His reply startled me a bit. It was simple yet deep. "I'm sorry to break this to you, Miguel. You might not understand it now until you're older, but we were just bodies to our leaders even before we signed the stasis agreement."

"That's...sad."

"Yeah... Yeah it is."

"Everyone! Listen up!" someone suddenly shouted.

I turned around to find a guard standing on a chair. He projected his voice by cupping his hands over his mouth.

"We got the green light to head out!" he continued. "Other guards will escort you outside. Please exit in a civilized and orderly fashion. All the resources you need will still be on the vessel for the time being. Feel free to enter and exit the ship as you please. We will continue to monitor the situation for your safety and protection."

I looked back to the window and saw occupants from vessel 3 coming out. A ramp extended from the ship to the ground floor. As the people came out in bunches, it was hard not to notice their dwindling numbers. Excluding Command from vessel 1, we started off with over a few thousand people. It waned into the one thousands and then hundreds once people were deployed for missions. Each ship used to have more than two hundred people at least. Now, each was lucky enough to have at least over a hundred.

"Is that really all of them, or is there more staying on their ship?" Miguel asked, peeking out the window as well next to Maria.

"These people are just like us. Only soldiers got to experience the outside during deployments. Even then, we had to be in suits and aware of those things at all times." I paused, trying to make out some of the faces but they were too far away. "I'd imagine they were climbing the walls for fresh air like the people here. No sane person would stay on the vessel right now unless they were in infirmary."

"Then what they said on the speaker was true. I can't make out the exact number, but it's less than a hundred people for sure— maybe less than fifty..."

"Oh, Dios mio!" Maria cried out while gazing at the lack of people. Her eyes became watery. I caught Miguel starting to look down, depressed.

I stepped closer to give her a side hug while still peering out the window. Just then, soldiers in exo-suits caught my eye coming out of the tents. I took a quick mental headcount and confirmed it was the original fourteen survivors of the battle. I could even see the familiar brunette hair flow in the wind. Seeing Leona at the distance rekindled my spirit as I refocused my attention to Miguel and Maria.

"Don't worry. Valeria is among them. I can't explain it, but I got a good feeling."

Miguel told Maria what I said. She solemnly nodded as she reassuringly stepped back from my grip.

"Follow us this way, folks," one of the guards said, approaching us. He directed us to the wave of people walking out of the mess hall.

We followed the others in silence, waiting to see our loved ones again. Witnessing the expressions of others who lost people they cared about after this battle reminded me of how fortunate I was. As we trailed behind, walking through corridors, I started to feel the coldness of the metal that supported this structure. Though it housed us and kept us safe all this time, mankind's inventions just didn't compare to the Creator's.

CHAPTER 15

I CLOSED MY eyes for a moment while walking down the ramp to savor the smell of the Earth entrenched meadow, tickling my nose. The breeze kissed softly as it gently grazed my skin. I not only smelled but tasted the freshness of the air entering my body and filling my lungs. The sensation pulsing through me as I felt Mother Nature again was nearly indescribable. I never did take my helmet off on my first mission. This experience was a welcomed treat. Before I knew it, I was hit with the stench of smoldering ash and death. It was so intense it made me prop open my eyes. However, as soon as I did, I found those forest-green irises consoling me again.

"Xander!" she said, standing at the ground floor where the ramp ended.

"Leona!"

I saw another soldier from vessel 7, waiting below in a suit for loved ones as well. I hurriedly made my way down to Leona, sifting through people. We hugged each other tighter than we ever did before. The material and reinforced capabilities of her suit nearly took the air out of me, but I didn't care. We stayed embraced in another for a minute. I was a tiny bit skeptical about us after remembering what my past self said to my brother about Leona. But after getting to feel her in my arms again and looking into her eyes, all doubt dissipated. I felt electricity every time we touched. It was palpable. We took a moment, examining each other.

"What happened to your nose?" she asked, slowly running her finger across the bridge of it.

A jolt of pain startled me as it spread throughout the nerves on my face. Judging by the sensitivity of the area, it must've been swollen. "Got hit by a guard." I gently took her hand away from my face. "It's nothing compared to what you just went through, though," I said.

She studied me, concerned. "You demanded answers for what happened out here, didn't you?"

"How did you—"

"It's the same thing I did when you were deployed. I thought I was losing you too."

I chuckled. "Aren't we the pair…"

She passed me a half-hearted smirk and looked away for a bit. "Look, I know I was being reckless… I wasn't trying to die or leave you alone. Comrades were falling left and right and…"

"You did what you thought was right for everyone," I cut in.

She looked up at me again, surprised.

"This thing we have… I rely on it now. That moment I awoke from stasis, I had no memory of you, and as far as I knew, I could've lived without you." I reflected for a second what it was like to not know Leona before. I felt like I was existing but not really living. "Once I recalled we had something, though, it was different. Ever since we reconnected, the thought of not having you in my life is impossible to think about."

Leona listened intently, harmonizing with my words. I could tell she felt the same.

I sighed. "But with that said, there are others who rely on us to help take back our world. Seeing you make that call to fight that possessed guy made me realize we can't be selfish with what we have. We'd lose each other and inevitably die alone."

She perked up a little. "So you've been thinking the same thing I've been, huh?"

"Yeah… To survive the next battles ahead, we're going to need all the friends and allies we can get."

"Which means trusting others. That's going to be hard after what happened out here…" She looked down, depressed. I sensed she was in more agony about the losses today than what she showed on the surface.

I examined the area. I recognized some occupants from vessel 7 interacting with vessel 3. No one really appeared to be in the talkative mood, but manners are ingrained in most of us growing up. Therefore, social cues were a must still among many even during times like this. Some people were conversing, being thankful for the opportunity to see and feel daylight again. Others broke down, reeling over the soldiers that were lost today. The sun illuminated both the fortune and tragedy this day brought. At a distance, I saw some of the surviving soldiers chatting with people they knew, trying to keep a level head. Others that didn't really know anyone had a harder time. I spotted Evan, for instance, locking eyes with us briefly while he was sitting at a tent a little ways ahead. I could tell he was too distraught for introductions. I caught a glimpse of a body under a sheet by the tent he was at.

"Is that who I think it is by that soldier named Evan?" I asked, pointing at the corpse.

Leona nodded.

"So did your idea to apprehend that possessed bastard pan out?"

"They don't know yet. The results are inconclusive as of right now."

"Ah…"

"Ahem!" I heard someone explicitly fake cough behind us to get my attention, followed up by "Owww!"

I turned around to see Maria pinch Miguel on the arm.

"Abuela wanted to give you two a moment and not be rude. I had to say something, though. I was starting to think you forgot about us!"

"Oh! Miguel and Maria," I said, scratching my head. "I was going to introduce you."

He studied me with suspicion. "You're lying, aren't you? You really did forget about us!"

I nervously laughed.

Leona did a facepalm, and I could tell she was slightly embarrassed by me, neglecting to mention they were with me. "I was wondering why you two were lingering around us for a bit. Please excuse Xander. He tells the truth most of the time, so he's not really good at lying," she said, crouching down to Miguel's level. "If he was, he would've known no introductions were needed since we've already met."

"You have?"

"When you and Henry were deployed, remember?!" Miguel exclaimed, frustrated. "We were with Leona when she complained about taking an inexperienced soldier in training—*you*, out on an important mission with such a small platoon. It was the whole reason we were isolated a month before in the first place. Why do you keep forgetting?"

"Oh, right! I'm sorry. My head is everywhere today."

I saw Maria whisper in Miguel's ear. He snickered.

"What did she say?" I asked suspiciously.

"She said, 'Why do you look stressed? Leona was the one fighting.'" He laughed harder.

If someone were to draw a caricature of me at that moment, I swear I would've had a blood vessel protruding from my head as I gritted my teeth. They were starting to annoy me. I let it go because I saw that their company made Leona crack a smile, even if it was brief.

"I really am sorry, by the way. I know I've said it before, but I really didn't mean for any of you to get caught up in my mess that day," Leona said to Maria and Miguel. Her expression reverted back to serious. "I should've gotten disciplinary action right alongside you and the others." Guilt riddled her face.

"It's okay. We told Xander isolation wasn't that bad. I was still with Abuela the whole time and—"

Maria interrupted Miguel, whispering something to him again.

"She wanted me to say that we know how some people have more privil...uhm..." He took a second to enunciate the word. "*Privileges* than others around here, but we don't hold it against you.

Henry used to sneak us snacks or extra supplies whenever he got extra."

"I still feel bad, though…" Leona replied.

"But you still…good person, Leona," Maria managed to say.

I smiled as I saw a flicker of hope return to Leona's eyes. "Gracias… Anyways, why have you two been with Xander?"

"We're trying to find my sister, Valeria. She was on vessel 3 last time we heard," Miguel said. He then pointed to me. "We figured after he yelled at Commander Brauns and didn't get in trouble, we would have a better chance at questioning authority with him by us."

Leona passed me a scolding look like the one I gave her when she told me she made a fuss about me during my deployment. I returned a nervous smile. Karma is kind of everywhere in life if you pay close attention.

"You're a glutton for punishment, aren't you? Try *not* to become a martyr, all right?"

"You're one to talk, *Ms. Reckless*," I said teasingly.

"I…" Leona let out a sigh. "Touché." She looked off to the side, sad. I knew she could tell I was joking, but I don't think she was quite in the mood. With all the emotions still lingering in the air, trying to say the right things was like catching sunburn. I couldn't tell what area was too sensitive to touch on yet.

Crap…too soon, I thought.

"Smooth," Miguel said, adding to the awkward tension. He reminded me so much of how my younger brother would tease me in this type of situation too.

"Shut up, kid" I replied.

He pouted. Maria noticed. I doubt she fully understood our little spat, yet she comforted and coddled him like most parents, taking the side of the younger one. Leona stood up and pinched the bridge of her nose in frustration. Her suit made noise as the mechanisms attached adjusted to her movement. We must've been low-key driving her crazy. If anyone around us was watching, we'd probably resemble a typical family, even if it was for an instant.

Suddenly, a small commotion came from a crowd by us. A man with a decorated uniform walked with a small entourage behind him.

All of us looked their way. The air shifted around him as his demeanor exuded dominance. His rigid walk was enough to make you want to straighten up in his presence. Among the entourage was an Alpha soldier still in the Juggernaut model suit, a few guards, Commander Brauns, and some other officials I didn't recognize. Another person with a decorated uniform trailed behind them. She was a woman who had her hair up in a ponytail. The sides and back of her head were shaved, leaving only her long hair, which was tied up and coming down from the top. Her petite frame and calm demeanor made her seem innocent at first glance. However, as they made a beeline toward us for some reason, the intense look in her eyes gave me the impression that she had seen some things in her time. The same went for the man with the decorated uniform. As he approached, white streaks were apparent among his dark brown beard and hair. A nasty scar came from the top of his brow, crossing his eye, and ended at the side of his cheek. His natural eye color was deep blue, judging from the one not affected by the scar. But the other that was affected was completely white. It's as if someone or something just stole the color from it. It kind of creeped me out.

Miguel, Maria, and I stood as spectators not knowing what to expect as the group stopped a few feet away from Leona. I glanced at Brauns who paid me no heed.

"Beta Squad Leader Madigan?" the man in the decorated uniform said.

"Yes, Captain Commander, sir!" she stood, poised in a salute.

Ah…so that's what Captain Commander Voorhees looks like, I thought.

"I thanked Alpha and the other soldiers for what they did today. You all truly fought against impossible odds," he said. He took a second to clear his throat. It could've been my imagination but something about his words didn't seem genuine—almost as if they were rehearsed. "However, *you* also pulled off the impossible. Our readings indicate that thing is still in Harper Walker. Though ill-advised, your actions have potentially brought us invaluable intel about the enemy. Well done." He stuck out his arm for a handshake. "We should all be proud."

Leona tried not to show it, but I could see she was livid by his comment. Her hand behind her back while she maintained her salute stance was balled up and shaking. I know the loss of Hunter, Chrissy, and others was eating her up inside. Heck, these people were complete strangers to me, and I couldn't help but feel a little guilty about not helping in some way. She hesitated to relax her stance and shake his hand in front of everyone, knowing how insulting it would be to the families and friends suffering the deaths of the deceased.

"Proud?!" I heard someone shout. They sounded enraged. I could clearly hear the distress in their voice even from here.

"There's nothing of my cousin left to bury!" I heard a woman chime in.

The crowd became louder and antsy. Captain Commander Voorhees pulled his hand back. I took note of Leona breathing out a sigh of relief.

"Saved by the riot," I mumbled sarcastically.

"Huh?" Miguel said with Maria close behind.

"Nothing."

We continued to spectate as Voorhees panned around to address the crowd. He took a deep breath before shouting the words, "Calm down, everyone! I assure you the lives lost today will not be in vain. We will take time to honor our fallen and commemorate their lives once we figure out the next step from here!"

"You could've at least let us say goodbye before turning them to ash!" someone yelled out among the commotion.

"Due to some of the states the bodies were in, it would've been too much to witness, especially with children present," Voorhees replied.

"And who's fault was that?" I saw a guy cup his hands over his mouth to project his voice to the officials. "It was because of negligence in background checks among *your* ranks that this happened!"

Some people nodded their heads in unison, feeding off of the ruckus and blame.

"Take responsibility for once!" someone else said.

"Yeah," another chimed in. "They were just expendable to you. You burned them like trash as soon as they outlived their use!"

The crowd began to protest in unison.

This really could turn into a riot, I thought. Leona stepped a bit closer to Miguel, Maria, and I as she witnessed the scene unfold.

"Sir!" We saw the Alpha soldier in the Juggernaut suit approach Voorhees. "These people just need more time. I don't think they're in a state to listen to anything Command has to say right now."

"Obviously," Voorhees replied in a snarky tone. He sucked his teeth. "Tch… Since when did I become a politician?" He turned to the guards around him. "Take control of the situation. The last thing we need is another fight at the moment, especially amongst ourselves."

"Yes, sir!" the guards boasted in unison.

I studied Voorhees's expression. Either he was very calm or disturbingly nonchalant about everything. Whichever the one, it was unsettling to say the least. I took a glimpse of Brauns again. He glanced at Voorhees oddly as well. I wondered if he was thinking the same thing I was.

The guards shouted, trying to calm people down. Brauns followed suit behind Voorhees along with the rest of the entourage, not engaging with the riot. The female commander trailed behind the line of officials.

"Hey! This is your chance." I felt Miguel tugging my shirt.

"My chance for what?"

He pointed at the female commander with the shaved sides and ponytail on her head. "To ask about Valeria. I'm pretty sure she's in charge of vessel 3."

"Remind me… How did this fall on me again?" I asked.

"Please!" he said innocently.

"Por favor!" Maria repeated.

A gentle touch on my shoulder made me look back.

"Friends and allies, remember?" Leona said, encouraging me.

I grunted. We made our way to the female commander with me at the helm. Leona didn't need to follow us, but I suppose she was curious about Valeria. I did tell her about my deployment with Henry, after all, and she did somewhat know his family. Maybe it would've eased her guilt knowing that a family she incidentally caused trouble to would get to rejoin with a member they thought could've been lost. She did already lose one kid today, Hunter, under her watch. I know it would've relieved her some to see us gain one.

I coughed as I cautiously approached the female commander. I had to be cautious not to get too close with some guards not too far away from her. After all, I didn't want to get hit in the nose again. "Ahem… Would you happen to be in charge of vessel 3?"

She stopped in her tracks and put up her hand. "Stop!" she exclaimed. "I know how distraught you all must be, but I will be forced to take action if you take a step further. Despite what you may think, I had no hand in keeping people informed of only select intel." She looked around, making sure no one else was in earshot. "In my personal opinion, the whole operation was a shit storm despite what Voorhees said. I sent three of my best guys, and they all died. If it wasn't for the youngest, we wouldn't be standing here. Screw Command as far as I'm concerned."

Her sudden shift from professionalism to casual behavior made me relax a bit. "We're not part of the riot. We're actually here to inquire about a possible trainee in your ranks?" I expressed it more as a question rather than a statement to not disrespect her in case it came out like a demand.

"Oh yeah? Who might that be?" she asked.

"Valeria," Maria replied anxiously beside me. "We look for Valeria."

The female commander crossed her arms and shook her head, not replying.

"Is she…?" Miguel couldn't get the words out.

"Please," Leona chimed in. "We have to know. Commander… uhm…"

"I'm Commander Bridgett, and don't worry. She's fine—physically anyway…"

"Isn't Bridgett more of a forename, Commander?" I asked.

"Yeah, it's my first name. So what? After fighting tooth and nail in a man's world for rank, I at least get to be called whatever *fucking* name I want. You got a problem with that?"

I shook my head. *Sheesh*, I thought. I was on edge again. Her petite frame and laid back manner was misleading. She had an attitude to boot.

Leona stepped up beside me. "Excuse us. We're not looking for trouble, but if you have information on Valeria, we'd really appreciate it." Leona directed Bridgett to Maria and Miguel beside us. "Her grandmother and little brother are right here."

I saw Bridgett glance at Leona's Beta squad insignia. "Ah… You're Leona, aren't you?"

"Yes, ma'am."

"They told me one of my youngest soldiers would be on your squad. It's a shame Hunter saw the end of the line here. That boy had potential. Now I got Valeria running around like her head's cut off, asking people what happened." She reflected, staring off into the distance. "I've been dodging her. In all my years, telling this girl about this is something I didn't have the heart to do. She's a good trainee too—a heck of a shot."

Miguel and Leona looked at her, confused, while Maria was trying to pick up on what she was saying.

"What did you mean about her being *physically* fine earlier?" I asked. "Did she have some type of mental breakdown?"

Bridgett's eyes widened. "My gosh… You don't know, do you?"

We were all perplexed.

"Know what, Commander?" I replied.

"Commander Bridgett!" Suddenly, a girl shouted from a distance, running toward us.

"Well, you're about to find out. She *might* have a mental breakdown after meeting all of you. I've gotta go."

"Wait—"

Before I could get another word out, guards came and ushered us to step back as Bridgett sped walked to catch up with the entourage she was following. I peered back at the girl who was shoving her way through the commotion of people.

"It's her!" Miguel said, anxiously jumping up and down.

Maria made a cross gesture with her hand, hovering over her body. "Gracias a Dios!" Her eyes became watery.

"Is that really her?" Leona asked Miguel as she came closer.

"Yeah! Just to let you know, she's kind of hyper and gets excited easily. It can be a bit much at first for people who don't know her."

"You tell us that now?" I said.

She stopped in front of us panting for air. Since she was Henry's sister, I knew they would have similar features, but I was shocked to see just how similar they were. She had short, light-brown hair like Henry. Though it was a bit longer, it was still generally a reminiscent style. She sported a fade on her sides while having a full head of hair, coming down a bit to her forehead up top. Though not as built as Henry, she was still slim and toned from the neck down. She could nearly give Leona a run for her money, judging from her athletic build alone.

Miguel wasn't kidding before, I thought. *She really does idolize her big brother.*

"Abuela! Miguel!" she shouted, surprised. She immediately hugged them. "I was looking for the commander, but thank God, I found you."

I smiled. "Looks like everything worked out," I said.

Valeria looked at me, puzzled. She then turned back to Maria and Miguel, talking in a low voice. "Quienes son estos personas?"

"Oh yeah!" Miguel said. He first pointed to me. "This is Xander! He helped us find you, I guess…"

I smirked and playfully looked irritated. He must've still held a little grudge from when I told him to shut up. Valeria giggled.

"And this is a kick-ass soldier who helped us get back on Earth."

Well, at least Leona had a better introduction than me, I thought.

"Hi! I'm Valeria. Nice to meet you!" She was nearly right in our face, smiling. Her hand was outstretched, waiting for me to shake it. She caught me off guard. Her naturally jubilant behavior contrasted with the depressing atmosphere people were experiencing.

"Uhm…hi," I replied.

Leona and I shook her hand, not knowing how to respond to her positivity.

Valeria turned back to Maria. "So, Abuela, where's Henry? Shouldn't he be with you two? It's not like any units are deployed right now."

Maria looked away, not knowing how to tell her granddaughter that her brother was dead. Miguel also looked down, not wanting to tell her.

"I was also trying to track down the commander to try and look for someone else."

"Who?" Miguel replied curiously.

"You don't know him yet, but we kind of became close…" She looked to the side, blushing a bit. "He's helped me cope all this time while I've been asking about you, trying to see how you were on vessel 7. I've especially been worried about Henry with the deployments and all."

I felt my heart about to rise out of my chest with anxiety as I began to realize why Commander Bridgett didn't have the heart to answer this sweet girl.

"But now I haven't been able to find him either since early this morning. His name is Hunter."

My eyes widened in disbelief as I remembered Hunter's words on the video feed when watching the battle on the ship.

I have someone I'm fighting for too. She doesn't know I'm here right now. She talks about how much of a hero her brother is, and here I am talking like we've already lost.

Miguel, Leona, and I stared at her with blank expressions, not knowing what to say. Maria was lost, trying to understand the situation. With vessel 3 having the least amount of people, the chances of coincidences like this happening were more likely. However, the chance that fate would make this poor girl experience the loss of two people she cared about at the same time was cruel. I understood what Bridgett was saying. I didn't have the heart nor the words to tell her to make this okay, and I'm not sure Bridgett even knew about Henry. Crushing this girl's happiness was one of the hardest things anyone could do.

CHAPTER 16

"**What? Why are** you all just staring at me like I have something on my face?" She wiped her face with her forearm just to make sure.

I remembered Hunter saying that vessel 3 was prohibited from viewing the battle. Valeria was in the dark about him and her brother.

Her eyes widened, realizing what our silence could mean. She covered one hand over her mouth as she said, "Oh no… Don't tell me…"

"Hunter was a part of my squad," Leona reluctantly replied. She hesitated to touch Valeria's hand to comfort her. "He didn't want to tell you that he was fighting. If it wasn't for him, the generator to the force field probably wouldn't be running right now." Leona took Valeria's hands into hers. Their hands were shaking. Valeria was frozen, listening in disbelief. "We'd still be in space, struggling to survive. He fought for you so that you'd have a chance to live."

"I-I…" She stuttered on her words, not knowing what to say. "A-and Henry?"

My heart fell to the pit of my stomach, sympathizing with this girl's pain.

"He was part of the platoon that got the relic for the generator," Miguel said. "Abuela and I…we…we didn't know what to do once we saw only two soldiers come back. Three left, but Henry wasn't with them."

She literally approached us, ecstatic about life. Now, I had to witness her expression morph from happy to disbelief and now pure frustration as tears flowed forth, streaming down her face.

"Hunter lied to me..." she managed to say, breathing heavily. "And Henry *promised*—he promised me he wouldn't ever leave me!" She started to shake in anger. I glanced at Maria who glanced back at me, worried. "I hate them!" she yelled. Some people around in the area broke their attention from the commotion and stared at us.

"You don't mean that," Leona said, still holding her hand. "You're just upset, that's all."

"If you would please excuse me... I think I need to be alone for a while..." she said as her bottom lip quivered.

I could tell she was holding on to what little composure she had left while still trying to be polite. Leona let go of her hands and attempted to hug her. Valeria suddenly slapped Leona's hand away from her. Miguel, Maria, and I were shocked by her reaction.

"I... I don't even know you. So please stop acting like you know me!" I could see the inner turmoil within her. She wasn't trying to be disrespectful, but she was fighting with sadness and anger at the same time. An array of emotions were mixing into one.

"I won't pretend like I know what you've been through or going through. However, I do know that your grandmother and Miguel have been searching for you all this time and didn't give up hope," Leona said. I saw Miguel explaining the situation to Maria in Spanish. "You don't have to waste time being angry at the situation. You can grieve with the people who care for you."

"I sorry, Valeria," Maria said in broken English. Her eyes began to water. "We're here now."

Maria attempted another hug, but Valeria quickly stepped away. "Just leave me alone!" She ran from us, fleeing in tears.

"Teenagers..." Leona mumbled. "I can't blame her. Today has been too much to take..." I caught her contemplating, most likely about everything that happened on the battlefield. It must've been playing like a movie in her head on repeat.

She turned around and started heading toward vessel 7. Her saddened expression worried me. I hurried after her.

"Excuse me," I said as I incidentally bumped into someone among the crowd.

I looked back and saw Maria was grieving while watching Valeria run from the area after just reuniting with her. Miguel didn't know what to do other than stare in the direction his sister was going.

I nearly tripped over myself, trying to catch up to Leona. "Wait," I said, grabbing her arm. "You've been through a lot too. Are you okay?"

"I guess I'm as good as I can be…all things considered."

I let her arm go and nodded. "Just don't grow quiet on me, all right? After the battle and seeing Maria again… I can't fathom what you're feeling right now, especially with Valeria—the girl Hunter sacrificed himself for."

She looked away, not wanting to think about it.

I placed my hands on the side of her face and directed it toward mine. "But… I'm right here! You don't need to bottle it up. Even if you want me to shut up while you just talk, I'll listen."

I felt the hands of Leona's exo-suit touch mine while she gave me a warm smile.

Mwah!

The way her lips felt after kissing mine let me know how sincere she was with her words.

"I'm okay, Xander. Really…right now, I just want to take this clunky suit off and shower the mess of today off of me. With my wounds and cuts, I'm pretty sure they'd let me use it instead of the bath. Besides, I've been through worse."

I slightly tilted my head to the side with a look saying, "No, you haven't."

"Okay, okay… I admit this *has* been the worst," she said, trying to dissipate some of her depression by smirking. "But I know I can get through it because I have you."

I caressed her face, thanking God she wasn't among the dead soldiers today. I noticed her glance over to Maria and Miguel. I peered over too. Miguel stared into space while Maria kept sobbing. They were utterly distraught.

"I'm not sure I'm in a state where I can talk to anyone right now, let alone help them with their problems," Leona continued. "My words won't reach Valeria, but yours can." She let out a deep breath. "You did agree to help Maria and Miguel reunite with their lost family member. It doesn't seem your job is quite over yet."

"Valeria isn't in a state to talk to anyone either. What do I even say?"

"You always manage to find the right words with me. Well, most of the time—other times you don't have a clue."

"Sounds about right."

We took a moment to study each other. If eyes were truly windows to the soul, then I feel like Leona and I were peering into each other's whenever we stared at another. It was as if no words were needed. We were simply taking in each other's feelings and emotions at that moment.

"We'll talk tonight, okay?" Leona said, breaking our trance. "I'm going to get some R&R. I still have to be on standby in case Command needs me to repeat details about the mission also."

"Okay, wish me luck."

"Knowing you, you'll just need to follow your instinct."

As she gave a reassured smile and walked toward vessel 7, I couldn't help but be taken aback for a moment.

"Follow my instinct?" I muttered. "That's the same thing my brother said I did in that memory flare. Is she starting to remember how we were in the past?" I contemplated for a second.

Eh, I'm overthinking it, I thought.

I made my way back to Maria and Miguel.

"Hey, take care of your grandma, okay? Don't worry. I'll go after Valeria," I said to Miguel.

He nodded. "Just to give you a heads-up… The reason we didn't go after her ourselves is because she can be a bit…*loco* like this." His index finger motioned in a circle next to the temple of his head. "She doesn't take being sad well… I guess no one does…but with her, it can be another level."

"Noted."

I ran through the grassy field with patches of ash remains, leaving Miguel and Maria behind with the crowd of people. Though it was residue, I found myself still trying not to step on them as if the bodies were still there. The riot from before calmed down as I jogged in the direction I saw Valeria last. It brought me to an abandoned four-story building. It was away from most of the people.

I cupped my hands over my mouth in an attempt to shout her name, but there was a good chance she would've ran away again. Instead, I focused and listened. There was nothing for a minute, but as my heart calmed down from pumping adrenaline through my ears, I heard it.

Sniff… Sniff… Sniff…

Low sniffles from crying sounded like it was hovering above my head. I turned around and looked up at the top of the building. I saw Valeria's figure, peeking from the edge of the rooftop. It looked like she was hugging her knees close to her chest, hiding her face.

How did she get up there? I thought.

I searched the sides of the building. An old, rusty fire escape ladder caught my eye.

Aha!

When I got closer, I noticed she raised part of the ladder so no one could climb it. She really wasn't taking any chances of anyone bothering her. Luckily for me, I knew some tricks from when I was a kid. I gave myself a bit of room for a running start. Then, I burst into a dash and used my momentum to step up the wall using my feet. However, my limit was two steps, so on the second, I kicked off the wall and caught the bottom rung with both of my hands. The atrophied throughout the muscle tendons on my right arm kicked in.

"Ahhh!" I cried out as a jolt of pain hit the right side of me in an instant. I almost forgot one of my arms wasn't 100 percent. I dangled for a moment, trying to figure out my next move. I tried to do a pull up to the next rung, but my right arm wasn't having it. Then, an idea hit me. I lifted my legs up to the bottom of the ladder. I pulled up as much as I could with my arms so my legs could weave through the rungs of the ladder. Once they got through, I was hanging upside down. Once I knew my legs were in position, I used my abdominal muscles to curl into a sit up. My hands managed to reach a higher rung of the ladder while my body was upright again, sitting on a lower rung.

"Well, that's my workout for the day," I mumbled.

I climbed the rest of the fire escape until I reached the top of the building. To my surprise, Valeria already had her eyes daggered in my direction. Even from here, I noticed that her eyes were red and puffy.

"Go away!" she screamed in a high shrill.

Her reaction seeing me threw me off. She took off one of her shoes and threw it at me. I ducked. She turned back around and curled herself into a ball, hugging her knees again.

Wow... Miguel still knows his sister well even after all this time apart, I thought.

Though I was scared to get her other shoe thrown at me too, I still proceeded across the rooftop toward her. There was debris scattered everywhere. Fortunately, I made it to her without a mouthful of shoe ware in my face, nor any sharp objects puncturing my foot.

"Why do you and that woman care so much about what happens to me?" she asked in a muffled voice. She was talking while still curled up. "I'm a stranger to you. Just go away..."

I sat down beside her on the edge of the roof. I peered down below as my feet dangled in the air. "I could, but after meeting your big brother, he doesn't seem like the kind of person that would want me to."

Valeria slowly raised her head away from her upright fetal position. "You knew him?"

"I was deployed on his last mission with him and saw how he died."

She looked at me. Streaks of tear residue streamed down her cheeks.

"A hero."

There was silence between us for a while as we both stared at the sunset. It radiated beautifully with the background. I almost forgot what this experience felt like. Though such moments were fleeting, it was still extraordinary nonetheless—like fireworks bursting in the air before fading into the sky.

"What now? Are you going to tell me about your problems and how it all gets better, so I can open up?" Valeria said sarcastically. "I'm not in the mood for a pity party."

I smirked and accidentally let out a snicker.

"Is my grief funny to you?" she asked, glaring at me.

"Not at all. It's just that Henry said something similar to me and another platoon member before he sacrificed himself to save me."

Her glare started to fade as her eyes displayed empathy.

"I've just met you, and I can already see how similar you two are." I stared at the sunset, reflecting. "You're both so positive. He focused on the task ahead, no matter the obstacle, while you try to be happy even during dismal times. I kind of wish I had that strength…"

She uncurled herself and let her legs dangle from the edge. A deep sigh escaped her mouth. "I know what you're trying to do, but I don't think venting about our shortcomings will help."

"I get it…but the thing about venting is that I don't have to say a word. I can just sit here and listen."

She leaned forward and stared at the ground below, not saying anything. I studied her demeanor as the sun highlighted the innocence on her face. I could tell she was just a normal girl doing her best to stay strong.

"Did you know Hunter like Leona did?" she asked, turning her head toward me.

I shook my head.

She gazed back at the sunset. "He liked me—maybe the first guy that ever really did. Others I came across in the past, before all this, liked me, but liked…*parts* of me, if you know what I mean."

I leaned forward to make eye contact with her as I solemnly nodded.

"He liked *all* of me—the way I dressed, the way I talked, the way my personality is…everything, you know…?"

The way she described Hunter reminded me of how I felt about Leona.

"And I liked everything about him…" She fiddled with her thumbs while kicking her feet. "It was just him and his father at first, but he was KIA during a deployment. I was lonely on the ship without my family...so was he. We became close... Nothing felt fake. Everything about our relationship was real...*love!*"

As she said those words, it was as if an invisible hand reached inside my chest and squeezed my heart. The sympathy I felt for her loss was indescribable.

"He made me feel special like Henry would when I was little. Hunter filled the hole I felt when my big brother wasn't with me." She ran her fingers through her hair, breathing in and out, trying to keep her wits about her. "During middle school and freshman year high school, I was picked on by the popular girls that developed early. I was a late bloomer."

"Wasn't antibullying laws being put into effect ever since 1999?" I asked.

She chuckled in an almost snooty way. "Adults never do get it. You can slap all the laws and policies you want on darkness. It still finds a way to creep out the corners of the shadows."

Her reply threw me for a loop. It was profound, yet so dark for a girl her age. Tragedy does tend to warp even the most innocent of minds.

"It didn't help that I was into sports and aspired to be strong like my brother, the local cop, either. Even Abuela made an offhand comment to me once, saying how much I looked like a boy at the time. Miguel was too young to know what I was going through, and he still is."

I see... I thought. *That's why she didn't want to talk about something like this with Maria nor Miguel.*

"Those girls were in a fantasy world...talking behind my back and harassing me when no one else was looking because I wasn't like them. But I looked behind the veil and knew what the world looked like. Henry was the only one who told me to forget what people think and just be myself. That's why I tried to be positive no matter what negativity came my way." Her eyes started to water. "But it's so hard... I'm sixteen, and I still feel like I need my big brother. Hunter was able to fight for me and die here on the battlefield without his father as a seventeen-year-old. Yet, I still feel like I need my brother..."

More tears came forth, and she curled herself into an upright ball again. I made an attempt to console her by trying to rub her back but realized it could've angered her instead. After all, I was still a stranger, and she seemed to value her personal space. It was a challenge even getting this close to her.

"Miguel told me about the time your brother saved you from your father," I said.

She turned her head toward me, still hugging her knees close to her.

"Your brother saved you from a horror that none of you should have even gone through as kids. It makes sense why you share such a bond with Henry."

"Did Miguel also tell you that I saw the whole thing?"

I raised an eyebrow, startled.

"Most girls my age wanted me to be like them—play the damsel, making myself pretty for the world to see like in the movies or shows. But this is reality, and I've seen what really happens to damsels. My mom was one of them."

I adjusted myself on the edge of the rooftop, continuing to listen intently.

"She couldn't be pretty enough, make more money to help out the household, or do anything right when it came to my dad. He'd work long hours at a job that paid him little, only to come home and hear my mom nag about all the problems we had." She paused, trying to regain her composure. A breeze blew by us and carried some of her tears through the wind. "Henry tried to help out with an 'under the table' job that only paid in cash. It still wasn't enough… It was just a three-way stalemate nearly every day as they argued to keep the roof over our heads."

Snap! She looked my way and snapped her fingers. It caught my attention.

"Then just like that, my father snapped. My mom was a damsel, waiting for someone to save her when dad came home and hit her until she wasn't moving. Once he noticed me and saw the horrified expression on my face, he lunged at me. His eyes were cold, soulless…like a man possessed. I ran to my room. My mom was raising me to be just like her. So when my father came at me with the hammer, I was helpless too. If it weren't for Henry, I…" Her voice trailed off, not wanting to think about it. "I watched as my brother stormed through my bedroom door and beat my father unconscious for him to stop coming at me."

I felt a tear begin to roll down the side of my face.

"The police came, and we never told Miguel the details. The monsters we face now are even worse than the ones we can become ourselves. Life taught me that playing the damsel in such a cold world will only get me killed. But Henry told me fighting fire with fire only makes things burn." She looked up, most likely reminiscing the memories of her big brother. "He tried to help with my PTSD whenever he could, took me out to the shooting range mostly and sometimes hunting. It was to empower me so I wouldn't feel helpless in a situation like that again. I got pretty good at it."

"Did it help?"

"Little by little, yeah… It was hard trusting people again. I mean if my own father could do that to me…" She let out a sniffle. "But I keep trying anyway. Henry encouraged me to take control of my life and be positive, no matter who makes fun of me and no matter what comes my way. But…as I keep facing loss after loss, I can't help but wonder if I'm meant to be cruel as those girls too to survive…and make it through this pain."

She let her feet dangle again as tears dripped from her eyes like a faucet and onto the ground floor below. Now I understood her perkiness when we first met. It was a coping mechanism to hide the pain. I was racking my mind, trying to think of something to tell this girl to let her know it was going to be okay. It was kind of odd to see such a physically capable person crying. But I guess deep down, we're all just children hiding our vulnerabilities, no matter how much we mature. At that moment, for some reason, I wished Burrel was with me. He knew how to put me at ease with normal conversation. Maybe I could chalk that up to his wisdom at his age, but I didn't have that ability. If he didn't walk away after the battle was broadcasted, maybe he would be by my side, doing the same for Valeria.

"I had a brother too," I started to say. "From what I could remember, we had parents who lived in a fantasy. I had to be the adult and make sure he succeeded in life while they pretended like everything was okay, although they argued all the time. The rest is a bit fuzzy, but I learned something."

Her eyes shifted toward me.

"Life can throw a lot at you, making you feel like you're suffocating under the weight." I gazed at the peak of the sun, lowering behind the horizon at the distance. Then, I started to think about Leona. "But it can also be rewarding, relieving you of some of that weight you have to bear."

Suddenly, Valeria shifted her body from the ledge and avoided me. She had her knees close to her chest again, burying her face in it. I thought I heard what sounded like whimpers.

I crawled over some debris toward her and said, "Hey, are you..."

"Hehehe..."

Before I let out another word, I was right behind her and realized it wasn't whimpering. "A-are you laughing?"

"Hahaha!" She raised her head and grinned from ear to ear. "I'm sorry... I don't mean to laugh at you. You just threw me off guard." She giggled some more. "I was expecting a sob story, but you talked about a memory you can't even fully remember and said some words that sounded like a commercial quote."

Wow... I really was bad at this, I thought.

"I don't think the wise guy thing really suits you if that's what you were going for," she said, still grinning and looking back at me.

I started to become agitated and a bit embarrassed. "Well...you did say you weren't in the mood for a pity party."

"Uhm... Thanks, I guess?"

What an ungrateful little smart mouth.

"Val! Xander!" I heard a voice below shout. It sounded like Miguel.

We peered down and found Maria yelling, "Valeria!" in a Spanish accent. Miguel was beside her.

Valeria quickly wiped her tears. "We're up here," she said, waving. Some of her high-spirited nature I first saw when I met her seemed to return. Though it wasn't exactly how I pictured helping her, at least she was beginning to face her despair.

"How did you find us?" I asked, shouting down below.

"I went in the direction I saw you go last after calming down Abuela. I thought I saw water dripping over here and then heard laughing out of nowhere."

Valeria and I smirked at each other for a second.

"We'll be right down," I replied.

As I started to walk toward the fire escape over the debris, I felt a tug on my arm.

"All joking aside, I get what you were trying to say." Her voice took on a sincere tone again, reflecting her losses. She looked back at the edge of the building for a second in Maria's and Miguel's direction and then back at me.

"Oh?"

"Yeah… Though I've lost people I loved, there are others to live for." She let go of my arm and looked off to the side, seeming shy about opening up. "I appreciate it."

"Don't mention it," I said.

"Just don't try to be something you're not in front of Leona, okay? She seems like a good person, and I feel bad about the way I was with her earlier…"

I looked back at her, stunned. I don't remember letting her know about our relationship.

"What? Oh, yeah. I might have caught a glimpse of how you two were around each other before I ran away."

"You're too young to be giving me relationship advice, kid. Besides, you're still a stranger to me too." I started down the ladder.

"Fair enough," she said with a satisfied grin on her face.

As the sun fully set and we reunited with Maria and Miguel, I couldn't help but notice how bright the stars were at night. It's as if no matter the tragedy, the world still tries to show you how beautiful it can be.

CHAPTER 17

LATER ON THAT night, all the people settled down. Both vessel 3 and vessel 7 occupants were trying to enjoy the little bit of freedom that came with our new base on Earth. I overheard some occupants chatting and reflecting about past events outside. Leona and I were walking past everyone with our plates of food, trying to find a quiet spot. Others were facing anxiety and couldn't be in the area where their loved ones took their last breath. Therefore, they stayed on the ship. Valeria was one of them. Considering he put her life before his own, Hunter deserved better. She not only lost her first love but her best friend who was helping her cope in the absence of her brother. Now, she had neither. Though she was trying her best to keep it together, she asked Maria and Miguel to spend time with her and catch up on the vessel 3 ship. Considering how strict the military was with our movements and monitoring us, according to Burrel, I was surprised they let us be out and about, interacting like this.

Hummm…

There she was again with that melody. "You hum when you're worried, don't you?" We walked side by side in the cool night air.

She parted her hair, avoiding eye contact to hide how shy she was about it. "That obvious, huh?"

"Where did you pick that up from by the way?"

She didn't respond, pretending not to hear.

"Guards are keeping a watchful eye," I said, switching subjects as not to embarrass her and push the matter.

Leona examined the area as she saw guards placed around key positions, making sure people didn't stray too far from base. "Though they gave us space to breathe, they're still being cautious."

"Why? It's not like anyone in their right mind would try and escape the force field. We all know those things are waiting for us out there." I caught the covering on my plate in my hand before a breeze blew it away.

"I'm thinking Command saw the riot with the captain commander earlier and is taking precautions. My guess is they want people to calm down and relax to boost morale and trust again, but at the same time make sure no one does anything reckless."

I sighed. "Not even rewards can be genuine with Command. Everything is calculated and controlled."

Leona and I grew silent as we continued walking. Our lives were truly depressing. Even though being on Earth again was a gift in itself, it came with baggage. We barely had recollection of joining a military organization that we're hesitantly putting our faith in. Comrades we've come to know on the battlefield seem to die just as we get to know them. Supernatural enemies invaded our home planet. Plus, we're only parts of who we were since our memories haven't fully returned. All of this was too much to take if you let yourself think about it.

"Over there," Leona said, distracting us both from our sad thoughts. She pointed at a hill. The moon shined on top of the grassy land, as if putting a spotlight on where we should sit.

"I didn't know you could be such a romantic," I teased.

She smirked.

"This could actually be a date if the world wasn't at stake and all."

"Aren't we so lucky..." she wearily said.

We hiked our way up the small hill and sat down with our plates in hand. The view was a sight to behold. Not only did the moon light up the night sky, but the glow from the force field really captured the moment. It was a perfect, romanticized spot we had all to ourselves to be with one another for a moment and away from everything.

"By the way, I ran into Commander Brauns on the ship earlier," she said, digging into her food with an old, scratched-up, rusty fork. It was the same as mine. Canned beans, some type of gross meat substitute, and stale crackers littered our plate. Though the meal wasn't ideal, the company was.

"Oh yeah?" I said, eating my food as well.

"Yeah, he told me about your little confrontation and what that R&A lady, Imala, proposed. They got the green light to do it."

"Huh, how about that…" I said, realizing what that meant for us and those still having to fight the war. "Sorry about getting worked up with him by the way. I didn't mean to cause more attention for us."

"Don't worry about it. I know I acted irritated with you earlier with Maria and Miguel around, but after having some time to rest, I know I would've done the same thing if I just saw you risk your life out here too." She gave me a warm grin.

I blushed a little. "So…" I said, switching gears. "What do you think we're going to learn tomorrow from R&A and the information they've gathered so far about those things?"

She looked off into the distance at the night sky. "I don't know… I've been through a lot of fights in my life, but fighting the silhouettes and possessed people are the only enemies to still give me nightmares. I looked at Harper's possessed body right in the face and saw something *otherworldly*…" Her eyes locked onto mine. She usually scarfs down all her food when I'm not looking, but a considerable amount was left while she held the plate in her hand. After what she experienced today, I couldn't blame her for not having much of an appetite. "Even when the other vessels join us down here, I'm not sure what we can do. We may be facing something beyond our understanding."

I looked down at my plate, picking at my food. "Yeah… I can't blame you for thinking that way. I have doubts myself. These things are…*unreal*." I bit my lip a little as I was thinking. "It's like as soon as we think we've figured them out, they do something that makes us question everything we knew. Like…didn't you find it odd that the silhouettes in the area ran away and came back with more just when the generator was descending?"

"Yeah. It's as if their primary target was the generator to begin with…"

"But how could they have known about it?"

"I don't know…"

"It's not like one of us could casually relay information to them. And everything that *thing* was spouting inside of Harper… How did it know all that stuff? And if the suits were made to repel possession, how did it still happen?"

"I don't know…"

"And that giant dark figure I saw on the drone's broadcast… It was so huge. All it did was stretch out its hand and the ground trembled… What *was* that?"

"I don't know, okay?!" Leona's plate of food dropped to the floor.

"Leona?" I asked, worried.

Her hands were shaking as she buried her face in them. "All I do know is, if Hunter and the rest of the remaining soldiers didn't hit that switch… I'd be dead, maybe worse."

I rubbed my hand across her back.

"I was fighting for my comrades up until that point. At that moment when I saw that monster, I only cared for my own life. I feel so guilty for being so selfish even for an instant." Her whole body was starting to tremble with anxiety. "But you had to be there… Just being around them… All I felt was darkness, not a spec of humanity in them."

I set down the little food I had left on the ground and embraced her head into my chest. Stroking her hair gently through my fingers made her calm down some.

"Chrissy, Hunter… All those who died before and *will* die are just fodder to them like the food we ate for their own *sick* enjoyment." She held me tight while we looked up at the moon—a light surrounded by darkness in the night sky. "I want to be with you, Xander, for as long as I can… I do… But after today, I can't help but think about how *hopeless* we are."

We sat quiet for a moment, taking in the small pleasures life still gave us.

"Burrel, Joselyn, Evan, Maria, Miguel, Valeria…"

"What are you doing?" Leona looked up at me while I was still saying other people's names.

"Naming off all the people still with us."

"Why?"

"Because we'll be screwed if we start thinking negatively. As hard as it may be right now, we have to look at what we still have." I grinned and caressed her face. "If I recall, a strong woman said to 'Cut the shit! We're all going to make it out alive. You start thinking that way, the enemy's already won.'"

Leona's eyes widened as she realized those were the same words she said to Hunter on the battlefield that gave him the strength to keep going. "I know my words gave him hope, but I can't help feeling it also led him to his death."

"At the end of the day, it was his decision." I sympathetically gazed into her eyes. "When it comes to the people we care about, we do reckless things… We can't help it. Love is unpredictable, after all."

She immediately gawked at what I said, and I saw her flushed with shyness. I was confused for a second, but then I realized what I implied. I instantly reflected the same reaction. I didn't mean to, but I unknowingly suggested that we loved each other.

Suddenly, she playfully shoved me off, turning her head away. She crossed her arms as she said, "Stop trying to act all cool and wise as if I didn't know that. It doesn't suit you," she said, changing the subject and steering away from our awkward tension. Her words were reminiscent of what Valeria said to me. "Besides, *I* said those words after all."

"You also said that I knew the right words to say most of the time, and from the looks of it, you were right."

I noticed her becoming flustered with embarrassment and irritated at the same time, not knowing how to react.

"You mad?" I said, poking her.

She didn't respond. I tried to look at her face and caught her blushing. She sat sort of cross-legged but her knees were up, covering her face in it. I giggled.

"Sheesh…you can't even let me be sad with you," she said in a muffled voice.

"I'm sorry."

She lifted her face and gazed back at me with her green irises and brunette hair flowing in the cool breeze. "It's okay. It's one of the reasons I let you stick around," she joked.

"You were pretty badass by the way."

"When?"

"On the battlefield. The way you looked at the drone to me…said you were fighting for something real…and raising hell for me. It was sweet."

She grinned from ear to ear, not able to hide her glee being with me. "I only did that so you could see who the physically dominant one in the relationship was."

"That has yet to be seen. I'm still in training and have been told I was a natural."

"Oh yeah?" she said in a patronizing tone.

"I might just get better than you."

"You wish."

I quickly placed my hand on her head and ruffled her hair. "Ha! You didn't see that coming, did you?"

"What the—?" Her eyes threw daggers at me. "Xander! You are so dead!"

I got up and sprinted down the hill. I heard her footsteps. I looked behind me and saw that she was right there. She tackled me to the ground, and we rolled down the rest of the hill, kissing and roughhousing as we laughed. It's like we were kids falling for each other under the moonlit sky. In hindsight, a little play is probably what Leona and I both needed to relieve some of our anxiety. Because with tomorrow fast approaching, it would change everything we knew about the world, putting us on edge.

CHAPTER 18

"SON OF A bitch!" Joselyn shouted as she leaned against a guard rail, holding her abdomen and out of breath. It was the next day, and she coerced Leona into sparring with her at the training room to gauge her mobility. I, of course, thought it was a bad idea. After all, I caught her holding her stomach several times yesterday during the broadcast, but Joselyn swore she was feeling a little better. She was wearing a tank top to where I could see the cast and bandages around her torso. Nasty scars were left on her stomach and back from her original wound. Having observed it, it was truly a miracle she managed to survive at all.

We thought about seeing Valeria across in vessel 3, too but decided she needed time for her raw emotions to settle. Due to the animosity between occupants and the military from the battle yesterday, the medical officials from the infirmary allowed visitors for the injured again as an additional attempt to calm the tension. Training rooms were also used as rehabilitation for the injured that were recovering. Various people were scattered among the room, doing different workout or rehabilitation routines. Without the pressure of training in a suit, the room was basically a huge space lined with metal panels. Some training equipment were in a few spots, but that was about it. Along with the musky smell, it was barely different from a modern gym.

"Does your abdomen still hurt that much after surgery?" Leona asked, lowering her guard. She put on a brave face, but she still had injuries healing from the battle yesterday as well.

"I can go another round in a bit... I just need to catch my breath," Joselyn replied.

These were two of the most stubborn women I've ever met, not wanting to show their pain. When I came to think about it, I haven't seen Leona and Joselyn actually converse. I saw when they occasionally greeted each other if we'd pass by through the halls but nothing beyond that. However, this was the first time I tagged along with Leona when she visited Joselyn. They probably had different interactions when Leona took the time to see her.

"Here..." Leona motioned for Joselyn to put her arm around her neck. "Lean on me for support."

Joselyn waved her off and shook her head. "I can do this," she said, panting. "I only really feel pain if I move a certain way." She let go of the guard rail and walked on her own, taking a break from sparring.

"I knew Leona was still visiting you, Joselyn, but I didn't think she was helping you through rehabilitation too," I said.

"That's what happens...when the medical team is spread thin," she said, wincing through the pain. "I'm tired of sitting on my ass not doing anything but resting. Sometimes you gotta run before you can crawl, you know."

I slightly tilted my head to the side and passed her a look like, *Really?* "To this day, that saying still doesn't make any sense to me," I replied.

Leona snickered. "Regardless, she'd be on her own if I didn't volunteer to help her."

Joselyn suddenly stopped her bravado and leaned her back against the guard rail. "About that, Leona..." Her tone became serious. "Now, I'm not saying this to be a prick. I really do appreciate these visits, but I hate being someone's charity case."

I raised an eyebrow, curious of what she was going to say next.

"I know you feel like you owe me still after I came back from that deployment with Xander...maybe even guilty that you can't do more for me..." Joselyn avoided our concerned stares and looked toward the floor for a moment. "But you're not obligated to check up on me. I'll be fine. Besides, with both of you here now... I'm kind of feeling like a third wheel."

Leona took a step closer to Joselyn. "I admit, at first, maybe that's why I came." She then put her hand on Joselyn's shoulder. "But that's not why I come now."

Joselyn smiled.

I was giddy inside myself as I saw that they had become friends.

"I just walked in on a moment, didn't I?"

We all turned around to a familiar voice. The cane he was holding tapped and echoed throughout the room. Because of his distinct characteristics, we were able to spot him right away among others around.

"Burrel?" I uttered.

He passed all of us a casual wave. Leona grinned while Joselyn nodded. I was about to go for a hug but realized how awkward that would be for a reserved guy like him. It was good I stopped myself as it could've been really embarrassing. I didn't realize how much I missed his presence even though it hasn't even been a full twenty-four hours since I last saw him. For some reason, it felt much longer. I shook his hand instead.

"Hi again, stranger," Joselyn said. "You didn't walk in on much, but I do have to ask how you managed to get in here? Guards are only letting in rehab patients and those who need to work out for more severe health conditions."

"Easy." He tapped his right leg with his cane. "Sometimes I tell them I feel pain in my leg and that working it out helps. They let me stroll right on in."

"Really..." I heard a slight suspicion in her voice. "I can't put my finger on it, but something tells me that there's more to you than meets the eye."

Burrel smirked coyly. "If that's true, I guess you'll have to wait and see."

"Okay, old man." Joselyn teasingly narrowed her eyes.

"I was wondering where you were yesterday," Leona interjected. "Xander mentioned last night before we went to sleep that you walked away after the broadcast. Glad to see you back."

"Yeah... I've seen a lot in my life but something about yesterday got to me, you know."

"Yeah, I know," Leona replied.

We all stood in silence for a moment, remembering the massacre of a battle Leona was in. Though we were trying to keep it together, I couldn't help but feel relieved. For some reason, I felt something special, witnessing all four of us around each other like this.

"Speaking of which, why did you come to see us now?" I asked.

He leaned more into his cane. I was still trying not to roll my eyes whenever I saw him with it, since I was the only one so far who knew he didn't really need it. "Well, you know how people gossip around here. I heard Xander made a scene and that R&A might disclose privatized information for the first time since we woke from stasis."

"This is my first time hearing about it," Joselyn said.

"Oh, right! You had to go back to the infirmary," I said. "I unexpectedly met up with Henry's family and might have confronted Commander Brauns in front of everyone about yesterday's battle." I scratched my head, embarrassed. Although Leona already knew, she still passed me a *What am I going to do with you?* look.

"W-wait! You what? Rewind. Henry's family met up with you after I left? I've been wanting to give my condolences for the longest time. What happened?"

"It's a bit of a story, Joss," Leona said. "I kind of came in during the middle of all of it. I'll catch you up later."

Heh, Joss... I didn't realize Leona gave her a nickname, I thought.

"So how did you manage to convince Brauns about a sanctioned R&A disclosure?" Burrel asked me.

"I didn't actually. It was a woman named Imala. I first met her while she was with Commander Brauns when Joselyn and I came back from deployment." I walked over next to Joselyn while answering Burrel and leaned my backside against the guard rail to relieve some of the pressure I felt from standing.

173

"I was there at Xander's bedside when she introduced herself," Leona added. "She was pretty nice. I didn't think she had the pull to convince the commander or Central Command, for that matter, about an open meeting to their discoveries so far."

"It is quite interesting," Burrel said, rubbing his chin with his free hand. "They don't even share much information with excavation and our department are the ones responsible for finding things like relics for our equipment to dig up and for soldiers to retrieve."

"Given that I'm trying to wrap my head around some of this news I'm just now hearing," Joselyn intervened. "I'd say it's unusual Central Command is letting this happen, but it makes sense given the circumstances."

"How do you figure?" Burrel asked, listening intently.

"This is just my two cents. I wasn't there, but I heard about the potential riot the people were about to start after hearing what Captain Commander Voorhees said about the battle."

"Yeah…" I crossed my arms, thinking about it. "Leona and I were there, and it wasn't pretty."

"If the guards weren't there, it would've been chaos for sure," Leona added.

"Exactly!" Joselyn exclaimed. "Being transparent as they possibly can is in the military's best interest right now. They're buttering up to us. It's the very reason why you're all allowed here while patients like me are doing rehab, though infirmary was so strict about it before. It's kind of weird."

"I noticed Captain Commander's expression as well," I said. "It's as if he was focusing on something else, although there was a crowd of frustrated and sad people after finally reclaiming a base here on Earth. You don't think something else is going on, do you?"

I looked directly at Burrel when asking the question. He knew that I knew he was holding back information, especially after the reactions he had when seeing the battle broadcasted.

"I'm not sure. Maybe R&A's meeting will answer some questions." I read his face and it was like he was thinking, *Not now. I'll tell you later.*

Leona took note of our split-second stare down. She put one hand on her hip and tapped her foot, slightly leaning to the side. "Is there something we don't know about?" She continued to examine our faces.

"Right," Burrel said. "I haven't told you yet."

I raised an eyebrow, trying to determine if Burrel was going to say what I think he was to Leona. He nodded, confirming that he would divulge his secret. Leona and Joselyn exchanged confused expressions.

Burrel hesitantly looked over to Joselyn and then back to Leona. "Let's step to the side, Leona. There's something I need to tell you." They took a few steps away from Joselyn and me.

"Uhm, okay," Leona replied, glancing over to us before talking with Burrel privately.

Joselyn backhanded me on my shoulder with a little force.

I immediately looked at her. "Ah! Why'd you do that?" I asked, rubbing my arm.

"What was that about?!" she asked, a little irritated. "Am I the *fourth* wheel now or something?"

I instantly put my hand up and shook my head. "No, it's not like that at all," I said, trying to clear the air. "Burrel is just a very private guy. Believe me, it took *this* long for me and Leona to get close to him. You really gotta earn his trust, you know? That's all, nothing personal."

"Hhm… I get that. It's not like it's my business anyway." I may have been imagining it, but I thought I heard a sadness in her voice, as if she was being left out. "Go on. I know you want to listen in." She stopped leaning against the guard rail and tried to walk on her own again.

"But your rehab…"

"I'm not some delicate vase about to break. I've managed on my own before. Besides, I got this rail for support if I need it." She gave me a reassuring smile.

I nodded. "We'll be right back," I said as I made my way toward Burrel and Leona.

"You can walk?!" I heard Leona whisper as I approached them. They were keeping their voices down since other people weren't too far away.

"That was one of the first things I asked too," I chimed in.

Suddenly, a slight sharp pain rose at the side of my arm as Leona playfully punched me.

"Ah! What's with people hitting me today?"

"Why didn't you tell me, Xander? And he's been training you too?"

"Don't blame him," Burrel said. Both of his hands rested on the top of his cane. "I asked him to let me tell you when I was ready."

Leona sighed, rubbing the bridge of her nose.

"I didn't mean to put more on your mind. I know there's a lot going on in there already." Burrel studied Leona's face, empathizing with her. "How are you holding up by the way?"

"I'm fine." Leona averted his gaze.

"No, really… Take it from me. Keeping that crap to yourself eats you up inside. I saw the horrors of that battle too, remember?"

Leona looked over to me, testing the waters to see if it was okay to open up to Burrel. I nodded.

"All right. Then I feel like crap! Seeing Joselyn again helps and, of course, Xander is always here." She smirked at me. "But the fight plays in my head like a broken record, especially Harper's possession and Chrissy's death." A frown replaced the smirk she had. "If I'm barely able to cope, I can't imagine how Evan's feeling."

"Evan was Chrissy's friend—the guy with the accent, right?" Burrel asked.

Leona nodded.

"Speaking of possession…" I interrupted. "What do you know about it, Burrel? You were the first one to point it out during the broadcast."

Leona raised her eyebrow, surprised.

"It's complicated." He looked around the room, examining the people in the area as he continued speaking. "I do know when I fought during the war, allies were possessed left and right. I don't know the details of it, but I do know the signs after seeing it so often. Hopefully, R&A will shed more light on it than I can."

"But you're from the old war, aren't you?" Leona asked. "That's when civilians worked with the military to overthrow the government and the rich. I read reports on it when I first started fighting those monsters before the stasis program was initiated."

Hmm.... I didn't realize Leona's memory had already progressed that far, I thought.

"So…wait! Were you on vessel 2 before you came to this one?" Leona continued.

Burrel solemnly nodded.

"You know what that means, right?"

"Which is why I'd appreciate you keeping this quiet for now," he abruptly said.

"Hold on. Did I miss something?" I said, bewildered. "What's so important about vessel 2?"

Bzzzzz!

Ugh! What horrible timing. How did I just become the third wheel?

Leona, Burrel, myself, and Joselyn who wasn't too far away, along with everyone else in the room stood quietly while waiting in anticipation for the announcement.

"Attention all remaining occupants of the eight vessels, including Central Command."

The voice was different from before. It was a little scratchy, but deep and of a male's.

"Due to our somewhat disarrayed state, the tactics of future deployments are being discussed as I speak. During this time, it was brought to my department's attention that due to our negligence of not sharing vital information with our comrades on the battlefield, hope was nearly lost."

"Duh! Obviously," we heard Joselyn say as we briefly glanced over to her. She had an exasperated look on her face.

"As head of the R&A department of all eight vessels, I take full responsibility for such actions. Please do not blame the military."

"I hope the military isn't trying to save their skin by putting him on the chopping block," Burrel commented.

"As vessel 4 is the next ship scheduled to descend due to their recent contribution of retrieving medical supplies, we thought it would be opportunistic to capitalize during this intermission. Therefore, occupants of vessel 3 and vessel 7 here on base are welcome to join us outside in one hour to get insight on what we know about the enemy so far. We are aware not everyone has this privilege since a majority of vessels are still orbiting Earth in space. With that said, we will use the drones from yesterday's battle to broadcast our session to those not on Earth yet."

"Not a bad idea," Leona mumbled.

"This session has been approved by Central Command while they strategize on our next move. We aim to enlighten those who sacrifice their lives for us to better prepare them for future encounters with the enemy. However, we do know there are others who are still sensitive to even be privy to such data due to traumatic experiences. Don't worry. This session is voluntary and not mandatory. We understand everyone needs time to cope before facing the next tasks ahead."

Burrel looked over to Leona almost like a father saying, *"I told you so"* since he just spoke to her about not keeping things in, and so did I the night before. She knew it, too, as she glanced over to me while I smirked at her.

"Yeah...yeah... I get it already," she said, stubbornly crossing her arms and looking away. It's funny how adults could still act so immature with their emotions.

"Thank you for all that you've done so far. We look forward to seeing you."

The speaker cut off.

"Is that it?" I asked.

"He's probably saving most of his speech for the session," Burrel said. "I'll catch up with you two at the meeting. I imagine Joselyn won't be able to come while still in rehab."

"You're coming with us?" I asked, surprised.

"Of course. I may have more years on me than you, but it doesn't mean I know everything."

I smirked.

"We'll see you later then, Burrel," Leona replied, waving slightly.

Burrel waved back to us and Joselyn, and just like that, he was gone again. I was slightly disappointed.

"Don't worry. We're *literally* going to see him in an hour," Leona said, rubbing my back. She must've noticed the change in my demeanor.

I guess I'll have to ask about vessel 2 later when we have more privacy, I thought.

The hour flew by as we spent most of it with Joselyn. Before we knew it, some people were exiting the ship for the meeting. Joselyn was disappointed she couldn't go, but Leona assured her we'd share all of the information we found out afterward before we left the training room. When we walked on the exit ramp of the ship that led outside, I heard birds chirping and passing overhead. Looking up at the sky, I could see the sun partially behind some clouds. The blue scenery above was like a beautiful canvas woven throughout the tapestry of atmosphere. Some gnats hovered around the patches of grass. They were usually annoying from what I could remember in the past, but today I welcomed them. Small things I did in passing in my life on Earth before, like breathing in fresh air, would be an experience I wouldn't ever take for granted again. I never thought I'd even miss the simplest pleasures about Mother Nature we all shared.

"It's unreal to me too," Leona said as she slipped her fingers through mine and held my hand.

I turned to her skeptically. "What has it been now? Several months, approaching a year? Within that time, I've never taken you as a big hand holder." I smirked.

She shrugged one of her shoulders. "Well, if the moment is right, I can make an exception." She turned to me and flashed a smile as we continued to walk amongst the crowd. "Besides, depending on what we find out, this calm crowd can turn into a riot again. I'd rather have you close in case this goes south. We're now in uncharted territory. There's no telling what we'll discover, nor people's reactions to it."

"You say the funniest things sometimes…" I held her hand slightly tighter. I saw her glance my way again through my peripheral. However, I kept my focus ahead. "We've been in uncharted territory since this whole thing started."

"Heh…" She looked straight ahead too. "True."

People from vessel 7 and vessel 3 were converging and mingling ahead. It wasn't as many as we thought would come. I'd say there were a little less than thirty of us in total from both ships with a quick head count. This wasn't including the other survivors from the battle yesterday we saw ahead as well. I guess other occupants were too depressed or still mourning over the losses. Either or, it was still up to us, who had the strength, to keep pushing on for those that didn't.

"Excuse me."

Leona and I both turned around to see a teenage boy with a few others around him, walking behind us.

"Aren't you Xander Williams from the platoon who got the relic for the generator?"

I nodded.

A young woman came forth from their small group with wide eyes, staring at Leona. "And you're the decorated soldier, Leona Madigan, right? You fought with the best here yesterday."

"Yep, that's me," Leona replied.

"We know the sacrifices were great, but you and the other soldiers made it possible for us to *rebuild*! It had to be worth it, right?" The rest of their group agreed with her.

Others around us, still feeling the weight of the deceased, began to scornfully stare at the small group talking to us. This was clearly not the time to do this.

"Y'all are like totally awesome people, and we just wanted to say thank you," the teenage boy said with starry eyes. "I'm in training too and hope I can contribute to the cause one day."

I glanced at Leona who was silent for a second, startled. A glimpse of sorrow lingered in her eyes. This boy and his aspiration no doubt reminded her of Hunter. She bit her lower lip, perhaps attempting to keep the emotion that came with his loss at bay. The young woman didn't help either. Her enthusiasm was reminiscent of Valeria's when she introduced herself.

"Thanks, but I don't think this is—"

"We're just glad that we could help and will miss everyone who fought with us, too," Leona interjected, cutting me off. The people's scornful looks disappeared, and they continued to look ahead while we all continued to walk toward R&A's set up. She was able to diffuse the situation.

Up ahead, there was a huge tent along with some equipment and displays. Officials in decorated uniforms stood and waited for us to gather around.

"You okay?" I asked Leona. We walked a little faster to get some distance from the group of people behind us.

"Yeah, I'm fine," she said, parting her hair. She then lowered her voice to a whisper as she said, "I know you're new to this whole soldier thing, but we have to put on a brave face in front of people. No matter how you're feeling, they look at us to get the job done. We represent the hope of the cause, Xander. Understand?"

I nodded as I understood where she was coming from. At the same time, I wondered just how many times she put on a brave face during the broadcast and times before. She was probably more affected by this than I realized as I felt her fingers shake a little between mine.

"She's right about that," I heard a familiar voice say right beside me.

I jumped up, startled to see Burrel walking beside me. I swear he had super hearing. He must've taken long strides with his cane to catch up to us and still make it look like he was handicapped.

"Damn it, Burrel! Why do you keep popping up out of nowhere?"

My flusteredness must've eased some of Leona's tension as I heard her giggle.

"I guess that's my thing," he said, half-grinning. He turned his attention toward the crowd in front of us. "Huh… Is that who I think it is, Leona?"

"Hm?" Leona looked ahead, and her eyes widened slightly. I took a look myself and spotted Evan a few feet away from us.

"Evan?" Leona blurted out.

He turned to us, breaking away from the few people he was talking to. I only heard bits and pieces of the conversation, but it sounded like they were giving their condolences to his loss. Vessel 3 wasn't allowed to see the broadcast, so it must've been our folks from vessel 7.

"Hey, Leona," he said unenthusiastically.

Leona, Burrel, and myself stood in front of him by the tent while a few more stragglers gathered around.

"I'm surprised you worked up the nerve to come… I thought you'd be taking a pod back to vessel 5 by now," Leona said.

"Yes… I thought so too, but Command thought it would be a better idea for the survivors not of vessels 3 and 7 to stay here and use their resources. Besides, other vessels are slowly but surely making their way down here anyway." Evan briefly examined Burrel and me. "I take it the young gentleman is the…'something real' you've been fighting for?"

I passed a half-hearted smile, not knowing what to say. Leona briefly nodded.

"I'm glad you have someone to help you work up *your* nerves… After Chrissy… I'm…" He briefly turned away. We could tell he was trying to keep his wits about him and not think about his friend's death. "Excuse me… Where are my manners? I didn't even ask your names."

He waited for Burrel and me to answer. In all honesty, it was kind of awkward for me to reply, seeing as he could break down in any second.

"My name is Burrel." He stuck out his hand to introduce himself properly. "I met these two on our ship, and it seems like we're always crossing paths now. So you may see me hanging around them at times."

The way he spoke to Evan was so normal and casual, as if he wasn't witnessing his depressed state. As I watched Burrel speak to him casually, I truly grasped what Leona meant before. The brave face Leona spoke of was the exact face Burrel had on right now. We have to be strong for people even if they are our own brothers and sisters in arms. Maybe the best thing we could do for an aching soul that experienced a situation that was supposed to be impossible was to act normal as possible.

"I'm Xander," I said after Burrel spoke. I shook Evan's hand as well. "Leona and I actually recalled being together before all this, but neither of us have fully gotten our memories back." I contemplated what to say next. Leona narrowed her eyes, perhaps trying to get inside my head. "I guess in a way we've been clinging to each other to not lose ourselves in this whole mess. The more we go through together, the more hope we have of reclaiming who we used to be, you know?"

Evan stared at me, amazed.

I felt Leona elbow me. "A little warning would be nice if you're going to say stuff like that in front of people."

"That *was* unexpected," Burrel added. "Have *you* been reading poetry lately?" His teasing remark was a shot back at me for what I said to him in the dining line before my first deployment.

"Sorry," I said, scratching my head, embarrassed. "I must've been thinking out loud some." I laughed a little to cover up the awkwardness.

"No... It's quite all right," Evan said, while waving my comment off with a hand gesture. "I think you just described everyone here. I don't even know you, and I can already see why Leona fought so hard to come back to you."

I felt Leona squeeze my hand. I glanced over and caught her blushing a little.

"You're *real*." He had a stern expression. "I like it!"

I smirked. "You're not the first person to tell me that."

Evan chuckled. "I'd imagine not...nor I suppose will I be the last."

"People! Gather around," I heard an official by the tent say. "We're almost ready to start here. We're waiting for Gerard Buckland—the pioneer and head of R&A, along with his two primary assistants."

Surprisingly, there were only a few people in front of us and the displays. There was even a table that displayed items I didn't recognize. On the far end, I saw an empty exo-suit displaying the inside of the cockpit. I saw Imala and some other officials I recognized in passing from vessel 7. The others must've been part of vessel 3. Drones hovered around the site, no doubt broadcasting to the other vessels still in space. The top of the tent gave us some shade from the sun's rays.

"Hey, so it looks like Evan could use some company," Leona whispered while Burrel stood beside me. "I'll be chatting with him and trying to get his head straight... It's the least I can do for Chrissy..." Her voice trailed off.

"I thought you wanted us to stay close," I replied, while we huddled between the crowd.

"We'll be right here beside you, guys," she said pointing to Evan that was a little further than an arm's length from us. "Besides, you have a friend that could use some company too."

Burrel smirked, slightly embarrassed. "I'm fine."

"What was it that you said to me about crap eating you up inside?"

He ignored her retort and didn't respond.

"I thought so."

I tried to hold in my laughter while she stepped away from us and conversed with Evan.

"Not a word," Burrel said, noticing my expression.

"I didn't say anything," I replied.

"Well, she seems like a keeper, huh? She can be strong and gentle at the same time...knows when to give you your space...and even puts people in their place when she needs to."

"Yeah...she seems like the total package."

Burrel narrowed his eyes. "But..."

I recalled the memory flares I had and how my past self was wary about going all in.

"Enough about me, Burrel," I said, ignoring it. "You frantically ran out during the broadcast yesterday. I needed—" I stopped myself before getting too emotional. "A lot of people needed a shoulder to lean on, man, including you. You don't have to be alone through this anymore. I thought Leona was going to die for God's sake!" I exclaimed in a whisper. "Just how much do you know about all this?"

"Switching subjects, huh? Fine. It's not my business anyway." He paused. I know he wanted to apologize, but his stubbornness didn't allow him to. He put on this tough act to hide his vulnerability, but it annoyed me sometimes. I thought of us as at least friends by now, but he still chose not to open up to me. "I imagine this meeting will cover all you want to know," he continued. "If not, I can fill in any missing facts you need to know. It'll surely be helpful, too, when training you before you go back on the field. How's the arm by the way?"

I moved my right arm and felt stings from the atrophied. "A little stiff, but nothing exercise can't fix."

"Good," he replied.

Just then, I saw Valeria, Miguel, and Maria amidst the edge of the crowd. Valeria caught a glimpse of me and passed a slight wave. She smiled at me, but I could tell it was fake. It could've fooled me as a stranger. However, after getting to know her life a little, I knew what lied beneath. She put on a mask that was a brave face, too, perhaps most of her adolescence. I pretended to look away after I waved back but quickly peered back over to her. A frown instantly replaced her smile as she stared off in the distance. Miguel and Maria didn't see me, but I saw their disheartening expressions. They probably mourned over the loss of Henry as a reunited family and tried to get Valeria in a good place after losing both him and Hunter. At any rate, they were clearly not in a mood to talk. Who could blame them? I let them be for now.

"We are ready to begin!" the official shouted. "Please! We ask that you give your undivided attention."

We all looked toward the officials and saw a man with a gray beard step forward. Along with his glasses, he appeared like a wise old man, like the ones you would see on movies and television. His eyes were stern and weary with bags under them. He also wore a different uniform than the other people in R&A. Their wardrobes were more decorated, but his was plain with only one badge. On first impressions, it didn't seem like he cared much about titles. Yet his posture was rigid with his hands behind his back. There were two thinly shaped men beside him. One had scraggly hair with a collared shirt. The collar was out of place, though, and it didn't seem like he focused too much on his public appearance, considering the tag and lining were inside out. His colleague was no different. He was dark in complexion with a scruffy beard and stood with his eyelids half open. We watched as he put what looked like eyedrops in his eyes. It must've been an old bottle he reused by putting water or something in it. These people must've had even more restless nights than the soldiers since their discoveries were crucial for our survival as well.

"My name is Gerard Buckland," the man with the glasses and gray beard said. "And today your life is about to change forever. We will divulge information to you that you were never supposed to find out. I was a historical researcher before this war started and have dedicated my life to finding the truth. The things I've discovered are unsettling. Whether you believe us or not, the data we will share is fact and can be backed by years of documentation, manuscripts, religious texts, records, and so forth. For example, all of us have negative energy inside of us and can be possessed at any time no thanks to the influence of our world."

My heart nearly dropped from my chest. I examined people's expressions around me, and I could tell they felt the same way. Leona and Evan had their mouths open in awe. The space surrounding the tent suddenly grew silent. Even people who were murmuring in the back were speechless. The two surviving Alpha soldiers and Burrel were perhaps the only ones besides the officials who had no reaction. This was information Burrel was hesitant to tell me. Can all of us really become those monsters like Harper at any given point in time?

CHAPTER 19

"**WHAT KIND OF** bullshit are you spouting, man?!" one guy from the crowd yelled out, waving his fist.

"Are you telling us that this whole cause is pointless?" a woman asked frantically. "Good people died yesterday so we could be back here on Earth! Family, friends…lost. Was that all for nothing?!"

The crowd around us started pushing and shoving, demanding answers. Leona looked over to me. This is the exact situation she was worried about before.

Suddenly, Gerard put his hand up and coughed. "Ahem!"

The official from before put his thumb and index finger in his mouth and blew to let out a whistle. The loud distinctive sound made people quiet down again.

Gerard sighed while patiently taking his glasses off and cleaning them. "You didn't let me finish. Anxiety, fear, worry, doubt… Your reactions are precisely why we thought it was in everyone's best interest to not tell you. These negative emotions are the very thing that let these monsters in and take hold of you."

I caught a glimpse of the man that yelled. He was frozen by Gerard's words, not knowing what to do or say, along with the majority of the crowd.

"Of course, as of now, you're safe from such influence due to the platoon of vessel 7 that retrieved the relic for the generator. Also, none of us will ever forget the combined effort of all vessels yesterday to establish this base for us."

Everyone quieted down again. Some people were staring at Leona, Evan, myself, and the other surviving soldiers before refocusing on Gerard. I even caught a glimpse of Valeria, Maria, and Miguel staring from a distance. I wondered if it was giving Valeria at least some comfort knowing Hunter didn't die in vain. I think everyone was starting to understand why every battle and decision had to be calculated up to this point, even if it meant leaving us in the dark.

"It was truly a feat of its own. Imala here..." He gestured his hand to Imala who was at the front of the line with other R&A officials. "Her and Commander Brauns brought it to Command's attention about having an open forum with you all because the very thing we tried to shield you from became our Achilles' heel in the form of Harper Walker."

Some more officials came forth with what appeared to be a stasis pod. Leona and Evan narrowed their eyes, upset upon seeing Harper's face through the glass window of the pod.

"I wholeheartedly admit that our negligence and arrogance of keeping you from the truth resulted in this. However, as some of you may find it hard to believe, these events did not have an impact on me to deliberate this meeting. It was always my intention to disclose our data once we set foot back on Earth."

Burrel and I narrowed our eyes. If that was the case, I wondered why being back on Earth was necessary to share such information. Gerard coughed again. He didn't appear to be in optimal health. Heck, none of us were, but his condition seemed more pressing.

"You see... The exo-suit and its features can only do so much. Yes, one of its designs was based on protecting the wearer from possession." He became more serious. "However, everything has its limits—everything! A soldier experiences a rush of adrenaline, stress, and other factors that lead to a release of endorphins while in the suit already. Commanders were given instructions to delegate to the leaders on the battlefield to keep you focused on the mission, decreasing the chance of getting overwhelmed with negative emotions."

I thought that was just a standard for any leader on the battlefield to stay on mission, I thought. But after thinking about it, Henry, from the get-go, did keep Joselyn and me on track during our deployment, even on the elevator. Was he instructed to do so? Did he know? I guess, either way, it didn't matter since his positive leadership allowed someone like me to be here now.

"As you can imagine, adding the knowledge of possession on top of it would've been disastrous. A lot more Harper Walkers could've been among us." People observed the possessed traitor in the pod as he said this. "With that said, not even we knew Harper's past to be so…deviant. As you probably surmised, it's the very reason we ran thorough background checks before accepting anyone in the stasis program."

"Apparently not thorough enough," Evan replied.

Leona was startled at his response but didn't interject. His feelings were understandable. Everyone lost something yesterday. For him, it was his best friend, Christine.

Gerard nodded. "We deserve that. I didn't want to share this information without being able to reestablish a footing on Earth. Progress we've made until now would've been all for naught if mankind succumbed to madness. This relic powering our generator is full of infinite energy. It has given a lot of us hope again." He paused, reflecting. "Now moving forward, I—*we* feel like to better combat this threat, you need to know the fundamental principles of our universe. I will give the floor to my associates, each a leader in their respective fields who can explain this even better than I can." He gestured his hand to his two primary assistants beside him and took a step back.

The one with the scraggly hair and inside out shirt stepped forward. "Hello…" His voice even sounded like it was dragging as he passed the crowd a tired wave. Upon closer inspection, their department was kind of full of oddballs. I even saw one of the officials with a hippy hairstyle and a uniform that looked a bit baggy on him. "I used to be a physicist at a noteworthy nuclear research organization in Europe. I'm sure at least some of you know of it. I left years ago before the war. They held back information from the public which unsettled me. Because of our…difference in opinion, I started to do my own research in the states. You may be asking what this has to do with us?"

Some around us, including myself, nodded, wondering where he was going with this.

"The answer is *everything*," he continued.

I began to listen intently. An old white board on wheels was put forth behind them by another official. I could tell it was hard to wheel it through the grass. It was meant for hard surfaces, after all. The board looked as beat as he did.

"Now, to explain what these monsters are, you must first understand the universe."

"Really, Hugo?" the dark-skinned man with the scruffy beard said. "Can we just call them what they are already? You know damn well they're demons."

We all reacted in astonishment. It made me think back to what that thing inside of Harper said to Leona after she asked what he was.

You refuse to admit it, but deep inside your bones to your very core… You already know the answer.

"Ah-ah-ah," Hugo continued, waving his finger. "That is pure speculation and conjecture, Thomas, and you know it! We will not be indecorous and make assumptions based on lack of facts."

"Lack of facts? Their behavior and characteristics coincide with that of demonology, scripture, mythological books… Need I go on?"

Hugo pinched his forehead, irritated. "Ugh… Thomas! Don't start with that—"

"Uhm!" Imala interrupted their little spout and came between them. "Perhaps we can call them *demons* just for simplicity sake? The specific terminology isn't something we necessarily have to agree on. We all know what you're talking about."

"Imala is right, you two," another official said. "Please refrain from your usual quarreling today. These people here and on the broadcast came for answers, not debates."

"Agreed," Gerard added.

The drones hovered around the area. I could feel the anticipation of everyone—even the occupants of the other vessels watching in space. Gerard nonchalantly observed the situation with his arms behind his back. He seemed neutral about what the enemies were. I wondered if he became leader of the department due to his indifference toward either side. Perhaps he only sought truth.

"I suppose I can go along with that," Hugo said. "Kind of like how people refer to our creator as 'God' but interpret the very existence of the concept very differently."

Thomas passed Hugo a scolding look. He must've had faith like Burrel and me, or at least believed in one god. I could tell they've been working with each other so long that they sounded like an old married couple.

"A realist and an optimist," Burrel uttered in a low voice next to me. "It sounds like the beginning of a bad joke."

"Heh… I wonder how often they're at each other's throats like that," I replied.

"Okay, back to the matter at hand before I was rudely interrupted." Hugo narrowed his eyes at Thomas before looking back at us. Picking up a marker from the ledge of the white board, he started to draw two circles overlapping. One on the right was red while the other on the left was blue. The slight screeching sound it made, along with its barely visible marks, indicated it was ready to give out at any moment.

"As I said before, the research I've worked on has everything to do with us. Imagine existence as a blank canvas—empty." He pointed to the red circle he made on the right. "I'm sure you've all seen it before. When someone is possessed, they become empty too, a shell of their former selves. To put it simply, negative emotions lead to emptiness and darkness is attracted to that very notion. For example, dark matter exists in a space we can't see—an empty world but still a part of this one."

Hugo briefly paused and stared at us. By the confused look on a lot of our faces, he could tell he was losing us. "Okay then, to put it in layman's terms, there was darkness at the beginning of our universe."

"Genesis," Thomas blurted out.

Hugo sighed. "Your point?"

"Everything connects."

Suddenly, a wave of pain hit my head like a passing migraine as I heard the words, "Everything is connected." I briefly saw my brother's face like from the last flashback. However, he looked more worn out and stressed.

"Ahh…" I groaned.

Burrel put his hand on my shoulder. "You all right?"

I nodded.

Leona took notice and momentarily broke her concentration from the session to tend to me. "What is it, Xander? You have a headache?" Evan looked back as well.

"It's nothing—just a memory flare."

"A what?"

"It's what Miguel called it when I had it the last time. It happens when I remember something vividly."

Leona studied my face, touching the side of my cheek, concerned.

"Shhh…" A person beside us hissed. "No disrespect, you guys. I appreciate you, and I'm sure you know a lot of this information already, but I'd like to know why our world is like this in the first place too."

"A lot of us are in the dark like you as well," I replied, regaining my composure. "We're all in the same boat."

"All the more reason to listen, eh?"

I nodded respectfully, not wanting to cause an issue. Leona and Burrel examined me one more time before turning their attention back to Hugo. There was a flicker of worry in Leona's eyes.

"So are you saying the darkness is what these demons are?" Someone asked Hugo in the crowd as I continued to pay attention to the conversation.

"These *demons* as you call it," Hugo said, nearly cringing at saying the word, "exist within this plane of darkness without form. But before we get ahead of ourselves, the left circle also comes into play— this represents light."

We stared at him as he shaded the middle oval where the two circles converged with a purple marker. He labeled the red circle on the right darkness and the blue one on the left as light.

"Look at light and darkness existing in two different dimensions," he continued. "However, there's a space where both exist—a space we call existence." He wrote existence above the purple shade. "That's us. Though darkness existed within this empty space first, when light intervened, it created a whole new world of possibilities. Whether you believe in the big bang, God, aliens, or other ideologies of how we came to be, we cannot exist in this plane without the light and dark—positive and negative."

Although some of this was going over my head, there was something that made sense to me. "Are you saying that these *demons* are physical manifestations of negative energy?"

Hugo smiled excitedly. "Ah! I'm glad some of you are able to keep up with this. Yes! That's precisely what I'm saying."

Leona, Burrel, and Evan looked at me, surprised.

"What? I might not have his IQ, but I can connect dots," I said.

Burrel and Evan smirked. Leona grinned coyly. I knew that face. She showed it whenever her competitive side wanted to leak out.

"So when the government facilitated the use of the particle accelerator, did it open up a gateway to this world of negative energy?" Leona instantly asked.

"Excellent question!" Hugo said enthusiastically. It's almost as if he woke up from his fatigue. "The answer is also yes! I'm glad to see we have so many bright minds left."

Leona glanced back at me and cockily raised her eyebrow as if saying, "*You're not the only smart one.*"

I smirked and shook my head. It's not like this was a competition. She could be a jealous type sometimes and act like such a kid. That playful side of her was cute to me, though—at least I thought at the time.

"Sadly, it was the same research center I worked at that was responsible for the development of the particle accelerator," Hugo added. "I already left years before the idea was at its final stages."

Everyone stared at Hugo in shock.

"If that's the case, why would the government do such a thing? How could they possibly benefit from bringing chaos into the world?" someone else interjected among the crowd.

Hugo, along with the rest of the officials, looked at each other warily.

"We don't know," Thomas said. "But here's what we do know…" He looked over to Hugo. "Do you mind if I get it from here, Hugo?"

"Of course not. You're the theologist. This is more of your forte anyway."

"Good," Thomas replied, stepping forward a bit. "As he said, our world is made up of light and dark. That bodes true with each and every one of us as well. Let me ask you, what is free will?"

"The ability to act and make decisions for ourselves," a woman shouted boastfully.

Thomas glanced back at Hugo and grinned. "People do catch on quick in this crowd." He looked back at us. "You are correct. Now, if we were born good, would we truly have free will?"

People looked around and pondered. It was a question that perplexed most. However, Burrel seemed to have an answer.

"No, because every decision we make would be a good one. If you eliminated our potential to make a bad one, there'd be no point in choices at all since we'd always choose a predictable one—a controlled one."

"You hit the nail right on the head, my brother with the cane." Thomas passed Burrel an upward head nod. Burrel returned it. It's like some people of the same ethnicity had this unspoken bond. I never really gave it any thought, but when I saw gestures like that, it made me wonder where that stemmed from—like if humans could connect on a level deeper than we thought possible. "I couldn't have said it better myself. The same is also true if we were born bad. That's why we all start off as blank as this white board before we make decisions that dye us into categories of light, dark, or the area in between," Thomas said, pointing at the white board.

"What does this have to do with demons and possession?" Evan asked. He appeared slightly agitated and impatient. "Why did that *thing* choose Harper, and why did my friend have to die?!"

The area within the tent grew quiet again, sympathizing with those we lost yesterday.

"I thought that much was obvious already," Thomas said. "With all the information we've dug up these past years, one thing is for certain—negative energy is determined by the decisions you make. And remember, these things feed on that negativity. So let's take you for instance...uhm..."

"Evan!"

"Evan, okay. Let's take you for instance. Even if you have no history of violence or destructive tendencies, the sadness you feel for your friend right now would open up a gateway for these demons to enter."

Evan started to listen to him intently as well as others.

"If media and other modern innovations existed right now, you'd suddenly find yourself on the news responsible for murder or another heinous act. You may not remember anything or blackout during the whole incident. People and law enforcement may chalk it up to you 'snapping' due to the loss of a loved one. However, it may very well have been a possession."

"What?" I said in a low voice.

"Is that what Hugo meant when he said all of us could be possessed?" someone said, worried.

"Yes," Hugo replied.

"Depending on your mental and spiritual state, these demons can enter and exit your physical being at any time," Thomas added. "Think of your body as a vessel or a portal, if you will. If you allow enough negative energy to inhabit you, a demon can use that as a gateway to enter our world through you—kind of like a pocket dimension. The same is true if too much negative energy lingers in one specific place."

A pre-teen girl raised her hand as if she were in a classroom while speaking. It was the same one that spoke to Leona and I earlier. "So haunted houses and demon possessions showed in movies, and stuff are like *real*?"

Thomas nodded. "Though law enforcement and so many others have encountered the impossible, they tried to rationalize it in their heads—dismiss it as something with a reasonable conclusion. There really isn't one." He looked disappointed as if speaking from experience. "So many people have claimed that their loved ones changed one day and looked possessed—something not human. However, we still ignored it. We have been programmed by our government to accept a common reality, one that's not even true."

Something clicked in my head. I looked over to Valeria. Even from here, I saw her eyes wide open in shock. I could tell she was thinking the same thing. The past traumatic event she shared with me about her father pinged in my head. *If that's the way possession worked, then was he also a victim of it?* I thought.

CHAPTER 20

"**THIS IS BULLSHIT,** man," one of the guys in the crowd said. I recognized his face. I think he was part of the other Beta squad when he regrouped with Leona and Evan on the feed. "What you're talking about is spiritual warfare. Demons or monsters like them don't exist. You've gotta be kidding me! Stop talking nonsense, and tell us what's really going on!"

Some people agreed with him and started demanding answers.

"Look around," Thomas said. "Does any of this look like a joke to you?"

"Tch," the soldier replied, sucking his teeth. "What do you make of this, Hugo? You're a scientist, aren't you? Give us the facts!"

"Though I disagree with Thomas's theory on demons, I will say this…" Hugo looked down, almost ashamed to admit it. "I have yet to find any viable information to contradict his theory as outlandish as it may seem to some of you. If anything, there is scientific evidence that possibly supports his claims."

None of the other officials interjected, not even Gerard. They agreed with Thomas and Hugo as well. The soldier didn't know how to react. It's like people's worlds were shaken once they saw theology and science not only coincide but agree on a common idea.

"Let me get this straight," I said amidst the stunned reactions. "Hypothetically speaking, if this force field didn't exist around us, we'd all be in danger then? After all, we're still feeling a mix of negative emotions, not only from yesterday but all the battles till now, not to mention our personal lives. Could possession really be as subtle as me acting normal one second and at someone's throat the next?"

"Hard to digest, isn't it?" Thomas replied. "You don't even need to show apparent signs like Walker here." He stood next to Harper Walker's pod and pointed at the black protruding lines from his face. "You could still look normal while still being under the influence of possession."

I looked all the way over to Valeria. Anxiety was apparent on her face as she stared back at me. Beads of sweat trickled down. Maria and Miguel glanced back at me and then back to her confused. Leona and Burrel took notice. I was probably the only one other than Valeria putting the pieces together and knew there was a strong possibility her father could've been influenced by possession. Not only that, but it begged to question just how much of society was influenced up to this point as well.

"As a matter of fact," Thomas resumed. "Most demons were invisible to the naked eye before the portal to their negative realm was open. It's because of all the negative energy we created in our world, that we can see them as physical forms now."

"How about those videos posted in the past online about possessions? Or things we've watched … Are those true?" A young man warily raised his hand while asking the questions. He seemed skeptical about the whole thing.

Thomas poised himself and smirked. "Well, of course, I can't speak for *every* video uploaded on the internet. But if you're asking if some of them had merit? I'd say quite possibly. Where do you think Hollywood got the idea for their movies based on possession? If we could stream those past movies right now, you'd see that most have the same symbolic references or based on someone else's account who also claims the same things as in other cases."

"Believe us. It's not simply coincidence," Hugo added. "The more research we do, the more we find that *coincidence* is just another word for connection, contrary to its definition."

"Okay, let's say your claims are true. Then there's something that still doesn't make sense," Evan said. "If possession has been possible or the very least cause for concern, then why hasn't it been broadcasted on mainstream news for decades? If almost anyone could succumb to it, why didn't it affect our world leaders or other representatives in government?"

I raised a brow as I saw Gerard form a slight grin behind Thomas and Hugo—the first positive expression he's made since we've seen him. "Whoever said they weren't?" Gerard asked rhetorically.

I couldn't physically sense it, but I knew a chill ran down everyone's spine after Gerard uttered those words like it ran down mine.

"I'm impressed by the individuals we have here today," Hugo added. "They're not only asking good questions, but the *right* ones."

"Does this go back to what you said about all of us being influenced by our world?" an old woman asked. "I'm guessing the government had a hand in forming the negative energy inside us, too?"

"More than a hand," Gerard replied. "I'd say they orchestrated the whole thing."

Leona glanced back at me, as if having a gut feeling our world was about to turn upside down more than it already was.

Another official stepped up. It was the guy with the hippy look and baggy pants. He also sported tinted glasses. "Mind if I cut in, Gerard, sir?" He had a lackadaisical demeanor about him. He acted as if he just woke up from a nap.

"By all means, this is an open forum. If you have something to say, go ahead and say it."

"All right, cool." He paused a second as he put what looked like a piece of gum in his mouth. "Sorry. Talking in front of people kind of makes me nervous. Gum helps. A team found this old pack on a deployment, and I helped myself to some."

I cringed, thinking that the pack of gum could've been anywhere before he put it in his mouth. Thomas did a facepalm, almost embarrassed to look at him. Most of the other officials kind of turned a blind eye to his behavior, too. Even Imala looked a bit ashamed to have him in the department.

"For Pete's sake, Galen," Hugo said, irritated. "Can you say your peace already and be done with it?"

"You know I'm fine with Gale, but all right. I get'cha."

Isn't Gale more commonly a woman's name? I thought.

"Let me ask you, guys, who ruled the government?"

"Us! The people of course," the soldier from last time said.

"That's incorrect," Burrel interjected. I was a little surprised to see him join in the conversation again. He was keeping his opinion to himself for the most part during this session. "The rich did." His eyes narrowed, and his tone became serious. It's as if he was personally affected firsthand by rich people's influence.

"Nice!" Gale chippered. "I didn't think anybody would be enlightened enough to answer that correctly. Yes! It was the rich. You'd be surprised how much money could buy in this world if you had enough of it."

"Are you saying the world was ran by the rich behind the scenes and not our government?" another soldier asked.

"Sadly, yeah. Once you realize that, concepts like the outrageous divide in social classes, taxes... even wars make a little more sense. If there was profit or something to gain from it, elitists weren't too far away from the scene." He parted his matted hair from his face as he continued to talk. "With that said, is it really such a stretch to think our world could be corrupted?"

I thought back to what Burrel said about the rich and how the vessels were originally intended for them. I couldn't say I believed the rich had their hands in everything like Gale said, but connections were becoming more apparent. *If they were heartless enough to build sophisticated ships only for them while the world suffered, what else were they capable of?* I thought.

"No. That can't be! The military was under the government, but soldiers didn't serve the rich. They served their country," Leona said. She usually isn't that patriotic when it comes to her military background, but it looks like what Gale said struck a chord. "What proof do you have?"

Gale's lackadaisical demeanor shifted to a more attentive one as he took off his tinted glasses and stared right at Leona. I think a lot of us were taken back as one of his eye sockets was partially closed. Upon closer inspection, I saw a hint of reddish flesh underneath and not a single indication of white for where the eyeball should be. Gerard,

Thomas, Hugo, Imala, and the rest of the officials' air toward him shifted, too, as they took what he was saying to us more earnestly.

"That look you're giving me right now," he said, pointing at Leona while the crowd listened intently. "That's the look I've seen more times than I can count when I tell people how messed up our system actually was. I might not look it now, but I used to be part of the National Security Agency—NSA for short." He paused as he stared at his glasses before putting them back on. "Once I found out things I wasn't supposed to and the injustices of our system, I took it upon myself to inform the public. The right thing, apparently, was a foreign concept to the higher-ups in charge. I was labeled a whistleblower, conspiracy theorist, and a traitor from the very country that's supposed to support free speech."

The crowd stayed silent, speechless. Leona was looking on in disbelief. I could tell gears were shifting in her head. Although, she did already know the government was corrupt while being a soldier before stasis. I wondered what her startled expression was about. Maybe she just didn't know the extent of it.

"I fled from my own home," Gale continued. "Russia was my refuge as I continued to act as an activist in issues such as propaganda, capitalization on illegal trade of goods, including prostitution, and so forth. Even then, I was pursued to be silenced, but I fought back and lost an eye." He pointed to his eye, reflecting on the event. "The more I dug into these issues, the more I found out we were influenced since birth to think and accept certain functions in our society as reality. I was recruited into the military at the R&D department, now called R&A, after they overthrew the government due to the particle accelerator cover-up. It was only after joining this department, or what's left of it anyway, did I discover that we were institutionalized to act and think certain ways to make this world negative. That way, demons could enter our dimension easier."

"Could you give us an example of something crucial you witnessed?" a person asked.

"One instance that allowed me to wake up to the real world was when I discovered a military program using taxpayers' money to fund experiments. It was under the guise of better understanding the enemy, getting inside their head, and extracting information. In reality, it was used to determine how to better control the minds of individuals around the world. They delved into what made the human mind tick. A lot of the human test subjects were involuntary or they neglected to give them all of the information." Some people were in disbelief. "Learning how to better control the mind makes you more susceptible to influence. This, of course, opens you up to being manipulated or taken over by other entities. They took what they learned and streamed symbols, imagery, and other tactics through the media to break the mind down and conform it to what they wanted. Fun fact, television shows were called 'programming' for that very reason."

"Months ago in excavation, we found bone remains way too large to be that of any person in existence," Burrel interjected. "In fact, by the sheer size of it, it was most likely determined to be that of a giant from centuries ago. Though it could be easily found in some areas on Earth, I don't ever remember it being broadcasted on news outlets—well, major ones at least. Did the higher-ups have a hand in that, too?"

"Yes," Thomas and Gale said at the same time.

"Go ahead," Gale said, returning the floor back to Thomas.

"Any discoveries that hinted at accrediting scripture, giving facts to what were deemed myths, or other major archaeological or historical finds were censored. Anything that remotely contradicted the reality that the government was trying to feed us was ignored or abolished."

"That would potentially mean a lot more concepts could be possible than we've realized," I said out loud.

Burrel nodded in my direction. Leona and Evan glanced back at me, realizing the impact of those words.

"Precisely," Hugo said. "And that's where relics come in."

"What are relics, really?" I asked.

The people of the R&A department smirked and glanced at each other.

"Our fighting chance," Gerard stepped up and said. "You see, there are historical artifacts throughout significant points or events

in time that emanate different types of energies. Through the contribution of many people, as well as trial and error, we were able to
develop a way to detect these energy signatures." He directed our
attention to the relics set on the table. They greatly varied from a
preserved skull fragment to a stone bound with special string. It was
bizarre to witness.

"Now, not all relics are good to use," Thomas added. "For
instance, objects used for occult practices or diabolical rituals only
strengthen those demons. However, objects used for sacred rites for
good, purity, blessings, and et cetera damage the demons greatly as
soldiers witness firsthand when harnessing the power through their
exo-suit."

"Wait," I whispered to Burrel. "Doesn't that mean we would
run out of relics? After all, if they're rare or uncommon throughout
the world, finding and using more would eventually put us in a corner, right?"

"Hold on. Did you think relics were useless this whole time
after using up the energy in the suit?" Burrel asked, staring at me
dumbfounded.

I nodded.

"Wasn't one of your training sessions as a soldier was to learn
the basics of how relics worked with the exo-suit?"

"I accidentally nodded off at that part. The lecture was boring."

Burrel sighed. "The military was well aware of that issue when
they were first introduced as a potential weapon against the enemy.
So R&D, at that time, came up with a solution to recharge that
energy through a multitude of processes involving alchemy, science,
and even reenacting rituals from what they could find in texts relat-
ing to the objects, believe it or not."

"Really? That's surreal. I'm still having a hard time believing any
of this is plausible."

"Excavation is crucial where relics are concerned as they pinpoint the energy signature," I heard Thomas say as I refocused my
attention to the forum. "Deploying electrical drills and soldiers to
retrieve it are imperative to the cause. As you know, exo-suits are useless without relics as part of the energy source to combat the enemy."

"How exactly are we protected in the suits from the enemy's influence?" Leona asked. She looked at the representatives of R&A pensively.

"Yes, I'd like to know how my dear friend was killed by that madman you have in that pod like a lab rat if we're supposed to be safe in these suits," Evan said, pointing at Harper inside the pod next to them.

Imala unexpectedly put up her hand, signaling Evan to calm down. "I can explain this one, sir," she said, looking at Gerard. He respectively nodded toward her direction. She coughed as she gave her full attention toward us. "Please don't mistake our nonchalant behavior for apathy. Me, personally, I try to carry on positively and smile every day because someone I lost asked me to. So believe us when we say we understand your pain. This department has lost people just as you. The difference is, we know we need to carry on because the information we discover is invaluable and gives the chance for more people to live."

I scanned the area in the tent and everyone was attentive to Imala's words. She was saying all this with a gentle smile, as if trying to wash away the negativity and disdain everyone was feeling from yesterday's battle. I even caught a glimpse of remorse from Evan's eyes as he tried to regain his composure from losing Chrissy. Everyone was angry, tired, hungry, and just fed up. However, I think deep down, people knew there was no reason to direct their frustrations to others who were trying to help us, despite them holding back information from us.

Imala whispered something to an official next to her. He went toward the outskirts of the tent, and an empty exo-suit with its interior exposed was brought up closer in front of us by some more officials. The backside of it was leaning against some type of dolly. Imala walked in front of the representative as she made her way to the suit. Upon closer inspection, I saw the inside was lined with some type of mysterious markings.

"What you're seeing here is the combined efforts of history, science, and theology working as one. The product is this exo-suit." The tips of her fingers ran along the markings of the interior. "These symbols have been tested and documented to prevent and stop the demons from inhabiting you to an extent. Of course, since they feed on negativity, if a person has too much of it, the symbols become ineffective as seen with Harper Walker here." She tapped on Harper's pod, which was next to the exposed exo-suit.

Ah, now I get what Commander Brauns was saying, I thought. Telling us this information would allow fear and doubt to creep in our minds, which would eventually create more negativity within us to allow the demons to take hold.

"Where did the idea of the exo-suits come from in the first place?" someone asked among the crowd.

Imala smirked. Some others behind her chuckled, including Gerard surprisingly.

"Sorry, it's just funny to think about how inventions are made sometimes," Imala said. "It started as an idea floating around on the internet from a young college student who was studying to be an engineer. He was inspired by a movie adaptation made from a video game. Because of it, he started developing real world theories and concepts and put it online. It caught the eye of a company in Japan and the top experts within their department were actually able to create a prototype of it."

Our last hope stems from the imagination of a kid, I thought. It was crazy to think about.

"Militaries from different countries saw the potential the suit had and patented it," Imala continued. "They thought it would be ideal to start making such suits to deter other countries from terrorist threats and prepare for potential wars if need be. They were buying the blueprints to make the suits their own and add their own weapons to it. I don't think anyone saw *this* type of war coming…" Her voice trailed off.

"So where were the markings derived from?" Leona asked suspiciously. "It's hard to believe the military would rely on such…*tactics* for battle."

"I hear your skepticism, Leona." Imala stared directly at her. Perhaps the eye contact was to let Leona know she was being sincere. "You'd be correct. When the war against these monsters started, no commander or high official would heed the use of these markings nor the power relic energy had. Unfortunately, a lot of good people suffered and died due to ignorance."

I caught Burrel by me, gripping his cane in frustration as if he experienced the event firsthand.

"But hopefully, you can believe me when I say that these markings are derived from occult practices."

Thomas and Gerard nodded in agreement. The rest of R&A stood poised. Some others among the crowd couldn't believe what they were hearing on top of the information they've already received. I even had doubts if I could accept what was being told to me.

"Wouldn't that make the markings negative since they were used for dark purposes among evil occultists?" the old woman from before asked.

"That is a common misconception," Gerard butted in. "Symbols and markings are like tools. They can be used to inflict harm, yes. But they can also be used to fix or help situations. These markings are based on universal principles such as numerology, geometry, astrology, and other concepts that actually give them its credence. Through such practices, they gain power. A lot of occult groups knew this and used them to advocate their own selfish agendas such as wishing death upon someone, political gain, money, power...among others."

"However, we use them to protect the wearer from the influence of malevolent or negative forces trying to invade the suit," Imala chimed in.

"I see," Evan uttered. He seemed to be a little more calm. "But even that has its limits, thus Harper as we see him now."

"It is a mystery..." Imala said to the crowd while pondering. "Though we ran thorough background checks before the stasis program, a man with such a dark past as Walker's managed to slip past us due to the old government's cover-ups and influences."

Hugo stepped out of position and examined Harper's pod closer. "It is perplexing to say the least. I don't even know how it's possible for him to stay in this possessed state. Our new readings indicate that the brain waves of the original Walker are still in there. However, it also shows the foreign entity drastically invading his mind—his very being as well."

"It begs to question how he's able to hold on to any semblance of himself still." Imala peered closer through the window of the pod, exposing Harper's face. "This may sound outlandish. I'm just speculating here, but what if he's struggling to keep the demon in him because he knows how crucial it is for our research?"

"Tch," Leona shunned away from the thought and sucked her teeth. "If someone like him is looking for redemption, it's too late. Being conscious while a demon invades his catatonic body is a fitting punishment for him if you ask me."

"I second that," Evan said. "The bastard can rot in hell."

Though Harper wasn't the best person, if he really was holding onto the demon with what little consciousness he had left, I wouldn't wish that on my worst enemy. Leona and Evan were just speaking out of anger, and I understood. Once she came back to her senses, I knew she would agree with me. She was a good person. Her moral compass couldn't be that off, could it?

Thomas coughed, trying to clear the awkward tension. "Regardless, Leona and her squad's contribution in capturing Walker is invaluable to our research. Who knows what else we can discover about possession and demons."

"Speaking of, what about that giant dark silhouette on the battlefield?" Leona followed up. "What *was* that?"

I looked over to Burrel who rubbed his hands on top of his cane restlessly. He seemed uneasy about the topic.

"Those beings are another discussion all together," Imala replied. "From what we know about them, the only thing that can topple it is an Arc Light—a previous exo-suit model. It was originally named the Arc Wing. However, we only have one prototype left, and it's been decommissioned for some time due to lack of resources to keep it functioning."

Leona was about to reply, but Burrel quickly stepped in and cut her off.

"So you're saying the best suggestion for right now is to retreat if any of our soldiers encounter it again?"

"Looks that way," Imala answered.

Burrel looked down, troubled and worried. This must've been another topic that hit close to home.

"With that said, that will wrap up our forum for today," Gerard said with a clap to get everyone's attention. "We're working on making duplicates of our documents to share with all remaining survivors among us. Therefore, if you have any more questions, please be patient as you'll be able to refer to our discoveries later on."

People started walking back to their vessels or loitering outside the tent. I spotted Valeria almost sprinting toward me. Miguel and Maria were barely tailing behind. Burrel, Leona, and Evan gathered around me.

"Hey, Xander!" Valeria said, panting as she approached me. "Those things they said… You don't think my father was…under possession, do you?"

"I honestly don't know what to think," I replied.

"What about Papa?" Miguel asked.

"Padre?" Maria said, confused.

"What are you two talking about?" Leona asked.

"It's a bit of a story. I'm not sure if she would be comfortable with me telling it to you, though," I replied.

"It's okay, Xander. I can tell her myself later." Valeria turned toward Leona. "I'm sorry for how I was yesterday. I—"

"No need. We're all angry and grieving because of the situation we're in." I could tell Leona was trying to process everything told to us just now, as was I.

"One thing is for certain," Burrel said, leaning on his cane. "After we get our footing again, we're going to have to be more prepared than ever for the battles ahead."

"You can say that again," Evan added.

They all started conversing amongst themselves. Though we faced a lot of tragedy, I saw a glimmer of hope the more people Leona and I got to know. I could even tell that the hard shell of distrust Burrel always carried was starting to come down now. As they started walking away from the tent, Harper's pod caught my attention. Some officials were still standing around it and monitoring it as they were putting other equipment away. I started to wonder if we were to peel the complex layers of ourselves off, were we truly good or evil? Or were we all just lost like Harper without a light guiding our way? I peered closer to his face. The black lines were protruding. His very complexion exuded a deep abyss of darkness and sorrow. No matter how far we've fallen as a race, was there truly still hope for us to come back?

"Xander! What are you doing? Stop staring at that asshole and come on," I heard Evan shout.

"Seriously, we need to get a move on. I can't promise to get you any food since we're sharing rations with vessel 3 right now!" Leona shouted.

Perhaps my questions were answered as I saw a tear run down Harper's face before I walked away.

CHAPTER 21

ABOUT SEVEN MONTHS had passed, and the territory we had inside the force field changed drastically. It turned out there were still certain people in pods to help out if we got a base on Earth again. Central Command released specialists and experts who knew specific skill sets such as agriculture, construction, and other fields necessary to rebuild. Here we thought we were the remaining survivors, but you could count on Command to always have a contingency plan in place. All the vessels were also able to successfully descend from space onto base. Some of Central Command stayed in vessel 1 in the sky and only came down now and again. I wasn't sure why. Because of our low number in soldiers, officials have been very careful in delegating supply runs for us. So far, we have been able to survey territories that have little enemy activity. Plus, guards around our perimeter shoot the enemies on sight with relic weapons in case they get too close to the force field. It really isn't necessary anyway since the enemy would cease to exist on contact. However, they can pile up around our perimeter, making it difficult to deploy for supply runs.

Leona has been one of the soldiers continually used for such runs due to her experience and success in previous missions. Thankfully, she had a break today. Needless to say, easy supply runs are the only missions we've been doing to minimize the casualties of the remaining soldiers we have. Others in training have been working hard to join the others on the battlefield. I'm one of those people as I continued my training in the exo-suit as well as resumed my side combat training with Burrel when I could. Tomorrow would be the first time in a long time I'd be deployed. Anticipation started to well up inside of me. My hurt arm from before was fully recovered, and my build thickened slightly. On top of the clean shave I gave myself, I kind of felt like a new man. Since the soldiers in training were imperative, we were treated like the rest of the soldiers and got extra rations now and then. Whenever I saw Maria and Miguel, I'd give them some if I had any extra to help Valeria out since she did the same for them. If they didn't need any, I'd share it with kids or those starving more than the rest of us. I guess, in a way, we were both trying to keep Henry's memory alive by taking care of the less fortunate and sharing what good we could. Reeling from Hunter's death also would've taken its toll if Leona and I didn't come say hi once in a while. Though Valeria was tough and positive, she was still a teenager. It was a lot to take in, especially for a kid.

"Ever since Joselyn recovered and got the green light to deploy again, she's been taking on more supply runs than me," Leona said as we stood in front of the large projector screen in our vessel as people walked by us. A past broadcast was playing that occurred the day after our R&A session to encourage us to work diligently.

"Yeah, she's been antsy for a while now to get back out there. I think she uses the deployments as a distraction," I said, rubbing Leona's shoulder.

"A distraction from what?"

"Well, she originally took a shine to us because we remind her of the relationship she had with her deceased husband, not to mention the loss of her kids." I gently pulled Leona closer to me.

"Your point?"

"I don't know what it's like to lose a child, but if I ever lost you, I'd be in constant grief. Since we remind her of what she had, checking up on her as often as we did probably didn't help her mentally. Come to think of it, it may have been part of the reason why she kindly said you didn't have to visit so much, especially during that time before the R&A forum."

"Oh… I didn't think of it like that," she replied as she contemplated while I held her from behind. "I see what you're getting at."

211

"Yeah, she could use a break from us." I chuckled.

"You know you're really good at putting yourself in other people's shoes and considering what they're going through. It's what I've always liked about you."

"Always?" I said, raising a brow.

"You know…since we came out of stasis," she said hastily.

"Heh…right," I said, laughing it off.

We refocused our attention to the projector. On it, the captain commander was on a podium outside addressing all the remaining occupants of each vessel. Other commanders from the other vessels were standing rigidly behind him.

"For those of you who are unfamiliar with me, I am Captain Commander Voorhees. I am the representative of vessel 1 and oversee vessels 2 through 8 that became our last refuge in space among the chaos happening on Earth. However, after releasing you from your pods in the latter of 2031, we have made progress. Through many sacrifices, we have been able to attain food and resources to sustain our remaining population. Thanks to the heroic efforts of a small platoon, we were able to retrieve a relic of insurmountable power."

I smiled with a hint of pride welling up inside of me as he said this.

"Afterward, we worked harder and were able to get medical supplies for the injured and prepare for more battles to come. Thanks to the combined efforts of our top soldiers, we were able to use the relic we retrieved to protect our home against the enemy and even learn more about the enemy by capturing one of them."

Leona grabbed one of my hands on her shoulder and kissed it as she heard this.

"Now we'll be at a point where we can cultivate land and acquire resources to live in a more humane manner. Make no mistake! Once we recover and regain our footing, we will expand our territory, reclaiming our world!"

"Yay!"

The crowd shown on the projector all raised their hands and shouted proudly. It was odd because during that time, they were against everything Voorhees said a day before. It was like politicians of the past. They could do something horrendous the day before, but the day after, as long as they say something the majority agrees with, people are on their side. The public can be easily swayed. Maybe because, as human beings, our feelings tend to be fickle most of the time.

"Earth is our home and freedom is our God-given right! So we'll pry what's ours back from the enemy's hands even if it be the devil himself!"

The crowd cheered even more. We turned our attention from the screen for a moment and saw a couple of people chatting beside us as they watched the speech on the projector.

"You realize which commander is missing on stage, right?" the guy asked the woman beside him. "Heisen."

"Oh! You're right," the woman replied. "He was the one through the drone feed Voorhees chewed out during the battle. What happened to him?"

"Since that Harper Walker guy was from his vessel, he got demoted, but no one has really seen him around. People were willing to blame anyone that day for all the lives lost. Heisen turned into a perfect scapegoat."

"But he didn't even know one of his own soldiers was possessed." The woman shook her head and scoffed. "No wonder why no one was mad at Voorhees anymore. Command gave someone else to point the finger at."

"It makes me wonder who wrote that speech for him," Leona commented in a low voice to me to not get overheard. "He wasn't as articulate with his words after the battle to get the force field up."

"Heh... Makes me wonder too," I said.

"I hear that. His words always get me as well," I heard a familiar Thai accent chime in down the hallway. I can't believe she heard us. How many people had good ears around here? It's like certain individuals had their ears closer to the ground than others, almost like spies.

We looked over to see Arinya, the original voice of the cryptic message when we first woke from the ship and the voice to Command's control system when the big battle for the force field happened. Her Asian features complemented her tanned skin tone nicely. Her complexion was so smooth and delicate you'd think she didn't experience any hardship throughout the war.

"Oh, hi! You're Arinya, right?" I asked. "It's really good to see the face behind the voice."

I looked over to Leona who gave me a threatening glare. Arinya scratched her head, embarrassed.

"Huh? What did I say?"

"Slow down there, soldier. I've seen Leona in battle, and I'd rather not get on her bad side. Perhaps you should keep your *suggestive* comments to yourself?" Arinya pointed out.

I immediately put my hands up in a defensive manner. "No! I-I didn't mean it like that at all."

Arinya chuckled. "I'm just teasing. I've been one of the personnel monitoring Leona's battles quite frequently. Just kind of happened that way, I guess... We know each other so no need to be so formal."

"Ah, I see. People just love pulling my leg, don't they?"

"I can see how it can be the highlight of someone's day."

"So what makes you walk with us common folk now?" Leona asked, smiling at Arinya and ignoring me.

"Like previously said before, we're all in the same boat. Command's vessel wasn't that different from the other vessels. Well, the level I was on anyway," Arinya replied.

"Hold on. There are different levels?" I asked.

"Yeah. Although they said they wanted to do away with most titles, there is still a considerable hierarchy within our vessel."

"So what does that make the Captain Commander?" Leona asked curiously.

I briefly studied what was on the projector as they replayed the battle it took to get the force field in the first place. Some of the drones must've been recording at the same time. I was kind of curious why recording needed to happen at all, but I wasn't too focused on Command's reasons. Replaying these things was the same tactic they used the first time we woke from stasis to give people hope. It was hard to believe that we hit rock bottom, not knowing what to do at that time. Now we're seeing the fruits of our labor as we continue trying to rebuild. Even now, during these times, life is truly remarkable if you think about it.

"He's turned into the spokesperson who relays information to the public," Arinya resumed to say, snapping me back to the conversation. "His orders come from higher-up. He hasn't really ran his own missions in quite some time now."

"Is that why he was mad months before—having to be the one to rally the occupants after the big battle for our base on Earth?" I asked.

"Yep. Imagine being a decorated war hero turned into a glorified frontman," Arinya said, empathizing. "I'd be a little bitter too."

"Hmm… I'm assuming there's no need for secrecy then, especially after the R&A forum. Is that why personnel like yourself are roaming around, eh Arinya?" Leona said.

"I've always liked how quaint but direct you are, Leona." Arinya smiled. "It makes you quite the leader on the battlefield. But to answer the question, yes. Pretty much all the information we know, you know as well now. No need for ambiguity."

"Thought so."

"So where are you headed to?" I asked.

"Oh, I'm one of the volunteers from Command who offered to check on production. You know…crop yields, material, labor time… all that boring stuff."

"Boring?"

"Yeah, yeah…don't get me wrong. I know production is important but checking to see if something like a tomato plant has grown a little less than a centimeter every day is tedious."

I nodded slightly.

"I'd rather focus on more exciting stuff like construction." Arinya slyly grinned at Leona.

I glanced at Leona as her ears perked up.

"It's a good thing I did that favor for you and got you a break from deployment today." Arinya eyed her nails while coyly glancing at Leona now and again. "They just finished your—"

Leona's cheeks flushed red with embarrassment all of a sudden. "Ahem! Didn't you just say you had to go check on production?"

"Okay, okay…" Arinya put her hands up, smiling while backing away. "I can take a hint. Sorry, Leona. It's just that teasing you two really is fun. Your reactions are priceless. But I'll let you be for now."

"See you around," I said, waving and slightly confused.

"It was good to finally see you too, Xander. After all, you're the man behind a stern woman like Leona that she can't shut up about."

"Arinya!" Leona yelled. She became red hot. Others around briefly stared at us.

Arinya giggled as she power walked away from us. "I'm going now. See you later!"

Leona stood, rubbing her forehead in aggravation for a moment. Then, she glared at me again. I looked back, perplexed.

"Uhm, Leona… If this is about what I said to Arinya before, I really didn't mean anything by it. I was just being polite."

"I know." Leona sighed. "I'm messing with you. Men are so clueless sometimes."

"Huh?"

She tugged my arm, and I followed her toward the ship's exit. "Anyways, I got us something today. It's a surprise."

Oh! Then why is she making such a fuss about it? I thought. *Women are so weird.*

I felt like a rag doll as she dragged me down the ramp and to the outside. As we walked, it was the first time I noticed that the base really did change. I usually glanced at things in passing before since so much was on my mind. However, a significant portion of the land was tilled. It made the landscape a tad more colorful and less desolate as I saw tomatoes, carrots, beans, and other foods from the crops. Though we made makeshift memorial stones for the deceased in a far edge location of the base, it was still hard not to think about the bodies that were cremated on the same ground. It's a thought I'm sure we all tried to push down. The eight vessels were kind of scattered at random places throughout the acres. They were so big, we kind of saw them as buildings for resources now rather than ships. I think the biggest relief to everyone was the newly built homes. Though it wasn't much to it yet other than a space for cots, it gave some people much needed privacy. They were still making more. I think I heard people, even soldiers, had to jump through special hoops just to get the ones already made early. All of these positive changes were boosting morale big time. I'm pretty sure it was part of the reason everyone seemed a little more enthusiastic about working, too, whether it be supply runs or building up the community within the base.

"You ready?" Leona asked as we approached one of the doors of the newly built homes. She was smiling from ear to ear.

"Wait a sec," I said, stunned. "How did you—"

"I was able to snag one due to capturing Harper. R&A was able to discover new information regarding possession. Long story short, they let me have this once it was ready."

I paused for a moment as I realized something. "So was Arinya teasing us because she knew we would have our own space to…"

"Yep," Leona said as she awkwardly looked away from me, still holding my hand. "I'm going to have to be more careful about opening up to her. She apparently loves throwing it back in my face."

I smiled and planted a kiss on her head full of hair.

She looked back at me and grinned. "Well, the door isn't going to open itself."

I chuckled. "Right."

As I creaked open the door, a wave of humidity hit us. It was like being blown back by steam. The smell of newly cut wood filled my nose. Not much was in the room except a cot in the corner and some of our personal belongings we've been dragging around while on the ship. My Bible, I low-key kept with me, was on a table stand beside the cot. I remember it was the only thing I was able to sneak in before stasis as the vessels' personnel, at the time, wanted all unnecessary items left behind to allow for more space on the ship. Sometimes I'd read verses to Leona. I couldn't tell if she listened because she was interested in scripture or liked hearing the sound of my voice. Either way, they were part of some of the rare peaceful moments we shared. Our space was similar to an old-fashioned cabin, only smaller with one room. I'm sure things like insulation, and other modern apartment features wouldn't happen until way down the line, assuming we survived and kept expanding.

"So…what do you think?" she asked with a slight nervousness to her voice.

"It's cozy," I said.

"I even brought the book you keep reading about symbols and markings from R&A on the counter by the cot."

"Oh, thanks. It actually has a lot of interesting stuff we could use against the enemy."

I took my shoes off and got up on the bed. Burrel got me kind of paranoid. Putting cameras in newly built private shacks would be even low for Command, but I wasn't willing to leave that to chance. I thought better safe than sorry.

"What are you doing, Xander?" She put her hand on her hips while speaking with a bit of sass. "Checking for cameras?"

I passed her an odd look, wondering how she pierced my thoughts.

"Burrel let me in on how they monitor us too. I admit, his paranoia kind of rubbed off on me, so I checked already."

I chuckled as I stepped down from the bed.

Click!

Suddenly, I heard the sound of the door locking. I spun around, and before I knew it, I saw Leona sprinting toward me from the other side of the room. I didn't know what to do as she tackled me to the bed.

"You are too excited today," I said, laughing.

"Of course I am! Remember what I said after your first deployment?" she asked, walking her fingers up my chest while we embraced each other on the cot.

I stared at her forest-green eyes, penetrating me with both lust and love. "To be fair, you said a lot of things," I replied.

She kissed me and said, "We have our own room now like I said we would."

I couldn't believe she held onto that idea of us for so long. It made me realize how much our relationship meant to her. Although

I knew it with her actions, her words affirmed it. She started kissing me passionately. I shyly grabbed her shoulders and stopped her.

"I'm excited, too, but Commander Brauns did tell me earlier today that I would need all my stamina for tomorrow's mission," I said. "So maybe we should cool it until after. Okay?"

All of the glee instantly drained from her face, and she backed away a little, disappointed. "Oh…right! Uhm…that makes sense. I didn't mean to make you feel uncomfortable or…"

"Hahaha!" I instantly busted out laughing. Her eyes threw daggers at me. "I'm just messing with you."

A sharp pain rose in my shoulder as she jabbed me. "Xander!"

"You see how it feels when you do stuff like that to me sometimes?" I asked teasingly.

Leona rolled her eyes while grinning. "Oh! Before I forget…" She pulled out two wooden rings. Judging by the craftsmanship, it must've been recently made. "I had someone in construction make these for me. They're really grateful to soldiers. Any who… I know it isn't exactly ideal, but I didn't want to disrespect your beliefs either. It's not like we can have a ceremony or anything." She studied my face, hoping for a positive reaction.

I played with the ring in my hand. A wooden engraving read, "L†X." I chuckled. "You *would* put your initial first." She smiled as she pecked my chest. "Why is the line at the bottom of the plus sign longer?"

"Oh!" She sat up a little, showing me the identical ring she had. "At first, I wanted to do that…you know, curly 'and' symbol." She traced the air with her finger to show me what symbol she was talking about.

"You mean the ampersand?" I asked.

"Yeah, that." She playfully shoved me as I laughed at her. "Don't be a smart-ass." She laughed too. "But like I was saying, I wanted to be different, so I chose the plus sign. I know I'm not the most religious person, but it reminded me of the cross, and I know your faith is important to you. So to symbolize what we have, our initials are on both sides of it to show that He"—she looked up when she said it—"is our center. What do you think? Too much?"

I was stunned, speechless, grateful, and excited all at the same time despite some festering doubts. The thought she put into something so simple blew my mind. Silence invaded the room for a moment as I studied her face, making sure we were both ready to take this new step in our commitment. Everything felt surreal. After all, how could we still be fortunate enough to find happiness surrounded by all this strife happening in our world? It seemed too good to be true, but I accepted it anyway. None of us were promised tomorrow, so we had to live today to its fullest. I kissed her on the forehead and slipped the wooden ring on my finger. It surprisingly fit. I wondered if she gauged the size of my finger while I was sleeping or something. I noticed hers slipped on with ease as well. She couldn't hold in her exhilaration as she climbed on top of me. We embraced each other passionately. Before melting in our touch, we took a moment to stare into one another's eyes again, penetrating one another's being.

"It's perfect. I love you, Leona," I said, holding her tight and continuing to kiss her.

She breathed heavily and dug her fingers into my back. "I love you too, Xander."

That moment solidified and conveyed exactly how we felt about each other. Looking back, it was crucial because from then on, neither of us knew just how hard our bond would be tested.

CHAPTER 22

THE NEXT MORNING was kind of embarrassing. The cabin-like spaces were good for privacy, but it also had a drawback. It was sort of in an obvious area on the base, easily spotted by others. If one person or family members went in, it was nothing to gossip about. However, if a couple went in, people could guess what they were most likely doing that night. Needless to say, we got noticeable looks from some as we walked to vessel 5 for breakfast. Leona and I were a bit uncomfortable as we made our way up the ramp to the ship.

"Maybe last night wasn't such a good idea," Leona said, loosening her grip on my hand.

"What do you mean?" I asked uneasy and a bit worried.

"Evan invited us and others to his ship for breakfast today. If these many people are giving us *the look*, then there's no telling what they'll say." She had her head down. I could tell she was starting to feel a bit humiliated. "I know you're a conservative person, and I like being private. I didn't mean to spring last night's *surprise* on you so suddenly. I wasn't thinking."

I gently lifted her chin with my free hand to look her in the eyes as we walked to vessel 5's mess hall. "Hey, look at me." Some people passing us were already giving us intriguing glances as if they knew a dirty secret we were hiding. Other than working to survive, there was nothing else to do on the base really, so word travelled fast. "We simply expressed how we felt for one another. There's nothing to be ashamed of. Forget them. I'm right here for you."

221

She gave me a peck on the lips, not caring about the gossip or stares surrounding us. "Thanks for always looking out."

"You got my back. I got yours."

Her loosened grip became tight again as she realized those were the words she said to me on the day before my first deployment. We both walked shoulder to shoulder, side by side with our heads held high, prepared for anything as we approached the table where we spotted Evan. I saw Burrel, too, with a few other people I knew in passing. There were others I didn't recognize, though.

"You two are sure looking chipper today," Joselyn said as she held two trays in her hand. "Don't worry about getting in line. We've had good production this month, and the servers were stoked that you two were coming. They let soldiers and families get some extra. These trays are for you two."

"Who uses the word *chipper* anymore?" I asked teasingly.

Leona playfully jabbed her elbow in my arm. I rubbed it in slight pain. "Thank you. You didn't have to Joss," she said.

"Are you kidding? After how many times you both checked on me, it's the least I can do."

We both smiled as we watched Joselyn set our trays down at an empty space for two at the center of the table. Evan motioned us over. Leona and I sat next to each other. Burrel was next to me on the right and Joselyn was next to Leona on the left. Evan sat across the table from us. The rest were seated in a manner comfortable to them. They actually spent time to figure out the most suitable seating arrangements for all of us. I realized the bonds Leona and I created and how blessed we were to have such considerate friends in our lives.

"Looks like you *did* seal the deal, huh?" Burrel asked, examining my wooden ring.

I nervously grinned and scratched my head.

"Good thing, too. I heard that once they instate expansion and things go well, they'll allow pregnancies again," Evan teasingly commented out of nowhere. "No more frozen eggs and vasectomies."

He gave Leona and me a devious grin, knowing he was putting us on the spot. Leona nearly spat out her water she was drinking.

"Can we just eat please and put our private lives off the table?"
I asked.

Evan chuckled. "Sure thing."

"I'll be sure to give you a hard time, too, when you go on your
next deployment." I smirked, but he shrugged it off. He switched his
gaze to Burrel who gave a half smile. Leona noticed, too. "What's
going on?"

"I kind of made a transition to excavation." He awkwardly
played with his food, avoiding our shocked expressions a bit.

"Oh," Leona replied, startled. I was taken back.

"It's just after Chrissy…"

"No, no…you don't have to explain." Leona tried to disguise
her disappointment.

"It's not the same, you know…"

"I understand." Leona took a bite of her food, avoiding the
awkwardness. "It's just nice to have someone to count on out there
on the field sometimes. But I get it… Fighting isn't for everyone."

Evan nodded and attempted a grin but relaxed his face again
after studying Leona's demeanor. We both could tell she was process-
ing it while digging into her plate.

I was relieved looking down at mine. Compared to times
before, the food was different colored lumps of partially edible crap
we scraped from reserves. Now the vegetation we were able to grow
outside made the tray more appealing to the eye and appetizing to
scarf down. You don't really miss something until it's gone. I never
thought I'd be so happy to dig into something like spinach in my
whole life. When food wasn't as scarce on Earth, I took veggies for
granted. Now, I felt my mouth watering, craving for any semblance
of real food instead of powdered mixes or outdated canned goods.

"I hear that Command has kind of been hush-hush about the
mission you're going on today," Burrel commented, respecting my
wishes and switching topics. "It's not the typical supply runs you've
been doing so far."

"Yeah, not even Joselyn or I know about it," Leona cut in. "And
we've been involved in Command's plans all the time lately."

Joselyn nodded in agreement.

"I heard rumors it has something to do with the water supply, but I really don't know. Considering how fast gossip spreads around here"—I passed Evan a judgmental yet teasing glare as I spoke— "those rumors could be true."

"You nervous?" another guy I barely knew said, sitting next to Evan.

"I don't know what I'm feeling... I guess anxious would be the more appropriate word."

"I'd say... Besides a few supply runs here and there, this will be your first time in a while on a real deployment," Burrel chimed in.

"Hopefully, you can complete this one without sacrificing an arm, huh?" Joselyn playfully giggled. I know she was trying to lighten the tension I had building up in me for the deployment, but she inadvertently hit a sore spot.

I noticed Leona playing with her food a bit, thinking back to that time. She really thought I was going to die. I grinned and tried to be a good sport for Leona's sake and keep up appearances, although I knew Joselyn accidentally triggered a scary moment for both of us.

"Yeah. I remember Dr. Ravi gave me a hard time because I said it hindered my training."

"He said the same thing to me when I had the hole in my stomach. Though, my stay in rehabilitation was much longer than yours. I know he meant well, but God does it feel good to get out there and stretch my legs again," Joselyn said, stretching out her arms next to Leona. "I felt as old as Burrel when I tried to move my body after the cast was off."

People at the table snickered at Joselyn's comment.

"I'm not as old as you think. Stress does it. You'd think war would make a man age, but no. These wrinkles are from women like you getting on my nerves," Burrel remarked.

Joselyn teasingly narrowed her eyes at Burrel. He smirked. I didn't realize how chummy they've gotten these past months. I remember Burrel telling me during our training sessions he would have small chats with Joselyn whenever they saw each other. They'd talk about us and then about things in general. It didn't shock me. They both loved to be in their lonely shells. If Leona didn't visit

224

Joselyn, I'm not sure if she would've ever opened up to anyone. And if I hadn't met Burrel, he'd still be eating alone, avoiding everyone. I'm glad they could give each other company as friends even when Leona and I couldn't. I'd hate to see either of them clam up and go back in their shells again.

"So, Burrel…can you answer a question for me, mate?" a guy said from across the table. He was a few spots away from Evan, chewing rudely into his potato while speaking.

"Ugh…another Aussie," Leona said, chuckling. "It's too soon."

Everyone laughed.

"Sorry if Harper put a damp on our reputation. They call me Luke. Me mum named me Lucas because, even as a baby, I was bright and picked up on things," he said, introducing himself to Leona. His calm, hazel eyes stood out in contrast to his matted hair. It's as if his demeanor and style conflicted. He then turned his attention back to Burrel. "For instance, Burrel knew some interesting stuff during the forum months ago. With some of the knowledge you had…did you start on vessel 2? Just curious."

Burrel subtly shifted to Luke. "I was. Why do you ask?" I could tell by the way he turned his attention to him that he was surprised. However, for people who didn't know him, they most likely couldn't notice. Until Luke mentioned it, I was so preoccupied with other tasks around the base that I completely forgot to follow up with Burrel about vessel 2 months ago.

"I hear that vessel was full of veterans from the old war. They could have intel and secrets not even we know."

I felt Leona grip my thigh anxiously over my cargo pants under the table. She knew some information about vessel 2 as well. I remembered her last talk with Burrel about it before the forum months ago. I guess it made sense considering how closely she worked with Command before the deployment to establish our base on Earth. However, it made me wonder why the mention of it put her and Burrel on edge.

All eyes were on Burrel now as we sat, eating at the table. Burrel breathed out easily as he relaxed his face. "Sorry to disappoint, but you must be mistaken. I wasn't a soldier. I was part of excavation on vessel 2 as well, and the guys I saw actually lost their memories of the old war. It didn't regress over time like their usual ones from what I've seen."

Why was it necessary for him to still lie about his background? I thought. He mentioned to me before he used to be a soldier. It's how he knew the skills he did to teach me. What was going on?

"Hm. I guess some rumors *are* just rumors then," Evan said, eyeing Luke suspiciously. I think he had the same feeling as me. We couldn't put our finger on it, but Luke was trying to stir up something—some type of information a lot of us weren't privy to.

"Heh. I guess not. My mistake," Luke replied, retreating back to his food as if defeated.

"So, Chad," Leona blurted out, switching the subject. She turned her attention to a gentleman at another part of the table. "How are you doing?"

Chad had tanned skin and sported a goatee. Leona waited for a response as he finished swallowing his bite of food. "I'm doing well, considering everything. Thanks for not calling me Chadron like usual. It's so formal, you know. Inviting me here to eat with you all was also very kind of you." He passed Leona a genuine smile.

"Don't mention it. It's the least I can do after what you crafted for me."

So Chad is the one who made these wooden rings for her, I thought.

"How's it been for you after waking from stasis? I know a lot of us who woke before had to take things slow. Me, especially, as I got random panic attacks the first few months," Leona said, continuing the small talk.

"To tell you the truth, it's unreal. Bits of my memory are coming back over time, as if I'm rediscovering who I am, or should I say... who I was?" He held his head. "Ahhh... I don't even know anymore. The last one I have is of me talking to my wife about the economy and how they delayed jobs like mine until they could get a handle on the enemy situation. People called them monsters, but my wife was a devout woman. She had Virgin Mary candles and prayed to God every day. She instinctively called them demons. I didn't know what to think. I still don't..." I noticed him rubbing a rubber band on his ring finger. "When I woke up, it wasn't on my bed at home. It was a cold pod. My ring was gone, and I still don't remember what happened to my wife, whether she's dead or…you know…" He looked down at his tray, staring at the leftovers. "I found this rubber band and put it on. After all those years of marriage, it kind of feels weird without something on it… Anyways, it felt good making you what I did… Reminded me of simpler times."

No one said anything. I think, in a way, all of us were trying to forget what we lost and somehow move on or at least put it in the back of our minds for a while. However, Chad brought it all back. I could tell on everyone's faces. I looked over to Joselyn who had her head down toward her tray too. If anyone could relate to Chad, it would be her. She woke up and discovered her family was gone too. It also started to make me wonder if everyone had significantly different rates of when their memories came back. Mine was still coming in slowly. I could tell because when having small talk with others around the base, they remembered a lot before stasis. I met one who nearly had full recollection of who they were.

"I'm sorry for your loss," Leona managed to say.

Chad raised his glass of water. "It's okay. I'm just thankful to share a table with some of the soldiers who advanced the cause."

Leona, myself, Joselyn, Evan, Burrel, and a few others smiled at him. He reminded us why the fight was still necessary—to reclaim our lives and our freedom.

"Speaking of the cause," Luke said, once again changing the mood of the table. "I don't mean to come back to this, but there's just something I can't shake from my mind, mate." He stared at Burrel, gesturing with his fork.

Burrel nodded. "I'm listening."

"Vessel 2 started off with more soldiers than anyone. You're telling me you didn't come across not one who had any recollection of the old war? That's weird, don't you think?"

"Yeah, it is." Burrel smoothly kept his composure. "But hell… relics, exo-suits, demons, portals… What about our predicament isn't weird, am I right?"

Luke flashed him a smile. "I suppose you are."

I felt Burrel's hand tap me on the side. "My bum leg feels a bit more tired today. Help an old man, would ya, as I take this to the trash." He was referring to the scraps and leftovers on his tray.

Getting the hint, I nodded back and said, "Sure."

I glanced at Leona who flashed a look back at me, concerned. What did they know that I didn't?

After passing by some people and being a little ways from the table, Burrel pulled me to the side. We were kind of in a blind spot within the mess hall. I guess he was still paranoid of any feed potential cameras could pick up.

"I need you to listen to me very carefully because what I'm about to tell you is confidential and dangerous. I know even Leona hesitated to tell you this," Burrel said with a solemn expression.

He was right. Leona hadn't told me anything. Were they afraid of such info leaking out that they waited to tell me until I was ready to hear it, or was there something more?

"I had to lie about not being a soldier. Besides Commander Brauns, only you and Leona know I was. You're the only ones I can trust."

"What does Commander Brauns have to do with this?" I asked. "He's the very man who sent me to die on my first deployment and was part of withholding information that cost lives on the battlefield. Why trust him?" I narrowed my eyes at Burrel.

"After I woke from stasis on vessel 2, I recalled a lot of my memories from the old war—the civil war when we attacked the government. Vessels 3 through 8 were basically sleeper cells until we could come up with a plan to combat the enemy. Therefore, a commander forum was held."

"A commander forum? As in all of the commanders of the ships in one meeting?"

Burrel nodded. "Veterans of the old war were also invited, but not everyone was awake from cryostasis. Only a select group that had significant details of the events or contributed to the fight more than others were there. I hadn't even told Leona this. She's only been cautious about telling you I was on vessel 2 due to the controversy surrounding it. Weird things happen to people when you know certain things before stasis." Burrel grabbed my shoulder. "An official above Voorhees recommended that the ships should run like our economy back on Earth where there was the elite, the upper class, middle class, and lower class. I was so appalled by his idealism, I didn't bother to catch his name. His argument was that it established order and caused less conflict if set up that way. Us veterans knew better after fighting the government. With that logic, it would create the same situation we were in now. Powers that are unchecked in any form of order only leads to corruption down the line."

"Did he listen to you?" I asked, staring back at Burrel's eyes intently.

"I thought he did. He shook hands with one of us and smiled like we were all on the same page." Burrel sighed and looked away a minute. "That's when I noticed some of my closest comrades were missing pieces of their memory during the old war. I asked around and higher officials were acting like it was just a natural process of stasis. However, you're supposed to gradually regain your memories and never lose them again." He clenched his free hand angrily. "Before I knew it, they were putting my pals back into their pods under the guise of their minds needing more time to acclimate to stasis before being put out. But I knew that was bullshit. They were fine until that commander forum."

"How did you walk away from that unscathed?"

"Little did I know there were still good people even when I thought they were all lost. Commander Brauns was one of the few commanders paying heed to what was going on and didn't buy into everything Command said. When they wanted to put me back into stasis, he proposed I'd be moved to excavation on his ship at vessel 7."

"Wait a minute! Are you saying you were awake before all of us on vessel 7?"

Burrel smirked. "Commander Brauns made it look like I was being put under stasis again but quickly got me out when we both returned to the vessel. He agreed with me and knew something weird was going on."

"So you've been his eyes and ears this whole time. Then that means…"

Suddenly, I remembered something Miguel said to me a while back. It was when I confronted Brauns in front of people after witnessing the battle Leona was in.

He likes you. If it were any of us, we would be punished.

He was lenient with me past times I spoke out of term too. Perhaps he *was* on our side.

"Listen to me, Xander!" Burrel said, snapping me back. "I know this is a lot. I can see the gears turning inside your head right now. But Commander Brauns trusts you. That means if he specifically wanted you for this mission, there's something important about it. Of course, he can't tell you directly. It'll blow his position as commander. But keep your eyes open. Now that you know this, you may pick up on things you hadn't before. Good luck on this next deployment. We both depend on you more than you realize."

CHAPTER 23

AFTER HEARING BURREL'S words, Commander Brauns sounded different to me. Instead of paying attention to the surface, I tried to dig deeper and discover any subtle hint or favor he was parting me with as my two other team members and I stood close to the force field in our exo-suits. Other officials were lined up with Brauns as well. Oddly enough, Commander Bridgett from vessel 3 was among them. I looked over to an Alpha soldier who sported the first exo-suit I was deployed in—the Infiltrator. I reminisced myself in it as I saw the guy stretching to work in the kinks. It brought back memories, but during this time, I've been going on supply runs with the Equalizer. Luckily, I was assigned to that suit now. Strangely, another Alpha soldier was with us which made me a little nervous, especially with their model. Whoever it was had a Juggernaut equipped. I don't know what type of mission this was, but to have two Alpha soldiers with us seemed serious. Usually, a soldier out of training would get two Beta soldiers and an Alpha.

"Apologies," Brauns opened. "We'd usually debrief for the missions while having someone like Arinya with you on comms. However, we're shorthanded and we'll be doing both this mission." He rubbed his eyes. He looked more stressed than ever but tried to hide it. "We're working on setting up a department for Control to monitor the battlefields while commanders tend to other important affairs."

"Are there only three of us, Commanders?" a female voice in the Juggernaut suit asked. Her faceplate was retracted, showing her complexion. I recognized her face as one of the surviving Alpha soldiers from the fight Leona partook in to get the base we now have on Earth.

"Patience, Squad Leader Rona," Brauns said. His hands were behind his back as he stood rigid as ever. "Your fourth member is running late. I would've never agreed with having *two* soldiers fresh out of training on one squad, but this girl was…persistent." He irritatingly shifted his gaze to Bridgett.

"Hey, don't look at me, Brauns. Now you see what I had to put up with when our vessels were in space," Bridgett said. Her stance was more relaxed than Brauns. It's like she didn't care one way or the other of how this war went. "That girl can work a nerve, let me tell you…but if it wasn't for Xander here, this would've never happened." She poked the chest of my exo-suit with her finger. Due to the armor and padding, I couldn't feel it of course.

"What do *I* have to do with the fourth member?" I asked through the communicator in my suit.

"I don't know what you did, but apparently she took a liking to you. So much so that she refused to do any deployments unless her first one was with you. Such a pain…" Brauns replied.

Bridgett laughed nervously, rubbing the back of her head. "What can I say? We women are a handful."

"Who is she?" I said anxiously.

"I'm here!" A voice blasted through our communicators in our suit, followed by panting. The two Alpha soldiers and myself held the side of our helmets, rattled by the sound. Some of the officials had communicators in their hands, so the noise wasn't right in their ears like ours.

"You're late, Rosenburg," Bridgrett said unenthusiastically.

It couldn't be… I thought.

The fourth member's Cavalry faceplate retracted to reveal Valeria.

"Great…just great," the guy said in the Infiltrator suit. I didn't recognize him. He must've been a newly appointed Alpha soldier.

"We have a bishop." He pointed at Rona. "A knight." He pointed at himself. "And two pawns. Pieces that can barely do anything out there while the kings and queens remain safe in their castle of a force field." His tone was sarcastic, but they were laced with truth.

"Hey, you do know I was part of the platoon that retrieved the relic for this force field, right?" I snapped back, kind of offended.

"Fine! A rook. You happy?"

Valeria scoffed at his comment. Calling us pawns wasn't only an insult to us, but he unknowingly slighted Henry calling me a rook since he was part of my first platoon too, deceased or not. I narrowed my eyes at him as my faceplate retracted. He put his face inches from mine. I didn't want to admit it, but my chess piece was pretty accurate. This would be my first real mission in a while after coming out of training. Calling me a rook also gave me reminiscent vibes from my deployment with Henry in the past.

"That's enough out of you, Colt!" another official behind Brauns and Bridgett said. "You will not further embarrass vessel 6. Our reputation is tarnished as it is due to Commander Heisen's negligence! Do I make myself clear?"

"Yes, Great Ambassador Judas." Colt bowed mockingly.

"It's Judea! Mispronounce it again, and this mission will be the least of your worries. There are still fates worse than fighting those monsters, understand?"

"Understood, sir," Colt replied, gritting his teeth. I could tell he was also holding in his pride as he said it.

Ambassador? I thought. I hope that was his real name because who arrogantly calls themselves Judea, as if he was meant to be worshipped? He must've been from Command—Commander Heisen's replacement. If we were all on one base now, what was the need for an official to still monitor the vessel 6 ship in the first place? And where was Heisen then? So many things weren't adding up.

"Commander Brauns and Commander Bridgett, may I have a word with you?" Rona asked as she stepped to the side with them on the grassy plain.

I shifted my attention toward Valeria. "What on Earth are you doing here? This mission isn't straightforward. It could be dangerous."

"Thanks, *Dad*, but I'll be fine," she said sarcastically with a smug smile.

"Valeria, I'm serious!" I tugged her arm in concern. "Why did you force yourself into this mission with me?"

She jerked away from my grip. "You and Leona have been there, checking on me this whole time. After Henry and Hunter risked their lives for…" her voice began to crack. "I just want to protect people I care about for once, okay?"

"But this is your *first* mission. Why put yourself at risk for me?"

"Do I really have to explain why? Without you, I would've joined Henry and Hunter on my own that day in my own way…" She avoided my glare. I think she didn't want to be shamed by my judgy parental-like eyes.

However, I stared back at her only with empathy, realizing she was thinking of suicide all those months ago. She wouldn't be here now if I didn't do something as simple as sit with a girl, listening to her troubles on a rooftop.

Her solemn expression suddenly shifted toward a more positive light, speaking to me again. "Besides, I have a war hero and two Alphas with me, right? I'll be fine!" She smiled confidently from ear to ear while giving me a thumbs-up.

I did a facepalm, irritated by her enthusiasm. "Ugh… Don't let your emotions cause you to lose focus out there, got it? Especially now that we know possessions feed on negativity even with these markings protecting us in the suits. Stick close, and follow the squad leader's command, all right?"

She giggled, unfazed by my doting tone. "Okay, okay! You worry too much. Geesh!"

"You don't worry enough!" If I wasn't careful, this girl would make me blow a gasket one of these days. I swear she took joy in stressing me out sometimes. I had to admit it was a bit amusing, though. It was like how a daughter would act with her father.

"If the objective is this serious, I don't see how babysitting two fledglings will benefit anyone in this mission," I overheard Rona say at a distance. Both Valeria and I pretended not to listen as we honed in on the conversation. "I say we drop the two greenhorns and get two Betas. Hell, I'd take Deltas."

"I hear ya, but it's not like we commanders make these decisions without thinking, you know?" Bridgett replied. Her tone came off kind of salty.

"I know. I didn't mean to undermine—"

"Listen, squad leader. Valeria, that greenhorn as you so put it, showed more promise than any other soldier on my ship in training." She spat out something she was chewing on the floor. "She can be annoying as hell, but her performance speaks for itself. She may appear scatterbrained at times, but her awareness for the enemy is uncanny. Also, her precision is terrifyingly accurate with a relic weapon, which is why she will be perfect backup for you in Cavalry."

"And Xander Williams shows more potential than anyone I've seen," Brauns added. "His instincts and natural fighting ability will serve you well out there. Not to mention, his moral code allows him to determine the right course of action when faced with challenges from what I've seen on and off the field. I know they seem wet behind the ears to you as an Alpha, Rona, but these aren't your run-of-the-mill trainees."

Valeria and I grinned at each other, trying to hide our contentment from the commanders' compliments from others. We didn't want them to know we were subtly eavesdropping.

"With all due respect, Commanders, lucky shots and morality don't win battles in war," Rona replied, unmoved by their praise. "We all know things like that only hold out for so long."

Brauns narrowed his eyes. "We appreciate your concern. We'll take it under advisement after we see the results of this mission."

"But—"

"The nerve of soldiers these days, I swear." Bridgett got inches away from Rona's face. "In case you didn't get the hint, girl, this discussion is over. Now get back in line for debrief!"

Rona looked toward Brauns who only agreed with Bridgett by motioning his head to join the rest of the squad. She stormed over to us, angrily holding her tongue. If I didn't know it before, I knew it now. He was on our side. And by the looks of it, maybe Bridgett as they shook their heads in unison toward Rona's actions. The other officials maintained their neutral stance as if nothing was happening. I only saw Ambassador Judea take note of it.

"Listen up. This is an important operation for our base." Brauns took lead while the other officials stood silent behind him. "As you know, vegetation is going smoothly, but supply runs for water like in the past isn't going to cut it this time. We need a steady source if we want to keep crop yields, morale, and other essential functions up on base. Fortunately, excavation found a river flowing into a waterfall with a fresh water source nearby. The plan is to make a dam. Not only will it allow us to have a reservoir of fresh water, but it also opens the possibility for a hydropower plant, producing electricity for us."

"If I may, Commander," I said.

Brauns nodded, allowing me to speak.

"Even if we survey the area and clear out the monsters, or rather demons as we're calling them, it won't prevent more from coming. How does Command propose we utilize the river with enemies constantly attacking soldiers, engineers, et cetera?"

Rona and Colt glanced at me, surprised. Perhaps they didn't expect a thought out comment from a rook.

Brauns smirked. "Good, Williams. You're thinking. You'll need it for this mission. We already received a signal from a relic deeper into enemy territory that resonates the same amount of energy the one your platoon managed to get for our force field. Until we can retrieve that one, we will use the relics we've acquired to keep temporary force fields up around the area where the river is with another generator. Since they won't have the amount of energy of the relic we use now for the force field on our base, they will have to be used in rotations, so they can be switched out and reused."

"I get it!" Valeria blurted out. "By using the relics with smaller energy in rotations, engineers, construction workers, and others will be able to build a dam once we clear the area out." She paused for a moment, contemplating. "But wouldn't that mean soldiers would have to be there around the clock to fend off enemy attacks until we can get the generator up so the relics can be used with it? It's not that different from what Leona and so many other soldiers needed to do just to get the base we have now."

Bridgett smiled. "I'm glad you two amateurs catch on fast. I am." Her smile then immediately went away. "But why don't you shut the hell up, and let Commander Brauns finish before disciplinary action is implemented for your constant disruptions during debrief!"

"Y-yes, ma'am!" Valeria and I both said in unison, straightening up.

Judea passed us a distasteful gaze. "I see why you chose them, but you could've taught them proper etiquette first." His tone was so arrogant.

Colt shook his head. "I really hope these guys aren't more trouble than they're worth," he mumbled under his breath.

Rona remained silent and attentive while Brauns continued to speak.

"As trainee Valeria put it, we are aware of this. Therefore, clearing out the area will not be your mission."

Rona, Colt, Valeria, and I were startled.

"Something is blocking our instruments from getting a more in-depth layout of the land. We're suspecting it to be interference from the enemy. Since we've already established they possess intelligence, it wouldn't be farfetched to say they're blocking any attempts of us expanding or fighting back." Brauns motioned to Rona. "That's where your squad leader comes in."

"I see," Rona replied, realizing what was being asked of her. She turned around to face us. "Listen. I understand this mission now. In the past, when we first started deployments while we were in space on the vessels, we used to have four-man squads with each member equipped with a different model. We went into a lot of missions blind, not knowing the territory. Hence, we had different models to adapt to any situation that may present itself to us."

"So we're going in dark and playing it by ear…" Colt commented. Rona nodded.

A wave of anxiety and fear hit me as their words made me even more concerned for Valeria.

"Isn't that all the more reason we should have two other team-mates with more experience?" Colt asked.

"We have our reasons," Brauns shot back at Colt intently. His eyes almost looked menacing, not wanting to hear any more on the matter. "One more thing. Before you go out there, keep your eyes open. Like you learned at the R&A forum, anything can happen and anything is possible. We're all in unknown territory now. Don't let negativity consume your thoughts. Keep each other in the right mind-set."

"Yeah, we don't need more Harper Walkers running around." Bridgett nonchalantly dug something out of her ear while she spoke.

Brauns and other officials passed Bridgett a look like *Really?*

"Not helping, Bridgett," Judea said, annoyed behind her. "Don't listen to her, soldiers. His was an exceptionally extreme case anyway."

"Hey, I just tell shit like it is."

"True, you never know what might happen," I heard Valeria say under her breath beside me. Her voice was shaky. I put my hand on her shoulder to calm her nerves.

"Attention!" Brauns boomed. Everyone became attentive again. "Use the suits as they were intended and follow Squad Leader Rona's lead. She has gotten multiple platoons through hell and back. That means Colt infiltrates, Rona draws enemy fire if things get hectic, Williams picks his spots and helps who needs it, while Rosenburg focuses on crowd control and targets from a distance. Got it?"

"Yes, sir!" Rona, Colt, Valeria, and myself replied in unison.

Does he only refer to people he likes by last name? I thought. It reminded me of the time he called Henry, Joselyn, and myself by our last names on my first deployment. Though Henry and Joselyn were missing this time, he still referred to Valeria by her family name. I admit that having her here was like still having a piece of Henry with me after he sacrificed his life for mine. And looking at how distraught she was but still willing to go through with the mission reminded me of Joselyn and how hard she fought to see it through.

"What is it? Why are you looking at me like that while the commander is speaking?" Valeria whispered to me. I didn't realize I was staring at her.

"Sorry," I replied as I jerked my head forward again, breaking eye contact with her. "Just…don't die out there, okay?"

"Okay," she said with reassurance. Though she tried to sound confident, I still detected uneasiness in her voice. I wasn't sure if she was trying to be brave for her own sake or for me at this point.

"Also, be aware of everything and anything out there. Eyes open for any clue we might find to help us in our cause," Brauns narrowed his eyes while saying this and glanced at me quickly to where no one could notice.

That must've been the sign!

"All right, team." Rona pressed a button on the side of her helmet and the faceplate covered her face again. We followed suit. "Let's make the folks we care about on this base proud, and find the thing blocking our attempts from getting what we need."

"I hear that," Colt replied.

"Yes, ma'am!" Valeria commented.

"Understood," I said.

"One more thing." Judea stood in front of the force field occupied by guards. They were shooting demons with relic weapons to get us a clear path outside without much enemy interference. "Command thought the drones worked out so well the first time we used them that they've been issuing one to follow squads on every mission. So whatever action you take will be monitored by us so that we no longer only have to go on the intel relayed by your radio contacts in your helmets. Good luck out there."

I know he said that to relay the information intended by Command, but the way he said it made it sound like he didn't trust us. I saw Brauns and Bridgett take note of it too. Just what was this shift and tension I was sensing between Command and some of its commanders? I wasn't sure what it was, but something was telling me I was going to find out.

"Let's move!" Rona shouted.

With that, Valeria and I followed closely behind her, running in our suits. Colt was already ahead of the line and slashed a demon in front of us while guards covered us from the sides. As soon as we exited the force field, I saw the light from the relic energy light up on Rona's Juggernaut suit. She slammed her fist into the ground, causing a massive shockwave of light around us. The small crowd of demons near the force field, blocking our exit, were gone.

"Wooh! That's what I'm talking about," Colt boasted. "I've been itching for some action."

"I know you're excited, but quiet down, Colt." Rona looked around to see if any other enemies were coming. We were surrounded by wildlife. "From here on out, we need to be discreet as possible. Your suit is the most agile and the fastest since it carries the least amount of weight. Since it was made for infiltration and reconnaissance, you'll scout ahead. Signal us if you even get a whiff of trouble."

He made a saluting gesture in his suit. "Whatever you say, boss." I couldn't tell if he was mocking her or genuinely responding.

"While I trail behind Colt, I want you two to follow closely behind me." She pointed at Valeria and me.

"We can do more than just back up," Valeria said through her communicator. "You can give us something actually useful to do."

I sighed as she spoke out of term. She completely disregarded what I said about following Rona's command a few minutes ago. Teenagers, I swear. Words go in one ear and out the other.

"Excuse me, little girl? Last time I checked, I was put in charge. Like Commander Brauns said, we need to play to the strengths of our suits since we're stepping in unknown territory. That's why Xander will be behind me in his Equalizer to help me fend off enemy attacks if we encounter any, and you will scout behind us and give us cover fire when need be." She adjusted some of the equipment on her suit. "Now, I'm not a smart-ass like you, but that seems pretty useful, doesn't it?"

Defeated, Valeria responded with her head down saying, "Yes, it does. Sorry, Squad Leader Rona."

"No more interruptions. We have to keep moving to the designated coordinates Command sent me. I know you're eager. We all are. But you need to keep your emotions in check if you want to stay alive."

We continued to follow behind Rona while Colt wasn't too far ahead. "Go ahead and say it," Valeria said to me through the communicator.

"Say what?" I replied.

"I told you so."

"I don't like rubbing things in. Just stay levelheaded, and keep your eyes open for any potential ambushes behind us."

She nodded. "It's just my brother and Hunter were so brave out here. I don't want to let their memories down by being any less than that, you know?"

"Yeah, I know. Your brother's sacrifice is what gave me the strength to keep fighting on my first deployment. And without Hunter's quick thinking, Leona and so many others probably wouldn't be alive right now. So yeah, I get it." I heard the sound of my suit crunching the leaves and plants I walked on while trying to search for the right words. "Just don't let your memory of them blind you into an early death. It's also important to be conscious of the choices you make now and not so focused on the ones your loved ones made in the past."

I heard a slight chuckle from my communicator.

"What is it now?" I asked her.

"Nothing. It's just...you stepped up from that commercial quote you said to me from the first time we met."

"Heh... I guess we've all been taking pretty big steps these past months."

"Shhh!" Rona said as she raised her hand for us to stop.

I saw Colt in his suit ahead, waiting for something to pass by. I heard it too. Rustling in the tall grass echoed throughout the area. I realized we were in an overgrown forest covered by evergreens and shrubbery. It was the most plant life I have seen since we set foot back on Earth. The sight of insects buzzing, squirrels scampering about, and vines intertwining with nature was peaceful to gaze upon. It was surreal how much life flourished without human interference. Witnessing the serenity of it all made me wonder if we deserved to live in the first place. After all, even though conspirators among our world leaders created this situation, they were still human, still one of us—still like me. As I saw my squadmates around me, I started to think that any one of us could throw the world into chaos depending on our circumstances and upbringing. Perhaps we were doing life a favor by not being a part of it.

Roar!

We braced ourselves for whatever was about to come out of the brushes. As the beast came out of the thicket with claws ready to pounce, we breathed out a sigh of relief as we saw a bear run the other direction, thanks to our weapons that were armed and ready.

"Just a furry nuisance," Colt said through the communicator.

"False alarm," Rona added, putting her hand down.

I laughed on the inside. Years ago, bears would've been something most people feared in our normal society. Now nothing fazed us unless they were demons.

"My heart nearly stopped," Valeria said behind me.

"Kill that feeling, girl, unless you want to freeze up when the real enemy attacks." Rona kept on and surveyed the area, not bothering to look back at Valeria.

"My name is Valeria."

"Good for you. You'll get a name on my squad once you earn it," Rona remarked.

Valeria tapped me on the shoulder and gestured in her suit as if asking, *What was that all about?*

I shrugged and kept trudging behind Rona. We kept walking in silence after that. I studied some of the huge trunks of the trees. I had to do a double take on one. It could've been my imagination, but I could've sworn I saw one with a pattern carving in it—a symbol. I wondered if it could've been hidden on other ones. But for that to happen, someone must've done it. It wasn't possible for anything in the world besides the demons to possess the intelligence to do this. Or was there even a darker mystery behind this war? Anxiety rose within me as I got a feeling in the pit of my stomach that this wouldn't be a simple mission. I could tell Valeria was mentally preparing herself for whatever was to come. The drone over us was camouflaged, but I could still hear its mechanical sounds overhead. Rona pulled up a small projection of a map on her wrist that showed we were close to the coordinates.

Colt stopped suddenly and looked back at Rona. "There's a cliff up ahead, boss. Is the area we're supposed to check out down below?"

All four of us got to the cliff and stared down at the unknown territory of the top of canopy trees from below. Beside the area was a waterfall—most likely the one Command wanted to use as a water source for the hydro-powered dam. Everything looked normal. Whatever was blocking Command's instruments from surveying the land definitely had to be down there.

Rona's device on her wrist pinpointed to the area below. "Damn... It looks like it."

"You were right." I turned to Colt. "We will *literally* be in the dark in this mission."

"You bet your ass I was right, rook. Try not to wet your pants." Colt mockingly held out an inactive flare from his suit. "I can give you a night-light if you want."

"Actually, that's not a bad idea. We can try out the new flare guns on the Equalizer," Rona said, turning to me.

"Lighting up parts of the forest?" I asked.

"Yep."

"Won't that alert enemies that we're here?" Valeria questioned.

"The hell with it! We'll be blind down there," Colt answered. "Besides, if things get too out of hand, we can stay by the flares to repel some of the demons away."

"There's a time limit, though. R&A increased the efficiency of the flares, but it's still on a clock." I think we all detected the obvious distress in Valeria's voice.

"I guess as soon as Xander shoots the flares, we'll have to hit the ground running to scout and get out of there. Won't we?" Rona spoke to Valeria in an almost patronizing tone.

I bet Valeria was thinking, *Why does Xander get to be called by his name and not me?*

"Well, rook. We don't have all day," Colt said, nudging me toward the edge of the cliff. I brushed his hand off.

As I stood there arming my flare gun, a thought occurred to me. I recalled something from the books R&A supplied our base with after the forum on demons. If I shot the flares in a certain formation around the forest, it might help us out later. I went ahead and did it. Suddenly, I felt a tug on my suit.

"What in the hell are you thinking shooting all six of your flares?!" Rona protested. "I meant for you to shoot a few. Flares should only be for emergency situations!"

"It's a contingency plan in case—"

"Plan?!" Rona cut me off. She tugged me close to her by the collar of my exo-suit. "Listen! I'm in control of this mission. You may see yourself as a hotshot because you got the relic for the force field, but you're still a novice, Xander!" Her voice cracked a little. "Do you have any idea how many families, friends, loved ones I had to look in the eye and tell them the person they cared for was never coming back? Your lives are on my watch! I'll be damned if anyone else gets killed while under it. Understand?"

At first, I thought she was all gung ho about being squad leader out of pride. But now I understood that her abrasive behavior came from a caring place, not a selfish one.

"Enough, Rona!" Colt shouted through the communicator, making his way down the hill. Valeria wasn't too far behind him. "As the girl said, those flares are on a timer. What's done is done. We gotta keep moving and take advantage of the flares unless we want to face a slaughter like the one for our base."

She grunted and pushed me away. "Try not to fall behind, and follow my lead. Got it?"

I nodded.

As we ran toward the ominous forest below, I could hear the rage of the waterfall cascading to the river. Mixed with the bird chirpings and other sounds of nature, it was quite serene. Though we were risking our lives to survive, I couldn't help but see the balance in all of it—God in every detail. I looked up and saw the drone going in and out of camouflage mode. I felt as if Command was trying to be the new eye in the sky and become God themselves by watching our every move. My paranoia was probably on overdrive due to the many unknown variables of this mission.

"Up ahead," Rona pointed to one of the flares attached to the canopy tree I shot moments ago. A mechanism from the relic flare latched onto objects after shooting to hold it in place. "We'll head for the tree and scout to see any potential interference from the enemy that might be blocking our instruments."

After catching our breath by the tree, we examined the area. The forest was dimly lit, adding to the anticipation. I couldn't spot anything possibly hindering our efforts to expand. Valeria was shaking a little with her sniper relic in hand. I briefly touched her arm to calm her nerves and let her know I was beside her. It seemed to help as she stopped fidgeting a little. Colt shrugged to Rona, not seeing anything either. In fact, it was a bit too calm, considering the world should've been overrun by demons. It was a miracle in itself that we didn't encounter any enemies at all reaching this area.

"Command, I'm not sure what we were supposed to find," Rona said, patching through with her communicator. "But besides the animals, it's dead out here."

"Keep your eyes open, squad leader," I heard Brauns reply through the communicator. "We can't come back empty-handed."

Colt scoffed. "We? As if he's out here with us. I wish some folks got off their high horses." I felt where he was coming from. I don't think I've ever seen a commander pilot one of these exo-suits ever since we got out of stasis, although most of them were known for fighting on the frontlines before the Earth was thrown into disarray.

Suddenly, birds were flying overhead, and other wildlife ignored us and went straight past us. We all looked around and tried to see what they were running from.

"Uhm, Xander…" Valeria poked a part of my suit that had less material on it so I could feel it. "Look!"

My eyes wandered the forest, and I could see the horrifying expressions I still had nightmares of from my first deployment. Those glowing eyes and eerie grins were in front of us, but they were also all around us. Numerous silhouettes were watching, ready to pounce on us like prey.

"Shit!" Rona shouted. "Command, are you seeing this?"

"We're surrounded," I said in disbelief. "They knew we were coming. It's an ambush!"

CHAPTER 24

"**BASTARDS!**" **COLT EXCLAIMED.** "They made us rats in a trap."

"How in the world are we going to get out of here now?" Valeria asked, retracting her helmet.

Though things looked bleak, staring at Valeria's frightened face reminded me of what Henry said to me during my first deployment. "We'll be fine." I armed myself with the relic gun strapped to the hip of my suit. "We just need to do our roles and get out. All right?" Valeria's frightened expression changed to a more optimistic one. She equipped the sniper on her suit and closed the faceplate to her helmet again in a ready stance.

"My thoughts exactly," Rona said. "I think it's pretty obvious what's been blocking the connection now. They must stay in the shadows and attack our instruments from afar to not be seen. They knew soldiers would come here eventually to try to investigate—"

"Then *bam!*" Colt blurted, finishing her sentence. We jumped from the sudden outburst. "Caught like a Venus flytrap. Just how advanced is their intelligence?"

"Judging from their tactics up to this point, I'd say the enemy is pretty sophisticated despite their grotesque looks."

"Shit… I thought you'd say that. We're gonna have to play it smart if we're gonna get out of this alive."

I examined the forest and took note of where all the lights emitting from the flares were. If Rona couldn't get us out of here, I'd have to use my plan as a last resort. I heard R&A based the design of these on traditional road flares, which only lasted fifteen minutes. They managed to add a few more minutes to it, but I'm pretty sure we wasted that time on our descent down to the forest.

EEEKKK!

Before we knew it, the silhouettes started closing in.

"Damn it! Brace yourselves!" Rona shouted.

Vworp! Vworp! Vworp!

I heard three relic shots fire from our side. I glanced over and saw Valeria use the sniper on instinct. Her body was tense, but she was a natural using firearms. She didn't even have to use the scope.

"Well I'll be...she really can shoot," Colt replied.

"Not bad, girl." Some silhouettes were closing in on us, but Rona created a shockwave by bashing her fist to the ground.

"They're getting bold. Even though we're by a relic flare, they're still trying to attack at a midrange," I said. "What do we do?"

"Command, any plans for extract?" Rona said through the communicator.

"Sit tight. We have reinforcements coming, but it will take a bit of time." Bridgett's voice shot back through the feed. "You have four capable soldiers between you. Find a way to hold them off until then."

Colt chuckled sarcastically, slashing some of the silhouettes getting near. "If we don't die first." I started growing accustomed to Colt's cynical nature as it held truth. Time was simply a luxury we didn't have.

Rona equipped the mini turrets on her wrists and started shooting in various directions around us. "We'll have to travel in a line and get back up the cliff for a better vantage point."

"And leave the safety of the relic flares?" Colt asked. One of the claws from the silhouettes was about to slash Colt. I shot my relic gun at it. He turned toward my direction. "Heh, don't think I owe you."

"We have no choice. They're trying to attack us anyway, though they are keeping somewhat a distance from the light," Rona replied. "We're in the dark down here. At least up there, we can see what we're dealing with."

"How do we get up there?" I asked, backing up Valeria and shooting beside her.

"We'll travel in a lined formation. However, we'll have a front guard and a rear guard. Xander, you take front guard with Colt. He'll slash enemies trying to target us while you shoot the ones getting too close in front of us." She slammed the floor again to disperse the enemy forces. Some of the demons around us shrieked as they dissipated. "The girl and I will take rear. We'll cover our flanks with turret and gunfire while I'll use the power of the Juggernaut to create shockwaves if too many get near."

"Sounds like a plan to me," Colt replied.

I couldn't help but think that there were so many things that could go wrong in a simple line formation while facing these many enemies. Though I suppose in any battle, a number of things could go south.

"Ahh!" Colt let out a ferocious yell as he struck one of the silhouettes. "Try to keep up, rook!"

I rolled my eyes in my helmet while shooting two that were getting close to him. "You might want to watch your sides, vet."

I heard him suck his teeth through his communicator.

"Enough, you two!" Rona said, spraying her turrets around the area. "How are you holding up back there, girl?"

"Uhm… I'll get back to you. We definitely need to pick up the pace, though, before we get—ahhh!"

At just that moment, I saw a possessed female bombrush Valeria behind us.

"No! Hold on!" Rona anxiously rushed over to her but was stopped in her tracks by more silhouettes. She was busy fighting them off with her gauntlets.

"Val!" I shouted. I ran back to her. Before the possessed female took her down, her foot got caught on a vine below. As she was going down, her foot looked like it went back in an unnatural position for a split second. I was praying that some of the material from the suit alleviated the pressure from the sudden shift in her ankle.

"You're breaking the formation!" Colt ranted behind me, swiping his sword at the enemies in front of him.

"The formation is already broken. One of us is down!" I shouted.

I hurried over to Valeria who was about to get hit by the possessed female. Colt trotted behind me, while Rona soloed the silhouettes around us by continuously spraying turret fire. Suddenly, I saw the possessed female put one of her hands up toward me. I remembered Leona's past battle with Harper when he was possessed and instinctively moved out of the way. Just as I recovered to see what was going on, Colt was a few feet in the air. The possessed female was controlling him with that same telekinetic ability Harper had.

"Balls! She has that ESP crap." Colt's body rapidly moved toward the possessed female's.

I dashed without her noticing. In the nick of time, I managed to slice part of her arm off with my shorthand saber equipped to the Equalizer. Colt used his propulsion in the air to capitalize on the opportunity with a decisive slash to her neck. Her head rolled over, and she was down. Rona immediately came over and stuck a flare to her Juggernaut suit to create a small field where the enemies couldn't infiltrate for a while. I wonder if other soldiers were implementing that tactic, too, after watching Chrissy on the replay feed during the battle to establish our base on Earth.

"You two aren't half bad when you're not squabbling like little boys," Rona said, catching her breath. "Stay close to me while we think of a way out of this."

We all retracted our faceplates.

I bent over to Valeria while in the small shield of light. "Are you okay?"

"Ugh…my leg!" she writhed in pain.

"Can you walk?" I tried to help her up only for her to sit right back down in agony.

"It hurts like hell," she yelped.

"Well, looks to me she can still move it, so it's not broken," Colt said, panting. "It must be a sprain."

"Fuck!" Rona exclaimed to the heavens, disappointed. "Give me a minute. I gotta think about our next move."

"I called it. I *knew* these two would be more trouble than they're worth."

Valeria and I glared at Colt. "Are you *seriously* trying to start crap right now?" I replied, infuriated.

"Rona and I *knew* you two would screw this up." Colt's face was pensive. "First, you use up all of our high-powered relic flares, and then she goes and hurts her ankle. We wanted better soldiers but *no*..." His sarcasm was deafening as he said "no." "Your *precious* commanders wouldn't have it. Now, look. We're handicapped!"

"Stop!" Valeria shrieked while in pain. "You're not helping the situation any more than we are."

"Oh, please. You have no right to talk, little girl. Who just saved your ass from being destroyed by that demonic bitch?"

"Shut up!" Rona shouted. "She's right, Colt. Look around us, would you?!"

We scanned the area, holding our breath. The only thing between us, and the swarm of silhouettes, glaring at us from a distance, was the small shield of light emitting from the flare on Rona's suit.

"Shit..." Colt uttered.

"Yeah," Rona replied. "This little spat you got going on isn't doing much."

"What do we do now?" I said. I tended to Valeria's leg, trying to keep it elevated and moving around some of the inner lining materials of her suit to give her ankle support.

Rona studied the drone overhead, still monitoring us. She then touched the side of her helmet to access her communicator. "Command, how long until reinforcements come?"

There was a short pause. "Commander Brauns just got word from the group coming to you that the ETA is a little over ten minutes," I heard Bridgett say.

"Damn it... This normal flare I started just has under five minutes left."

"We could run over to one of the high-powered ones the rook used to buy a little more time," Colt said.

"Too risky," I shot back. "The ambush got us off guard. I don't think any of us kept track of how long those flares have left. Plus, we've used a lot of our relic energy in our suits. We can't waste any more arbitrarily."

"I'm sorry, rook. When did you become squad leader?"

I grunted.

"Give it a rest, Colt," Rona quickly said. "He makes good points."

"Then what other option is there?" Colt shot back.

"You all could leave me."

All of us turned to Valeria, surprised after she suggested that.

"What on Earth are you talking about?" I asked, looking at her as if she was insane.

I could tell she noticed the concern on my face. "Listen, it only makes sense. There's no need to bring the whole team down just because of one squad member, right?"

"Don't think like that! No one has to die. We'll think of something."

"I'm with Xander on this one, girl," Rona chimed in. "There's no need to sacrifice yourself. It's my responsibility to get you all back to base safely."

Colt was uncharacteristically quiet, observing the situation.

Valeria scooched over and gave me a hug. "Tell Abuela, Miguel, Leona, and the others that I said thank you for everything. I know this is hard to accept, but do it for me, okay?" She released her hug and smiled as her eyes became watery.

Rona walked over, crouched down, and got into Valeria's face. "Stop talking like that, you hear? I'll find a way. Just give me a minute!"

I was speechless. I couldn't fathom what brought this on or why a girl her age was so ready to die without even getting a chance to live her life. But then it clicked. It was so obvious. I started to remember significant moments and what she said to me.

It's so hard... I'm sixteen, and I still feel like I need my big brother...

Even Hunter was able to fight for me and die here on the battlefield...

Without you, I would've joined Henry and Hunter on my own that day in my own way...

"You've been planning this from the very beginning, haven't you, Val?" Valeria, Rona, and Colt jerked their heads toward me as I spoke. "You didn't come along on this mission because you wanted me around for your first deployment. You came to say goodbye, didn't you?"

She looked away from my doting glare and couldn't say anything. To me, her silence said everything.

Oh, God, please let me get through to this girl, I prayed in my head.

"You've been having suicidal thoughts this whole time... What you're proposing to us may not be killing yourself per se, but it might as well be the same thing since you want us to leave you here to die."

"Is this true?" Rona's voice was laced with concern.

"You don't get it, Xander. I wake up every day and miss them. It's like I'm already dead! Please, just let me go in peace. I only want to see them again." Tears began to stream down Valeria's face.

"You're right. I can't possibly know how you're feeling, but giving up is never the answer. Henry and Hunter wouldn't want to see you again."

She looked up at me, almost surprised at what I said.

"Not like this."

Valeria looked away, ashamed. Though she didn't want to admit it, I could tell she knew I was right.

"Okay." Rona stood up. "Enough of this sob session. Time is running out, and we need a way to escape these things!"

"I have a plan. But it's going to take all of us doing our parts—playing our roles."

"Shut it!" she unexpectedly shrieked. Now, Valeria, Colt, and I fixed our gaze on Rona. "You still don't seem to get it, Xander. *I'm* the squad leader, not you!"

"I understand. But it doesn't mean we can't—"

"No!" She cut me off. "Before we were one base, people spoke about vessel 3 having the lowest number of soldiers all the time because of how much they contributed to the cause. Newsflash, they weren't the only vessel doing it! I practically carried vessel 8 who had the lowest morale out of any ship."

"I had no idea," I said in a low voice.

"Do you know what it's like to try and inspire a platoon? To encourage people who are so food deprived due to shortage that they can barely stand without feeling like they're about to faint? To be the last one standing on most missions only to tell their families their loved ones didn't make it?"

"I'm sorry, but—"

"No! You don't! So you all are going to follow my lead because, so help me God, no one is going to die again under my command."

"Rona! I had to stand idly by while her brother got punched through the chest by a crazed, possessed man." I pointed at Valeria.

Valeria looked toward me, surprised. I never did tell her the details of how Henry died.

"I know what it feels like to be helpless. I had to do it every day for months as my arm healed and soldiers were fighting battles I should've been in." I got right in her face and sympathized with her. "All of them, risking their lives for people like me who can't even do anything! So yeah, I get it. But you can't carry the team on your back. The only way we're doing this is together."

Rona grew silent. I could tell all of her anger and frustration came out of a place of love. She was just tired of losing people.

"Fine. We'll go with your plan," she managed to say. "But if everyone doesn't come out of this alive, Xander, then it's on you. You hear me?" She poked her finger to my chest. Sincerity and compassion filled her eyes.

I nodded.

"All right." Colt finally said something. "Let's end this drama scene then and get on with the details, shall we? You have the floor, rook."

"Thanks," I said sarcastically. "I'm sure you're all familiar with the Star of David."

"Yeah, Jewish symbol. What does that have to do with anything?"

"Well, it's also mistakably known as the Seal of Solomon because of their resembling features. It's actually its predecessor. It's a strong symbol because King Solomon built the First Temple of Jerusalem dedicated to God, and he was the last known king of a unified Israel."

"What's with the history lesson? We're on a clock," Rona said impatiently.

"Because these markings in our suits, preventing us from possession, are based on histories like this one. And if you've noticed, I shot six flares. Six points for—"

"A symbol," Valeria commented.

"Yes. With the books of research R&A made available to us, I learned that in western occultism, the Seal of Solomon is believed to trap and relinquish demons in the area of its casting."

"You want us to create a giant one right here," Rona realized.

I solemnly nodded.

"How are we going to do that?" I was startled Colt was actually paying attention, considering he was so dismissive to me this whole time.

"I'm glad you asked." I smirked at him. "You'll be the one actually drawing the symbol while we support you since your saber can cut through the ground. My shorthand saber is too short and inefficient to do the job."

"How can I help with my limited mobility?" Valeria asked.

"From the cliff we came down earlier. Your strength is shooting, which is also good because that sniper weapon was made to scope out enemies and target them from afar." I made a gesture with my finger to draw two shapes. "Also, as you know, the Seal of Solomon is a six-pointed star. The easiest way to draw it is by depicting a regular triangle and an upside down triangle overlapping one another. You'll be guiding Colt to the points from the cliff while attaching your relic flare to you so enemies won't be able to get close. And, Colt, you do the same while dragging the saber on the ground to draw lines. Then, you'll finish it with a circle enclosing the symbol."

"What about our roles?" Rona asked me.

"We're going to—"

Suddenly, we witnessed the silhouettes around us go to one spot, huddled together. It revealed ten possessed people surrounding us. Before we could even comment on what was happening, the silhouettes formed together into the dark giant shadow I saw way back on the feed during Leona's battle.

"What the…" Colt didn't know what to say and neither did any of us.

We looked on in awe as we saw two giant glowing eyes peer at us from up high. The dark giant outstretched its hand. The trees, vines, and branches around us shook. We all began to lose our balance as we felt the Earth quake beneath our feet.

This can't be happening, I thought. *Am I really going to die here? Is this how Leona loses me?*

CHAPTER 25

"**YOU HAVE GOT** to be kidding me…" Rona mumbled in disbelief.

"H-how is this possible?" Valeria asked in a panic.

All of us were holding onto the vines on the ground for dear life as the entire forest continued to shake. Luckily, the possessed people surrounding us kept their distance, although they were losing balance too. I hope they only had uncanny strength and not telekinesis, although the former wasn't that less to deal with. Considering the dark, giant shadow was using its ability on them too, these creatures didn't seem to care about their own. They truly were void of life.

"I'm not an expert, but R&A did say that these beings were negative energy to their core. When possessing people, they have a form. But without a form, they're just energy." I struggled, trying to keep my grip on the vine. I had no idea what that giant silhouette was doing. "What if they could amass into each other as one entity of that energy since they're technically not held back by the material world?"

"That's a cryptic thought," Colt replied.

"It's the only guess I got."

"I was there too," Valeria added. "R&A also mentioned that this thing was so powerful only a previous exo-suit model could take it down. It was the arc of something."

"The Arc Light." I saw Rona trying to access her communicator with one hand while the other was trying to stay steady to the ground. "It was a model that concentrated all the relic energy from the artifact powering it into one decisive beam. It used so much power that solar energy was needed as well. Flight was one of its capabilities to better absorb the solar rays in the atmosphere."

I passed her a questionable look, taken back that she knew that information. *She wasn't part of the old war, was she?* I thought.

"What? You're not the only one who's read some of R&A's archives, Xander."

"Touché," I replied.

"Command, come in! We need the visual the drone is picking up. What is that thing doing?"

"Do we have an Arc Light thing lying around we can use?" Colt asked rhetorically, while Rona was patching through to Command.

"I don't know how to say this, Squad Leader Rona," Bridgett sounded surprisingly sympathetic. "But that thing made the forest a floating landmass."

Valeria snapped her gaze over to me, full of worry.

"I'm sorry, Commander, but could you repeat that?" Rona frantically asked.

"That thing has you several feet in the sky! Unless you can find a way to damage it and retreat, this isn't boding well for any of you."

The communication cut out.

"Damn it!" Rona shouted. Suddenly, she let go of the vine and shot her turret at one of the giant's glowing eyes, enraged. "After all this crap we've been through, I'll be damned if I let it end here! This is only supposed to be a fucking recon mission!"

To our amazement, the giant silhouette was actually stunned. We felt the force of gravity as the landmass crashed hard back to its original position in the ground. The possessed people around us fell hard too.

"Well, Xander. It looks like we got our roles," Rona said, standing up.

"Yeah, we'll keep 'em busy down here while you two execute the original plan." I was trying to speak calmly as possible while my heart was nearly jumping out of my chest.

"Are you sure about this?" Valeria used her long sniper rifle like a crutch to stand and alleviate pressure from her sprained ankle. "Can the symbol we draw even work on whatever that thing is?"

"I'm with the girl on this one," Colt said. "Your plan accounted for the usual enemies, but none of us were expecting this."

"What choice do we have? If we don't do nothing we're dead." It was encouraging to see Rona on my side. "And I refuse to let anyone die today. Besides, the light on my relic flare is dimming. If we're going to do something, we need to do it now."

At that moment, an eerie chill ran up my spine as an inhuman, loud voice bellowed and echoed throughout the forest area.

"You all will fall!"

We froze in fear as we realized it came from the giant silhouette. It seemed to be holding its eye with its shadowy hand. A gust of unnatural force blew the wind right past us. It wasn't remotely human, but I knew a display of power when I saw it. It was merely flexing its strength, intimidating us. Negativity crept within the confines of our minds. None of us knew what to do or say. We were being taken over by doubt and fear. It's as if the air shifted. Whatever wisps of hope was there, started to fade into the darkness of this creature. Colt's words during the debrief floated around in my head. We really were fighting in the dark. However, a light touch on my arm allowed me to slowly turn my head and look hope in the face again. It was Valeria.

"You and Rona are right. We can't let each other die here if we want to move forward from all of this. But the only way we're going to have a chance of pulling this off is together." Her face became stern, but there was a blissful optimism to it. "It's what they would do." I knew she was talking about Henry and Hunter. It was unworldly—her change in her demeanor. Parts of the sun's rays broke through the canopy of the forest and shined on her. It's as if their spirits were with her. She put her faceplate on and immediately sniped two possessed people on the path back to the cliff directly in the head with finesse. "Let's do this!"

Rona smiled back at Valeria with a new sense of vigor. "Let's." Her faceplate retracted back on.

"That's the stuff, kid." Colt smirked, almost proudly. "We're gonna need that moxy." He put his faceplate back on.

There's that positivity I knew and we desperately needed right now, I thought. I let my fist out to her. She bumped it with hers as I uttered the words, "Together then." We nodded to each other, and I put my faceplate back on. She started limping her way toward the cliff. The eight remaining possessed people started running toward her.

I caught Colt's hand before he was about to throw his relic flare to stop them. "What's the big idea?" he asked.

"Look. She has her own," I said.

She started up toward the cliff as she stuck her relic flare to her suit to avoid enemy interference. Rona shot some still following her and aggroed the remaining around us so they could focus their attention to us.

"You're going to need yours for when you start running and drawing lines in the dirt with your saber," I continued.

"What do I do in the meantime?"

"Help us fend off these guys until she's in position." Rona was baiting them more to us by throwing some Earthly debris from the floor. "I've been using my relic energy more than you, guys. I need to save some for the big guy." She hid behind a tree out of the giant silhouette's line of sight. We followed suit.

"What are you thinking?" I asked.

"If you can get them here where I am, I can do a big shockwave and eliminate the negative energy within them, incapacitating them."

"Easier said than done," Colt remarked.

I nodded. "There's no guarantee that the giant is going to stay still either." Just then, I looked up, and an idea hit me. "Wait a minute! We're in a forest."

"Yeah, so?"

"Let's use it to our advantage."

Colt and I perched ourselves atop tree branches, praying that the thick ones we chose could support both our weight and the suit's. Rona stayed behind the same tree from before. I could tell her flare was dimming fast. I hoped Valeria's was staying up as she made her way to the cliff. I spotted one of the possessed people searching for me below.

Clink!

What I thought was an old bear trap actually snagged one of its legs. It began to make noise. I quickly shot my relic gun at its head. It went down before it could alert the others. Upon closer inspection, it was actually a somewhat new makeshift trap. But who could've possibly made that? We knew the demons had intelligence, but why would they need to build such a thing considering what they can do? *Could someone have recently made it? It wasn't possible, was it?* I thought.

"Seven," I said through the communicator to indicate how many were left.

"Six," Colt communicated a few moments later. I saw him drop down silently and stab his saber through another possessed person's neck.

I exhaled, realizing I was holding my breath the whole time. But then, I heard it.

EEEKKK!

I peered down at the one that was dead below me only to find another piercing its evil eyes straight through me.

"Shit!"

It rammed the tree trunk with its shoulder.

Crash!

To my dismay, the tree trunk actually gave way to its incredible strength. I jumped off just before it crashed onto the ground. It never ceased to amaze me how strong these things actually were. I immediately ran toward Rona's position. Colt wasn't too far away either as I saw two chasing him. I glanced behind me to find only three chasing me. *Where was the sixth one?* I thought.

Rumble! Rumble! Rumble!

I felt the quake of the giant silhouette's footsteps getting closer to us. There was no time to wait for the sixth. As soon as we got to Rona, she would have to do the shockwave. I saw her in my sights. She observed both of us. I could tell she figured out we were shorthanded.

"Is that all of them?" she asked.

"No, but just do it!" Colt exclaimed, panting.

"He's right! We'll have to worry about the straggler later." I felt a tug pull me back. One of them must've had telekinesis. I spun around and quickly sprayed some shots from my relic gun and the force let me go.

"These things are gaining on me. Do it now, Rona!" Colt was in full sprint toward her under the tree.

I mustered the rest of my stamina and dove toward her. The sound of anxious, monstrous stomps on the ground came toward us. Rona lifted her gauntlet and gave one decisive pound to the ground. The five possessed people that chased us were now incapacitated before us. I knelt before the trunk of the tree, trying to catch my breath. Colt leaned his back against it, exhausted.

"Ha…ha…ha…" I could hear his frantic breaths through the communicator.

Just then, the sixth one appeared from behind one of the trees next to us and lunged for Rona in an instant. She tried to equip her turrets, but I could tell she wasn't going to do it in time. The moment it was right in her face, a shot rang through the forest and just grazed Rona's helmet, piercing the tree. The sixth one was down. I could hardly make it out, but I followed the shot back to its origin through tiny cracks where the canopy's branches were touching each other.

"How on Earth did she scope that?" Colt asked.

"Commander Bridgett was right. She is one hell of a shot," Rona said, amazed. "Not only did she get the enemy but avoided hitting me too with such a narrow opening."

We barely made out Valeria waving on top of the cliff. She made it! The aura her flare made around her allowed us to spot her somewhat. It looked like she was taking a knee to relieve pressure off of her ankle some.

"Mira! Up here! Looks like y'all needed help," Valeria boasted through the communicator.

"Hehe…don't get cocky, girl." It was unreal to hear a slight chuckle from Rona, especially to Valeria. She's been antsy about this mission the whole time.

"Well, I hope you caught your breath." I shifted toward Colt. "Because she's about to run you wild."

"Heh… She wouldn't be the first girl in my life to do that," he joked, trying to prepare himself before he had to dash to draw the symbol on the ground.

Rona and I both peered over the sides of the trunk and saw that giant silhouette coming straight for us. My gaze then shifted toward her direction. We were right by each other. "Whenever you're ready, squad leader."

"Haaa…" I heard her exhale deeply through her communicator. She glanced at the level of her relic energy on her wrist. It was low. I glanced at mine. It was mid-low. Colt studied us too, realizing if we didn't pull this off, that was it. The mission would be over, and we'd be gone. She nodded to Colt, giving him the signal to proceed with the plan.

He attached his relic flare, our last one between us, to his suit. "On your mark, kid," he said to Valeria through the communicator.

"Roger that," Valeria responded. "Start heading to the relic flare emanating from the tree closest to you. You'll start drawing the lines from there."

Colt nodded to us and took off running toward the flares. I examined the flares around the area I shot before the mission even started, and they were dimming. It made me realize that Rona's flare was gone. It was all or nothing.

"Well, like Valeria said," Rona lastly focused her gaze on me and gave the signal. "Let's do this!"

We stepped out of the shadows from behind the tree and charged toward the giant silhouette.

"Did Rona just call me by my name?" Valeria asked in disbelief.

"Focus!" Rona, Colt, and I unexpectedly replied in unison.

"Right, my bad."

As Rona and I ran toward the danger, a force pushed us back, making it harder to approach. Branches and twigs from trees nearby snapped off from the sheer pressure of the wind.

Vwip!

"Argh!"

Valeria got us out of a tough spot again as she shot one of her other relic weapons equipped to her right in the giant's eye. Rona immediately followed up with turret fire to the same eye. Its giant hand drew closer to us. Now, the force of the unseen pressure was propelling us toward him again. I shot my relic gun at its hand, but it had no effect. Colt noticed and stopped drawing lines for a moment. He leapt on a branch and used the propulsion to get to its wrist. He slashed it, sinking deep into its shadow-like arm. It momentarily stopped its telekinetic ability as the semitransparent gash recovered its opaque darkness.

"Now we're even!" Colt exclaimed to me through the communicator after he landed. He went back to where he was and resumed drawing lines on the ground with Valeria's direction. I could hear her directing him through my communicator as well, but I had to focus too. I pushed it to the back of my train of thought as background noise.

"Thanks, but now what? It's not like I can slice through its neck like you did before," I replied.

"Grrr...."

A low, ominous grumble coming from it alerted us.

"I think all we managed to do was piss it off." Rona's voice exuded a slight tremble.

First, there was an unnerving silence for a few seconds. However, as Rona and I looked on, parts of its monstrous, dark figure separated into the regular silhouettes again. Now, we were faced with a small flock of the silhouettes as well as the giant. I swiped my shorthand saber and shot my relic gun to keep them off while they swiped at our suits. Colt was still able to run and continue drawing lines due to the relic flare still attached to him. For the silhouettes to be able to get that bold and close to him, even with the flare still active, showed me how desperate they were to get rid of us. As he was running between the trunks, I could tell the flares attached to the trees from before were losing its light. He must've noticed that too, which is why he was sprinting into high gear. He had to get this done before Valeria wasn't able to see them and direct him to the points he needed to make. I saw some go straight toward her. Luckily, she was the safest.

Behind her was the direction we came from with what looked like wardings on the trees, so I doubt any enemies would sneak behind her. Plus, her relic flare attached to her was still active, along with her impeccable aim. She was focused and doing the impossible by guiding Colt with her scope laser from the sniper in one hand and taking out silhouettes with her other relic gun on the other. However, I knew she couldn't keep that up for long.

"Shit! I'm out," Rona said as she shot the last turret fire her last drop of relic energy could muster.

"It's fine! I'm almost done," Colt said. I caught glimpses of him between the shrubbery from afar as he appeared to be making the enclosed circle to finish off the symbol.

"I can vouch for that," Valeria added. "It really does look like the Star of David from here, though I can barely make it out with the trees in the way."

"Get out, you two!" Colt was trying to speak while running in between pants. "You might've been a know-it-all so far, rook, but I don't think even you know how this seal is going to react once it's complete and this *thing* is in it. Assuming that your plan works, that is."

"You're right," I realized. Rona and I immediately hauled our asses and ran to the direction that led to the cliff above where Valeria was.

"What about you?" Rona asked Colt through communication while running beside me.

"Don't...don't worry about me." Colt's nonchalant attitude suddenly filled with sincerity. I could tell by the tone of his voice. "I'm not like all of you. I cared about no one. The amount of bodies I stepped on just to survive even sickens me sometimes..."

No one replied through communication for a moment, trying to digest what Colt was saying and what he was about to do. The silhouettes that were chasing us became part of the giant dark figure's body again. I noticed it eerily focused its attention solely on Colt. It must've known what the seal was when it saw the pattern the lines were in on the ground.

"I don't deserve to live like the rest of you." Colt was now speaking while wheezing and breathing heavily through the communicator. He was at his limit. "So let me do one goddamn thing with my miserable existence and allow all of you to get out of here in one piece."

"Colt! No!" Rona shouted.

We were able to make it halfway up the cliff. Valeria managed to limp to us the other half. I started to go back for him, but Rona and Valeria pulled me back as we saw the monstrous hand of the giant figure reach for Colt as he was enclosing the circle. Its humongous hand swiped at him but missed. The moment Colt was finished drawing the last stroke of the circle, debris from the giant's swipe flung toward his back. He was knocked down.

Suddenly, the lines in the ground making up the seal began to glow.

"Aaarrrgghhh!"

We were bewildered as the giant held itself and began to moan. It crouched over, almost human-like as if it was hurt. I shifted my attention back toward Colt. Luckily, he was outside of the seal's area of effect.

"Colt, get up!" I shouted through communication.

"I can't," he writhed in pain.

A change in the atmosphere set in again. Dread iced our veins as we saw the giant try to separate into many silhouettes again to escape the seal.

"You've gotta be shittin' me… There's no way we can get out of this one. We're spent," Rona said, defeated.

The warding behind us carved on the trees, I thought. But then it occurred to me we'd be leaving Colt behind. Just then, a miracle happened. I saw rays of shots from relic fire blanket the sky and pierce through the swarm of silhouettes. Soldiers emerged from the wooded area behind us.

"The reinforcements are here!" Valeria shouted excitedly.

"Well, I'll be… I can't believe it." Rona was stunned.

"We're here for extract, Command," one of them said.

The light emanating from the seal grew brighter.

"No. Colt is still down there!" I exclaimed. "I have to get him!" I jerked out of Rona's and Valeria's grip.

"Xander!" Valeria shrieked.

An intense flash of light shone from the seal, blinding the area with its radiance. It was as if everything came to a shrilling halt.

CHAPTER 26

"**CRAP! I'M JUST** getting static from video feed from the drone," Bridgett said through the communicator.

"Was the drone damaged during the battle? We've been trying audio feed for a bit now too, but no one is responding from their side," Brauns replied.

"Commanders, this is the head of the reinforcement unit. Do you copy?" a voice stated.

"Yes, Commander Brauns here!" Brauns sounded anxious. "What is the status of the squad you retrieved?"

"Yes, we're curious to know," Ambassador Judea added. A hint of sarcasm laced his words. Compared to Bridgett and Brauns who were hiding their distress to maintain their professional appearance, Judea didn't seem to care one way or the other.

"Two are injured and the other…" Static interfered with the signal.

"We couldn't make out that last part, soldier," Bridgett followed up. "What was that?"

It was as if I could feel their heartbeat from the other side of the line as the reinforcement head said, "The other two are fine. The mission was a success. We're heading back home now."

"Thank goodness—I mean ahem," Bridgett tried to cover up her worry and regain her composure with a cough. "Tell Rona's squad they did a fine job. We'll be waiting for your arrival."

"Subtle," Brauns sarcastically commented in a low voice.

Valeria laughed beside me. "She's always tried to sound tough when she was running vessel 3, but I annoyed her because I knew deep down she was a big softie."

"Your comms to our line are still open, you know," Bridgett shot back.

"S-sorry, ma'am," Valeria responded, embarrassed. She quickly cut the line off while using a stick to walk, taking some strain off of her injured ankle.

Rona shook her head and couldn't help but smile. We were listening to the whole status report through our communicators while walking. The reinforcements surrounded us, making sure we got back safely. All our faceplates were retracted as we spoke to one another. Colt was on my shoulders as I had to fireman carry him.

"I can't believe you did something so stupid and came back for me," Colt said right in my ear as his body dangled on top of me. Holding the weight of him and his suit was a bit harder than I thought. Lucky for me, his Infiltrator suit was the lightest model. I couldn't imagine what it would be like if he was wearing something like Rona's Juggernaut. "After that thing flung a chunk of dirt to my back, I felt a sharp pain in my spine. I couldn't move from the waist down and still can't. At that point, I knew I was dead weight."

"You were anything but dead weight," Valeria immediately pointed out. "A bit of a prick at first but far from dead weight." She smiled.

Colt sighed, reflecting the situation.

"You're right," Rona cut in. Her Juggernaut was riddled with scratches and damages. Come to think of it, my Equalizer might've been in worse shape. "We were both pricks to you. We thought you'd be the ones to be dead weight, but you ended up saving us..." She paused, trying to wrap her head around the series of events. "Especially you, Xander. Without your plan, we'd be... And the way you went around the symbol when it flashed to get Colt. It was lucky the light stopped after that giant, dark thing vanished."

"It left charred marks on the ground where Colt drew the lines in too, a permanent sigil. None of the remaining silhouettes would dare go near it either, but we were able to go past it just fine afterward." I stopped myself before I went on a rant into my own deep thoughts about the whole thing. "Anyways, what's important is that we all made it out under your command, right?"

Rona's eyes widened a bit, realizing those were the words she said to me when we were arguing. "Yeah..." Her eyes became hopeful. "It's crazy how this whole thing played out. I mean what are the odds of only four of us surviving an onslaught of those demonic monsters? After the immediate ambush, we should've been wiped out, but all of us had a role to play."

"What are you getting at, Rona?" Colt asked her while speaking right next to my ear.

"I was a skeptic. Even with everything going on, I refused to believe in a higher power because of the senseless slaughter around us. But now..." She looked up to the sky. The wind blew leaves around us as if God was responding to her newfound faith. "I don't know. What I do know is, something was watching over us today, I can't explain."

I smiled, touched by her optimism. The others grew quiet, not knowing what to think. I noticed Valeria turned away from us, almost ashamed. Rona took note of it too. I wondered if she was feeling guilty now after trying to die purposefully on the battlefield.

"You have faith, don't you, rook—I mean... Xander?" Colt asked. He stopped being an ass and called me by my name like Rona did before with Valeria. *Miracles keep happening today, don't they?* I thought. I turned my head to meet his face beside mine. It was weird talking to someone's face that was upside down with their body on your shoulders. "I could tell by the way you carry yourself."

I nodded, continuing to listen.

"Believers I met in the past were the first ones to go down during battles. I stepped on them too to get ahead and not die by the wayside." He was silent for a second. "Let me ask you, is this my repentance? After standing on so many bodies, is the man upstairs taking my legs away as punishment? I should feel sad knowing I could never walk again, but I'm just relieved I still have my life after looking for death."

Valeria honed in our conversation. I could tell she was sympathizing with him.

"Maybe it's because I feel like I deserve this," Colt continued. "What do you think? I do, don't I?"

I sighed, praying for the right words. "It's not my place to judge you nor what you did to survive. Heck, we're all clinging to life, hoping there's something better along the way. But you don't have to let your past define you. What you do from here on out is what matters."

"Heh… Not a bad pep talk," Colt remarked, half grinning.

"It shouldn't be much farther," one of the reinforcement soldiers said out loud.

"I'm surprised we haven't faced any enemy attacks," the head of the reinforcement unit said.

I'm not, I thought. We were still walking in the same wooded area with some of the hidden markings on the trees. Even if the others spotted them, I'm sure they would think it was only old etchings from people of the past. But from what I could tell from R&A's research so far, they were ancient symbols. Someone made these. The fact we haven't been attacked by demons proved they were, in fact, wardings. This, along with the makeshift trap from earlier, was too weird. Something fishy was definitely going on.

Valeria started walking closer to me. It looked like she wanted to say something.

"Let me carry him the rest of the way, Xander." Rona picked up on Valeria wanting to speak to me privately. "You two have pulled your weight enough. Besides, I have the Juggernaut suit. It's more fortified to do the heavy lifting." I nodded and slowly transitioned Colt from my shoulders to hers.

Colt laughed at himself, looking at Valeria as he did it. "Not dead weight my ass, kid."

Valeria smiled back awkwardly, not knowing what to say as he was literally being treated like dead weight, being carried from one person to the next. She didn't speak until Rona got the chance to go a little further up, away from us.

"So… I suppose you were right about me wanting to say good-bye to you today."

"Does that mean you want to talk about it?" I asked. The sound of leaves crunching at the bottom of our suits' soles filled some of the quiet pauses between us.

She stared down to the ground while walking with her stick in the Cavalry.

"You don't have to say anything if you don't want to. I can't pretend like I know what you're going through, but damn, you scared the crap out of me, Val."

"I know… I know… I'm sorry." She still couldn't look at me. "It's just I was so sure of myself, you know? I started thinking I was a coward because I didn't have the guts to take my own life myself."

My heart ached for her. To think she was in so much pain that her thoughts went to such dark places killed me inside.

"I saw this mission as the perfect opportunity to say bye to you and end this hurt I was feeling. Then the way you and the others wouldn't let me die sparked something in me." She took in a deep breath while continuing to walk and shifted her gaze toward me. "After the fight was over, I started thinking like Colt. Maybe letting me live was divine punishment for wanting to die in the first place."

"No matter what we go through, life isn't a curse. It's a gift." I narrowed my eyes at her sincerely.

"I know that now. After hearing you talk, I understand I've been letting my past weigh me down despite how hard I try to move past it."

"Don't be too hard on yourself. Change is a process."

"But it's been months, and I've still been feeling this way. Will it ever go away?"

"Holes that loved ones leave within you never go away. That pain is a part of you as pain is part of life. But the more you strive to walk forward, the more others can fill those holes along the way."

Valeria gave me a big smile. "Thanks, Xander. I really don't know what I would do if you weren't here."

"I wouldn't like to think about it."

She randomly poked me in my arm. Her perky enthusiasm reappeared like flicking on a switch. "Speaking of holes, wouldn't you have left a huge one in Leona if you ended up dying alongside Colt, risking your life for him?"

"Leona knows what type of person I am. She'd be stricken with grief, but she'd understand."

"Hmmm… I wonder about that." The way she said it made me kind of wonder too. "Psst…" She hissed in my ear.

"What?"

"Look what I found while we were walking." In her hand was an MP3 player that had a few scratches on it. "It even has a built-in speaker and has juice still! I'm totally smuggling this in and playing it at the base. You think it has reggaeton?"

"Woah… Weren't these pretty much obsolete once cell phones could store music? I can't believe you spotted this, with power still, no less."

"I know, and it's all mine!" she chippered.

She was excited, but I was dumbfounded. There was no way that device would still have power after all these years if it was deserted on the ground when the war began. The markings, the trap, and now the MP3 were all too coincidental to be random. All these clues lead to one thing. People were here. We all thought the remaining population were either killed by the demons or evacuated with us in the vessels all those years ago. Even Command iterated it as a fact while we were living in space. However, what I found contradicted that "fact" we were fed. It was a lie. There had to be survivors this whole time.

CHAPTER 27

WE WERE APPROACHING the force field. Guards within the vicinity and the reinforcement unit, alongside us, were shooting silhouettes and a few possessed people at the entrance. They protected our squad as we entered. It was like having our own personal escorts. Judea and Bridgett awaited our arrival. As we made our way back to base, I noticed Brauns was absent.

"Good work, all of you." Bridgett shook Rona's exo-suit hand and panned to all of us. "You see why we recruited who we did?"

"You took a gamble, ma'am. We nearly died." Rona was clearly exhausted and not in the mood for Bridgett's eccentric behavior.

"But you didn't, did you?" she said, rubbing it in.

Rona shook her head.

"On the contrary, our groupings are based on complicated algorithms to produce the optimal results for a mission," Judea interrupted.

Bridgett turned to him. She looked surprised.

"We're more than numbers for just your show, Ambassador," Colt said after Rona put him down to sit on a wooden platform.

"Clearly. Our results indicated you shouldn't have survived. However, we still would've got the intel we needed from the drone feed nevertheless."

Rona, Colt, Valeria, and I first exchanged glances and then shot furious glares at him.

"And you still had us out there?!" Rona shouted. "What's wrong with you?"

"What's wrong with *you*? You all forget your place. You're soldiers! At the end of the day, you protect the majority—always have." He couldn't contain his smug face. "You all know better that most wars require sacrifice. Your grouping had the highest probability of success to get the information we needed to keep seeing many tomorrows. Be proud, not angry!"

I saw Bridgett tense up, startled toward the ambassador's words. She seemed to want to object, but his rank in Command made her hold her tongue.

"Don't you dare tell me how to be! I can't feel my fucking legs!"

"Hey, Colt." Valeria knelt beside him. "Maybe this isn't the time to…you know…be you."

"What's he going to do? Numb my top half too?"

"Tch…" Judea actually chuckled at his comment. It made me sick. He pointed at some of the soldiers from the reinforcement unit. "Hey, you. Get him back to infirmary. He's served us well."

"Yes, sir," they said in unison.

Colt seethed in frustration. Rona was livid. I think Valeria was still trying to process the whole thing as was I.

"Ambassador." I eavesdropped on Bridgett talking to Judea in a low tone as they stepped to the side. "I wasn't aware we had algorithms choosing squads."

"Oh, of course," he replied simply. Bridgett seemed confused and disappointed. "What? You don't actually think we condoned you and Brauns's stunt by putting two rooks on a squad, did you? We only went along with it because the odds supported it. Everything is calculated and quantified."

Bridgett narrowed her eyes at him as he walked away. Rona relaxed some. It seemed to ease her worry knowing Bridgett was unaware of Command's tactics as well.

"I'm going to go to the deployment deck to take this suit off. Good work, you two. I literally couldn't have got through that mission without you," Rona said.

Valeria and I waved.

"Oh, and thank you."

"For what?" I asked. My faceplate was retracted.

"I've been wallowing in my own crap for so long, I forgot what hope felt like." Rona smiled before walking away.

I think what she said described all of us. Bridgett resonated with her words too. Suddenly, I saw Burrel, Maria, and Miguel walking toward us.

"Abuela!" Valeria said excitedly. However, the greeting wasn't mutual.

Slap!

Maria smacked Valeria right across the face. Bridgett and I looked on in shock. Burrel and Miguel scratched their head nervously.

"I tried to calm her down before we got here," Burrel said, leaning on his cane.

"Estas loca! How dare you scare me like that, Val? Don't you die on me too." I didn't know whether to be more shocked that Maria knew what Valeria did or that her English was getting better.

"How did you know, Abuela?" Valeria asked, as confused as we were.

"Oh, right," Bridgett said. "Your squad is one of the ones we forgot to inform. The drone following you around not only had audio and visual feed for us, but for monitors set up at the central hub station still being built."

"I do remember Imala saying way back how they were sharing all they knew, and even Arinya mentioned again how we were all in the same boat," I replied.

"Yeah, and to prove it is part of our transparency plan. Basically, you see what we see. We all need to trust each other, right?" It was visible she felt awkward saying that, considering the interaction that just happened between her and Judea. "Having people view the battles on the day we established the base had both a negative and positive effect. So we let the decision be yours. If it's too traumatic to watch, you don't have to, but if you want to see your loved one out on the battlefield, you're more than welcome."

"Thanks, Xander," Miguel said, tugging the arm of my exo-suit. "If Abuela and I didn't meet you that day, I'd probably not have a sister either." The realization crept in his eyes, filling it with sadness.

"Try not to think about it. Okay, Miguel?" I said, patting his head. "What's important is that she's here now."

He wiped his face, nodding.

"I'm so sorry, you guys," Valeria said, embracing them.

"Well, I'm taking my leave. You two keep training. I want to see great things from you." Bridgett started walking away toward another area of the base.

"Yes, ma'am!" Valeria and I shouted, watching her go.

"You mind if I steal Xander for a second?" Burrel asked, stepping closer to us.

Valeria shook her head while still embracing Maria and Miguel. Maria mouthed the words "thank you" to me while I stepped away with Burrel, but her demeanor to me seemed cold and unenthusiastic. She didn't even smile. I smiled anyway and waved them off.

"Not that I'm unhappy seeing you, Burrel, but if you all had access to view our battle, then I'd expect Leona would be running here worried out of her mind," I said after we got some distance. "What gives?"

"I asked Leona to meet you later as I had an important report to go over with you concerning Brauns. It wasn't a lie. Commander Brauns is absent for a reason. He told the ambassador he was called on another assignment, but it was a cover-up." Burrel got closer and spoke to me lower. "By the way, Leona didn't fight me on it. As a matter of fact, she seemed a bit moody. I know you came back in one piece, but we both saw you about to die on that feed. Did something happen between y'all?"

"Not that I know of." I took a mental note of what Valeria said to me about Leona on our way back here.

"Hm… Anyways, after observing your battle, he wants a private meeting with you with me accompanying you to talk about what really happened."

Anxiety ran through my veins. I wasn't sure how to feel. "Do I have a choice?"

"You always have a choice. If you're uneasy about it, I can make up an excuse."

"No, no… I trust you, Burrel. If there really is something else going on, then you're sticking your necks out for this." I exhaled. "I just hope our suspicions are worth the risk."

CHAPTER 28

BURREL AND I descended down a familiar pathway. The area was laced with metal panels and a metallic staircase that led down to a secluded spot.

"We're meeting in the old training spot on vessel 7, eh?" I asked as I walked down the stairs beside him. I was no longer in my exo-suit and had normal clothes on now.

"Heh…funny. Even after all the vessels landed here on base… after expanding our territory and resources on Earth, this is still the only safe place I can think of without eyes constantly watching our every move."

"I'm surprised the guard wasn't bribed by now and let others in."

"That's something else you can thank Commander Brauns for. I've been the only one with authorized access as long as no one else was around." Now I understood why the guard let him in so easily numerous times before. It was more than them being old war buddies. "You remember way back when I told you the mind was fragile, and I didn't want to tell you everything I knew yet?"

"Roughly."

"Well, things are picking up, and I don't know how much time we have left. We need as many allies as possible. Besides, you took the R&A forum pretty well."

"Uhm…okay, but so did everyone else. And time for what exactly?"

"Everything will make better sense soon."

We finally made our way to the spot. He took out a device from his pocket. It appeared to have a projector lens attached to it. He tossed it on the ground, and the lens ejected, pointed to the nearest wall, and emitted some type of holographic light. Suddenly, a light image of Brauns appeared along with Imala beside him. It looked like they were sitting down somewhere at another location on base. I always wondered why Imala was with Brauns, but there were too many mixed emotions within me to question it at that moment.

"No way… Is this hologram technology?"

"Holography, yes," Burrel answered.

"This is not a recording, is it? It's showing them in real time."

"You are correct, Xander," Imala's light image responded. I jumped back, startled. "Our apologies for meeting you under these circumstances. The commander's private quarters was the safest place we could think of to discuss certain matters with you without suspicion." Imala smiled as if everything was fine and not weird at all. I was still confused.

"I know when society was still intact that such a thing was in the works but not to this degree. They only showed stuff like this in movies. It's been an actual thing this whole time?"

"There's a lot those in power keep from those without," Brauns stated.

"You would know," I said sharply.

Imala's smile faded as everyone grew quiet. Burrel stood beside me, waiting for either Brauns or I to speak to clear the air.

"I'm sure you have a lot of questions, Williams. Go ahead and ask them."

"Okay. If you really are looking out for us, then why did you act like a prick at times?"

"I was doing what I had to do to keep up appearances."

"You sent me to die on my first deployment!" I exclaimed.

"Take it down a notch," Burrel said, touching my shoulder to calm me down. "The corridors echo, remember?"

"That wasn't entirely in my hands. You see, Command only gave me the authority to gather three soldiers that day."

I didn't know what to say. I started to realize the situation was more complex than I thought.

"The excavation team that picked up the signal for the mysterious relic with an infinite amount of energy was from vessel 3, Commander Bridgett's ship." Brauns folded his hands on the desk through the hologram. "However, they were spread thin and asked another ship to do reconnaissance, and, if possible retrieval. Command wanted to drop the discovery all together."

"What? But it was the first major discovery in a while that could turn the war in our favor," I said in disbelief.

"I thought it was odd as well. So I volunteered our vessel, vessel 7, to do it. Command was still adamant on dropping the finding, but I was persistent. A retrieval like this would've required more man power as there was no telling what way the mission would go, especially if the demons spotted the platoon digging an artifact with that much power. But I don't have to tell you that part."

I narrowed my eyes, reflecting that day and how the demons surrounded Henry, Joselyn, and I at the perfect time. Come to think of it, there was only one demon in that desert at first for miles. Even if the demon I slayed with the Infiltrator did shriek for backup, there's no way they would've come that fast unless they were already prepared for soldiers to arrive. The thought was mentioned before about them being tipped off. But was it really possible?

"But despite my efforts," Brauns continued, "they only gave me the green light to deploy three soldiers just to shut me up."

"Is this a joke? So the mission was hopeless from the very beginning?" My head was spinning.

"Unfortunately," Imala replied grimly.

"We were never supposed to retrieve it… And you knew that all along?"

"I didn't want to give up, so I did my job and made a tough call as commander. If there was even the slightest chance I could change all our fates, then it was worth the risk." Brauns's light image looked away to the corner of the screen for a moment, not wanting to look us in the eye.

"That's why you recruited Joselyn and Henry. They were potentially two of the best available on our ship at the time. But why choose me and not Leona or any adept soldier not on a mission at the time? Wouldn't it have been a better choice?"

"Like you said to me on that day, you were expendable. And at the time, we had a limited amount of suits. Anyone who had to power the excavation machine while piloting the Infiltrator was a sitting duck. I couldn't risk one of our best taking that role." He adjusted himself and briefly averted my gaze as if mustering up the fortitude to say his next words. My teeth grinded together. "Besides, you had the perfect motivation to get through it due to your relationship with Leona. I knew you'd fight tooth and nail to at least survive long enough to retrieve the relic."

I scowled at him. "Is there nothing you won't do to get a mission done? You manipulate people for your own ends. How are you different from the rest in Command?"

"Cold, I know. There's a lot of things I've done to ensure the survival of humanity I'm not proud of. Burrel can attest to that."

Burrel passed me a solemn nod.

"But I had limited options considering our enemy may be the very military that saved us from total extinction. I had to make the calls. From what I've seen, you're a reasonable man. I know you understand that, Williams."

I took a step away, infuriated. I could feel their eyes burning in the back of my head, concerned. As much as I hated to admit it, he was right. We were in an impossible situation. Who knows what type of decisions I would've made if I were in his shoes.

I turned back to him, distraught. I was leaning on a wall and crossed my arms. "The only reason I'm not storming off right now and relaying this secret meeting to officials is because of Burrel. I trust him. He's been there for me whenever I needed him."

"Yeah… He's done the same for me too." Brauns eyed Burrel for a second, appreciating him.

Burrel maintained his composure, but I knew he was grateful to be recognized by both of us.

"But what about you?" I followed up.

"What do you mean?"

"Why bring me into this fold? I'm not one of the adept soldiers, nor do I have any knowledge of the old war like Burrel does. So why me?"

"Ah…that's what you mean." Brauns tilted his head slightly to the side, looking away from me. "Well, Burrel trusts you…you show a lot of promise…you've pulled off feats in missions…" Suddenly, he exhaled and shook his head. "No, that's not it. You deserve the truth from me, not more lies like the higher-ups have been feeding you." He leaned in closer from his chair on the hologram. His change in demeanor made me want to listen more intently. "It's your eyes. It's you."

"I'm not sure I follow…"

"The moment you were surrounded by those demons on your first deployment, I expected you to fall, despite your strong desire to make it back to Leona. However, you showed me something else. I heard the audio from the communicator. It wasn't all about her or what was precious to you. You fought for a higher purpose—for everyone. Ever since then, whenever I see your eyes, you have the determination of someone that will fight the world if they had to, to do what's right."

Imala shifted her attention to Brauns beside her in the hologram. She seemed surprised by his sudden enthusiasm to share how he felt. Burrel was taken back by it too.

"Which is what I'm trying to do now, but my position has my hands tied. Alone, I have to make tough calls. But if I have more people I can trust, then I can share the burden, and those hard decisions may get a little easier. I'm trying to build that trust."

"Joselyn and Henry taught me what was really important that day through their actions." I shifted weight more to my other leg since the other one was feeling the pressure. I didn't get a chance to sit since my deployment. "Besides Burrel, Leona and I were pretty much loners. I was a stranger to my comrades. They didn't know me. Yet, they were willing to put their lives on the line, not for just people *they* cared about, but for others. I realized Leona and I weren't alone.

There were still good people among the survivors worth putting our necks out together for too."

"Are you implying you need to see action on my part for you to trust me? Is this private meeting not enough to convince you?"

"This could be a trap for all I know. You could be setting up false pretenses to lure people Command suspects not complying by their rules."

"Fair enough." He sighed. "I'll share this piece of information with you then. I'm sure Burrel has told you he's been my inside man for quite some time. He is one of the few people besides Imala I trust. Do you know why?"

I shook my head.

"Bring up the documents of the veterans from vessel 2, Imala, and explain."

Her light image hologram held up pictures of old war heroes. I've recognized some in passing before. "Being part of R&A has its perks, like inside information on confidential documents. Well, might as well call us by our original name R&D since we're able to develop things again. They didn't know I was capable of hacking this far into their database." She held up the pictures more so I could see. "These vets should have full recollection of their memories by now, but they don't. In fact, it's as if their original memories were distorted and only come in small fragments over long periods of time."

What she said hit me like a ton of bricks. It was the same way my memories have been coming in.

"We suspect Command did something to their minds while they were in stasis. It was fortunate I kept Burrel from experiencing the same fate that day, or he would've wounded up as another statistic," Brauns commented.

"How many times do you want me to say 'thank you'?" Burrel joked.

Brauns smirked.

I couldn't believe what I was hearing. If the military was truly capable of something like this, then we really were in trouble. Fighting among ourselves while fighting those monsters out there would get us all killed. If Brauns was telling the truth, unless we banned together and did something about it, then we'd succumb to the will of our opposers on both fronts. But what he said wasn't enough for me, not even having Burrel here to vouch for what he said. There had to be another way to validate his trust. I shifted my focus toward Imala.

"Imala, may I ask you why you joined Commander Brauns?"

Imala, Brauns, and Burrel exchanged glances. "Is that really important right now?" she asked, confused.

"I'm curious. I could be presuming too much, but from what I can tell about you, you seem like a reasonable person with a conscience."

She placed her hand on her opposing arm and avoided eye contact. It was as if she was consoling herself. "I don't like to talk about it, but do you recall the friend I mentioned during the R&D forum who's no longer with us?"

"Vaguely," I replied.

"Well, she was trying to convince me that certain details and missions Command was delegating on vessel I didn't add up. Being a part of the discoveries by being in the action was important to her because she was the type to analyze everything. Therefore, she was one of the few officials at the time who chose to fight on the battlefield more than develop and coordinate like us." She bit her lower lip, holding in her emotion. I think I saw it quiver a little, but it was unclear through the hologram. Brauns appeared sympathetic. "When she tried to confront an official about it, she passed away under mysterious circumstances. The military labeled her insane and said she committed suicide. But the strength in that woman was undeniable. The timing was too coincidental for Command not to have a hand in it. Brauns thought the same thing, and I've been working with him ever since."

"Everything is calculated and quantified," I responded, remembering Judea's words.

"Precisely!" Imala perhaps said that with more enthusiasm than she thought. She caught herself off guard but regained her composure. "You sense it too, don't you?"

"Yeah, I do. But those exact words were said by Ambassador Judea to Commander Bridgett when my squad returned from deployment a little while ago."

Brauns and Imala were taken back. Burrel perked up. "How bold of him to say," Brauns uttered. "It's like the higher-ups are not even trying to hide their intentions anymore. I've been trying to steadily open Bridgett's eyes to get her on our side, but she thinks it's nonsense. So I left it alone and decided it was something she needed to see for herself."

"You don't have to worry about that. I think her eyes are definitely open now. Ambassador Judea didn't have a shred of empathy as he told us our squad groupings were based on algorithms."

"Algorithms?!" Brauns shot up in surprise. Imala's eyes widened. "As if we were mere pawns?"

"Colt had a similar reaction while Judea smiled and ordered the reinforcement unit to take him to infirmary. I'm pretty sure Colt is most likely a paraplegic now. Judea said we had zero chance of surviving anyway. So the fact all of us made it back in one piece was a miracle in itself."

"How heartless…" Imala said, putting her hand over her mouth.

Brauns was baffled. "I can't believe this… So my efforts to get you a part of this mission were in vain. It was all part of their plan anyway."

Burrel stared down at the metallic floor, shaking his head. "Why, oh why, did Judea replace Heisen?"

"He was a good man," Imala added.

"Wait a sec… Was Heisen a part of this too?"

"Sort of," Brauns said to me. "Like Imala's friend, Heisen suspected Command was hiding something as well. Through other like-minded individuals I recruited, Heisen tried to reach out to me. Among them were guards, mostly vets, who were aware of their memory fragmentation, placed in key positions."

All of this is starting to add up, I thought. No wonder why Brauns and Imala looked more exhausted than most. They were working two jobs—their own and keeping tabs on everyone else.

"However, I suspect the officials accompanying him on vessel 6 probably caught him up to something, and therefore, he 'disappeared,'" he continued, using air quotes when he said the word *disappeared.*

"Are you saying he was the scapegoat for the Harper Walker incident and is now missing because the military *suspected* something, yet couldn't prove it?" I asked in disbelief.

"Politics, huh," Burrel said sarcastically. "You see why I hate it?"

"I fear they're acting no different than the government did," Imala commented.

"As bleak as things look, I can't say the mission was a complete loss." Brauns briefly scratched his nose. "Xander's squad did come back intact. Plus, you gave us a way to expand with less of a mortality rate."

"True." Some of Imala's anxiety was swept away as she relaxed some.

Burrel furrowed his brow.

"How do you figure?" I asked.

"I was right beside Bridgett before your mission concluded. The symbol you used to eradicate the giant demon was clever. We can use that concept with the original plan to create the hydro-powered dam and expand. We wouldn't need the relic with the infinite source of energy if we power our makeshift generators long enough for our soldiers to implement the sigil around the area, preventing those monsters from getting through. Also, during supply runs or other missions, squads can implement the sigils in other areas so that territory can't be inhabited by demons any longer."

"I see," I realized. "By drawing the seals during or after the missions we do, we'd be slowly expanding the areas we can move freely in, also expanding our reach and land."

Brauns and Imala smiled.

"Plus, we could use this tactic to steadily migrate our forces to the signal emanating the same energy frequency as the relic we use for base." Brauns started to sound more confident again.

"It'd open up a lot of possibilities for us," Imala added. I grinned, starting to feel good about our potential plan to take back our home. "We wanted to try out the seals in this manner before, but implementing it during battle was too risky. At the time, we had little soldiers as it was and still do. However, thanks to your efforts, Xander, we don't have to wonder if the seals would work over wide ranges anymore."

"You defeated one of those things without an Arc Light?" Burrel asked in disbelief.

I nodded proudly but tried to stay modest as I could.

"You really are a natural, son."

"Well, I was skeptical about implementing the idea at first, but what made me sure of it were markings my squad passed by in the woods."

"Markings?" Brauns questioned.

"Yeah, they were definitely manmade. Traveling through them protected us to and back from the location designated for the expedition." I stopped leaning against the wall and stepped closer to their hologram. "At first, I thought maybe they were just left by people in the past, but upon further examination, the etchings seemed somewhat fresh. There wasn't much weathering to indicate they were there for a long period of time."

"You think the demons made them personally? Why? They could've just ambushed Rona and your squad before you even found out they were intercepting our instruments." Brauns was perplexed, trying to make sense of it.

"No, you got it all wrong. The enemy didn't make it, nor do I completely believe it was the demons messing with our equipment." I paused, wondering if I should trust them enough to tell them what I discovered. The more I thought about it, the more my hands were tied. If I didn't choose which side to be on now, it'd come back to bite me sooner rather than later. I briefly looked over to Burrel. I can say without a doubt with all the advice and guidance he's given me, I had faith in him. And if he had faith in them, then it had to be enough— hopefully. "I thought it was crazy to think about at first, but I also spotted what I thought to be a bear trap while fighting some possessed enemies. Like the markings, it barely had wear and tear. Judging by its little rust and somewhat pristine state, it also couldn't have been too long since it was placed. If that wasn't enough, Valeria found an MP3 player nearly charged fully and still functional."

"It can't be," Burrel uttered, realizing what I was implying.

Imala exchanged glances with Brauns before stating, "You're saying there are survivors still on Earth, aren't you?"

Brauns stared at me intently.

"You both know something, don't you?" I realized.

Imala seemed like she wanted to say something, but she looked toward Brauns for approval. He nodded. "This is technically confidential information—well, pretty much everything we're speaking about has been confidential up to—"

"On with it, Imala," Brauns interrupted before she went on a rant.

"Right! Well, one of the things my friend confronted Command about that didn't add up were odd sightings some squad leaders would include in their reports after expeditions. Back when vessels were competing to get the most jobs done for extra supplies, ridiculous things were done to boost morale I know, but there was a time vessels 4 and 5 were neck and neck."

Burrel leaned into his cane, and I rubbed my chin as we both listened intently.

"She was in excavation and claimed soldiers at times saw a campfire smoldering or a personal belonging left behind, not integrated with the Earth like other old stuff. Reports from vessel 5 concluded similar events as well as others here and there. Command prohibited such reports and chalked it up to conspiracy. When she made a bigger deal about it, that's when she was labeled a nut, unfit for her position."

"I'm sorry that happened," Burrel said as he saw emotion exuding from her face from her lost friend.

"Me too," I added.

She gestured a "thanks" through her subtle yet solemn body behavior.

"It begs to question, though, if there really are people out there, how have they been able to survive this long? And if they are theoretically behind destroying our tools to survey the land, then why? Why block off communication from us if we could help them?" Brauns stated.

"I've been toying with those questions in my head too. Perhaps they use the markings or discoveries in an innovative way we never thought possible," I said.

"Markings on the trees used as wards certainly point to that," Imala commented.

"Exactly," I resumed. "And come to think of it, there were plenty of people around the world who did believe in demons and stories from theology wholeheartedly. And there were plenty of people who spoke out against an organized society ruled by government who only had their own interests instead of the people at heart. Perhaps they don't trust us. It's fair given that before stasis, there was a civil war, fighting back the government." I pointed to Burrel beside me with my thumb. "Heck, Burrel was part of that resistance."

"True," Burrel agreed. "They have a right not to trust us. I mean, look at us now. Even *we're* conspiring against the military as we speak."

"Point taken," Brauns replied.

"Speaking of trust," I said, "If you wanted to gain mine so badly, then why did you let Valeria tail me and put her in harm's way?"

The tension lines on Brauns's forehead creased as he narrowed his eyes to me. "Didn't you say before that Judea said this was all planned out anyway? Besides, Bridgett is the one who recommended her."

"Cut the bullshit, Commander!"

"I'd watch my tone if I were you, Williams," he glared.

"Hey!" I stomped my way inches from his hologram.

"Watch your step," Burrel warned as he put his hand on my chest to stop me before I accidentally stepped on the device. I briefly glanced down. I initially thought he was telling me to keep calm.

"You told me I deserved the truth!" I continued. "You have no idea what that girl has been through. I know how much pull you have even without the people you're rallying to oppose the military. Burrel told me how you were able to convince an official above the captain commander to put him on vessel 7 before they planned to wipe his mind. If you wanted it bad enough, Valeria wouldn't have been on the mission, or you would've at least found a way to delay the deployment until you could think of an excuse. So tell me why!"

Concern was plastered on Burrel's face. He probably didn't know the paternal-like affection I felt for Valeria was so strong. On second thought, looking back at the worry in his eyes as he stared at me and seeing as he's had my back this entire time, maybe he did. Brauns's holographic image sat there, pensive. Imala, being herself, awkwardly attempted a nervous smile to lighten the mood.

"With all due respect, Brauns, if he's going to be in on the fold with us, he deserves to know the reason behind your actions." Brauns glanced at Burrel, surprised. I guess Burrel was so grateful and loyal to Brauns this whole time that he didn't expect Burrel to be on my side about this. "We've been putting him through a lot without his awareness. We at least owe him that much. *You* owe him that much."

Brauns clasped his hands and let out a deep breath. "Fine, but you won't like what I have to say." I stood silent. "I not only assess a person's physical attributes on the battlefield, but their mental ones as well. The psychologists on board not only help people maintain their sanity through this chaos, but they also help commanders assess the logistics, capabilities, and outcomes of soldiers on a squad."

"What does this have to do with anything?" I asked.

Brauns put his hand up, gesturing for me to be patient. "Valeria is a naive kid who desperately clings to a male role model to fill the void her father left. First, Henry. Then, Hunter. And now, you. In the beginning, you acted like a loner, but deep down, you're an optimistic man who clings to his faith. The amount of people that have gravitated toward you is proof of that. But because of it, you always want to see the best in someone and save them even if it seems hopeless. The way you went out of your way for two strangers on your squad during your first deployment…" I gritted my teeth, knowing where he was going with this. "I thought, imagine if he was on a squad with a person he actually cared for. With that, I knew you'd come back alive to us during this mission and would go through hell, making sure she did too. Thus, ensuring the success of the reconnaissance and ensuring the safety of two soldiers, including you. You exceeded even my expectations and brought the whole squad back alive."

"You used the life of a kid to motivate me?" My anger was boiling. "And the eerie details you know about us… You spy on us too! How are you any different from Judea and the other higher-ups in Command or hell, even the government itself?!"

"Like I said to you the first time we came face-to-face, you knew what you signed up for when you accepted the stasis program. And like I stated before, my position requires me to make hard decisions I'm not proud of." He stood up from his chair and stared back at me with sincerity in his eyes. "You want to know the difference between myself and those with power? I use my influence *for* humanity's survival. They use their influence *against* humanity, for their own agendas. I assure you that you can trust me, Williams, because that is a line I will never cross!"

I scoffed at him. "And what if Valeria succumbed to possession because of the negativity inside her? What then?!"

"Actually," Imala butted in, "thanks to the contribution Leona gave us of Harper's possessed corpse, we've learned quite a bit. We initially thought possession was solely based on negative emotions since the demons feed on it. However, that's not the case. There have been tests coinciding with archives indicating that demons can even possess virgins or the pure-hearted. The person doesn't have to be completely malicious."

"So what, these monsters can either corrupt the innocent or guilty now?"

"Like the world we live in, it's not that black and white. Harper's case really was a rare one. It might be the case that the demon chooses who to inhabit based on its own preference alone."

"Is there not a common thread that links all the possessed people so far together?" Burrel asked.

"Afraid not."

"But these things feed on negativity without a doubt, so there has to be something negative about the person that makes them want to latch onto their body," Burrel followed up.

"Perhaps, but we don't have the time to talk about that right now," Brauns said, putting the discussion back on track.

"Okay, then. So who can I trust so that this secret resistance, or whatever we're calling this, is all on the same page?" I asked.

"Well, the guards Burrel speaks to are a no-brainer."

"Do they have that uhh…memory fragmentation?"

"The official name we're giving it is SMS—suppressed memory syndrome," Imala answered. "And yes, most of them. We would call them 'repressed' memories but seeing as the higher-ups most likely had a hand in it, 'suppressed' seems more appropriate."

"Okay, the guards with SMS. Who else?"

"Us four in this room, of course, as well as a number of adept soldiers and inhabitants. We steadily try to see who is trustworthy like Burrel has been doing with you."

I folded my arms and glanced over to Burrel. "Is that why you took a shine to me?"

He smiled as he said, "You know that wasn't the only reason."

"No bullshit, right?"

"Exactly. No bullshit." He gave me a look, knowing I was referring to what he said to me back in the mess hall before my first deployment.

"Come to think of it, Burrel, wouldn't Leona be one of those adept soldiers?" I then switched my gaze to Brauns. "If you wanted to motivate me, why didn't you have Leona go on the mission with me instead of Valeria?"

"She doesn't know everything," Burrel quickly replied.

"Why not?"

"I'm a little hesitant," Brauns interjected before Burrel could get a word out. "She was a soldier to begin with before all of this. I fear when it comes to you, she could be a liability."

"What do you mean?" I asked, perplexed.

"I think I can answer this one. Relationships aren't really your thing, Commander," Imala said. Brauns nodded for her to proceed. "Leona's track record is impressive, but as far as we can tell, her mental state was sporadic, for lack of better term, on Earth until she met you. She has seen a lot of bad things in her position. We only had mission reports to go on. Apparently, her performance was on the decline for a time when society was intact years ago. However, after she met you, it came back up."

"Okay, please put it in plain terms. What are you saying?"

"She might not want to admit it, but even now, as her memories are progressing, she's co-dependent on you as she was in the past. God forbid, if she died, you still have something to hold onto…your faith. However, if it were the other way around, we believe she would have a mental breakdown."

"This is ridiculous," I stated.

Burrel held my shoulder. "Xander, I didn't tell you this because I felt like it wasn't my business, but when she thought you weren't coming back from your first deployment, she was devastated. So much so that she caused that chaos in the mess hall that got people like Maria and Miguel on disciplinary action. It was my idea at first, but she took it to another level. She was hysterical. For a short period, she was out of her mind with grief until your pod came back to the deck." He looked at me, concerned.

"Come on! Seriously? If someone you loved died on you one day, you'd be out of your mind with grief too. Don't give me that crap."

Burrel, Brauns, and Imala avoided my gaze for a minute, reflecting on my words.

"Okay then, Williams. It's your call," Brauns said. "Do you believe we can fully trust Leona?"

"Ahhh!" Suddenly, I held my head in pain, falling to the ground. "Hey! Xander!" I heard Burrel shout before the room faded to black.

* * * * *

"Do you really think you can trust that woman, Leona?" I heard a familiar voice say in the darkness. I knew who it was, but for some reason, I couldn't place my finger on it.

I scanned the area and found myself in a kitchen. Everything was neat and tidy. A woman in the kitchen was cooking something on the stove, and the red light to the oven was on. The place smelled like heaven. I couldn't remember when I last smelled thyme, chopped onions, potatoes, olive oil, rosemary baked chicken, and other fixings she was whipping up. The aroma wafted up to my nose, making my mouth water and toes curl with just the thought of taking a bite. It was as if the crisis never existed. However, a burning sensation at the pit of my stomach washed away my hunger. I was angry, but I didn't know why.

Then, I realized I was in another memory flare as my lips moved and words came out of my mouth without me doing so. When I spoke, I instantly remembered who this woman was in my life. "Ma! I don't want to have this discussion again. She's a good person and hasn't done anything to make you think otherwise. You don't like her because she isn't Christian? It's the twenty-first century. Let it go!"

"That's not the reason, Xander!" she said, furiously mashing the potatoes.

"Then what is it? She's coming over in less than an hour." I leaned my bottom against the counter across from the island in the middle of the kitchen. "Is it the fact she's in the military? Because her service is almost up."

"It's part of it, but... You know what? You wouldn't understand." She plopped the bowl of mashed potatoes on the island and went to check on the chicken in the oven. "Just trust what I'm saying, okay?"

"'Trust what I'm saying?'" I repeated. "What am I supposed to do? Say, 'Hey, Leona, things are going great with us, but I have to break up with you due to my mom's silly women's intuition.'"

"It's not silly!" she exclaimed, putting on oven mitts with animal designs. She passed me a stern expression, but I couldn't take her seriously with those on.

"I beg to differ with those foxes on your hands you're using to fish out the chicken in the oven," I smirked.

She glanced at her fox design mitts and gave a sarcastic glare that replied "Haha" to my joke. She set the tray of chicken down on the counter, giving it some of her special seasoning.

I crossed my arms. "C'mon, Ma... What's really going on here? You can tell me."

She braced her hands on the edge of the island after she put the chicken back in the oven. "Hehe…" Her giggle tickled the air. I raised an eyebrow in question. "The Lord is working even when you think he isn't."

"What does that mean?"

"Do you know foxes are predators to chicken? And predators sneak up on prey when they least expect it. They do it because it's in their nature. They haven't been taught or shown another way. And foxes mangle the chicken after killing them and partially bury it sometimes." She paused, reflecting. "That's how my heart felt like after I was madly in love, and I don't want the same thing happening to you."

"That's a reach." I raised an eyebrow in question. "Are you actually comparing the relationship you had with Dad to Leona and me? That's ridiculous, Ma. It's not the same."

"In some ways it isn't, but in other ways it is."

"You can't be serious."

"I know it's hard to see when you're blinded by affection. Trust me, I know. But I see the way she looks at you. She tries to hide it and play it cool, but she admires you…idolizes you… It's like you're her world."

"Isn't that a good thing? I thought you'd be happy your son finally found a woman who truly cares for him."

"I thought so too when I was young, but too much of a good thing can become bad. We all have things to sort out on our own and our own journey to go through before we find peace. You were able to find that peace through God, Xander. That's why you can love without it being toxic in a relationship." She stepped closer to me. "But she's been through *a lot* in her life. She met you before she could sort out her own baggage she was carrying, and because of that, she sees *you* as her savior. She's a soldier for crying out loud who was an orphan as a kid! Think, son! It sounds romantic at first, but one person can't be your everything, or you start depending on them for everything."

"Is that the reason you're saying things between you and Dad got so bad?" I clenched my teeth. "You just loved each other *too* much?" I said it sarcastically.

"I don't want to get into this right now." She went back to checking on the food, deflecting.

"Where was the love when you cheated on him?" My anger was boiling to the surface again.

She stormed my way, holding a ladle to the broth she was making. The ladle waved in my face, expressing her gestures as she spoke to me. "I don't care how old you are. You have no right to speak to me that way. You hear me? I did my best to raise you and your brother, Sam."

"I raised Sam!" I yelled. She was taken back by the boom of my voice. "You and Dad were too busy pretending like everything was perfect, although your marriage was crumbling. Faking it in front of us didn't help either. It did more damage than good."

"Excuse me?" Her eyes narrowed, enraged by my outburst. "We put a roof over your head, clothes on your back, and supported Sam through college! I wonder to this day why you didn't follow in his footsteps."

I banged my hand on the counter behind me. She jumped up, startled. "Because I had to step up as a big brother and do your jobs!" I felt a refreshing release finally getting this off my chest. "When he got bullied in elementary, I walked him home while you both went to counseling. When he had trouble getting his first job, I was there to give him a recommendation to work where I was. I consoled him while you and Dad had your 'private' arguments about your finances and relationship behind closed doors, although we both heard. And granted, you both provided money for his tuition, but you weren't there when he was blowing the money on drugs due to his depression over your divorce. And you weren't there when his GPA dropped to a 1.89 his sophomore year. I was!" I narrowed my eyes at her. "I gave him extra cash because he didn't want you two to find out and put more stress on you. Hell, I even encouraged him to get his grades back up and graduate when no one else could!"

Her mouth was open in shock. "Well, I'm sorry I was *such* a bad parent to you." She looked away.

"Ma... You know I didn't mean—"

"Hush, boy! You've said your piece."

We stood in silence. She made her way to the dining room table in the next room over and sat down. I followed her, feeling guilty. I leaned my back against the wall on the opposite side of the table. The lights overhead from the ceiling fan dangled, as if highlighting our moment of truths.

"I guess your dad and I were so wrapped up in each other, we neglected our sons sometimes," she pondered. "But that's what I'm saying, love isn't selfish. And as long as she loves you as hard as she does, she'll block everything and everyone else out, unable to see her own faults." She sighed. "Like I did."

I took a seat in a chair near me. "Ma, I'm glad you got better and lean on the good book now more than ever. But sometimes, your love is smothering. It's like you're trying to make up for all the moments you weren't there. I appreciate you looking out for me, but if Leona really is the person you think she is, then you gotta let me see that for myself."

She shook her head. "Why is it so hard with you? Your brother listens to me, no questions asked. Now, he has a wife and a good career in LA. But you? You have so much potential, but you squander it, working a job that isolates you from most people—from the world. And why you turned down the management position is beyond me..."

"Ah, here we go." I rolled my eyes, leaning back in my chair.

"I'm serious, Xander." I refocused my attention to her. "You could use me and your dad as an excuse all you like, but you've had plenty opportunities to do more with your life. Now, you're a regular blue-collar worker who can do so much more. I'm glad you found God after your incident, but something is still holding you back." She tapped her finger on the table. "You'd think as your mother I'd know what it is... I mean, you came from my womb for goodness sake, but we couldn't be further apart. What is it? Why don't you want to do more?"

I stared down at the table, pondering the question. "I can't explain it well, but I feel like I'm meant to do something else other than be another productive member of society." I peered out the window beside us. "This world is so fake to me... Propaganda on the news... Food we eat laced with by-products in order to make the companies who sell them richer... How people are so vain on social media and think society revolves around them... Lack of loyalty in relationships..." I saw Mom hurt a little by the last one, although I didn't mean for it to be another shot at her. I let out a deep breath. She refocused on me intently. "I'm sick of it all. Sometimes I feel like the world needs a reset. Maybe then everyone will start to see what really matters in life...faith, hope, and love."

"Referencing Corinthians 13:13, huh?" She smiled. "Maybe now I'm starting to get you a little bit."

I smirked. "Sometimes I wonder if God chose Noah to build the ark because he was thinking the same thing as him."

Her eyes widened after I uttered those words. "I forget how deep you are at times. But not expressing those thoughts are what's making you alone and keeping you from others in the world. Don't be afraid to share your beliefs—this side of you! If you do, I guarantee good things and good people will come to you."

"That's why I'm with Leona. She's a loner, too, who understands and is tired of the fake things in this world. Believe it or not, Ma, she gets me."

She clasped her hands in a prayer and murmured something, looking up before turning back to me. "Listen, I'm not saying she's not meant to be with you. Contrary to what you might believe, I loved your dad very much, but he never got the chance to find himself and go through his own journey. Instead of becoming a part of each other's lives, we *were* each other's lives. We made mistakes and grew apart because of it. Your significant other should never replace your life, only become part of it. Until she finds her own solace, she'll only disappoint you, Xander, because she doesn't really know what love is yet."

"Now I'm the one not understanding you. I don't know what you mean, but let's just agree to disagree."

She sighed, defeated. "Why do I bother sometimes?"

Ring! Ring! Ring!

The sudden noise from my cell phone made us jump.

"Leona's ears are probably ringing from us talking about her so much, and she called to cancel this get-together," I teased.

"Oh, don't be so melodramatic. It's probably Sam calling. He should've been here already."

I picked up the phone only to hear frantic pants. "Hey, Xander. Tell Ma I'm running a little late. I'm in tow with the Mrs. right now."

"What's taking you so long? I wanted you here already so Leona can greet everyone when she pulls up."

"I'm sorry, but you know those articles I've been working on, covering important figures like celebrities and politicians?"

"Yeah."

"I've found a lot of dark crap connected to them, and I mean like dark-web dark, man."

"What do you mean?"

"What is he saying?" my mom asked, impatiently interrupting.

I waved her off, gesturing that I was trying to listen.

"These people are into some twisted shit..." I heard Sam say, speaking faster than his tongue could keep up. "Child abductions, pedophilia, trafficking, cannibalism, cults, rituals, mind control programs, media influence, propaganda—"

"Woah, woah, woah...slow down! How do you even know all this?" I asked.

"Okay. So other reputable sources spoke on these types of cases before, but it wasn't taken seriously due to payouts and lack of evidence. However, there has been one case made public that's opening Pandora's box to what these rich people are really doing behind the scenes." I heard a car door close in the background noise of his phone. "Apparently, there was this well-known accountant who dealt with these types of people's money. The guy had so much wealth, he bought his own island. Reports from witnesses and victims led police to believe suspicious activity was occurring on the private land. Guess what they found."

"What?" I asked, a little annoyed. I wasn't seeing what this had to do with him being late, but I was a bit interested.

"Evidence of trafficking underage girls. And it's not even scratching the surface. So many well-known figures are connected to this guy and into other sick stuff you wouldn't believe."

I rolled my eyes. "Stop with your crazy conspiracies and just get here, would you?"

"He's on again about that, huh?" my mom said, standing up from the dining room table.

I nodded, uninterested.

"Eh... There are some things you have too I wish your brother did, like your level head. I'm a check the food and set the table." She walked away from the dining room and back to the kitchen.

"You and Mom, I swear..." Sam replied, overhearing our mom talk about him. "Don't you still research messed-up things like this in our society as a hobby? Why is this so hard for you to believe?"

"I look up GMOs in foods, toxic wastes in our environment, political lies to keep the masses under control... Real stuff, Sam."

"This *is* real, Xander!" he blasted through the phone. I pulled my head away from it for a moment, startled. "The things I just said are part of those political lies. I was one of the reporters covering those stories and got suspended until further notice without pay."

"Really?" I said in disbelief.

"Yeah... We got some savings, but... I tell you, man, it was surreal. My boss was all gung ho about pushing these stories until some rigid guy in a black suit showed up. He looked important. Before I knew it, myself and the others in the department, ready to expose these people, were dismissed as if nothing happened."

I shifted uncomfortably in my seat, concerned. I was speechless on the other side of the phone, not knowing how to react as he continued talking.

"My boss has the other writers doing fluff pieces now, stroking the egos of celebs like you said on the Ferris wheel that time ago." He scoffed. I guessed due to the irony. "They control the media, man, while secretly promoting negative stuff like sexual perversion in shows, movies, and videos and other deviant behavior. It's laced in every aspect of our lives now. Magazines, pop culture, you name it." He cleared his throat, regaining his composure. "And it's being orchestrated within the very depths of our government and society by these 1 percent rich elitists. It's like they're purposely trying to make our world dark for some unknown goal. I know I sound crazy, but whether you believe me or not, Xander, I do know one thing for sure."

"And what's that?" I asked skeptically.

"Everything they're doing… *Everything* is connected."

* * * * *

I held my head in pain again. I opened my eyes to a white haze surrounding my vision. Burrel was standing over me, eyes full of worry. Brauns and Imala were perplexed, not knowing what was going on with me.

Why did I remember this specific moment of my past now? I thought to myself. *Was my subconscious trying to tell me something? Was Leona connected to whatever my brother was spouting?*

"What happened, Xander?" Burrel asked, helping me to my feet.

"I had a memory flare."

"A what?"

"It's what Miguel said people call it. Maybe he made it up."

"A memory flare… Your memory…" Imala's hologram uttered. "Wait… Holding your head in pain is the same symptom the vessel 2 vets experience during their SMS episodes. Don't tell me…"

"He has it too," Brauns said, finishing her sentence.

"But how?" It seemed Imala was as clueless as I was concerning my scattered memory.

"There's no way he could have it." Burrel let me stand on my own. "He doesn't have any military background. He was just your average joe."

Brauns rubbed his chin. "It would appear there's a deeper mystery going on here."

"How long has this been going on, Xander, and when does it occur?" Imala asked.

"Fragments have come steadily ever since I woke up from stasis, like my childhood and whatnot," I replied. "But I noticed if it deals with events even loosely related to Leona or the government, I have these...*episodes* like the one you just saw."

"It's a miracle it never happened on the field," Brauns commented.

"Would that make him compromised from going on further missions, Imala?" Burrel asked, concerned.

"It depends." She shifted her gaze to me again. "Is there a specific trigger for this that you can tell?"

I took a minute to ponder. "Well, with one I was talking to a kid named Miguel who told me about the backstory of Henry, his brother. It made me reminisce about mine, and the episode happened. With this one, you asked me a similar question my mother asked me in the past, and I blacked out to that moment."

"Could adrenaline suppress it or perhaps the release of endorphins? That could explain it. No—no, let's not get ahead of ourselves." Imala was thinking out loud and caught herself about to go on a rant again and stopped. "Let's take a step back. What was the question that triggered it, Xander?"

I remembered that it was the one about trusting Leona. However, I didn't want them to know. "I don't recall exactly," I lied. Besides, Leona has done nothing to prove otherwise.

Brauns, Imala, and Burrel passed each other uneasy glances.

"Hey," I continued. "I'm sure it's nothing."

"I think we should still take precautions," Brauns said. "Before going on missions, I'd like you to take a neuro suppressant. The last thing we need is for you to have one of these episodes while on the field. You've been lucky so far."

"Good idea, Commander," Imala answered.

"So what's the plan from here on out?" Burrel asked.

"We'll play it by ear while steadily expanding toward the strong signal emitted that's similar to the one holding our force field up on base," Brauns instructed. "Slowly incorporate people you can trust

100 percent and discuss it among us first. If there is even a sliver of doubt you feel for them, then keep silent."

"Then, I guess we keep our cool and pretend like the military isn't out to get us?" I asked.

"I think that'd be best." Imala smiled, trying to ease the tension we all felt.

Burrel took a deep breath and then exhaled. "I just hope we can keep our suspicions under wraps long enough before it implodes in our faces."

We all felt the gravity of those words as we prepared ourselves for what was to come.

CHAPTER 29

"**You sure she's** still over there?" I asked Burrel as we walked toward a construction site after concluding our discussion with Brauns and Imala. Part of it was built while other parts of it still needed work. The construction crew must've been done for the day as it was dusk, and we saw equipment lying around at a distance.

"Yeah. Leona said for us to meet her at the central hub station once we were finished with the meeting."

"Hmm… I wonder why she wants to meet here instead of a vessel or at our place."

"Beats me."

We walked a little further. Sounds from monitors perked our ears as we heard the effects of battles projecting from them. To think we had electricians awake from stasis, too, that could get this job done. I really wondered now what other type of things Command could be hiding. As we entered the building, a thick, concrete pole with a large diameter ran from the floor to the ceiling of the room. Monitors were placed all around its circumference from above. Some other people were around, witnessing the mayhem of other squads on expeditions. Though I understood the purpose of wanting to see your loved one make it out okay, it must've been torture constantly worrying if it was their moment to fall. The thought alone could kill anyone on the inside.

"Hey, slackers," Valeria said, waving and smiling wide. She was standing next to Leona who was staring at a monitor above. A brace supported her ankle where she got injured from our mission. It was odd. Usually, Leona's attention would be directed toward me first when I entered a room. But this time, she didn't pay me any mind.

"Don't let this cane fool you. I got enough fight in me to show you up and then some," Burrel teased, smiling.

"Right…" Valeria said sarcastically, nearly condescending. Only if she knew how right he was.

I went for a quick peck on Leona's lips, but she averted it by turning her head. The kiss, to my dismay, planted on her cheek instead. "Everything all right?" I asked.

"I'm fine. Just watching Joselyn," she said while continuing to stare at one of the monitors. She crossed her arms. I watched with her for a moment, wondering what this strange tension between us was.

"So how's your grandma doing?" Burrel asked Valeria.

"Well, after giving me an earful and nearly biting my head off, she calmed down." A nervous smile formed on Valeria's face. "How do you know her by the way? I know we've greeted you sometimes when Xander was around, but I don't remember you two really talking."

"Oh, it's nothing. I was with Leona watching you and Xander on the monitor. Your grandma and your little brother happened to run into us, watching you at the same time. Leona spoke to her more, of course, since they've met before. She also understands her a bit better than I can." Burrel scratched his head.

It must've been an awkward moment between the four of them trying to converse while watching Valeria and I risk our lives. I imagine Burrel had a hard time conversing with Maria, who barely knew English, and Miguel, who was less than three times his age. Leona must've been trying to act civil as possible while worrying about us.

Wait, could that be it? I thought.

While staring at the monitor with Leona, I noticed Joselyn's improvement. She was more proficient at combat and using the exo-suit than last time. Moments after, her squad leader called in for a retrieval after the mission's success.

"Wow, she's gotten good, hasn't she?" I asked Leona, trying to open up a conversation.

"Yeah, Leona told me a little bit about her while we were waiting for you two to get back," Valeria interjected. There's no way she was that clueless about social cues. "She kind of reminds me of Leona out there, seeing her in action."

"I agree. Plus, she's levelheaded and doesn't take any unnecessary risks," Leona said in an aggravated tone. She then glared directly at me.

Burrel gestured for Valeria to step closer to him. He could tell things were about to get heated.

"What's that supposed to mean?" I asked, confused. "Why are you acting weird?"

"Take a guess!" she shot back sharply. I've never seen her like this.

"Look, I know my mission must've been shaky at moments but—"

"Shaky?!" She scowled at me furiously as if I betrayed her or something. "The screen literally flashed! That was the scariest minute of my life—it felt like hours. Something that didn't have to happen in the first place if you didn't try so hard to be a damn hero!"

"Me?!" I fired back. "Last time I checked that thing inside Harper Walker is still here because of you. You could've ran away with Chrissy while her flare was still active, but you chose to stay and capture him."

"That's different!"

"How?"

"I've been a soldier for years, Xander! It's been my job."

"So you only do it because it's your duty?" I narrowed my eyes judgingly.

"That's not what I'm saying!" she yelled. Some people turned their heads. "I have more experience and a better chance to walk out of those situations alive. You, on the other hand... You're—"

"I'm what?" I cut her off.

Her chest was heaving in frustration, glaring back at me as she stood silent. Burrel and Valeria observed the situation nervously. Valeria, especially, was saddened.

"Go ahead. Say it! You think I can't hack it, right?" My blood started to boil as I started to think she didn't believe in me.

She turned away for a moment, holding her palm against her forehead, frustrated. "What I'm saying is…you're still new to this. Besides the supply runs, you've only been on two serious deployments, including today's where you were lucky to come back alive at all." She was inches away from my face, trying to penetrate me with those green eyes like she usually did. "When you went back for Colt, did you not think of me at all? I got us these wooden rings"—she raised her hand to my face, showing her ring—"to let you know *you* were my endgame if we survived all of this. How can that happen if you're just willing to lay down your life for anyone?! You must've known how that would make me feel."

I glanced toward Valeria and Burrel. I could see anxiety creep into Valeria as she started shifting uncomfortably. Her words, along with my mom's, echoed in my mind.

Speaking of holes, wouldn't you have left a huge one in Leona if you ended up dying alongside Colt…

She met you before she could sort out her own baggage she was carrying, and because of that, she sees you as her savior…

"Okay. Let's cool it. We've all had quite the day," Burrel said, trying to intervene. "Besides, it's best not to do this in front of the kid."

"You risked your life for others all the time even before you met me," I said to Leona, shrugging off Burrel. I had to see for myself. I had to see if their women's intuition was a thing. "I have to start somewhere, and we're both soldiers now. Don't forget! I was the one in the beginning after stasis staying behind and worrying about you too. But I knew it's what you *had* to do. So what makes what I do any different from what you do?"

"Ugh! Don't you get it?" Leona said, trying to keep her anger in check. "I can't…" She exhaled, struggling to get something off her chest. "I can't…"

I took her hands into mine, trying to console her thoughts. "You can't what, Leona?"

"I can't live without—"

"Stop!" Valeria shouted. Burrel, Leona, and I stared at her, surprised as well as some people nearby. She paused for a moment, perhaps startled she uttered anything at all. "Uhh... I'm sorry. It's just I've been through enough of this growing up... I..." She stopped, gathering her thoughts. Guilt riddled my core as I realized we must've brought up moments of her past from when her mom and dad argued. "Burrel's right. We're all stressed out right now, and we all need to chillax." She eyed all of us, regaining her composure. "Follow me. I kind of wanted to plan a little get-together anyway."

I let go of Leona's hands, and we both avoided each other, not knowing how to respond to Valeria nor the argument we just had. Burrel spotted our awkward behavior toward one another. He came over and put his arms around both of us.

"What could it hurt, you two? You both could take a load off."

I didn't respond, not knowing how to process what just happened. One minute we were fine, and the next, we were shouting in each other's faces. *Why is it like that with women?* I wondered.

"Sure..." Leona hesitantly uttered.

We walked in silence for a bit as Valeria led the way. I noticed that she didn't put much pressure on the leg with the brace while walking; to not further injure it. Construction was happening almost everywhere as far as my eye could see. The base was really picking up momentum. As I saw people roaming around and doing their part to make this area easier to live in, I caught a glimpse of a somewhat decent society again.

"Where are you taking us exactly?" Burrel curiously asked Valeria. I continued examining our surroundings. Something about it looked familiar.

"Don't worry. It's not too far. The spot is kind of sentimental to me." She briefly flashed Leona and me a smile. "I understand if Leona can't remember. She had just come from that crazy battle for our base. I think Xander would remember, though."

It hit me. "I thought I recognized some parts. This whole area is where we first met you, isn't it?"

"Wow…things really have changed, huh?" Leona muttered. She realized it might've been a window toward a conversation with me and immediately stopped talking, ignoring my passive glance.

I shrank on the inside. The situation was uncomfortable. Pretending to be cordial while there were things left unsaid wasn't my thing. It irritated me. We came to a building that looked refurbished. I could still see rusty metal pipes along the walls on the inside in contrast to the new ones installed. A tune engulfed the space we were in, encompassing us in a refreshing melody as we made our way further inside. We hadn't heard music in what seemed like ages. As I scanned the room to pinpoint the source of the sound, I spotted Maria and Miguel in the corner. Miguel was moving his hips to the song with a device in his hand. Maria was sitting on a wooden crate, clapping and tapping her foot.

"Miguel! No toques mi MP3." She nearly bulldozed Leona and me to get to her brother. I was surprised how fast she could move on that ankle when she really wanted to get somewhere. "You're going to break it." She took it from Miguel and examined it for damage. "Who showed you how to move like that anyway?"

"Abuela!" he said excitedly.

Maria giggled.

"Ah, you two are so embarrassing," Valeria said, putting her palm on her face.

A typical teen would say that, I thought. She'll reminisce about these moments and laugh, though, once she gets older. That is, considering if we all survive that long.

"It's so cool, Val! There's a bunch of songs to choose from. I can't believe you found it," Miguel said. I didn't notice it before, but he was getting a little taller. He was at the age where most experience a growth spurt.

"Yeah, yeah… I'm glad you had your fun. I'm turning this off to save battery. I don't know how I'm going to charge it yet."

"Loosen up," Maria said. Her English was slowly but surely improving.

"Really? After the crap you just gave me—"

"Unh ah! Cuida tu lenguaje."

"Sorry..." Valeria said in a low voice. I approached behind her with Burrel and Leona following. "Ugh...she's picking up on too many words. I can't even curse around her anymore," I heard her mutter.

"You curse around your grandma?" I asked.

"Oh!" Valeria was startled, not realizing I was so close behind her. "Pretend like you didn't hear that, okay?" She rubbed her head and gave a nervous grin.

Leona moved away from me and went toward Miguel and Maria, showering them with hugs. She was trying to avoid my company. Come to think of it, she was acting a bit curt with Valeria as well. It reminded me of how she was when we were first getting to know each other on vessel 7. She was close yet distant, keeping up emotional walls. *Could she still be harboring some resentment toward Valeria when she brushed her off when they first met?* I thought. Valeria was understandably upset. Leona couldn't still be carrying that. If so, women sure knew how to hold a grudge.

"Señor Burrel!" Maria waved at him happily. He was standing right next to me, but it was as if I didn't exist.

He returned the wave. "Burrel is fine." He took steady steps with his cane as he walked over, giving her a side hug.

"Gracias por consolarme mientras veía a Valeria arriesgar su vida," Maria replied.

Burrel was already looking toward Miguel to translate. "She said thank you for comforting me while my sister risked her life." Miguel reached out his arm to give Burrel a fist bump. Burrel smiled and returned it. It made me smile on the inside too.

"Oh, no problem at all," Burrel replied.

"No 'hello' for me, Maria?" I said, poking fun. Maria turned her head to the side and ignored me. I stared back, confused.

"Can you blame her?" Leona asked me, comforting Maria. "You two nearly died out there. Maria nearly lost another grandchild by having Valeria with you."

I was taken back. "Hey, I didn't expect her to be there in the first place. It's not my fault Val—" I stopped myself before placing the blame on Valeria. After all, she was just a kid who's been through a lot. It wasn't fair blaming me, but it wasn't fair for me to place it on her either. I glanced over to her for a second. "Never mind," I finished.

I sat on the floor, away from some of the group. Valeria looked uneasy and a bit guilty. Burrel walked over and sat beside me. Leona continued talking with Miguel and Maria.

"Don't take it too personal," Burrel whispered. "Anxiety is high, and they need someone to blame right now. None of this is your fault."

I saw Valeria eavesdropping on our conversation. She fidgeted her fingers as if pondering over something. The next thing I knew, she warily climbed some of the steps that ascended to the next floor.

"Where are you going?" Miguel asked, concerned.

"Nowhere. I just got something to get off my chest." She stopped atop one of the steps and eyed each of us with sincerity. "Ahem. Abuela, Miguel, and Xander can probably guess why this is my favorite hangout spot. But Burrel and Leona..." Each of them looked up as she said their name. "This is the spot Xander talked me out of my dark thoughts."

I gave a passing smirk, watching her full of humility.

"It was the corniest thing I ever heard." That spark of glee instantly turned to a frown as she continued to speak. What she said next embarrassed me. "He tried to bring up something from his past that related to what I was going through, but he couldn't even fully recall it." She let out a nervous giggle. Burrel chuckled. Leona and Maria stayed silent while Miguel snickered. "I didn't even know him...or you, Leona." She brought her attention to Leona. "But you both helped me. You were strangers. You even somehow reunited me with my family I searched months for..." She focused on Maria and Miguel tenderly for a moment.

I grinned, understanding what Valeria was doing. Leona stared at her pensively.

"I envied both of you. I could tell even then how much you cared for each other without you having to say it. You got to see each other...hold each other... It could've gone so differently like with me. I thought I was going to hold Hunter again, but..." She tried

312

not to choke up. "Anyway, I would've embraced him and wouldn't let go without a second thought. But you didn't." She focused on me, gripping the railing of the stairs. I could tell she was holding back a dam overflowing with emotion. "Leona came back fighting for her life, and Xander still came to check on me... I think I opened up to you that day on this roof"—she pointed above us—"because you reminded me of Hunter. It's something he would do. I'm sure you saw firsthand what type of person he was."

"Selfless," Leona replied, reflecting.

Valeria nodded. "Just like you both are. And if I could guess, you encouraged Xander to check on me because you already knew it would eat at him if it didn't." She panned over toward Maria and Miguel who Leona was standing beside. Leona was focused on her, surprised she knew.

"How did you know that, Val?"

"Because he's a good guy. I may be young, but I'm not stupid."

Leona snickered. Burrel and I cracked a smile. Maria was focused, trying to pick up on any phrases she could. Miguel continued looking up toward his big sister.

"No matter how much time passes, the younger generation is always watching us," Burrel muttered under his breath, staring at Miguel. I focused on him too. He peeped at us for a moment, wondering why we were focused on him. "They get wiser just by studying what we do." He brought his attention back to Valeria who spoke again.

"Though good people can get on our nerves, too, and can make us feel alone at times because of how selfless they can be for everyone else..." Valeria held herself as if she felt a cold touch saying it. "We love them all the more for it."

Leona bit her lower lip, not wanting to admit it to herself.

"It's because of that care that I'm here now. Xander saved me yet again today and the rest of our squad because that's just who he is. I'm not really sure what I'm trying to say... I kind of feel like Xander when he tried to speak to me the first time." She let out another nervous giggle.

It was silent for a moment as no one knew what to say. I couldn't exactly read her mind, but I suspected she was trying to return the favor of my help by getting Leona to talk to me again. I caught Leona stealing glances at me in the corner of my eye but didn't react. Just when I saw Valeria about to speak again to fill the uncomfortable silence, Burrel chimed in.

"I remember my first months on vessel 7." He quickly passed Valeria a look, saying "I got this." Valeria gave a slight nod and listened intently. "It was lonely… I woke up from one hell to find out I was in another one." We all focused on him. "Like most of us, still surviving on this godforsaken rock, I lost people dear to me. There was this hole that hurt worse than some of the chronic pain I felt." He rested his cane beside him. I imagine he was referring to pains he got from battles in the old war he was still keeping secret from the others. "Then, came along Xander. I had a nephew who…" Burrel stopped himself midsentence before giving away anymore of his past. "Well, that's not important, but I ended up talking to Xander because he was one of the few that understood the world we were in now."

Burrel averted our gaze as he shared. I didn't know about his nephew until now. I wondered if that was the real reason he took such a shine to me.

"Then I met Leona," he continued, "who I could tell thought the world of him." Leona flushed, trying to hide it. "Before I knew it, more people started gravitating toward them. And the more I was around them, the more the hole within me became a bit more bearable each day." I looked over to Maria. She seemed to understand that last part as I saw her steal a glance at me too. If I could take a guess, she was probably remembering all the times Leona and I checked in on them to see if Valeria was okay. "Anyways, that's all I'll open up about. I'm not good at these things."

Leona and I tittered at the same time. I recalled when Burrel used to sit alone when we ate in the mess hall, although he knew he could sit with Leona and I at any time. She probably was remembering something similar. Burrel could tell it was toward him and smirked at us. We caught each other staring at one another but didn't look away this time.

"Anyone else have anything to say?" Burrel asked the room.

"Yeah, I do. Why in the world are you all sitting in the dark?"

We all turned around, surprised at the refreshing voice and an unfamiliar racket that snuck up behind us.

"How in the hell did you find us here, woman?" Burrel said smugly.

Joselyn stood in the doorway with minor bandages and bruising. I could see one cut just below her knee with the pants she was wearing that was torn at the legs. She was dragging a barrel with her. Leona smiled, seeing her come in. I didn't even notice that dusk turned to dark so quickly.

"You're not the only crafty one here, old man," Joselyn teased. She brought the barrel to the middle and sparked a fire with two stones. Crafty she was. "To be honest, I just asked around. Some patrols and people at the hub station saw you walk this way. You're lucky the guards on duty don't care about people in construction sites much when the crew is off. If it was anyone directly in Command, they'd have a fit since there are no cameras installed yet to monitor our actions here."

"Won't this fire draw attention to us here or cause some type of hazard?" Leona asked, peering out one of the uninstalled windows, worried.

"Screw it. The worst thing they can do is tell us to go back to our quarters. People around here need to loosen up a little." She stood next to Leona, leaning her back against a wall.

"That's what I say," Maria uttered, still sporting some broken English. "Ella me gusta."

Valeria was now sitting on the stairs, rolling her eyes and shaking her head, letting out a cheeky grin. Miguel wasn't minding us anymore as he did shadow puppets on the wall, using the light the fire from the barrel casted. Burrel couldn't help but chuckle and do a facepalm. Examining the room and how everyone acted with one another, it was like we were a functioning dysfunctional family.

"Good to see you, Joss," I said, sitting Indian-style on the ground.

Leona smirked, noticing I adopted her nickname for her. "Yeah, how did the mission go?"

"Smooth," she said, crossing her arms. "Don't get me wrong. Fighting these monsters, demons, or whatever you want to call them, suck! But getting to stretch my legs again and actually do something after being in the infirmary for so long is such a relief." She looked up and back to me as if a weight came off her shoulders. "I was starting to feel like a shut in. No offense, Burrel." She looked over to Burrel teasingly and smiled.

He narrowed his eyes at her, amused. "None taken. If my next excavation project is assigned to your squad, I'll just make sure the location is crawling with enemies to give you more 'relief.'"

Joselyn laughed, along with Leona and Valeria.

I shook my head, grinning. "I hear ya," I said to Joselyn, picking up on her reply from Leona before. "It felt good to finally make a difference again." I caught a glimpse of Leona, resonating with my words.

"Yeah, I didn't know things would change this much after being on that deployment with you, Xander." Joselyn scanned everyone and focused back on me. "I was eavesdropping a little bit out there. And since we're doing this whole telling stories around the bonfire thing," she teased sarcastically while glancing toward Valeria who started it. "I got one." She eyed Leona empathetically and, if I didn't know any better, I'd say there was a glint of envy too. "When I woke from stasis, I didn't remember much, but for some reason, only God knows, my husband's death was still fresh in my mind."

Our smiles faded as we focused on her words intently.

"I was hysterical. The head shrinks calmed me down, and I tried to focus on training and the expeditions I went on. But it was like, I couldn't be free of that thought—I couldn't breathe from him unless I slept. It still haunts me even now."

I saw Leona sympathizing all too well with her words. The way she studied Joselyn as she spoke, I could tell losing me was her biggest fear.

"But then something caught my eye." She endearingly examined both Leona and me. "It was you two. The way you were with each other… I would walk around the vessel doing my own thing, and I would catch moments where I could tell the love you had was the love I lost." Leona and I took note of her envious eyes, understanding her pain. "In the beginning, I saw Xander waiting for Leona every time she was deployed, hoping she'd come back. I'd catch him in the training room, working to the bone, while I was walking by because I knew he wanted to be out there with her one day. On deployments I had before with Leona, I could tell she was fighting harder than most of us to get back to him. I even saw her sneak snacks sometimes for him so he wouldn't go hungry at night."

Leona and I passed each other tender looks, recalling what we did for each other. Valeria watched us, looking on earnestly.

"In the smallest ways possible they could, they watched each other's backs like my husband and I did for each other." She chortled as her eyes began to water. "So when I saw Xander's helpless eyes when he spoke to Commander Brauns and realized he was expendable, there was no way I was letting a love like that die again…" She wiped some tears away, regaining her composure. "Before I knew it, Xander was saving *me*. I blacked out and woke up in the infirmary where Leona checked on me whenever she could."

"It was the only way I knew how to say thank you at the time," Leona responded.

Joselyn crouched down and wrapped her arm around Leona who was next to Maria on the crate. Leona tried to shrink away from Joselyn's affection. Though she seemed mildly irritated and looked as if she wanted to say, "Get off me," I could tell she found comfort in it. "I know… You were a stern woman, Leona, and you still are on the battlefield. Showing any type of compassion to me, I think, was as much as a surprise to me as it was to you. It made me wonder how exactly Xander was able to crack such a hardened shell."

Leona was silent for a moment. Then, she startled me as she mustered up the courage to speak to me directly. "I thought I was alone. When they told me the world changed, I was hysterical at first, but I calmed down faster than most. From the bits of memory I still had, I could tell I was alone most of my life and fought to get anywhere. People came and went. So even as I regained my memories of being a childhood orphan who eventually joined the military, the world's state didn't mean much to me. It was just another fight I had to face."

Joselyn took her arm off Leona and touched her hand.

"Then Xander came. From what I could remember, guys I met betrayed my trust or wanted one thing." I saw Valeria and Joselyn relate to what she was saying. "So I stopped bothering with them. But Xander, being the person he is, came to me with such concern in his eyes for how dangerous the missions I was going on were. I thought it was some male chauvinistic crap…" She grinned. "But the more he pressed, saying we knew each other in the past, the more I recalled what we had. I got snippets and couldn't recollect memories entirely, but remembered the feeling… It was deeper than normal people dating… It was…*real*."

I smiled at her. "I think 'no bullshit' were your exact words."

"Yeah…" she said endearingly. "It was no bullshit. Everything felt natural as if I could do or say anything, and you wouldn't look at me any differently for it. Most guys would be intimidated by a woman who could take them out, but not you. You liked me all the more for it. Your compassion, your kindness, everything about you… It was foreign to me…" She smirked. "It still is, and it drives me crazy sometimes."

I couldn't explain it, but for some reason, the room felt warmer, and it wasn't due to the fire crackling from the barrel. Even Burrel's iced neutral expression to these sentimental moments broke some.

"Not to sound weird, but why are you like this, Xander?" Valeria questioned, descending down from the steps. "Who were you before all this? I don't think I ever asked you that."

"Come to think of it, neither have I," Burrel stated.

"I bet you worked for the police like Henry," Miguel said anxiously.

"Maybe or a firefighter, something to do with helping people, right?" Joselyn chimed in.

All eyes were on me now like I was some type of alien. Valeria's question reminded me of the time that dentist asked me in the bathroom before the speaker on vessel 7 interrupted us. The only one who didn't seem curious was Leona. Did she already know? I always wondered just how much of her memory returned.

I exhaled, looking down, ashamed. Then, I refocused on them again. "Don't mean to disappoint you. I know you're all looking for some exciting past I must've had, but I was boring like everyone else, blending into the background." Their ears perked up as I continued. "Believe it or not, I was just a warehouse worker."

They all looked at me, astonished.

"I know, boring, right? I wasn't exactly living off of check to check. I made enough money to save, but I wasn't going to live in the suburbs anytime soon." I chuckled to lighten the mood, but they all stared at me, confused.

"I don't get it," Burrel uttered. "You have rare qualities and so much potential. Why would you settle for something so average?"

"I was tired."

"Tired?" Josclyn asked.

Leona studied me keenly, as if understanding where I was coming from.

"Our world was descending into chaos long before these demons came. Children were missing every day, school shootings rose rapidly, people worshipped celebrities, and students ultimately went to college to work for corporations, making them richer. The less fortunate needed help, and all everyone could care about was working more and making more money."

Everyone was quiet.

"I was tired of it all. The way mainstream news ignored important issues to carry out someone else's agenda for advertising or propaganda... I thought the world was doomed anyway, and no one understood that. I was tired of how fake everything was and wanted something real. Until then, I wanted to be left alone, and the warehouse gave me a perfect opportunity for that." I cleared my throat. "I'd stack boxes on a barret, wrap it, and then go to the next order from morning to evening. No one bothered me."

"That is lonely," Valeria said, almost sounding sorry for me.

"It was..." I said, reminiscing. "Fortunately, from pieces I could remember, Leona understood where I was coming from, witnessing the horrors of this world better than most." I saw Leona reflecting what I said. "I can't remember exactly how yet, but by some miracle, we found each other before this whole war began."

"Huh… Not to get too personal, but there are still layers to each other both of you have yet to peel off. Am I right?" Joselyn said, being nosy.

"I guess you are," Leona said. A part of me worried about what that exactly meant.

"Anything else you recall?" Burrel asked curiously.

"My parents and my brother."

Leona widened her eyes, almost surprised. *Weird*, I thought.

"My parents disagreed about a lot of things, even my name." I scratched my face. "My mom wanted to call me Alexander for the biblical meaning. However, my dad thought it was too common and wanted me to stand out more from everyone else. Xander was the final verdict."

"One who assists men," Maria said out of nowhere. We were surprised she knew. "I research Bible names. It means that."

Valeria smiled as her grandma chimed in. "Suits you."

"I don't know about that," I replied. "My brother was trying to tell me about his crazy conspiracies happening smackdab where he was in Los Angeles, but I didn't listen." Regret filled my heart as some blurred memories of him became clearer as time went on. "Maybe if I didn't choose to seclude myself—maybe if I sought to get a job where I could make a difference like him, I could've done something to prevent the predicament we're in now."

"Like what?" Leona asked me. "You're only one person. You can't take on the world."

"I don't know…"

The room went quiet again. What I said made everyone reflect about the crisis we were in again. The only noise was coming from Miguel, making sound effects with his shadow puppets.

"Not alone anyway." Burrel smirked. I looked around, and so did everyone else, except for Leona. She appeared worried.

"Val! Let's put on some music. I'm bored," Miguel whined.

"Great idea!" she said excitedly. "I'll worry about charging this thing later." She whipped out her MP3 and put something on we could dance to. She scanned the room and could tell no one was in the mood. "Come on, guys. We do need to loosen up a little. We don't know what tomorrow is going to bring, right? We might as well live up today before it ends." She started moving her hips to the beat while being cautious with her ankle.

We watched as Valeria was dancing with Miguel. Miguel was wagging his bottom, off tempo, and just moving awkwardly. They lived it up.

"Ah, what the heck," Joselyn said. "Might as well enjoy this get-together before it gets shut down by some dutiful patrolman." She started synching her body with the melody. Her eyes shifted to Burrel. "Don't worry about 'getting up,' Burrel. We all know men your age have performance issues."

Leona's worried face nearly vanished as she covered her mouth to keep from laughing.

"Hey, I know my brother is too young to get that," Valeria said, cheeky and flustered, "but I'm not. Gross! Don't say that again."

"You know what?" Burrel said, getting worked up while grinning. "You got one more old joke, woman. I'm serious."

"Ooh, I'm scared," Joselyn teased.

Burrel joined the little dance floor they were making, but the most he did was tap his cane and occasionally attempted a two-step. He was so good at milking that "injured" leg. Even Maria joined, dancing along with Miguel.

I gazed at Leona. She gazed back at me. Seeing the people we brought together and how much they cared for us made everything else seem trivial. I walked over to her.

"You want to continue this little dance we have going on?" I let out my hand.

She smiled and took it. "I know you wanted a slower pace at first, but things picked up kind of fast, huh?"

"Yeah, if you told me we'd have wooden rings and our own place when we were in space on the ship, I would've called you a liar."

She rested her head on my chest and sighed as our feet went with the rhythm. "I'm sorry, Xander. I know you did nothing wrong. I just don't want to lose this."

I swung her around before embracing her again. "I'm sorry too. I didn't realize how upset you'd be."

We kissed and stared into each other's eyes again. This moment made me realize how important all the bonds we made were. That's why I decided to tell all of them about Brauns's suspicions afterward, including Leona. My mom, Brauns, Burrel, Imala, and other past occurrences that contradicted the Leona I saw now *had* to be wrong. I saw too much good in her for it to be bad for me. But I had to admit, something was different. It was her eyes. The forest-green irises that consoled me like before didn't have the same effect. For some reason, the connection—our souls weren't intertwined as before.

CHAPTER 30

IT FELT LIKE a pipedream at first, but there we were about to dance on the battlefield like we did in that building some time ago. To think, our numbers dwindled down to the hundreds while we survived off of rations in space. Now, we've reclaimed enough territory to start establishing the human race as a viable species again, although we were still endangered.

"Squad Leader Madigan. This is Control. Do you copy?"

"I copy, Arinya. Awaiting further instruction," Leona said as she spoke through the communicator in her exo-suit, the Juggernaut.

"Roger that. Your commander for this mission wants to say a few words."

"Understood."

"Madigan," I heard Brauns's voice boom. "You think you have an adequate line up?"

We had the faceplates of our exo-suits exposed. She smiled as we peered at Valeria who was confident and Joselyn beside her who was ready to go.

"I can't think of any other soldiers who would have my back more, sir."

A glint of pride swelled my face as I mouthed the words, "You got my back. I got yours." Leona couldn't hide her glee.

Brauns suspected there would be heavy fire, so this was less of a reconnaissance mission and more about, survival. We were knee deep in unknown territory since we've expanded. However, where the signal emanated for the powerful relic Brauns told us about in our little impromptu meeting with Burrel and Imala, was in an abandoned city. Some buildings were leaning against each other. Things like bags, a stroller on the sidewalk, jewelry, money, and other personal belongings were abandoned. It was hard to believe we cherished these material items. Now they meant nothing. We even saw colossal holes in the pavement where roads should've been. It made me wonder just how catastrophic the battle for Earth was, and we were the ones still fighting the war.

"Good," Brauns replied, snapping us out of our little sight-seeing. "Other soldiers have surrounded the perimeter and put up wards. Still be on guard. Darkness tends to slip between the tiniest cracks. I'm making sure our defense is airtight."

"They cover our sides, but we're exposed from above. Not to mention, the demons that could still be lurking within the perimeter," Leona said, concerned.

"I'm well aware of that, Madigan. However, our forces are spread thin. Though we're in a base not too far, about a third of our battalion alone is fighting to defend our other bases and your surrounding perimeter. Others are on supply runs or other expeditions, trying to expand." He paused, speaking to someone. I heard Imala's voice in the background but couldn't make out what she was saying. "Command might've given us the thumbs-up to pursue this signal, but they didn't give us a whole lot of support to do it. That's why you four are there."

"We understand, sir, but anything could be out here," I interjected. "Records show that this city was one of the hotspots where supernatural phenomena showed up the most."

"Williams, you're on this squad because of your sharp tact. Due to your innovation with the markings and your success on missions, we've been able to expand and reclaim more territory with a significantly less fatality rate. Your strategic disposition will be vital here."

"Understood." I exhaled, trying to remain calm in the Equalizer suit. "No pressure," I said under my breath. Leona took notice and briefly caressed my elbow.

"And like we discussed in the debriefing earlier, Madigan's track record of success and experience as a soldier is crucial in leading the helm of your squad," Brauns continued. "Fairbanks has improved significantly enough to do supply runs on her own if she had to. Her resourcefulness and adaptability will aid you greatly. Not to mention, Rosenburg has the sharpest aim among all of you as well as a natural instinct to detect where danger is."

I know what he was doing. It was pep talk, but it worked. All of us sported our suits with more confidence.

"You and Burrel have given me reason to rely on this party. You're the only ones I can trust to see this through. Understood?"

"Yes, sir!" we all said in unison over the communicator.

"Good luck!" we heard Burrel shout through the communicator as static indicated a channel change. Previous tech we had, such as our communication system, had become more efficient with a few tweaks and upgrades.

"Burrel?" Leona questioned. "Won't officials start asking why an excavator is on a command line?"

"Don't worry. Brauns has this on a private line. I'm back at our original base, working with R&D on something they're tinkering with."

"Manual labor?" Joselyn said. "Whatever you're assisting with, make sure it doesn't *tinker* with anything in your body, old man."

Valeria giggled, sporting the Cavalry suit.

"Ha-ha..." Burrel replied sarcastically. "Your old man jokes are played out woman."

"You would know," Joselyn teased.

"Hey, just in case I don't make it," I cut in. "I want you to know—"

"Save the dramatic speech for when you come back, okay?" Burrel said, avoiding the possibility we may very well die.

"I got you."

The channel switched back to Brauns. "Switching back to Control. Watch yourselves out there."

"Keep us posted on any changes to your situation." Arinya returned to our channel. "Oh, and Leona and Xander...be careful," she added. The anxiety in her voice as she said the last bit made me a little uneasy.

"Roger that, Arinya. Thank you," Leona replied.

The communicator went silent. And with that, we prepared ourselves for what lied ahead. Leona pointed her index and middle fingers to her eyes and then to the abandoned city we were walking into, signaling us to keep our eyes open.

We walked briefly in silence until Joselyn asked, "It's been a while since we were on the same squad, Xander. How does it feel?"

"How does what feel?"

"To be surrounded by two—" She paused and patted the head of Valeria's Cavalry suit. "I mean, three females who can knock you out?" She smiled, trying to lighten the mood.

Leona let out a chortle while Valeria grinned. I rolled my eyes. I did feel a little singled out since I was the only male on this squad. It made me wonder about capable guys like Evan. If he didn't switch over to excavation, would he have advanced like us too or be another casualty? Considering how much we've all been through, maybe I should just be thankful I was still alive and kicking.

"Make fun all you want, but don't forget who saved you on our deployment," I slyly retorted back.

Joselyn narrowed her eyes at me playfully, but I could tell she was annoyed.

"Okay, okay… Settle down, you two," Leona said dotingly.

Valeria adjusted her helmet as she spoke. "This is unreal. We're actually Beta soldiers now, and Leona and Joss are Alphas! I wish Henry could see me." She looked at me with pride but with a hint of worry at the same time. "I can't believe I'm with you, guys, especially after what Commander Brauns suspects. Do you really think Command could be our enemy like you said, Xander?"

"Shhh!" Joselyn put her finger to her lips. "Do you really want to take the chance of them hearing you over the communicator?"

"Don't worry. I turned it off for now," Leona said. I heard her humming a bit. She must've been more nervous than she was letting on.

I sighed. "I don't want to believe it either. But a while back, during that meeting I told you all about after you and I had that deployment," I said, motioning my finger between Valeria and me, "Commander Brauns was adamant. Him and Burrel alone brought up enough suspicion between the both of them to suede me, and that wasn't even counting Imala's or other people's accounts about Command's odd behavior at times."

"Potentially fighting two enemies on the same front would be like trying to look left and right at the same time," Leona said while observing the area in front of us.

"That's why you have comrades by you to watch the blind spots you couldn't otherwise," Joselyn assured. "Besides, who's to say the two enemies aren't one in the same?"

"The military working with demons?" I asked. "Why?"

"Why did the government work with demons and create this hell we're in now?" Valeria shot back rhetorically.

"Good point," I replied.

"Oh well, no use in speculating about something we don't know yet," Joselyn shrugged.

"Agreed," Leona said.

"By the way, you two must be psyched about finally being deployed together." Joselyn pointed to Leona and me. "You were getting antsy about one another being on the field so much. Now, you can finally breathe out here side by side, right?"

"It must be a relief," Valeria chimed in. "I wish I had that chance." I bet Hunter would've liked that chance too.

"The anxiety is still there," Leona replied. "After all, our lives are still on the line, but at least we can bear the burden together out here. Wouldn't you say, Xander?" Leona playfully elbowed me.

"Yeah, you're right," I said. "But this anticipation is killing me. These demons love negative energy, and we're in a city that's a breeding ground for it."

"What do you mean?" Valeria asked.

"Well, one of my hobbies when we still had a society and internet was looking up corrupt acts of our nation. These buildings were made on the graves of Native Americans, slaves, and colonialists.

They fought battles, fires, fevers, epidemics, hurricanes…you name it. If the odds weren't already stacked against us, the dark energy this place still has will certainly do it."

Valeria gulped nervously.

"Stop, Xander!" Joselyn exclaimed. "You tryna give the poor girl a panic attack?"

"I'm just stating the situation so we all know what we're prepared for."

"Shh!" Leona put her Juggernaut's fist in the air, gesturing for us to halt. She was looking at something on the upper story window of a building by us. I briefly equipped my faceplate and activated the magnification setting on my visor. Judging by its irregular movements, it appeared to be a demon, but it was wearing something familiar. It jerked its head toward our direction.

EEE—

Vwip!

Valeria sniped its head from a distance before it could finish its disturbing shriek. It fell out the window and crashed onto a car a few feet ahead of us. Control's drone, following us from above, uncamouflaged to get a better look at it.

"Is that a dated exo-suit?" Joselyn questioned.

"Control, you gettin' this?" Leona asked through the communicator.

"Yes," Arinya replied. "If I'm not mistaken, it's wearing a suit from the old war."

Our jaws dropped as we witnessed multiple eyes in the windows of buildings near us. Possessed demons broke through the frames. It was a mix of normal possessed civilians and those who inhabited old war veterans in their exo-suits. Shards of broken glass rained down on the pavement.

My heart began to race. "It's a good thing you sniped that guy." I briefly turned my attention toward Valeria before pressing the button for my faceplate to come on again. "We would've been walking in, surrounded."

"If silhouettes heard its abrupt cry, they shouldn't be far behind," Leona said, frantically arming her wrists with the mini turrets.

Valeria braced herself and put her faceplate on, although she was visibly anxious.

"Don't worry," Joselyn stated calmly. "Us three gals are more than enough to take this horde. Xander is just our tagalong."

Valeria laughed but with a bit of unease. Joselyn sounded a lot more confident than she was letting on. When I peered over, the same tense demeanor I saw from when I first deployed with her was riddled through her movements. Seeing that alone made me second guess this whole venture as my confidence faded. I'd found out later on, so did my faith in us.

CHAPTER 31

THE SILENT CALM before the storm was broken. A barrage of attacks scattered from our weapons as Leona and Joselyn equipped their faceplates. We spotted a small group of cars and immediately ducked behind them. Things already looked bleak, and we weren't even near the signal yet, according to its energy signature.

"Leona, be careful," Arinya said through communication. "Some of them are suited with the Barricade."

"The what?" Leona asked.

"It's a model from the old war. As you can imagine, there was civil unrest among different parts of the world when it was apparent these things manifested themselves inside human hosts. The military worked with police departments, supplying them with exo-suits that had shields."

Leona and I peered over the car and saw several possessed people with shields as large as the person's body. "Hence the name *Barricade*, I'm guessing," I commented.

"Correct. It sported not only a shield but a gun that took relic energy, of course, to take down the demons. However, its design is really meant for large crowds of those things. They were originally paired with Infiltrators. The shields side by side would create a barricade while the Infiltrator was able to sneak behind them and catch enemies off guard or enter vicinities by surprise."

"What are the chances the enemy could mimic our strategies?" Leona said, still peering behind the cars. Valeria and Joselyn were still shooting.

"I'd say pretty high, considering that we know they have intelligence."

"Shit…" Leona aimed her turret.

"What is it?" I asked.

"See for yourself."

I poked my head out again and saw Infiltrator suits peeking behind the gaps of the shields. Valeria and Joselyn were shooting at the possessed people around them. "You gotta be kidding me."

"Makes sense," Joselyn shouted over the relic shots. "You remember Harper, right? That demon had all of his thoughts and knowledge. It wouldn't be a stretch to say these things have the skills of those vets either."

"What's the plan, Leona, because we're looking kind of screwed here," Valeria said anxiously.

"Okay, listen up!" Leona shouted. "Valeria, some of these possessed people may have telekinesis. We can't rule that out. Prioritize your headshots to those who outstretch their hands. It's an obvious habit they have before doing it."

"Got it!"

"Plus, even if they are in suits, the electrical energy should be way past its use by now," I added. "Suits have a default function where the faceplate is retracted, and its locking mechanisms open when out of power. It's to prevent the pilot from being trapped and suffocated in it just in case."

"Good. That'll make my shots stick a heck of a lot easier," Valeria said, equipping the scope to her relic gun.

"Xander," Leona resumed. "You watch our flanks, and use that head of yours to scout out any weaknesses we can use against them."

"My pleasure," I replied.

"What about us?" Joselyn asked, pointing to herself and Leona.

"You stay close to me, Joss," Leona said. "Like Xander said, their suits' energy is long gone, so we don't have to worry about relic guns or saber swords from them. The suits need electrical energy for the relic energy to activate and the weapons to function. I'll get close and break their guard with the Juggernaut's impact. As soon as they're open, strike with your Equalizer."

"Understood," Joselyn nodded.

Leona and Joselyn waited for an opening before moving from behind the cars and into enemy fire. I caught sight of a possessed person trying to flank us. My aim improved significantly as it was down with one shot. I gestured my head for them to move forward as Valeria and I made an opening with the relentless shots we fired. Leona charged out first with Joselyn on her tail. Leona's Juggernaut was shielding Joselyn from random objects the possessed were throwing. Some had telekinesis and used it to hurl heavier objects like street sign poles and a fire hydrant at us. Some of the objects would've done serious damage. Ducking behind the cars was the only protection Valeria and I had against them. The Juggernaut was making leeway. One of the possessed saw it and outstretched its hand to manipulate her movements. Luckily, Valeria saw it and placed a direct shot in between its eyes.

"Good shot, Val," Leona said through the communicator as she swept the area with turret fire.

"Thanks, just doing what I can," she replied.

I needed to do what I could too. Right now we were in a tight spot. We needed to move forward, but more kept coming. There had to be more I could do than just shoot the ones trying to flank us. I had to think. While observing the area while still shooting at the enemy, I tried to find some solution to this situation. Even though Leona was getting close to the ones wearing the Barricade, we still had to push through this horde even if they put them down. But how in the world were we going to do that? After all, the relic energy supply was rerouted through our suits these past months for improved energy efficiency, but it didn't mean we had an infinite supply of it. We'd run out soon if we kept this pace. And it wasn't like I could draw a big symbol and make them vanish like last time. There were too many to implement a distraction for me to do it.

Think, Xander. Think! I thought.

Leona was right in front of one of the Barricade's shields. The possessed person tried to push her back, but she countered and pounded her gauntlet to the shield. The blow made it stumble back. Then, it hit me. The shield! Arinya mentioned they were originally used for large crowds of demons. However, how did normal shields push them back? It's not like regular objects could affect them. My eyes drew to the design that made up the shield's surface. Could it be some type of marking that affected them on contact? Only one way to find out.

"Val," I said, who was just a few feet by me behind the cars. She was still diligently taking out any suspecting demons powerful enough to do telekinetic abilities. "I don't mean to make you work overtime, but I saw you wield two relic weapons before without sacrificing accuracy."

"What do you need?" she asked, still focusing.

I peered over the hood of the car. One of the possessed in a Barricade veered away from the formation and was coming closer to try to flank us on my side. Leona and Joselyn were so focused on the ones in front of them, they didn't notice the other that split from the group.

"I may have a plan, but I need to test something first. Lay down some cover fire for me."

She nodded. "Be careful."

I took in a deep breath and exhaled sharply. Then, I went in full sprint toward the Barricade one near me. Valeria's shots whizzed by me as other possessed people tried to bombrush me. I could never get over how good of a marksman Valeria was. Anyone that came close to me, she took out with a headshot while still sniping the powerful ones. It let me get enough time to kick the Barricade's shield. The demon was knocked back. A possessed person right behind him, who was hiding from Valeria's shots, tried to pounce on me. However, I took out my relic gun and shot it point-blank in the chest. Before the demon in the Barricade had enough time to recover, I stabbed my relic saber into it. It yelped out in pain before its essence dissipated from the dead vessel of its human host. I pried the shield from the suit containing its corpse.

"Good!" I said to myself. "The shield isn't integrated with the suit. We can easily take it off."

"How is that good?" Leona asked, panting from fighting. I didn't realize my communicator was on.

"Yeah, it's not like we're strong enough to push them back," Joselyn added. "All these guys have insane strength."

"*Die!*" a possessed person groaned as it lunged toward me. I instinctively put the huge shield up to block. As soon as it made contact, the sound of skin synging hissed through the air. To my surprise, wisps of smoke emanated from the shield, and the now lifeless corpse of the demon that tried to attack me was on the ground.

Joselyn stared briefly in disbelief. "What did Xander just do?"

Leona tittered while holding back one with a Barricade. "He gave us a new game plan." She kicked the Barricade's shield, knocking it back. "Slip behind him, and take it!" she ordered Joselyn.

Joselyn shot a few enemies by her with the relic gun first to create some space for a moment. She then grabbed the wrist of the demon inside the Barricade and jerked its arm forward. Using the momentum of the tug, she managed to land the short relic saber between the crevice of the armor, piercing the skin. It cried out as its essence vanished from the human vessel. Using the hand still placed on the wrist, she yanked the shield from its grip before it fell to the pavement. A demon on her right tried to hit her with a powerful hook, but she put up her shield to block it. It also synged on contact.

"Woah," Valeria said through the communicator. "We can bombrush the enemies with these."

"My thoughts exactly," I replied. "We'll run through them like bulldozers until we reach the location of the energy signature."

"Then what are we waiting for?" Leona jerked a shield away from another Barricade and shot it point-blank in the face with her turret. She tossed the shield to Valeria still shooting behind the cars. Due to the large frame of the Juggernaut, she could pick up and heave heavier objects than we could. "Let's move!"

Valeria joined us on the frontlines, carrying the shield. I looked over to Leona who was panting more than us. She was doing most of the hand to hand combat since her suit was made to aggro enemies.

I could tell she needed a break. She picked up a shield too from one of the Barricades on the ground.

"Hey, Leona. Since you're carrying the most weight with the Juggernaut suit, stay behind us. Your suit is going to be the slowest when we sprint through these guys," I said, trying not to overstep her squad leader role.

Valeria touched her suit's shoulder. "Yeah, you kicked ass," she said in her usual mirthful way. "You're good at calling the shots."

Joselyn shot some enemies still coming toward us. "Yeah, you're not the only Alpha, you know. Take a breath. You'll think of something while I pick up your slack."

"Fine, guys! I can take a hint. I'll stay close behind and pace myself. But keep moving! There's no time to waste." I could tell she was a bit annoyed but appreciated our concern.

We all nodded in unison. I positioned myself front and center to make sure I protected Leona.

"Aww, look at him being all chivalrous," Joselyn pointed out, putting her shield up.

"It'd be cute if a small demon army wasn't around us," Valeria chipped in.

I felt my cheeks grow hot with embarrassment.

"Shut up, and stay on guard, you two!" Leona shouted, coming to my aid.

"Yes, ma'am!" Valeria and Joselyn straightened up quickly.

"Looks like Xander isn't the only one being protective," Joselyn commented in a low voice slyly. I might not have seen her face through her helmet, but Leona must've been blushing.

I headed the charge as we sprinted with our shields straight down the road. Leona stayed close behind me. Valeria was to the left of me while Joselyn was on the right. The three of us formed our own little barricade with our shields. Leona was tracking the location of the signal.

"It's just a little ways ahead. Keep pushing," Leona said.

As we made our way down the road, we had to outmaneuver some demons as they were cleverly trying to get around our guard. One tried to sideswipe Valeria, but she had another weapon cocked and ready on her wrist, blasting it away. A big possessed one tried to ram Joselyn's shield with a pole. She deflected the hit and stabbed it when it was staggered. Another tried to jump over my shield. I lifted my shield, and the top of it caught its neck. While it was startled by the pain, Leona shot it in the face with her turret. Its body synged down the shield. I pushed it off and kept going. Just when we thought we were making some leeway, we hit a literal roadblock.

"No way," Valeria said as we saw the huge hole in the ground up ahead. It was deep. It looked like something sunk a building as we saw rubble from its structure buried down beneath.

"Damn it!" Joselyn yelled. "What could cause a crater that big?"

"Probably those colossal silhouettes we've seen before," I answered.

EEEKKK!

"Shit! Speaking of silhouettes..." We all saw what Leona was looking at as a swarm of them were headed straight toward us.

We looked around and panicked as the possessed people began to surround us too. They were delaying their attack, as if savoring the moment.

"What do we do now?" Valeria asked anxiously.

Leona started to pull out a familiar device attached to her armor. "I really didn't want to use this now, but these relic flares may be our only option out of this mess until we reach the signal."

"But even when we reach it, these things will follow us. And the flares don't light forever. It's not like we can fight 'em all."

I heard the faint sound of Leona gritting her teeth through the communicator. Our hearts raced as we were running out of time and options. The horde of possessed and swarm of silhouettes were closing in on us. Just when Leona was about to activate the relic flare, one of the demons shrieked in pain and fell to the ground. Then another shriek was heard and another. We witnessed the possessed falling in groups around us. We began shooting at the silhouettes rushing toward us.

"What's happening to them?" Joselyn asked Leona.

"I don't know."

Then, we found the answer. People with strange tattoos, charms, and weapons in hand came out of the shadows around us. They were helping us fight back the enemy.

"No way," Valeria said in disbelief. "Who are they?"

My jaw dropped in my helmet. "It's them. It has to be... They're survivors!"

CHAPTER 32

I OBSERVED SOME of them while we were fighting the horde back. How did they survive this long, and how were they harming the demons? At first glance, I thought the tattoos were just that, but upon closer inspection, some of the designs looked familiar to me. They were markings. Using it the way they were on their bodies would keep them from being possessed as well as protect most from the demons' power. Strange charms were wrapped around their weapons that varied. I saw a woman carrying a makeshift wooden spear. A young man shot one of them in the head with a bow and arrow. Even a little girl hit one directly in the eye with a slingshot. Perhaps the most innovative ones were the blades and guns they used. Symbols were etched on the sides of their blades as they stabbed the demons. They dissipated the same way as we used our relic weapons. Some bullets littered near me. The craftsmanship didn't look manufactured. Symbols were etched on them. They were handmade. Finding the metal to melt these down into shots while trying not to be killed out here was a task in itself. I could tell by their weary, rugged states they had it even harder than us.

"So are we just going to keep fighting and pretend like people didn't come out of nowhere to help us?" Valeria asked, pushing some demons back with her shield.

"It's not like we can stop, Val," Leona answered, making an impact on the ground with her gauntlet. Silhouettes around her dissipated. "If we let up the pressure even for a second, we could die."

"We need some type of tactic." Joselyn was slashing and shooting any of those things that came her way. She planted her shield in between a thin crack on the road to be more on the offensive. "We'd die keeping this up, too, running out of power or stamina. Heck, maybe both." She started panting from exhaustion.

We found ourselves swiping at anything and everything that came toward us. The enemy pushed us back near the edge of the crater. Valeria and I peered down below to something unusual. There was a crane and debris from the collapsed building laid out in a pattern. Then, we heard the sounds of something spraying all around us. I looked up to see a few more survivors from the other side using spray cans like graffiti. It hit me. The pattern from the debris below was an alternate Seal of Solomon. The people spraying the graffiti were adding to the seal, making it wider. It was ingenious.

Grrr...

Suddenly, I heard a low, guttural sound near me. I instinctively moved out of the way. It was a demon trying to impale me with a sharp, metal object. When it missed, it went straight for Valeria. I was about to lunge to her, but another possessed person grabbed my shoulder. I swiped at its head with my short saber.

"Val!" Leona screamed. She immediately shielded Valeria with her Juggernaut. The demon managed to stick the object in between the crevice of her armor. She yelped in pain.

"Leona!" I shouted.

"Son of a bitch!" Joselyn said as she stabbed her saber into the demon that attacked.

Valeria stood there in her Cavalry in shock as Leona clenched her tight in fear. I knew she cared for her, but her reaction was so unexpected. Even some of the survivors looked on surprised.

"Are you two all right?" I asked, rushing over.

Leona immediately let go of her as if she did something she didn't want to, catching herself. "Uhh, yeah. Just a close call, that's all."

"Well, all of you, shape up." Joselyn got her relic gun ready. "More are coming."

Right when we were preparing ourselves for another round, we heard, "Move!"

"Away from the sigil!" a woman shouted from the top of her lungs. "It's almost done!"

I scanned the area and saw graffiti marks around us and where we were standing. We were so focused on staying alive we didn't even notice. Joselyn got the shield she stuck in the ground earlier. We followed her and ran in the survivors' direction, ramming oncoming demons with her shield. We were headed to a nearby building. Valeria and I assisted Leona, who was wounded. A flash of light from the sigil blanketed the area within its reach. All the surrounding demons, both the silhouettes and possessed, were gone. The only thing left were the burnt etchings from the markings the graffiti caused and lifeless bodies they inhabited.

"Is this run-down building secure?" Leona asked, taking a squat near the wall. She retracted her faceplate, and we followed in suit.

"She's 'bout secure as can be," a woman with blond hair and markings on her body said. Her country accent threw me off a little. However, we were down somewhere in the south, so it did make sense. She had on a stained tank top and ripped jeans. "Dis place is warded up real good. It's a safehouse before we get home down below."

"That's enough out of you, Maggie!" A man with stained teeth, a ripped shirt, and worn-down cargo pants came out from among the group. Some people were even wearing older versions of the exosuits. To think they had to fish out a dead corpse from it to put it on. We were a little over ten feet away from them and still smelled the culmination of their body odor. I wondered if some of these people still had their sanity being out here for so long. "What in the hell do you got our guys doin'? You know we don't fuck with military."

"It's Margaret to you, asshole," she said. "They were cornered, Chris!"

"Not our problem." His demeanor was stern. I noticed a cross dangling from his neck.

"What's with the stick up this guy?" Joselyn turned and asked while helping me put pressure on Leona's wound.

He stepped toward us. "Piss off, you traitor!"

Valeria stepped in front of Joselyn and us. She pointed her relic weapon at them. "Traitor? Look, we're grateful you helped us, but we didn't ask for this crap. We've done nothing to you."

"Aint that rich? Don't play dumb with me, sweetheart. You've only come for our supplies."

"Supplies? We didn't even know you all existed until this very moment," Joselyn replied. "Why would you save us in the first place just to have us sit through this shit?"

Chris eyed us, confused. "You didn't know people like us were alive?"

"I told you not all of the soldiers were the same," Margaret said.

"Hey!" I shouted. "I know there are a lot of unanswered questions here, but let's take a breath and prioritize." Leona's wound on the side of her torso had blood seeping out. "Do any of you have any kind of antiseptics?"

"Not here, but we salvaged quite a bit from where we stay."

"Don't you dare show these yellow bellies where we coop up!" Chris said, coming face-to-face with Margaret. Everyone among their group looked uneasy as if not knowing which one of them to agree with. Leona observed the situation while taking steady breaths, conserving her energy.

Smack!

Joselyn clasped her hands and rested them near her face, agitated. "Okay, we're clearly not getting anywhere here. So let's hear it! What's your deal?"

They were silent for a moment, contemplating whether they should speak or not. Chris veered toward Margaret. "You're the one being *Ms. Friendly* out here. You tell 'em!"

Margaret crossed her arms and gyrated her neck with attitude before replying, "She asked *you*."

Chris turned to Joselyn who raised an eyebrow, wondering if he was going to speak or not. All eyes were on him. "You seem to have a level head on your shoulders," he said, gesturing his head in my direction. "Tell me, why are you people here in the first place if you supposedly didn't know about us and our supplies?"

I was freaking out, holding the pressure more tightly around Leona's torso. Margaret took pity and tore off a piece of fabric from her tank top, showing scars from past battles on her abdomen. She handed it to me. Chris must've definitely been the leader of their little group as she stopped arguing with him and waited for my response. So did the others behind them. However, for her to have swayed the people to help us fight off those demons, means they must've respected her enough to go against his wishes, even if it was for but a moment.

"Fine, if it's the only way to get some help for her around here," I briefly looked at Leona. Perspiration clouded her face. She was fading bit by bit. "We have technology capable of tracking relics—old artifacts we use as energy in our suits."

"Yeah, we know how the energy is used," a teenage boy in the small crowd commented. "We've been surviving before your people left us in ships to head out in space."

"Left you?" Confusion plastered my face. "We were told the stasis program was voluntary."

The teenage boy was perplexed too. Chris and Margaret glanced at each other with unease.

"Keep talkin'," Margaret said.

"We got an order from our commander that a relic with unlimited energy was in this area. We've been trying to reclaim our world bit by bit from these monsters. But the world is big, and there's a lot of these things out here."

"Hmmm… We did find a pebble that was unusual." Margaret rubbed her chin. "No matter how hard we threw it, it didn't break, and we have a guy with us who used to be into petrology, the study of rocks basically. He said it could date back further than we could comprehend, yet there were no signs of erosion or wear."

"We can beat the bad ones with the pebble, Momma?" a little boy asked a woman beside him. He looked to be six or seven.

"Hush!" she replied, embracing him tightly to her. If the psyche of some of these adults were bad, I couldn't imagine what the children had to endure or learn in order to survive. Shielding their innocence must've been next to impossible dealing with a threat like this.

"Where is it?" I asked, continuing the discussion.

"In our bunker below," Margaret answered.

Bunker? I thought.

"That's most likely what we're looking for," Leona managed to say. Valeria nodded in agreement as she leaned against the wall.

Margaret seemed worried and spoke to Chris in a low voice. "We should tell 'em what we found wit' it, Chris. Some of these soldiers clearly don't know."

"Know what?" Valeria asked.

"Yeah, I'm curious," Joselyn added.

Chris hesitated, wondering if he should divulge their information. "Listen up 'cuz I'll only say this once. I don't trust the damn lot of you. Nearly a couple years back, we were rummagin' for supplies. This is after we fought like hell to avoid death from these monsters out here—after the military left us, that is."

Leona, Joselyn, Valeria, and I listened intently.

"We were out here bustin' our asses against these things, and as soon as we know it, a pod lands in the area." He gestured with his hands to show the pod landing. "Then these hotshots come out of it and clear the damn place of monsters, real stoic-like. We were psyched. We thought they came to save us. Then, just like that... bang!" He made a gun gesture with his hand pointed at us. "They turned their guns on us."

"Oh my God," Valeria uttered, shocked. "They stole your stuff instead of rescuing you?"

"Damn straight. The assholes called themselves Alphas. One guy looked me straight in the eye and said, 'This is survival of the fittest, and orders are orders.'"

Leona, Joselyn, Valeria, and I all passed each other uneasy glances.

"You two know anything about this?" I asked Joselyn and Leona, who I still held the pressure of the fabric on.

"Why ask us?" Joselyn said a bit defensively.

"You two were on deployments before I was when we woke from stasis."

Leona adjusted herself while she was sitting against the wall. "If it was a couple years back like he said, there were soldiers awakened before the rest of us in stasis. They were some of the best on Earth the military used to get necessary supplies now and again. It provided officials what they needed like food and resources to keep working until they found a way to turn the tide of war in our favor."

Joselyn and Valeria were startled. The others among the survivors' group didn't appear surprised.

"The military has possibly known about survivors for that long?" Joselyn questioned in disbelief.

"I did encounter signs of survivors on that mission a while back Valeria and I went on."

They raised an eyebrow to me in question, especially Valeria. "You suspected it this long and didn't tell us?" she said. "What else is everyone hiding from us?"

"You did sound like you expected it when we first encountered them. I'm with Val on this one, Xander. Come on, like what the hell?" Joselyn commented.

"It was the only thing about this mission Brauns has us going on that I left out. I had to be sure." I felt their ridicule through their stares. "I spotted it north from here in the woods."

Valeria crossed her arms, a bit upset with me. Joselyn seemed to understand a bit more. Leona didn't seem to mind one way or the other. Perhaps it was the pain, or she was simply used to sudden intel on the spot as a soldier. Who knows?

"That sounds like Slick's group," a girl from the small crowd said. I think she was the same one who used slingshots against the demons—such brave children.

"Mmm, mhm," Margaret nodded. "We don't know his real name, but we trade with him sometimes. His group grows vegetation out there. The name Slick caught on since he always escapes danger by the skin of his teeth."

"Last time we spoke to him, he said he had to move." Chris still eyed us suspiciously. "Said the military was building a dam or whatnot near his spot."

Valeria and I exchanged glances. Some unanswered questions were coming together.

"Wait," Valeria intervened. "Trade? Our world is taken over by monsters! Why aren't you working with them? There's no way you can keep existing in small groups like this. Who knows how many other survivors are out there. We're in an organized military and *still* struggling to stay alive."

Chris chuckled. I noticed him caress his cross, reflecting. "You must be naive, girl. You know how many people we lost, trying to convince others of the same thing?" His eyes suddenly grew cold. "Even in a crisis, people are selfish as hell. Like your Alpha boy said, 'survival of the fittest,' right?"

Valeria averted her gaze from him and crossed her arms, not knowing how to retort back.

"I'm curious," I said, changing the subject. "What could you even trade or have after living in an abandoned city for years?"

It looked like Margaret wanted to say something or show us where they hid out, but Chris held her back. "We ain't tellin' you nothin'. So you can go on and get where you came from."

"Ahh…" Leona groaned in pain. Her injury was getting worse.

"Look, I can tell you still have faith, right?" I asked.

He looked down at his cross, tucking it back into his shirt and then focused back to me, not saying a word.

"I have faith too. Believe me when I say we're not trying to steal from you. We've been using unique relics as weapons and protection against the enemy just like you use those markings on your bodies and equipment." They seemed surprised I knew what their tattoos and etchings were for. "I'm sorry for what those soldiers did to you in the past, I am. But I'm telling you right now, we are on the same side." I motioned back and forth with my free hand. "If you have what we need, then please, help us!"

Chris pondered for a moment. The rest of the group looked on in anticipation. "So you really didn't know the stasis program wasn't voluntary?"

I shook my head.

"I remember it like it was yesterday. They coerced people who they thought would comply with their rules and pretended like they had an option." He snickered smugly. "They came as saviors from our government. But for us, people who were already aware of how corrupt they were, well…" He raised his hands and scanned the room as well as the doorless frame to the outside, desolate city. "Let us all be damned." He sighed. "Fine. I'll get your artifact, and we'll stitch her up too. But that's it, you hear me?"

Valeria, Joselyn, and I nodded in agreement.

Leona accessed her communicator. "Control, patch me through to Commander Brauns."

"Copy that. One second," Arinya said through our communicators. I heard a brief static sound.

"Brauns here," he said.

"Did you get all that?" Leona asked.

"Unfortunately."

"Don't beat around the bush with us," I said sternly. "Did you know about all this?"

"Like I said before in our meeting back then, I won't lie to you, not anymore." There was a brief pause. "I strongly suspected it."

"Oh, God…" I heard Joselyn say under her breath. The survivors could overhear our conversation through our communicators. Valeria and her stared at the floor, ashamed. These people had every right to distrust us, the military—the same pricks in charge we were still working with.

"But like you said, Xander, I had to know for sure. I couldn't act on my suspicions without being certain. Now that we know, we need to do everything in our power to help these people."

The survivors heard Brauns. Some of them looked skeptical, others relieved, especially Margaret. I saw a glint of hope in her eyes. Chris noticed her expression too, but he remained neutral. He almost looked concerned, not wanting her or the others to get their hopes up.

Suddenly, a blast of static interrupted our connection with Brauns. We placed our hands against our exo-suit helmets in slight pain. My ears began ringing.

We heard someone else on the other end. "Ah… It's unfortunate you all heard that tidbit of information." His voice sounded familiar.

"Isn't this that Judea guy?" Valeria asked.

"Ah, shit…" Leona said. She took the words right out of my mouth.

"Indeed, my dear," Judea mocked. "And you're deep in it, I'm afraid."

"What the hell do you think you're doing, Judea?" Brauns replied over the communicator.

"You tell me, Commander." He chuckled. "I mean did you really think we weren't noticing your every move? Why do you think most of Command stayed in vessel 1 in space? We're the eye in the sky, watching all of you scurry like ants."

"That's what I never liked about you higher-ups. You look down on us like you're God, and we're the ones invading *your* world. It's *our* world! You self-absorbed pricks." Brauns was usually levelheaded and occasionally frustrated, but this time, he sounded livid.

"Oh my, someone's true colors are showing," Judea teased.

"You're one to talk. Tell me! How long did you know?"

"For some time now, actually. Why do you think I tagged along that day when you *personally* sought to Xander's debriefing with Valeria? You pretended to dislike him before then for appearances, but we knew something was up." Judea giggled. It's like he couldn't help but laugh at how cruel he was being. I was starting to wonder if he was possessed himself. "The newest confidant you recruited, Bridgett, was there too. I know you both had exceptional rooks you tried to make sure were prepared, so it did make sense. Though, it was still a stretch. Standard officials *were* doing debriefs for missions at that time while commanders were coordinating strategies."

"We thought the military freed us," I said, interrupting their heated exchange. "Are you saying we just fell into another form of control?"

"Oh, yes! Since the very beginning." Dread ran through my veins as Judea continued speaking. "We like doing things subtly behind the scenes. It's easier for people to accept change that way." Valeria and Joselyn looked sick to their stomach.

"You mean hiding your true intentions and lying," Brauns said.

"Precisely!" Judea spoke as if none of what he was divulging was a big deal. "You see, resistance is messy and causes complications. It's better to avoid it. First, we tried manipulating people to forget their past, but the process of erasing memory became intricate. Erase too much and it starts messing with other things like cognitive functions. Plus, we had some persistent people like you and Commander Heisen, among others, catching onto us when you were all in pods. So we only got to most of the veterans from the old war."

So Brauns wasn't the only one back then who suspected foul play, I thought. I wondered who else could be on our side.

"Next, we tried to naturally weed out the ones who would potentially stop us by continuing with the stasis program as planned, and hone in on those individuals. After all, we were all on ships together. If a battle ensued on board and damaged the vessel, we'd be stuck in space, waiting out our inevitable death as well." He loved hearing himself talk, freaking narcissist. "It took suspicion off of us while biding our time to get rid of those pests. But then, excavation had to find the holy grail of all relics. Ugh…"

I listened intently.

"We tried to shut down the idea of an expedition for it, but no… Brauns *persisted*!" I heard the hiss seethe through his teeth like a snake as he said "persisted." "Then lo and behold, Xander's team managed to retrieve it with only three squad mates by *some* miracle!"

Joselyn and I stared at each other, realizing the success of our mission was more pivotal than we thought. I then glanced at Valeria, remembering Henry's sacrifice.

"We thought your hope would be snuffed out after being annihilated on the mission to get the generator working for the force field, powered by that relic. However, a punk kid from Leona's squad suggested to kick the jammed lever!" He laughed hysterically. "And by some dumb luck, it worked."

"Huh…" I uttered. "You're speaking as if you didn't expect anyone to work that lever." Valeria perked up, listening to me. Then, it hit me. "Did one of you higher-ups jam that lever before the mission began?"

"You always did catch on fast, Xander. I see why Brauns took a shine to you, as well as Burrel."

He knows about Burrel too?

"What? I thought that Harper guy was responsible," Valeria said. "You son of a bitch! Are you telling us Hunter didn't have to die?" Joselyn tried to calm her down. Leona and I sympathized with her pain.

A static sound could be heard, indicating another channel patching in. "You're all sick!" Burrel chimed in. "Is there no level you'd stoop to?"

"Ah, Burrel. Nice of you to join the party. It's about time you stopped hiding your involvement in all this." Judea spoke so smugly. "And as I told your commander, little girl, everything is calculated and quantified. I do have to thank Leona, though." We all stared at Leona in question. For a brief moment, I thought she betrayed us, but she looked confused as we were. "She gave us the opportunity to truly test the limits of demonic possession through Walker. We're close to controlling it. You're about to see in any moment now."

We heard something outside break the sound barrier. We peered through a glassless window frame and spotted one of the pods we used to use for deployments in space descend through our atmosphere.

"There's no controlling this supernatural phenomenon," Imala said through Brauns's channel. "R&D, my department, has tried to understand it and couldn't."

"Hmm… I wonder about that. At any rate, we get to test our project and eliminate you pests too, killing two birds with one stone."

"Why are you doing all this?" Brauns asked. "What's the point?"

"Ah, ah, ah… Confidential information is not for traitors to know." He let out an eerie cackle before he cut his channel.

"Burrel, don't! It's a prototype," I heard Imala say in the background of Brauns's channel. I barely made out what she said. Then, his channel cut off.

And just like that, right when we felt like we were making progress in reclaiming our world, it was like we were back to square one. I looked down at my hand that pressed on Leona's abdomen through her suit. It was stained a dark red. Her face was pale as she took slow, steady breaths. Joselyn was too in shock to act or say anything. She was staring off in space, holding Valeria close. Valeria's eyes were red and puffy from crying. She eyed the survivors staring at us who I almost forgot were with us. They heard everything. I scanned the room and saw shocked, confused, worried, and hopeless faces. The images of their expressions burned a hole through my very being. I didn't know what to say as we stood in silence.

Chris looked at Valeria. For the first time, I saw empathy from him. "I told you, girl. People are selfish."

Margaret's glint of hope disintegrated into disappointment.

Boom!

Suddenly, a crash came from the road outside. Static invaded our eardrums again.

"Leona, can you hear me now?" Arinya asked. "What was that static interference from earlier?"

"Huh? Are you telling me you heard none of what Judea said?" Leana asked.

"Judea? Ambassador Judea? No. I wasn't even aware he was on a channel. Mine was briefly cut off."

How convenient, I thought.

Rawr!

A deep, guttural, inhumane growl was coming from the road. Joselyn peered outside. "You have *got* to be kidding me…"

Bang! Bang! Bang!

Something powerful and loud echoed outside. "What is it?" I asked.

"I think some type of demon is trying to break through that pod," Joselyn replied.

"Go ahead. I'll hold it," Leona said to me, placing her hand over mine that was holding the makeshift bandage fabric.

I pressed my hands tightly against hers while touching my forehead to her suit's helmet. "We're going to figure something out, okay?"

She weakly nodded. I looked out the window and terror ran through my spine as I saw a person break through the heavily fortified pod. I wondered if I could even call it a person. Its face was full of black lines, along with grotesque black veins coursing through its body. Despite underwear, the possessed man was naked. But there was something different about it than other possessed people we came across. Its bones shifted within its body, moving in eerie positions, not possible for a human. Its diaphragm was convulsing. Perhaps the most disgusting of it all was its face. The skin on it was constantly moving, and I briefly caught outlines of what seemed to be other features of faces. It was as if there were multiple beings in him, trying to tear out of his body.

"Leona, you might want to check this out," I said, jaw dropped.

"Oh my word," Chris said, staring through the doorless entrance of the building. "What on Earth is that?"

Leona patched through to her communicator. "Arinya, do you have eyes on the target? You see what they're seeing?"

The drone uncloaked itself. Some of the survivors in the crowd were taken back, not knowing we had tech to that capacity still. As it hovered overhead next to the unknown demon, Arinya's next words shook us to our core.

"Th-that can't be... Wh-what the hell is going on?!"

"Arinya, listen!" Leona said, trying to keep it together. "A lot of crap just happened, and your drone is all the support we got right now. I'll explain everything later if I get the chance, but tell us what that is. You seem to know, and we need to know what we're up against."

"I-it's him. It's Heisen... It's Commander Heisen!"

All of us were speechless. Goosebumps morphed my skin, pressing against the inner linings of my exo-suit. Everyone at base wondered what happened to Commander Heisen. Now we knew. This was a direct message from Command. They made him an example—a statement saying, "If you cross us, this is your fate." If they were capable of going to these lengths to satisfy their own end, then that changed the entire landscape of the war. We weren't only fighting demons now, but also human monsters without any sense of remorse.

CHAPTER 33

"IS HE STANDING on the sigil we made?" Margaret said, amazed.

"Yep. Not a damn thing is happenin' to him," Chris replied.

"What did they do to him up there in vessel 1?" I rhetorically asked. "From the looks of it, I think his body is a host for a bunch of those things… His strength is probably on another level."

"Fuck…" Joselyn choked out.

"I don't get it," Valeria said, freaking out at the sight of Heisen. "If they were against us the whole time, then why do the R&D meeting and other things for us?"

"Textbook manipulation," Leona managed to say through her pain.

"What?"

"In other words, standard mind control," Joselyn explained for her. "They tell us what we want to hear to get our guards down, all the while, betraying us when our backs are turned. Perfect control."

Valeria balled her fists in anger and fear. "There has to be something we can do! This can't be the end."

"The hell it is," Leona said. "Not while I'm leader of this squad." She armed the gauntlet of her Juggernaut. Relic energy laced the lining of the fist. I wondered what she was doing. Before I knew it, she used the heat off of the gauntlet and pressed her balled fist against her wound to cauterize it. "Ahhh!"

"Leona, you shouldn't be—" Joselyn tried to tend to her, but she brushed her off.

"Don't, Joss!" Leona commanded. "Look at them!" All the survivors were worried and scared. I even saw a hint of it in Chris. "Our military did this... *We* did this!"

"But we didn't know..." Valeria hesitantly said.

"Not an excuse!" Leona mustered all the strength she could and slowly stood again. "We have to make this right." She witnessed Heisen's possessed state for the first time through the window frame and glared at him intensely. It was lashing out at structures and objects on the road, barely able to contain its destructive malice. If we didn't do something soon, he'd probably tear down the building we were in and what was left of the city.

"We'll help you," Margaret said. "After all, we hold up here now. We can't have it fall apart."

"No," I instantly intervened. They stared at me as if I was insane. I remembered Leona's words from way back as I examined their frightened expressions, especially the children's.

I know you're new to this whole soldier thing, but we have to put on a brave face in front of people. No matter how you're feeling, they look at us to get the job done. We represent the hope of the cause, Xander. Understand?

Watching Leona fight all those times gave me the strength to stand by those words. "It's our job as soldiers to protect our people from foreign threats," I continued. "People before us may have failed in that aspect, but that doesn't mean we have to."

I walked toward Leona, who was standing on the sidewalk near the entrance of the building, ready to fight. She smiled proudly at me as we both knew what the right thing was to do.

Margaret looked like she wanted to stop us, but Chris held her back. "Maggie, we have kids with us. Teaching them to fight small demons was already extremely dangerous. I know you always want to help, but this... We can't risk it."

"But I didn't have our people save 'em just so they could die! I have enough on my conscience."

"Hey, not to sound heartless, but let them do what the military signed them up to do." He looked toward me, touching his cross and nodded in our favor. "Protect us." I nodded back, acknowledging his restored faith, even if it was just a little.

"Go now and hide! We'll take care of this," Leona ordered them. They quickly opened a hatch I didn't notice before. They went to some type of underground shaft a few at a time. That must've been where their bunker was.

"Are you two crazy?!" Joselyn shouted. "That was a nice show you put on, but we're not equipped to handle this either. We're going to die!"

"We were dead as soon as we joined the cause," I replied, smirking to her confidently. She stared at Leona and me in utter disbelief. "What happened to your sarcasm? You usually make light of these types of situations."

"I…uh…" She wanted to say something, but seeing how determined we were, she knew no words would reach us.

"Xander's right. If we're going out, then we're going to make a difference doing it," Leona said.

We deeply looked into one another's eyes, bracing ourselves for the fight ahead. Part of me couldn't believe it. I was finally standing next to Leona on the battlefield. It was the one thing I wanted ever since we reconnected on vessel 7. Knowing that my hard work and faith weren't all for nothing was an achievement in and of itself. Being able to face an enemy side by side with the one I loved was all the peace I needed before death.

"I'm with you," Valeria said, standing behind us. She wiped the last traces of her tears.

"Val? Have you gone insane too?" Joselyn questioned.

"There's no way I'm dying without a fight, knowing Henry's and Hunter's death could have all been for nothing! This is mierda!" she shouted at Joselyn with such ferocity. Anger, love, and loss fueled her fighting spirit. "If I can still make their sacrifices mean something, then that's what I'm going to do."

Joselyn was utterly shocked we still had the will to keep fighting against all odds. Leona, Valeria, and I examined the possessed Heisen. He jerked his head to us, aware of our presence. We instinctively put our faceplates on and prepared ourselves.

"Joss, I get that this is a lot, but make up your mind now." Leona stayed focused on Heisen's movements. "I don't blame you for losing your nerve, but if you're not going to fight, then get out of harm's way."

Joselyn scoffed at Leona's comment. Her confidence returned as her fear dissipated. I guess Leona got to her. "Lost my nerve? Did you two forget what I did?" We exchanged glances, confused at first by her comment. "Just because you got Val to lose her sanity along with you doesn't mean you get to underestimate me." She rose to her feet with a new sense of determination. "Don't forget that I was the one who helped Xander make his way back to you after his first deployment, and I'm on equal footing with you as an Alpha too. Bonds we formed like the one I lost won't be in vain again, not while I still draw breath."

Joselyn took her place by our side as all four of us stood armed and ready against the enemy.

"About time you stood with us," Leona egged on. She was oddly content in this grim situation. So was I, getting to fight next to those I cared about.

"We never did settle our sparring matches when I was in rehab," Joselyn teased.

"Well, I was going easy on you."

"And I was handicapped."

They chuckled at their little commentary as Heisen lunged straight for us. We dodged out of the way. A crater formed on the ground from where he punched.

"Not good," Valeria commented through the communicator.

It snapped its neck toward Valeria's direction. Her eyes widened. I took a shot with my relic gun at the nape of its neck, but no effect. The blast made him jerk his head toward me now. He sprinted full throttle with insane speed. The momentum alone caused its own draft and dust to pick up near him.

"Xander! Catch!" Joselyn threw one of the Barricade shields we left on the ground earlier to me.

I caught it and braced myself for this demon's impact. Unlike the other demons, when it made an impact with the shield, nothing happened. Heisen's possessed state thrusted his shoulder through my guard and broke the shield. I was blown back a few feet from it. Just when it was about to follow up, Leona rammed her Juggernaut suit into it. The unexpected attack pushed it back a little.

"On your feet. We got this!" Leona shouted to me, getting the mini turrets on her wrist ready to fire.

As I stood, Valeria and Joselyn stood next to Leona as they hailed down a barrage of relic shots to Heisen. I joined in and started shooting too.

"Hmph!" Heisen grunted as he outstretched his hand.

"Damn it. Telekinesis," Leona said.

We all braced ourselves for it, but nothing could've prepared us for the sheer magnitude of force coming from just the motion of his hand. Resisting it was useless. We were blown away, crashing right into cars and buildings behind us. Glass windows shattered on top of me after I slammed into a truck. Parts of my exo-suit were dented. There were body parts aching I didn't know I had.

"Ah! The hell with it!" Joselyn had her shield equipped before being sent into the corner of a building. She managed to get up from some of the rubble and charge straight toward Heisen. She shot her relic gun in one hand while shielding herself against objects Heisen threw with his telekinesis with the other.

"Joselyn!" Valeria screeched, while sunk in the indent of the hood of a car.

"Back me up, Val!"

Valeria dusted herself off and used her sniper shots from her wrist against its head. As she approached him, her other hand was equipped with a relic gun, attached to her suit, that looked like a shorthanded pistol. It steadily chipped away at other parts of its body. Leona and I glanced at each other and followed in suit. Before Valeria and Joselyn could get close, the demon used its ability like a repulsion. The force was so strong we saw a kind of translucent force blow away debris and objects from it, using its body as the epicenter. It blew Joselyn and Valeria back.

Leona and I kept pushing forward. I scraped up another Barricade shield on the ground and threw it to Leona. However, it switched its repulsion to attraction. I felt myself being tugged toward it. Like the fight she had with Harper, she purposely let herself be pulled by the attraction. I held onto a jutted out crack in the pavement for dear life. She rammed her shield into Heisen, causing him to stop the ability. Then, she used the impact of her gauntlet and banged it on the back of the shield. The shockwave created by the sound dazed him for a bit. She was always able to think quickly on her feet. It gave me the opening to come behind and slice his throat with the shorthand saber.

As I saw the flesh from his neck separate from his head, for a split second, I saw the real Heisen. His eyes were misty, full of grief. I stopped in my tracks as he uttered, "End my life. Please!" It was in the demon's reverb rather than his own voice. Talking after slicing his throat should've been impossible either way. The way demons manipulated the human body was surreal. A tear streamed down his face, full of wounds. We put so many cuts and holes in him, he was barely recognizable. It made me think back when I saw Harper in his animated state after the R&D meeting. He was in pain too. Even the demon inside of him said he was feeling every strike inflicted on his body. I'll never forget the first possessed guy I slayed in the Infiltrator on my first deployment. I wonder how much pain he endured before I ended it. Humanity was suffering more than anyone could possibly fathom.

Suddenly, as his body was falling to the ground, it stopped itself. The way it returned to its upright position was impossible. All of its wounds healed right in front of our eyes. The demon waved its finger and shook its head, mocking our attempts. It levitated all of us from the ground by our necks by some invisible force. It was like invisible hands were clenching my throat. He didn't even out stretch his arms like last time and probably never needed to. We realized we were just being toyed with like Walker did with Leona and Chrissy.

"Choke on your own fragility," he said in a demonic voice.

"Flares…" Leona managed to gasp.

We instinctively knew what she meant and equipped our relic flares to us. Surprisingly, it was able to loosen the invisible grip as we landed back on the pavement.

"Thanks, Chrissy," Leona said in a low voice, trying to catch her breath, "for pioneering this idea. You and the others we've lost can't be in vain…"

"No matter," Heisen uttered. His voice sent eerie chills through my veins each time. "Your relic flares may cancel out our tricks, but we can still pummel all of you with our bare hands."

Leona didn't respond. She charged ahead, and we followed. Attempt after attempt proved pointless. I tried an attack with Joselyn but failed. Leona and Valeria combined their rapid fire, but fell short. We tried rushing him together but got pounded into the pavement. No matter what we did, every tactic failed. He licked his lips as if savoring every satisfying moment he had torturing us. His body was still creepily convulsing, as if trying to break out from inside its shell. We struggled to get to our feet again, although we had nothing left to throw at him. Most of our relic energy in our suits ran out. I only had one shot left. Their faceplates immediately retracted due to loss of power.

I tasted iron in my mouth and discovered it was full of blood. Valeria was so exhausted from fighting, she vomited. It reminded me of when Joselyn vomited on our first deployment when we landed. She, herself, has come a long way since then. Leona and her still stood, ready for the next attack, although they had nothing left in their tank. I thought we got the worst of his beating. However, I was wrong as we watched in awe as he lifted an eighteen wheeler diesel truck.

"No way…" Joselyn commented.

"What's the plan now?" Valeria asked, dusting herself off. "Leona? Xander?"

We were both speechless. Neither of us knew what to do at this point.

"Die!" Heisen said, getting ready to throw it. I shot at the tank full of gas before he got the chance to hurl it our way. The heat from my relic shot instantly ignited the fuel and exploded, leaving him a scorched corpse under it.

"Good going, Xander." Leona leaned against me, thinking we could finally be at ease.

However, our hope soon turned into despair as we witnessed Heisen's burning flesh emerge from the fire.

"That's impossible…" Valeria uttered nervously.

"I don't think that word applies to the world we're in anymore," Joselyn said, defeated.

We continued watching in horror as pieces of its flesh melted and fell to the road. There was no longer any semblance of Heisen left. After most of its flesh was singed, a walking skeleton was left in its wake, along with a black aura surrounding it. Suddenly, I felt my body tremble as the aura first manifested itself into a huge silhouette, breaking what was left of the skeletal body to broken bones. Then, a gust of wind hit us. I thought it was going to turn into a colossal silhouette like we've seen demons do before, but not this time. It had a form and features. It towered over us, making the six-story building it stood next to seem like a mere object by it. I don't know if you could even call it skin, but the membrane acting as it was moist, black, and void of color. Its long limbs were disproportionate from its small torso. I couldn't even look directly at the face. It was sickening. Two faces emerged on either side of its face. It had no lips, only jagged edges that looked to be its teeth. The eye sockets were void of light or soul. I wanted to move, shout, run, do anything besides stand there. I'm sure the others wanted to do the same, but fear had us frozen.

It laughed, looking down at us. "Futile," it said in an even deeper and unworldly voice, "defines your weak species well. You think you can defeat us…" It then looked up to the sky. "They think they can control us…" I wondered if it was referring to the officials in vessel 1 still in space or something more ominous. "But we'll laugh last in the end. You've faced small fry 'til now. The negative energy here fills us." It did some type of ritualistic movement foreign to us, getting a euphoric feeling from the negativity. "There are places much worse and others more powerful."

"No…" I managed to spit out in a defeated tone. I felt a tear stream down my cheek.

"Ahh… You see it now, don't you? How small you are? It's like we said…*futile*."

We dropped to our knees, shaken to our core. Our will to fight vanished. Whatever we saw as reality before was broken.

"Don't kneel. Bow!"

An invisible force pinned our bodies to the road, making us eat dirt. It felt like a ton of pressure was on my back. None of us could move nor say anything. This was really it. Brauns and our allies were probably occupied, trying not to get captured. The higher-ups most likely cut off our communication to Control. Judging by Arinya's last response, she was as surprised as we were about Heisen. She probably didn't know anything about this and was an innocent bystander. A lot more people still on base were perhaps the same way. We were the main soldiers good commanders like Brauns depended on to fight back such oppression, and we failed. That was the one thing I couldn't get out of my head—how much of a failure I was. After living a simple, mediocre life, I finally had a chance to make a difference, and it all ends with me being flattened to death. What was the purpose of that? I shifted my head just enough to be able to look to the heavens.

Tell me…what's the point of this? I thought. *Please, tell me!*

I watched as the thing was about to raise its foot and stomp on us.

"Hey!"

It placed its foot back down, looking at someone. Leona, Joselyn, and Valeria strained to see who it was too. Our eyes widened in shock as we saw a child. It was the little boy from before who asked about the pebble. He was holding it with a cloth. Tears leaked from his eyes like a faucet as he walked past the demon's huge frame and toward us. It grinned, amused at the sight. Snot hung from the boy's nose as he kept sniffling. His body was trembling so bad I could see his clothes shaking from where I was pinned down.

"This will beat the bad one, right?" he asked, staring at us in sheer terror.

I was so paralyzed at the spectacle happening before me, I didn't know how to reply. They really did have some brave children with them—braver than me. All I did was freeze when I saw this colossal monstrosity before me. He walked by it with no hesitation and absolute faith. His mom came rushing out of the building we were in before, trying desperately to retrieve her son. However, Margaret and a few others who came out restrained her.

"Get off me! That's my baby!" the woman cried out.

"It's too late! It'll kill all of us if we don't go back," another member shouted.

"Then go, and leave me with my son!"

The demon stared down at the boy. "Amusing, but you'll be crushed all the same."

"Nooo!" I yelled, straining to get up. It lifted its foot again, ready to stomp. Snaps and cracks emitted from my body. Bones were breaking from me resisting the pressure, but I didn't care. My knee buckled as I jerked my body to move, but I ignored it. Parts of my armor fell to the ground too, but it didn't stop me. I don't know if it was adrenaline, will, or something else, but I couldn't let that kid be in harm's way.

"Xander!" Leona shouted as she witnessed the pain I was in, diving toward him.

I don't care what happens to me, I thought. *Just please spare this boy. Protect this light in him, allowing him to stand up to darkness... God, please!*

I wrapped my body around his, preparing for the inevitable. Fortunately, fate had other plans. When I didn't experience the instant death from being stepped on, I opened my eyes. Standing in front of me was an exo-suit with wings, blocking the stomp from the demon. Its design was sleek, and it had interesting contraptions laced with its armor more complex than our models. However, it didn't seem stable as sparks flew everywhere. Light from relic energy was on every lining of its structure, making it shine. If I didn't know what an exo-suit was, I probably would've mistaken it for some type of angel.

"Back off!" a male's voice shouted. A mini force field surrounded him. The initial activation was so strong that it actually made the huge demon stumble back. "You ugly piece of sh—" He looked back briefly to the boy I still held in my hands. "Eh, you get the gist."

I recognized his voice from anywhere. Relief and surprise replaced my fear as I said, "Burrel?"

The faceplate on Burrel's exo-suit retracted. His expression was at ease yet stern at the same time. "Stand back. This vet is going to show you how it's done."

CHAPTER 34

BURREL DROPPED SOME type of device he was holding. It was about the size of a standard box. "Keep an eye on that for me," he said to me before he flew forward with the exo-suit to face the demon head on.

"Burrel?" Leona questioned, straining to sit up. "Could that really be him?"

Joselyn was able to get to her knees again. "Does this mean I can't say any more old jokes?"

"I'd say so," Valeria replied, trying to catch her breath. "I can't believe he's able to pilot that thing. What is it?"

I recalled something Imala mentioned during the R&D meeting some time back.

The only thing that can topple it is an Arc Light—a previous exo-suit model. However, we only have one prototype left, and it's been decommissioned for some time due to lack of resources to keep it functioning.

Didn't she also say something to Burrel before in the background of Brauns's channel about a prototype? I thought. Perhaps this was it. However, this demon we faced now was more than the giant silhouette we faced before. It had a physical, tangible form. Also, it was more powerful than any other we've ever encountered. Could this Arc Light prototype, barely functioning, really topple this monstrosity? I stared at the kid within my embrace. He was shaking, scared to death. I sure hoped it was enough.

I watched Burrel as he took on that thing. It swiped at him with its elongated arms, but Burrel dodged with an aerial maneuver. "You can't win," the demon said in its eerie voice. "All we see is another insect waiting to be crushed beneath us!"

"Funny," Burrel replied, putting his faceplate back on. "You know how many of your kind I've taken out? I should be saying the same to you." An energy sword, longer than the one I wielded when I piloted the Infiltrator, emerged from the wrist of his exo-suit. He immediately flew toward the crevice of its shoulder and sliced off one of the demon's arms.

"Argh!" it cried out. Some type of black substance spouted it out of its wound instead of blood. I wondered what it was. Before it had time to recover, Burrel did the same thing with the rest of its limbs. "Hahaha!" It let out a deep, menacing laugh. "You've done nothing."

We watched in horror as its limbs started to grow back.

"What is it going to take?" Joselyn said.

"I don't know. We already gave it everything we got," Valeria replied.

"Maybe not." Leona pointed to the kid still in my hands. He held up the pebble to me.

"Here. Use this," he said in his toddler's voice, still shaken.

Burrel descended in the Arc Light next to us. More parts on his suit were sparking. "I flew here as fast I could before it ran out of power, but no matter what, it needs a stronger relic to function to at least part of its capacity."

"So the relic inside that suit can't cut it?" I asked.

"Afraid not. I need to think of something quick before that demon's limbs grow back." Burrel, Joselyn, Valeria, and I observed the demon regenerate as we racked our minds for a way out of this.

Leona, on the other hand, kept her focus on the pebble. "Margaret!" she shouted across the road.

"Yeah?" Margaret said, while still consoling the boy's mom with the others. The demon's giant frame was still in between us and them.

"That pebble the kid brought out… It's the one you were talking about, right? He didn't grab it randomly from the street or something, did he?"

"Yep. Little rascal took it when we were preoccupied and what-not. Why? What're you thinking?"

"Get to safety! If this doesn't pan out, we're all done for."

"Hurry and run to your mom, okay, while the bad one is down," I instructed the boy.

He nodded obediently and waddled over to his mother before I took the pebble from him. Suddenly, the demon tried to swat the kid with the first limb Burrel cut off that grew again part way. Burrel used what looked like a mini cannon from the side of his suit and shot it away. "I told you to back off."

"Grrr..." The demon growled in response.

"Xander, you know what I'm thinking, right?" Leona asked.

I nodded and then focused my attention to Burrel. "You know the hatch that houses the relic in our suits? You wouldn't happen to have the admin key, would you?"

"Nope, but I never needed it," Burrel replied confidently. "I know how to access the emergency override. It was placed just in case there was a negative response to a relic, affecting the suit."

"Is that possible?"

"Remember the R&D meeting when Thomas said not all relics are good? How do you think they know that? Inventions aren't per-fected until trial and error," he said. I briefly wondered what experi-ments past engineers, scientists, and researchers did to give us these weapons to use against the enemy today. Burrel opened the hatch with ease that had the current relic in it. It was some type of dated carved piece I couldn't make heads or tails of. "One of the perks of being a spy." He let out his hand so I could give him the replacement. "I'm guessing you're going to give me the one in your suit?"

"Nah, I'm spent. I may have something better, though." I gave him the pebble.

"A pebble? Seriously?" He looked perplexed.

"We've trusted you all this time, right? Then...trust us now."

Burrel looked over to Leona who agreed with me. Joselyn and Valeria looked on, waiting to see if the relic would actually work. I'd be lying if I said I didn't have my doubts too, but sometimes you have to cling to hope even when there's no reason to.

"We will enjoy breaking your bones and tearing your flesh!" the demon yelled as it tried to get up with its limbs that were growing back.

Burrel immediately put the pebble into the hatch. "All right. If I don't make it..." He put his hand on my shoulder. It seemed like he was about to say something else to me, but changed his mind. "Tell Joss she's a pain in the ass."

"I heard that!" Joselyn said. Even while bruised, beaten, and broken, she had enough energy to retort.

"Judging by the way the power is routed through the suit, those cannons on your sides are the strongest in your arsenal to finish this, aren't they?" I asked.

"Fingers crossed." He ascended into the sky, using the jets and wings on the suit. It was still sparking, but it was responding better than last time. The demon unexpectedly used what was intact of its growing limbs to leap off the road and into the sky where Burrel was. I saw Burrel's helmet point toward the sky while in the air before aiming his mini cannons toward it. "Please let this work," I heard him say through what was left of my staticky, damaged communicator. "It's all or nothing."

He stared the demon right in the face as it opened its mouth to consume him. Beams of brilliant light emitted from the cannons, shooting point-blank in the demon's face. It was unbelievable. The demon we fought tooth and nail just to get a dent in was being disintegrated right before our very eyes. The pebble really was a powerful relic to be able to give the suit that much power. It made me curious about its history, but I found myself just relieved that fortune was on our side. Seeing the suit shine its power in the sky reflected our very situation. Although the world was being consumed by darkness, all it took was a spec of light to show us the way again.

"The kid's not around, so I can say it. Take this, you piece of shit!" Burrel shouted as the beams from the cannons continued to rain down on the demon.

"Hahaha!" the demon bellowed. "Futile! We're one of many. You think you've won?" Most of its being disintegrated into ash, except for the last part of its face. "The one you called Heisen...

You wanna know what his last thoughts were?" All our ears perked up before he was completely wiped away. "You all have no idea what you're up against." It said it in Heisen's voice. I couldn't believe it could still mimic it even though his body it inhabited was obliterated. The demon's hysterical laughter echoed through the city before Burrel ended him.

"I can't believe we pulled through," Valeria said, still in shock as Burrel descended.

"Believe it." Burrel's faceplate retracted. Then, he unexpectedly shot the drone following us since the beginning of the mission. The suit was now completely shot. He had to take himself out of it as it wasn't functioning properly.

"Why'd you do that?" I asked.

"After what went down at base, we have to assume we're compromised."

"What do you mean?" Leona asked.

"Well, after that little chat Brauns had with Judea, Command ordered everything on lockdown and made Brauns, as well as his conspirators, public enemy number 1."

"And here I thought this couldn't get any worse," Joselyn added, defeated.

Burrel sighed. "Until we can find a way to meet up with Brauns—assuming he can survive the fight, that is—we're on our own."

"Wait a minute. Brauns is in a suit?" I asked.

Burrel nodded.

"That bad, huh?" Joselyn followed up.

"Yeah. Imala told me over comms. He was on one of the expanded bases while I was on our original one. I rushed over here as soon as I heard Judea's crooked voice."

"Worried about us, old man?" Joselyn teased.

Burrel smirked.

"Hey! Over here!" Margaret shouted. "We'll patch you up in our bunker, but leave your weapons behind, including your suits."

"Leave our suits?" Valeria questioned. "I know we're out of power anyway and this area has markings, but what if the demons find a way to take them?"

"That's true. What's your call, Leona?" Joselyn chimed in.

"I'm not sure. We do need medical attention, but I don't exactly trust those survivors either." Leona, as well as the others, were struggling to stand with all their injuries. I was hurting too. I'm sure it would be a lot worse once the adrenaline settled down.

"I don't know about these survivors, but we won't have to worry about the demons." Burrel took the pebble out of the hatch from the Arc Light with a cloth from the ground the kid left and walked over to the device he carried here.

"What is that by the way?" I asked.

"It's a compact generator. It has the same capabilities as the one that powers the main base now that Leona and so many others fought to defend a while back." He tinkered with the box-looking device before placing the pebble in a slot. "Excavation and R&D have been working together to get resources for new projects to aid in the war. After soldiers made areas safe by implementing seals in the area like Xander did on his mission, it made it safe for excavation to explore. We ended up finding a lot of stuff for this device and the Arc Light."

"But it was still in the prototype stage, Burrel," Leona said. "I briefly heard Imala say that to you through the comms. It could've been one of our only weapons to stop demons like this one."

Burrel gazed at each of us with sincerity. "It very well could have been. No use in crying over spilled milk now. What's done is done."

I know he was too prideful to say it, but I don't think he could bear the thought of losing us. He was more attached than he cared to let on. In hindsight, it probably worked out for the better. If the Arc Light prototype stayed on base, Command would no doubt find a reason to confiscate it. It may be a hunk of junk now, but it still had components worth fixing if we could use it again.

"That should do it." He turned the generator on. To our amazement, it really did work like the one on our main base. A force field of light expanded throughout the abandoned city. Demons we saw from a distance, not wanting to get close to the markings in the area, dissipated. Bodies that were possessed fell to the floor too. "That takes care of the demons, fortifies this area until we can make our next move, and saves the survivors. Anything else I can do for you?" he asked cockily.

Valeria finally let out a smile like usual even if it was a slight one. "Thanks, Burrel. I don't want to think about what would've happened if you didn't show up."

"Yeah, just don't get full of yourself," Joselyn retorted.

"You're welcome," he replied, staring right at Joselyn and rubbing it in.

Leona watched them bicker as she shook her head and laughed. The exhaustion was probably making her hysterical too. "Let's take this crap off. If they wanted to harm us and take our stuff, they had plenty of chances to do it. I say we see what they're about."

"I agree," I said with a half-smile on my face. Despite everything, I think I was just happy we were at least going through this grave situation together. Leona smiled back. I could see the relief in her eyes—the relief that she didn't lose me.

We made our way to the building, approaching the hatch of their underground bunker. Since Burrel had the least injuries, he was walking faster than all of us. It wasn't a sight I was used to. Margaret opened the hatch, knowing we were coming. To our surprise, there was a set of stairs, but they weren't cement covered or made of cheap material. They were decadent. There was dust, sure, but it was clear that whatever was down below wasn't made for ordinary people like us.

"Hold on a second," Joselyn said. We all focused on her. She was studying Burrel. Something was different about him, but then I realized he didn't have his cane. He limped slightly but nowhere to the degree of needing the cane. "You can walk?" Valeria widened her eyes after Joselyn asked as she noticed it too.

"Oh yeah… You didn't know?" Burrel asked, scratching his head.

"I thought I told you he could after I informed you all about Brauns's suspicions of the military," I added.

"You said he was spying for Brauns but not that he could walk," Valeria said in disbelief.

"Huh… Must've slipped my mind."

"Slipped your mind?" Joselyn looked as if she would blow a gasket. She looked over to Leona. "Can you believe this?"

Leona first examined Burrel, then glanced at me, and then back to Joselyn. "It is what is," she said, shrugging. She did already know from when Burrel revealed to her he was from the old war before.

"Have you all gone crazy from hysteria? Like what the f—"

"Language! Children are down here," Margaret cut in while leading us down the stairs.

"You got some of these rugrats facing demons and whatnot, and you're worried about my pottymouth? After seeing this crap, their innocence is long gone by now." Margaret ignored her and kept walking us down a hall. Even the walls seemed pristine, minus the dust. Plus, there were actually lights running on electricity, allowing us to see. Joselyn focused her attention back to Burrel. "So what the heck, Burrel?!"

I covered my face with my palm, embarrassed. Leona subtly shook her head. Burrel kind of shrugged her off. Valeria walked a bit faster to catch up with Margaret. "I'm sorry. We're all kind of out of it. She's not usually like that."

"What's she usually like?" Margaret asked.

"Ehrm…" Valeria looked behind her only to witness Joselyn's eyes throwing daggers, daring her to say something bad about her. "So uh…this is surprisingly a nice place," she said with a forceful glee to her words, changing the subject.

"Yeah," I followed up. "How does this place still have power?"

"It runs on a generator originally paid for by rich snobs," Margaret answered. "It can last up to forty years, depending on how we use the power."

We all glanced at each other perplexed. Burrel spoke up. "I'm guessing this was their version of a panic room when sh—" He stopped himself before he cussed like Joselyn. "I mean when dung hit the fan."

Margaret chuckled. "It's okay to talk as you like. She was right. They have lost their innocence. This place is full of colorful vocabulary. Some of the others and myself try to take it down a notch for the lil' ones and protect some of that purity, but they still say what they want anyway." She scoffed. "And about this place being a panic room, you have no idea." She approached a metal door that had some type of metric scan. "It had top-of-the-line kitchens, recreation rooms, bidets—heck, one bedroom is so spacious it could shelter around twenty people." She opened the metal door without using the scanning system. "Oh, and this thing was a pain to get open before we took it. We disabled the security a long time ago. It only worked for them."

"Took it?" Leona questioned.

"That's another story…"

As she opened the door, we were shocked. There were a lot more people down here than we saw helping us on ground level. Men, women, and children were scattered in numerous places around the bunker. I couldn't even tell we were in a bunker due to the spacious rooms. Couples, families, and friends were together, trying to survive. Skin was hanging off some, deprived of nutrients. It reminded me of myself whenever I looked in the mirror back when I was in space. The walls had childish drawings but eerily accompanied with manufactured markings etched on the walls. It suggested that those considered upper class in our society, the ones with money, knew about the demons' weaknesses long before this world went to hell.

"My gosh…" I realized something. "A lot of these people were in the city years ago before the demons attacked, weren't they?"

Margaret solemnly nodded. "Mostly, includin' myself. Havin' all these mouths to feed ain't no walk in the park, I'll tell ya that. It was easier in the beginnin' when the fridges were stocked, but you know how that goes… The snobs hoarded a lot of it, but it eventually ran out."

"How have you been holding up?" Burrel asked.

"Scavenging and trading here and there, but it ain't enough. Believe it or not, this is only about a third of the people we had."

"Lo siento!" Valeria commented. "If we only knew…"

"Like Burrel said before, no use in crying over spilled milk," Joselyn said. "We're here now. That's what matters."

"We did employ that force field," Burrel added.

"It's a start," I said.

Valeria nodded, reassured. "Thanks, Joselyn—I mean, err... Ms. Fairbanks?"

Joselyn chuckled. "You've been through more than most your age. As far as I'm concerned, you're mature enough to be considered an adult. Don't make me sound old like this one over here." She pointed at Burrel. He grunted. "Call me Joss, Val."

Valeria grinned.

"I thought you said no more old jokes," Burrel said.

Joselyn smiled gleefully. "I guess I can't help myself."

Burrel rolled his eyes.

"You mentioned there was something along with the relic you found," Leona intervened, ignoring us and stepping closer to Margaret. We were walking from room to room with eyes on us. "What is it exactly?"

"That's where we're goin' right now. It's with Chris. I think it might answer a lot of your questions as it did for us."

Leona seemed concerned. It was silent for a moment as we continued to follow in agony. My lower back was throbbing, and I felt several of my ribs dislocated. Not to mention, random pain throughout other parts of my body. I had to distract myself from the hurt. I came closer to Burrel.

"So way back when you started training me... Is this what you meant when you said there were so many things I didn't know?"

Burrel looked ahead sternly. "I'm pretty sure we still barely scratched the surface." We listened to him intently. "I think the term *woke* became popular in o'ten maybe eleven.... Hell if I can remember the year." He tittered. "I became woke as an adult, but in the '80s I thought it was a bunch of bull, making up wild conspiracies to blame your problems on something other than yourself. Back when I was a teen, I was brash, stubborn, and hated authority. The world was full of people telling you what to do. I had a habit of drowning them out with music."

"Really? You? The veteran soldier who afterward became a spy for the cause?" I asked, surprised. "Did you rock the emo look too?" Leona and Joselyn snickered.

"We all have our stupid phases when we're younger. It's not until later we figure out we need to find ourselves, our place on this little rock of ours." Burrel glanced over to Valeria. She formed a half-smile, paying heed to those words. She probably empathized with them the most. "When I got the stupid out of my system, I needed a purpose, or I'd isolate myself like Xander over here." He pointed at me with his thumb. I smirked at his comment. We rested at a pair of double doors in a hallway as Margaret stopped in front of them to listen to the rest of Burrel's story. People passed in and out. I recognized some of them with bandages that helped us with the demons from earlier. It must've been their infirmary. "The military gave me that purpose," Burrel continued. "I joined the marines, eventually making it as an aviator. They put clothes on my back, food in my belly, and money in my pocket…they even allowed me to go back to school. All I had to do was protect people—my country from enemies trying to harm them. Best believe I straightened up real quick."

"What made you suspect something wasn't right then? When was your epiphany about the world?" Leona asked, holding her abdomen. She probably related to Burrel the most, seeing as she joined the army at a young age.

"During the draft. You know that Selective Service thing men have to sign when they're eighteen, or they basically can't do anything in this country except live with their parents?"

"Yeah, when I signed mine, I thought it was unfair," I said. "Men had to die for the government's wars at a moment's notice? What kind of twisted and sexist crap was that?" Leona, Valeria, Joselyn, and Margaret glared at me. "No offense."

"I don't think you want to play the sexist card here," Joselyn replied.

"Yeah, after years of male oppression, you should let that one go," Margaret chimed in.

"I'm just saying." I defensively put my hands up.

"You see, I didn't even think like that," Burrel continued. "I thought people should be proud to protect their home—the same one that values freedom. Little did I know it was another form of control." He shook his head, disappointed—maybe more at himself than anything. "I should've seen it, but I was one of the soldiers that volunteered. First they said the 'aliens'"—he said it in air quotes—"were on our side. Then, they said they were our enemy. So I signed up to fulfill my purpose and protect the people from them. Propaganda is a son of a bitch!" He couldn't look us in the eye. "Apparently, the aliens were manipulating people and making them speak in tongues. These people were the same ones we labeled conspiracy theorists."

"No...don't tell me," Valeria uttered, putting her hand over her mouth.

Burrel slowly nodded. "We were ordered to take them out on sight, although they didn't exhibit any of the paranormal abilities we see now. The government said the outlandish things they were saying about them were the initial symptoms of the aliens' influence." He nervously rubbed his hands together. "Those people were spouting nonsense to me at the time too. Corrupt leaders within our nation, criminals running the world, mind control experiments... You name it."

My ears perked up as it reminded me of what my brother said to me in one of my memory lapses.

"The one that did it, though—the one that 'woke' me up was a song."

"A song?" Leona asked.

"Yeah... During this time, the world was under martial law. The government said they wanted to stop the spread of the aliens' influence before it started. So we spied on people and raided their homes if they exhibited any of the 'symptoms' as they put it."

"My god..." Joselyn uttered.

"I went into this one home and shot a person down. It didn't even matter who they were or if they had family or not. I blindly followed the hand that fed me. Before I saw the light fade from their eyes, though, they said demons were real, and they manipulated *everything*, including the news, media, and even songs." He chuckled. "Of course, I thought they were batshit crazy. But I still had that habit of listening to my music to drown out the world. You know what I heard this time and I mean *really* listened to?"

We all looked up at him.

"The lyrics. The beat always soothed me, but when I dissected the words, they were satanic and gave praise to dark forces. A sense of clarity began to take root in me. I did my own research, and that's when I started taking these conspiracy theorists' words to heart. I found out everything the government did was connected, to empower these aliens we later discovered were demons for their own selfish means." He was quiet for a moment. "Everything...the music we listened to...what we watched...how we perceived relationships...*everything*, even how we think were influenced by these satanic people in high places. All to turn our world negative and prepare these demons to come."

Everything is connected...

My brother's words rang true in my head. I began to miss him and regret I didn't believe him all that time ago. Margaret seemed angry but understood at the same time. I had no idea the events leading up to the war were already this bad. Civilians who were trying to do the right thing and fight for truth were snuffed out like nothing.

"The government was making us eliminate those who were speaking the truth about them. More soldiers and people like me started to realize things weren't right. Sects within the military began to defect from the commander in chief, joining the people to overthrow the government. That's when the civil war began." I caught a glimpse of his eyes beginning to water. I've never seen Burrel shed a tear before. The guilt he was holding in must've been overwhelming. "I can't tell you how many innocent people were caught in the crossfire of the government's mind games. However, we were so busy fighting amongst ourselves that we failed to focus on the real threat—the demons. After we overthrew the government, the demons capitalized on our divide. And as you saw, there are different levels to them in strength. The silhouettes are of the lowest, but there are invisible ones all around us if we're not protected by markings or relics or of course…" He looked up to the ceiling of the bunker as we knew he was referring to God.

We were surprised. "So we haven't even been fighting the cream of the crop?" I asked.

"Not even close," Margaret added. "Some of the demons we've seen were so horrific, they're beyond words."

"Why do you think the military only deployed us in areas with the least demon activity so far? They don't want people knowing how bleak things *really* look." Burrel paused, regaining his composure. "We fought back with the invention of the exo-suits later, but by the time that happened, the billions of people turned into hundreds of thousands."

"You damn straight!" Chris burst through the doors. We were all startled. Was he listening to everything? "And want to know what happened when the military took over?"

Burrel stared at him a bit confused but stayed silent. Maybe he felt like he should take all the blame.

"Chris, please—" Margaret tried to intervene.

"No! These assholes need to hear this…"

Margaret backed off, seeing Chris seethe with rage.

"You still have that stick, huh?" Joselyn said in her sarcastic tone.

"Shut up! You have no idea… The stasis program was bullshit! If you wanted to fight, then sure…you got in, along with your loved ones. But they mainly took the people they thought served a purpose."

The construction workers, electricians, and others preserved in stasis afterward made sense now. I thought it was for the people, but they planned to rebuild from the start. I narrowed my eyes, confused. *If that were the case, then why wasn't my brother nor mother here?* I thought. I did recall Burrel saying to Brauns I was just an average joe. So there was nothing special about me to be able to join the stasis program. I couldn't see my past self wanting to join the war. After all, I don't ever remember having a desire to be a soldier. Then, I stared at Leona. *Leona's always been the soldier.* My eyes widened as some of the truth started to sink in. *Was I only able to be on vessel 7 because of her?*

"The rest of us were left here to die!" Chris resumed. "We had to fend for ourselves. You want to know what we found in this place?" He turned his attention to Margaret. "Did you tell 'em?"

She shook her head.

"We got a tip from one of the survivin' groups that the rich were down here, livin' it up. Of course, we didn't believe them until we saw it for ourselves. There are bunkers like these set up in every major state!"

We examined the room. I realized why there were wards here. "They were going to let everyone die," I uttered.

Chris nodded. I couldn't imagine what they had to go through to claim this place from the greedy hands of the rich.

"But why?"

"All of your answers are on here!" He shoved a device into Burrel's chest. He took it into his hands. "Now, get out!"

"Chris!" Margaret exclaimed. "They saved our lives."

"Who told you to bring them down here anyway?" I wasn't aware she didn't discuss it with him first. "Does that mean they get a pass?" He clapped slowly and saluted to us mockingly. "Congratulations. You did what you were supposed to do years ago." He focused on Margaret again. "You say they saved our lives? Look around. They took them too!" We all looked down, ashamed. Even though it wasn't our fault, we still fought for an organization willing to subjugate its people like this. "What they did out there is the *least* they can do."

"They're hurt, and it's not like they knew about everything." She looked at us sympathetically. "And I can tell they're still going to be in pain even after their injuries heal."

Chris looked away from her, not wanting to acknowledge the wisdom in her words.

She grabbed his face and made him look into her eyes. "They took a beating within an inch of their lives to protect us, Chris. For God's sake, they even got a force field workin' to keep the demons at bay. Patching them up and sending them on their way is the least *we* can do."

He contemplated for a moment. "Fine, but that's it!" he declared. "If you tell anyone else this place exists and put our people in danger, so help me God, I will hunt you down like the dogs you are." He stormed past us with his cross dangling from side to side against his chest.

"Hey, Chris," I said.

He stopped, narrowing his eyes.

"I get it. Your anger… We can't fix the past, but if it means any-thing for our future, I just wanted to say thank you."

He exhaled, trying to calm down. "I can tell you're a man of faith too, right?"

I nodded.

"Then, you shouldn't be thanking me." He looked down to his cross and continued walking away in the same direction. It's as if he was saying, "You should be thanking Him."

I smirked, realizing no matter how dark things got, there was always hope.

"Leona," Margaret said. "You should go in first. You took a direct hit to the torso and suffered more injuries afterward. Luckily, this place has the best medical supplies, and a few of our survivors were doctors and nurses. They're helping others in there, so you could only go one at a time for now. You should be in good hands."

"I don't—"

"I know you're about to be stubborn and say you're fine for our sake," I cut in, "but please, just go. You've done enough. I don't want to lose you either."

She smiled at me, defeated. "I guess I can't refuse when you say it like that." I hugged her close to my chest, and she kissed me before she headed in. "Okay."

"Smooth," Joselyn teased.

"Give it a rest, would ya?" Burrel said to her. "Stop being your-self for, like, five minutes."

Joselyn playfully gave him a scowl. Valeria chuckled.

"Speaking of," I said, turning my attention to Margaret. "I don't mean to pry, but you and Chris bicker like an old married couple. Have you two…"

"A long time ago," she replied. "No ring or nothin'. We grew apart after all this, barely seein' eye to eye. This craziness we live in now will do that to ya. We're stuck with each other now to survive. But it's the past. No use in stirrin' it up."

"But the past shapes who we are now, and it's not like we're promised a future. If there was anything to mend between you two, wouldn't it be worth it now? In the midst of all this craziness?"

Her eyes drifted to the side, thinking about what I said for a moment. "There's some things I need to tend to around here. If you need anything, just ask around for me, and someone will come get me." She walked away, avoiding my question. They say love is the one emotion that can withstand the test of time. I wondered if that was really true.

"Hey, uh, Joss," Valeria said. Burrel and I focused on them. "I didn't want to say this in front of Leona, but you're closer to her than I am."

"So is Xander and myself," Burrel said.

"Yeah, but I think it's more of a girl talk," Valeria replied. Joselyn raised an eyebrow in question.

"Oh, say no more." Burrel started to walk away from the hallway and into another room.

She grabbed his arm. "No, not like that." She giggled, holding her side in pain as she did it. It probably made the pain worse. "You don't need to leave for this one."

"Okay," Burrel replied, bewildered. I wondered what she wanted to ask.

"I keep staring at Leona's cauterized wound. Back when she defended me from that demon's attack, don't you think it was odd?"

"Well, she does take her role as soldier and squad leader seriously," Joselyn said.

"But it was the way she grabbed me... Like I was this delicate flower that couldn't be harmed. I don't know... Maybe I'm thinking too much into it, but she never did that with anyone else, and it's not like we're close. In fact, sometimes I think she's still mad at me about the way I was with her when we first met." She shook her head. "I'm just being silly, right?"

Joselyn glanced at me first before speaking to Valeria again. She sighed. "Don't tell her I said this, but there was a moment when

Burrel, Xander, myself, and her were in the mess hall of vessel 5. Evan teased Xander and Leona about having a baby."

"I remembered that. It was awkward." I scratched my head, still embarrassed about it.

"No one else noticed, but I saw it. The longing in her eyes when she wiped off the water from her mouth she spat out. When Burrel and Xander stepped away for a bit, I asked her about it."

"What'd she say?" I asked curiously.

"You know her better than anyone. She was tight-lipped about it at first, but she admitted she did wish for that life." She crossed her arms and focused back on Valeria. "The military froze our eggs and gave guys vasectomies while in stasis to make sure pregnancies weren't possible, as you know. Xander is probably the closest thing she can get to a normal life to save her from being alone in this hell, which is why she's so close to him."

"Are you saying she cares for me more than she's letting on?" Valeria asked.

"Yeah, I learned not to take her random cold shoulders to heart. She'll talk to you, sure, but keep her distance at the same time. Don't take offense. She does it with everyone, including me at times." She paused briefly to clear her throat. "I can tell it's more to protect herself from getting close to anyone and then losing them. I was a mom myself, so I know that look of longing. She probably sees you as the child she probably will never have."

"She never expressed that to me," I said. "And she practically tells me everything."

Joselyn rolled her eyes. "Men are so oblivious sometimes… That should tell you that you're the exception and how much she loves you. Not everything has to be put into words. You should be able to tell at times. I mean, be in her shoes for a second, Xander," she replied smugly. "Telling you that would put unnecessary pressure on you and the relationship, especially knowing it's something neither of you can provide for each other, at least right now. The best thing to do would be to keep it to herself so as not to lose you."

"How would she lose me? Where is all this coming from? Women's intuition?" I asked, remembering my mom acting like she knew more about Leona than me.

"Make fun all you want, but it's a real thing. I noticed the way she steals glances at Valeria and then looks at you with that longing in her eyes. Putting all that pressure on one person, seeing them as your whole life, can unintentionally drive them away." She leaned against the wall. "Because of that, don't be surprised if there are things she still hasn't expressed to you. I got a keen eye for this stuff."

Joselyn was spouting similar things my mom was saying in my memories. Even Burrel was agreeing with her. I do recall him warning me about Leona's attachment to me as well. What was the universe trying to tell me?

"Wow..." Valeria said. "I didn't know she possibly saw me that way."

Suddenly, the doors flung open. A gentleman in a white lab coat walked out. "Are you Margaret's strays?" he joked. "Come, we can take another."

We went in one by one until we were all patched up. By the time we left the bunker, it was beginning to be sunrise. Margaret saw us off as we ascended up the stairs to the hatch. "Thank you for everything. Be safe," she said.

"We should be telling you that," Leona replied. "I know Chris doesn't exactly accept us, but if we can help in any way, let us know."

Margaret passed her a walkie-talkie. "It's how we communicate to each other when we're out here scavenging or fighting. Be in touch."

We nodded as she closed the hatch.

"What do we do now?" Valeria asked. She spotted our suits at a distance. "It's not like we can drag them all the way back to base and help Brauns."

"One problem at a time," Burrel said. He pulled out the device. Upon closer inspection, it looked the same as the holographic device he used to communicate with Brauns. "First, let's see what's on this thing."

"Yeah, I'm itching to know too," Joselyn added.

"Hopefully, it can give us the reason why we're going through all this in the first place," I said.

As Burrel placed it on the ground on a nearby hill up the road, we found out it did give us the answers we were looking for. However, it changed our perspectives and our trust beyond what we could have ever predicted.

CHAPTER 35

STANDING ATOP THE hill was a sight in itself. We could see flashes of relic fire from a distance. The vantage point allowed us to somewhat scope out the situation. With all the battles going on between other squads, avoiding the crossfire to get to Brauns would be difficult. If we went through the safe areas we claimed around the base we placed markings on, Command probably had personnel ordered to capture us on sight or worse due to being "traitors." Plus, getting there was another matter entirely since our suits were out of commission. I spotted them standing in the middle of the road in their powered-down neutral states. The scratches, scrapes, and worn-down plating is a lot like how we felt inside. How we managed to survive this deployment with every surprise thrown at us was a mystery to me. After viewing whatever was on this device, getting back to base and helping the others was definitely our first priority.

"Well, here goes," Burrel said, snapping me out of my train of thought. "Ready?"

He panned around each of us. My arms were crossed while my finger was tapping my elbow anxiously. Valeria gulped, getting ready for anything. Joselyn was steadily tapping her foot, waiting for Burrel to activate it. Leona appeared calm, but I could tell she was a bit nervous. She was humming that same tune again like she's done before but very low, almost to a whisper. We all nodded in agreement. Burrel pressed the button to activate it, and a technological light shined all around us. The details it depicted were in greater depth than the hologram Burrel used before when communicating with Brauns. Two Caucasian males in suits were in what looked like a pristine room. Elegant tapestry covered the walls, the furniture was illustrious, old books covered the shelves, and famous paintings added to the ambiance. We took a few steps back to not be in the way of the projector's light. When we had a better picture of what we were looking at, we spotted a desk in the middle of the room, along with two chairs. One of the men was pacing around the room while the other sat in one of the chairs in front of the desk.

"This looks like some secret private meeting," I said. "They record themselves?"

"When I was researching some of what the rich did behind the scenes, they'd record each other for dirt on one another," Burrel replied.

"Why?"

"The stuff they did was basically on the level of a national crime syndicate. A lot of their activities were blatantly against the law." He crossed his arms. "If one of them got caught or tried to rat the others out, they'd use their involvement in dirty deeds as blackmail to stay silent, along with threats to their loved ones or anyone or anything they cared about. It's kind of like their own system of checks and balances but for the rich and corrupt."

"They're disgusting…" Valeria uttered with a sickening face.

"No argument here," Leona said. Joselyn also showed disdain on her face.

The man in the chair began to speak. "You know, when I joined this 'brotherhood,' I didn't think I'd be cleaning up PR's mess."

"You gotta love the perks, though, right?" the other man now standing next to a window said. He grinned deviously while speaking with a British accent.

"Brotherhood?" Valeria questioned, interrupting our focus. "Like Boy Scouts? All they're missing is matching uniforms."

"They practically have on the same suits." Joselyn snickered with Valeria.

"Shh!" Leona hissed.

Valeria and Joselyn went silent as if getting in trouble. I don't know why, but it reminded me of an irresponsible aunt being a bad influence on her niece.

The one with the British accent got out what looked like a glass bottle of scotch. He started pouring his companion a glass within the hologram. "Gabriel, was it? What degree are you?"

"Thirty-first, Arthur," Gabriel answered, taking a sip from the glass.

"Oh!" Arthur said, pouring himself a glass. "You've just gotten into the rabbit hole then? Good. I can speak candidly with you."

"It's not like Alice's story at all, though. Just when I think I know everything there is about what we do, there's always more." He chuckled. "But I don't have to tell you that. You're as high on the rung as any member gets."

"True. A whole new world opens up as a thirty-third." Arthur walked around the room while taking sips of his glass too. "You think you're above the sheep now? Just wait."

I tapped Burrel on the shoulder while observing the hologram. "Are these degrees they're talking about some type of code among the elite?"

"I don't know," Burrel replied. "Maybe they're ranks for whatever cult they're in." I noticed Leona, listening intently.

"It never ceases to amaze me how the gullible masses believe any story we fabricate and feed them," Gabriel resumed on the hologram.

"Well, that's how sheep are. They follow anyone they see as the shepherd. But that's how it goes with the uninitiated." Arthur swirled the drink in his hand, staring out the window.

"Ah, but more people are starting to question this wool we put over their eyes."

Arthur scoffed. "Categorizing them as conspiracy nuts is how we always blew it off…" He shrugged his shoulders. "And it worked!"

We all passed each other uneasy glances.

"Yeah, but after those public scandals, especially one of our own getting caught up in his own private island…" Gabriel paused to gather his thoughts. "We can't sweep it under nor brush it off. You and I both know I'm here right now because your country's prince is tied to those allegations."

My eyes widened in shock, remembering what my brother said about the rich guy who owned his own private island.

"You okay, Xander?" Leona asked, touching my shoulder.

"Yeah…just, uh…missing my brother, that's all."

She was startled by my response.

Arthur's holographic image sighed. "I miss the good ol' days when you could rile up the public and make them go to war with a few speeches and some terrorist threats."

Valeria's mouth gaped open. "How long have they been doing this? They talk about our lives and sacrifices like strategies on a chess-board." We all resonated with her words.

"The big social media conglomerates are working on censoring the people's first amendment online, but political figures not part of our inner circle are getting in the way." Gabriel said this so casually as if it was another day in the office. I couldn't believe the little to no remorse they had. "Until then, we have to deal with this press back-lash. So how do we spin this to make it believable to people before pitching it to our Grand Masters?"

"Oh, please! This is child's play." Arthur took a seat on the opposite side of the desk. "Let the lawyers do what we pay them for while the prince denies all accusations. Evidence is just another tool we can tamper with." It made me wonder how many things they got away with over the years, using their power to corrupt the system. "The real issue is Korea."

Gabriel shot back a confused look. "Korea? I don't think I follow."

Arthur poured Gabriel a second glass. "Take it." He pushed the glass to him, urging him to drink. "You're going to need it after you hear what we really got planned. I'm not really supposed to tell the lower ranks, but since you're thirty-first, there's not much harm in it."

"Do tell." Gabriel grinned.

"Well, you know we orchestrated the virus this year, right?"

"Yeah, it was supposed to be one of our plans for population control, wasn't it?"

Joselyn gasped. "I remember that. Some relatives I knew got affected by it when 2019 was about to end. Then, it boomed every-where in 2020." We were all in shock, realizing how close to home their words were hitting.

Arthur's hologram continued. "Correct. At first, it was doing its job. People died here and there who contracted it. Plus, the quarantine caused unemployment to rise significantly, and some people died, trying to survive on the streets. Things were going smoothly. However, due to the quarantine, the people who stayed indoors caused another baby boom like in 1946."

"Is that what this alien fiasco is about?" Gabriel asked.

"You're sharp. I like that." Arthur deviously grinned again. "You see, the plan is to feed these alien conspiracies and make them real. We introduce them as friendly immigrants. Then, *wham*!" He smacked the back of one of his hands against his palm on the other. "We have them attack when the public's guard is down. Little do they know that they're actually the demons we've been harnessing negative energy with."

I think all of our stomachs dropped to the floor after hearing him utter those words.

"How will the Grand Masters pull that off?" Gabriel replied. "The only demons the public is privy to are of rare cases where they manifest and conjure through pocket dimensions. The people who have claimed to see them are just labeled insane. No one believes them anyway." Gabriel's eyes widened, getting a thought. "Unless our branch sects or cults learned how to manifest more of them through our rituals."

"Even better than that," Arthur said gleefully. "They did it with science. Remember what our nuclear research center right here in Europe is developing?"

Gabriel's jaw nearly dropped. "The particle accelerator! They're going to create a rift between the barrier of our world and the demonic one."

"Bingo!" Arthur pointed at Gabriel like he won the lottery.

"I still don't understand what Korea has to do with this." I noticed Gabriel was trying to follow his train of thought.

"I'm not sure who passed on this information to them, but they know about relics."

"The same ones used during ancient times?"

Arthur nodded. "They are the leading country in robotics. I heard they found a way to harness the raw energy relics have into these armored-like suits people could potentially pilot."

"Are you serious?"

"As a heartbeat. They're working with Japan to potentially pitch the idea to the military to combat this foreign threat. Some of the people within their departments were raised in the ancient ways and know the abilities these 'aliens' are exhibiting are demonic and not extraterrestrial. Word can spread." Arthur chuckled. "It always astonishes me how history repeats itself. People believe the crusades were just men fighting over religion because that's what we put in their textbooks. However, we both know they fought with crosses on their shield and sigils on their armor to combat demons. To think, we could be entering that age again."

"It would throw a wrench in our plans for sure if people knew how to fight them."

"Where's your faith in our doctrine, my brother?" Arthur said this to Gabriel as if he was preaching gospel. The twisted concept of this made me want to punch him in the face, even if he was just a hologram. They wholeheartedly believed in their wicked deeds as if it were religion. "Don't worry. Everything is calculated and controlled. Our one-world government will rule all the powers that be because we are initiated. That's why we have contingencies."

"Please excuse my behavior, Arthur. I didn't mean to sound doubtful toward our mission." Gabriel crossed his legs in his seat uncomfortably now as if he was nervous. So even guys that high up in their rank were afraid to sound disobedient. "Besides, if the public knew exactly who, or rather I should say *what*, was controlling the government behind the scenes, they'd submit to their will like we have."

What did he mean by that? I thought.

"Yes, in their infinite wisdom, should the public find out how to combat the demons, we would play it in our favor. We capitalize on the propaganda of a civil war between the military and its people opposing the government. While they're distracted with that, some of our higher-ups will infiltrate the military right under their noses. As soon as they think the military is on the people's side, our guys take over their command." He laughed hysterically while taking the last sip of scotch in his glass.

"We do what we've always done and hide in plain sight."

"Exactly! We'll let the war between the demons and the public get so bad, we'll take the remaining population to space with the original vessels we constructed for us elite in case of a unified uprising. They'll think we're doing it for a fighting chance, but it would really be to reprogram the minds of the people who are subordinate and comply with our rule. Then, we get rid of the demons and rule this world, using the remaining population as a manageable labor force to serve our needs." He leaned closer to Gabriel from across the desk. "Imagine it... We'd control docile people who wouldn't have the will to stand against us. We'd be gods in the new world."

"Let me get this straight!" Joselyn exclaimed, interrupting our concentration. "They put us through all this shit for a power grab?"

"No... That can't be why. It's too sick to think about," Valeria said.

"This is insane..." Leona added in disbelief. She held her head, not knowing what to make of this.

"So the military and the government *are* one in the same." I looked over to Burrel. "You had an idea that this was their endgame, didn't you?"

Burrel nodded. "Brauns and I had a pretty good idea behind their motive if they were against us. All we needed was proof. I guess we found it."

"But how would we get rid of the demons?" Gabriel's hologram asked, resuming their conversation. "I know there are bunkers below to protect the rich in case of an orchestrated end-of-the-world event."

"Ah, so they told you that much already?" Arthur asked.

"Yes, but the relics we have can only take on the first level of demons—those invisible to the naked eye and the dark shadows that look like silhouettes." He set his empty glass of scotch down. "What about the more problematic ones? The ones that manifest actual physical forms?"

Arthur pulled out something from his desk drawer and held it in his hand. "I was waiting for you to ask that." Whatever he was holding was wrapped in cloth. He unraveled it on his desk to reveal a pebble, the same pebble we used in the generator to make the force field around this city. I examined the others around me. They were attentive now more than ever.

"What is that?" Gabriel observed it, scratching his head.

"It's more powerful than a relic. It's a holy artifact."

Gabriel was speechless at first. He reached to touch the pebble, but Arthur immediately swatted his hand away. Gabriel was startled and confused.

"Don't touch it! It's for your own good. Some of these things are so powerful that when interacting with organic material made from this Earth, it immediately cancels out negative energy." Arthur was very cautious around it. "My guys working for me found it in an archaeological dig. This cloth is man made from synthetic materials. Without it... Well, you know how much negative energy courses through us with all the rituals we've been a part of."

"I'd imagine things like cannibalism and trafficking to harness the negative energy for demons to pass through our world more feasibly wouldn't be considered 'holy,'" Gabriel said sarcastically. "What's so special about that pebble anyway?"

"When they first found it, one of my guys accidentally picked it up with his hands and died a day later. It could've been pure coincidence but considering where it was found and what our instruments picked up, there were no more doubts." Arthur cockily leaned back in his chair. "The positive energy on this thing was off the charts. Are you familiar with the Philistine warrior from Gath? He was taken out from it by a simple man of faith."

"David and Goliath..." I uttered the same time Gabriel's hologram did.

Arthur's image eerily sneered back right before the hologram cut out. The circuitry began to malfunction. Burrel started banging on it.

"Easy, Burrel," Joselyn said. "That thing does have some years on it. It probably ran out of juice."

"No! There has to be more information we can dig up. There has to—" Joselyn comforted him by patting him on the shoulder. Burrel put the device down. He stayed on his knees as if defeated. It was the first time I've seen them interact without teasing one another.

"We're out of options, old man. I think it's about time we accepted it."

"Yeah, I'm with Joss," Valeria said. "Besides, I think we learned everything we needed to know and about all I could stomach." She held herself, shaking a little in fear.

I felt goosebumps myself. We stared at one another, realizing what this meant. This war we were fighting *was* spiritual despite whether people believed in God, deities, or some higher power or not. If these elitists had enough wealth and knowledge to believe in it, then it had to be real. Ironically, my faith was reassured with confirmation from people who served darkness. I thought back to my very first mission. The relic I picked up had to be a holy artifact as well. When it escaped my grip from the box and fell to the desert sand, a wave of light extinguished all the demons around me. I wouldn't be alive if that didn't happen. If it was that powerful just by touching Earth's surface, it made me wonder what significant event in history that piece of wood I saw was from.

"This can't be possible... Can it?" Leona asked us.

"Like we learned in the R&D forum, anything is possible now," I replied.

"No...rather anything was possible from the start." Joselyn shifted uncomfortably. "They changed our perception of reality through media and other influences to make us believe it wasn't. While we were distracted by whatever lie they fed us, they worked to control us like puppets in the shadows."

"Xander was right..." Valeria stared down at the floor. Any hope she had seemed to diminish after watching the hologram. "Everything about our past lives were fake. My mom, dad, and brother arguing to keep a roof over our head… Bullies I suffered through in school…" She looked each of us in the eyes. "Everything each and every one of us went through… It was all for this? To be slaves to power-hungry pendejos?!"

We all grew silent after hearing Valeria. Our past lives did seem pointless when looking through the bigger scope of things like we were doing now. This situation has been our actual reality ever since we gave up faith and put powers in the normal hands of people. You think humanity would've learned from the times of monarchy, appointing kings and queens to rule over entire lands only to become corrupt eventually. It's the same thing that happened within our government. Even with a system of checks and balances in place, power corrupts even the purest of intentions.

"There was one thing I was hoping this thing would explain," Burrel said, tucking the device away in his pocket.

"What would that be?" Leona asked. "I think we got all the bad news anyone could take for the day."

"Try years," Joselyn added sarcastically.

"It was what Arthur said about programming people—mind control, basically. I thought the plan was to tamper with our memories while we were in stasis. After all, Brauns, myself, and a few others found that out when most of us were in pods. We thwarted those plans." Burrel rubbed his chin. "But by the way he was talking…"

"You think there's something else to it?" I asked.

"I can't put my finger on it, but he spoke as if people were being mentally conditioned already before the stasis program even began. I've heard of military funding rumored to be used for experiments such as mind control by CIA and other private government sects."

"What's your point?" Leona questioned curiously.

"It's a thought I can't shake. If those experiments were successful, then can some of us still be influenced, perhaps by other methods?" Burrel shook his head. "Ah…maybe I'm overthinking it. We should be focusing on how to get out of this mess."

Leona started to hum nervously, trying to think about the next move too. Suddenly, my brother's past words pinged through my head. "Ahh!" I shouted. The amount of pain surging through my head made me fall to my knees. The others rushed to my aid and started shouting at me to see if I was okay.

"Xander! Don't leave me!" They were the last words I heard Leona speak as I held my head before everything went black.

CHAPTER 36

TWILIGHT BROKE THROUGH dark clouds. A missile overhead roared as it hit an area far away. I realized I was reliving another memory as wind from the blow back rushed throughout a city filled with screams. Dust and debris filled my nostrils. I covered my mouth and nose so as to not inhale some of it. Glass shattered from the buildings I stood next to. People standing close to them got cut or worse from the shards that rained down.

"Xander! Grab my hand!" My mom shouted. I grabbed it while my brother, Sam, was right next to her, holding onto the other one. Sam's other hand was holding his wife's, Nadima.

"Was that some type of nuke on the next town over?" Sam asked. "Is that going to happen to us?" I could barely hear him over the panicked noises coming from people around us.

Nadima spoke through tired pants. She was doing her best to keep up with her protruding belly. "Although I'm a second-generation Arab American, my grandfather always warned me about trusting this country... He said America's crime and government were like two ends of the same snake."

"I agree with him. Look at the state our nation is in. I wouldn't be surprised if the powers that be orchestrated this whole thing."

"I don't know about that," I said amongst the disarray. "But this city hasn't been taken over by those monsters yet. We still have a chance."

"Your brother's right. Now is not the time for you two's wild ideas," my mom said, scolding Sam and Nadima. She examined the people and destruction around us. "I can't believe it's gotten this bad. Lord, help us!" my mom said as we approached a line made up of military personnel.

They were all in older versions of the Barricade and Infiltrator exo-suit models. I saw some of them from a street over, pushing back the possessed people. A number of them were around the downtown perimeter at a distance, keeping the silhouettes at bay as well.

"You're going too fast, Sammy!" Nadima was panicking. She held onto his hand for dear life.

"Don't leave your wife now, boy!" my mom shouted at Sam. "You know she's carrying your baby too, don't you? I don't need to lose a daughter and a grandchild now."

We made it near the military line and let Nadima catch her breath. Sam stared at us with worry in his eyes. "Sorry, Ma. Sorry, Nadima." He clenched Nadima's hand tight and kissed it.

"Tell your brother to put his head on straight, would you?" Nadima said to me, trying to lighten the mood to our dismal situation.

"I've been trying all my life. You got the ring, so he's your problem now," I teased.

"Speaking of women and our problems..." Sam was scanning the area, looking for someone. "Where's Leona?"

"She said she'd meet us here," I replied.

"I don't see her," my mom said, checking the military group in front of us. "Shouldn't she be here with these soldiers, evacuating people? She *did* volunteer for evacuation."

"Maybe she got programmed," Sam chimed in.

"Sam, really?" I remembered that I started to really question his sanity at this point. "We're fighting for our lives here. You can't give this conspiracy crap a rest for one second?"

"Maybe that's how your brother copes with stress." My mom was petrified and shaking. I knew scolding us was her way of coping too. "We're all on edge right now. Leave him be."

"Don't defend him, Ma. It'll just get worse."

"Seriously, man. You know those mind control experiments they show in spy movies and stuff? It's a real thing." He held Nadima tight while we waited for our turn to speak to the military line other people bombarded. "If you break down the mind far enough, you can control it with code words, melodies, or specific sounds."

"You see what I mean?"

My mom rolled her eyes, ignoring me. They were all getting on my nerves, but as we were on the precipice of the end of the world, I was thankful to be around my family. Despite how crazy they drove me, I loved them all the same. While reliving this memory flare, I got the feeling that's how Leona felt when she saw Joselyn, Burrel, Valeria, other friends, and myself interact with each other.

"Excuse me, sir," Nadima said, approaching one of the military officials. "How much longer do we have to wait for evacuation? I'm pregnant and need to rest in a less-stressful environment right now." She was sweating and nervously talking to the guy in the Barricade exo-suit.

"My apologies, ma'am." The communicator on the suit amplified his voice. "We're having people wait because we're sorting the ones that are part of the cryostasis program."

"The what?" I asked.

"Months ago, you should've gotten an application from the state to join the program. If so, we would've sent you a notification if you were qualified."

"I don't remember getting any type of thing like that."

"Maybe you missed it," he snarked.

"Uhm, excuse me!" Sam interrupted anxiously. "What if we didn't apply? What happens to us then?"

The military official walked away, pretending not to hear my brother.

"Oh, God…" my mom uttered with her hand over her mouth, realizing what that potentially meant.

"Hey!" Sam shouted. "Don't you walk away from me!" He shoved himself through some people to get to him. The surrounding military personnel took notice. "We have families. You can't treat us like this!"

One of the military men punched him while wearing the exo-suit. "Do not cross this line unless we say so! Qualified people only!" he yelled.

"Sammy!" Nadima shouted, rushing to his aid.

I was about to rush to his aid, too, but felt a warm hand tug my arm. "Ma?"

"Your brother and sister-in-law might be right. These people might actually be two ends of the same snake."

"Whether that's true or not, does that mean we should give up on trying to live?" I asked among the ruckus.

"I keep thinking about that Noah thing you said for some reason." She looked toward the military fighting the demons off from the distance. "I think I see God's plan too now, but this time, maybe we're not supposed to get on the ark."

Nadima and Sam made their way back to us. Sam's nose was bleeding. We took a few steps away from the angry mob the crowd became so Nadima could tend to Sam. She began murmuring a prayer while clenching him tight. My heart began to break seeing my brother and his wife in such distress.

"What do you want us to do, Ma? Surrender to the enemy?"

"No, Xander. Surrender to God. Maybe this is supposed to be our end."

I shook my head, refusing to believe it. "Please, don't talk like this. You know we already lost Dad..." I choked up for a second. "We can go with the military and find a way to live."

"You mean exist," my mother refuted. "Let's face it. We've all had our suspicions about those in power. We just denied it and looked the other way. But we all know power corrupts. How they've treated us then and now is proof of that. Your brother has been one of the few to speak the truth, no matter how ridiculous it sounds. He's saying the same thing we're thinking."

I stared at Sam as he listened to us, dazed. I was hoping he didn't have a concussion.

"Call me crazy too, but I have a bad feeling. We're fighting monsters *with* monsters, Xander! Both sides are corrupt."

"Your intuition again, huh?"

She nodded at my remark. "If we join them, we'd be fighting with that corruption, and in turn, lose ourselves in it. I've heard of facilities giving out lethal injections. Wouldn't you rather die together with family than lose each other to this chaos?"

"I…"

"Xander!" Suddenly, I heard a familiar voice call my name. I looked up to see those green irises, staring back at me in the Infiltrator suit. The faceplate was retracted.

"Leona?!" I said, surprised. "Come on! She's here. We'll definitely get in."

I caught a glimpse of my mom with a somewhat disappointed look as she released my arm. Nadima and Sam helped each other up and urged my mom to follow me. We reached the military line again. I hugged Leona as tight as I could, although the armor pieces from the exo-suit hurt me a little as it dug into my skin. Surprisingly, the military officials didn't stop me when I went over the line. I gestured over to my family that it was okay to cross. I smiled at Leona, relieved to see her. However, when she stared back at me, I saw a hint of contempt.

"None of you are registered with our stasis program." A military personnel prevented them from crossing. "There are only limited spots available. I'm afraid you cannot pass."

"What?" my mom asked frantically. "Then why is my son allowed to cross?"

"His registration now checks out."

My mom, Sam, Nadima, and I stared at each other blankly. "How? When?" I asked, confused.

"It's okay, Xander," I heard Leona say in my ear. "I'll find a way to get them on. Stay on one of the transport vehicles until I can figure this out."

I immediately jerked away from her. "What are you talking about? I-I can't just leave my family."

"You're not leaving them. I'm finding a way!"

"Okay. Until you do, I'm staying with them."

Her mouth gaped open at me as if I made her heart sink. "These things are close to surrounding us. You'd be in more danger the longer you're out here."

"I'll take that risk then until you can get all of us out of here."

"So you're going to give up with them and possibly die? Xan—"

"They're my *family*, Leona!" I said with authority. My mom, Sam, and Nadima were watching us, along with a handful of surrounding people.

Leona looked as if I was ripping her heart out of her chest. "I thought I was your family too…"

I shook my head, not knowing how to respond to her. I started to walk away.

"Xander! Don't leave me!" She screamed the same words at me in this moment as she did before I blacked out to this memory.

Then, out of nowhere, I heard the word I'd never forget, "Swarm!" one of the military guys shouted. Suddenly, some type of electrical barrier surrounded those on the other side of the military line, including myself and Leona. It must've been laced with relic energy to protect those registered for the stasis program. A swarm of silhouettes blacked out the twilight amidst the clouds. I'll never forget the sickening sounds of flesh getting scraped apart by those things as they cut the crowd on the other side of the line into pieces. Leona and I stood with silent, horrified expressions as what was left of my family was gone on the cold pavement of the road.

* * * * *

A white haze surrounded my vision. Hot drops of liquid fell on my face. I could see Burrel, Joselyn, and Valeria, examining me with concern. My head was being rocked in Leona's bosom.

Hmmm… Hmmm… Hmmm…

I heard the hum again. It was the same one all this time—the same habit she had. It was the same melody I woke up to on the day of my first deployment. Everything made sense to me now. My own intuition was trying to tell me something, but I wouldn't listen. I was blinded by her love. The little changes in moods, the offhanded gestures, and the feeling that she was keeping something from me that I chose to ignore. Every hint was trying to tell me something. Everyone's words echoed like a drum in my head, including Leona's.

When we do remember everything, will that break us apart, or will it strengthen what we already have...

Your significant other should never replace your life, only become part of it. Until she finds her own solace, she'll only disappoint you, Xander, because she doesn't really know what love is yet...

She's co-dependent on you as she was in the past...

I'm sorry, Xander. I know you did nothing wrong. I just don't want to lose this...

I've heard of military funding rumored to be used for experiments such as mind control by CIA and other private government sects...

If you break down the mind far enough, you can control it with code words, melodies, or specific sounds...

I... I don't want to lose you...

Everything is connected...

I instinctively yanked myself from Leona's grip. They all looked at me perplexed, including Leona.

"Xander, you're okay!" She first said with joy in her voice. Then, she stared at my shocked expression, penetrating her very core. "What's wrong?" Concern plastered her face.

"You've remembered everything since we woke from stasis, haven't you?"

The others passed us a look of shock, not knowing what was happening.

"W-what are you...?" She attempted to get close to embrace me.

"Don't bullshit me!" I exclaimed, putting my hands out in front of me to distance myself from her. "Out of everything, what we have is supposed to be real. Just tell me. How long have they been controlling you, and how much do you know?"

I could tell the others' hearts fell to the pit of their stomach as Leona averted my gaze, ashamed and held herself in contempt as she said, "I never thought it would happen this way."

As soon as I heard those words, I felt the love within me that stirred from the mere sight of her boil into hatred.

CHAPTER 37

"**LET'S JUST ALL** take a breath here," Burrel said, trying to calm us down. "Anxiety and stress are high. There has to be a misunderstanding."

"Yeah," Joselyn added. "I don't know what's going on, but you know what type of person Leona is. Surely there's an explanation. Right, Leona?"

Leona couldn't look her in the eye.

Joselyn gasped.

Valeria was riddled with worry.

"So your memories are fully restored, huh…" Leona managed to say, still avoiding eye contact. "What makes you suspect I know anything?"

"It was your hum. You've been doing it ever since I met you in the past. I'd wake up to that same melody when we lived together before society went away. You never told me where it came from. I had no reason to believe it was nothing more than a habit, but you were so secretive about where you picked it up from…" I paused to gather my thoughts. "Then, something my brother said caught my attention. I admit it's a huge speculation on my part, but he said mind-control techniques could be done by code words, melodies, or specific sounds. And after we woke from stasis, you were humming that same tune again. The only way you can know that melody is if you've had your memories back this whole time. Stop me if I'm wrong."

Leona didn't respond. Burrel and Joselyn stood in shock.

"Xander, this is ridiculous!" Valeria interrupted. "This is Leona we're talking about! The same person who risked her life for other soldiers…the same person who stuck her neck out so we'd have a base on Earth to call home…the same person who checked on Joselyn in the infirmary whenever she could…the same person who shielded me from a demon…the same person who loves us and loves you—"

"Stop!" Leona shouted. Tears streamed down her face as she witnessed our distress. "Just, please stop…"

Valeria gasped and backed away a little, not knowing how to react.

"Judging by your reaction, I'm guessing you knew you were being controlled by Command this whole time. Are the tears even real? Who triggered your programming?" I questioned. I thought back to what Arinya said.

I've been one of the personnel monitoring Leona's battles quite frequently. Just kind of happened that way, I guess…

"Arinya was the main communicator giving you commands on your missions," I resumed. "I suppose she used that same hum to trigger your programming?"

"Despite what you may think right now, it's not that simple. Nothing with the military nor the government actually is. I'm pretty sure she was a proxy—a middle man being manipulated by them too. You heard her reaction when she saw Heisen. She didn't know about him…neither did I."

"Bullshit!"

"I'm telling you the truth, Xander! I didn't know everything."

"So you're telling me you didn't know my family was going to die after you registered me for the stasis program?"

Leona was taken back that I knew.

"Lord, have mercy," Burrel uttered in surprise.

"Oh, God…" Joselyn uttered.

Valeria was speechless.

"Yeah, Burrel, Brauns, and I suspected something was fishy about my suppressed memory as well as how I got into the program in the first place. There was nothing about my life the military would be interested in except for *you*." I pointed directly in her face, fuming with anger. "What did they offer you, hm?"

"Like I said, I never thought it would happen this way... My whole life I suspected I was being manipulated by the military—a pawn on a chessboard. But I didn't care." She scratched her elbow, reminiscing about her past. "I grew up as an orphan, so men and women I served with became my family... Eventually, I'd lose them too, either to battles or when they went back home to their own families. I stayed in the military because I thought as long as I served a purpose bigger than myself, I could be content being alone."

I listened intently with rage still bubbling to the surface. Joselyn and Valeria appeared sympathetic. Burrel kept a steady eye on her.

"But then, I met you. You saw this world for what it was...a fake load of crap! You wanted something real for once you could hold onto and never let go. So did I." She wiped some of the tears from her face. "So when officials told me about the stasis program, a way out through the hell the government put us through, for the first time, I wanted to live and not just exist. But... I wanted to live with you... They said they'd take care of it. I didn't know Sam, Nadima, and your mom were going to be left out!"

"What did you think was going to happen?!" I shouted from the top of my lungs. They all stared at me, surprised. They've never seen me lose my cool like this before. "It was a *de*population program! The less people they boarded on the vessels, the better, especially if they had no use for them. I was their insurance policy for you to join the cause, so you could fight the demons after they took this world for themselves."

"I didn't know!" Leona shouted back. "We literally learned their plan barely over five minutes ago."

"And I'm just supposed to believe you had no idea of the government's true intentions? That you've been keeping the truth about your memory to not lose me?"

"What was I supposed to say, Xander? Huh?! My memories are flooding back, and oh, I accidentally got your family killed."

"So you're saying it's better that I found out now?"

"I just…" She grabbed her head, frustrated. I noticed Valeria's eyes getting red and tearful, seeing us fight. "Ugh… I knew it wouldn't last, but I just wanted to live the fantasy a little longer. You were content with dying with your family. But what about me? After everything we've been through… You didn't even give me a second thought."

"Oh, so that makes it okay?"

"Damn it, Xander! Just because you have faith in God"—she glanced toward the sky and then back to me—"doesn't always make you right."

"How long have you been holding that in, huh? I knew you wanted to say that to me all this time. Does it feel good to finally get it off your chest?"

Leona scoffed at me and shook her head.

"Stop!" Valeria shrieked. She held her ears, trying not to listen to our shouting match. "It's like Mama y Papa all over again." She ran down the hill with the wind blowing the tears from her face. Seeing us must've brought back her trauma of witnessing her own mother and father fight in the past.

Joselyn stared at us for a moment, concerned, before running after her. "Val! Wait!"

I could see the pain Burrel felt for both of us exude from his eyes. "Look, I've known you both for quite a while now. So I don't have to tell you that you're doing this at the worst possible time when everyone is depending on us." He shifted his attention toward Leona. "Now, I don't know what to think about your situation nor this whole mess we're in." He then shifted his focus toward me. "But what I do know is that this doesn't work without trust." He pointed at both of us. "So I'm going to let you two be while I work on getting us out of here. I know emotions are high right now, but please, remember who you are and why we're here in the first place." He walked away from us to sort this out ourselves.

Leona and I stared at each other but not affectionately. There was this intensity between us now, blocking our hearts from connecting again.

"Xander… Listen to me. I'm sorry."

"You're sorry? Tell me then, and I mean honestly. Would you do it again if that meant not losing me?"

She wanted to speak, but I noticed her bottom lip quiver. I knew she wanted to say no, but if she really loved me, she wouldn't lie to me again. So she stayed quiet.

"Unbelievable. Well, thank you for finally being honest."

"Do you really expect someone who loves you to just sit idly by and watch you die?"

"My mom did. She was able to let go and believe that was what fate intended for us. She was happy she'd at least die peacefully with her loved ones at her side."

"Die peacefully? Accepting death without much of a fight is the same thing as suicide! We scolded Val for doing the same thing."

"That was different."

"Was it?" Her eyes started to console me. I stubbornly avoided staring back at them. "You saw their remains like I did. It was a *fucking* massacre. There was nothing peaceful about that!"

"Don't."

"And if that were the case, why didn't you ask me to die with all of you then?"

I avoided her glare, trying to think of the right words. "It was your life, Leona. I had no right to even suggest that to you."

"You chose people you fight with, bicker with, and don't even understand you."

"They were my family, Leona! You never understood that because you never had one in the first place."

Leona gasped. "So there it is…"

"There it is…" I said unapologetically. I felt my eyes become watery.

She wiped a tear from her face. "You knew if you asked me, I would've died with you in a heartbeat." She shrugged her shoulders, trying to wipe away the rest of the tears. "The fact that you didn't do the same for me and at least try to fight by my side… How was I supposed to live with that?"

"I don't know, Leona… People move on every day. You should've done the same."

I could tell I deeply hurt her by how casually I said that. However, I was hurting as much as her as I said it. The reason I never asked her to die with me and my family, whether it be by the demons or lethal injection, was because I loved her too much for her to end her life for me. I was too angry to admit it and let her think otherwise.

"So where does that leave us then, Xander?"

I was silent for a moment, observing her brunette hair flow in the wind and the sun reflect the complexion of her skin I loved so much. And, the green irises staring back at me, allowing me a glimpse into her soul, weighed on my heart. Then, I reached out my hand to hers. Hope appeared for a split second but vanished as soon as the color on her face turned pale, realizing I was holding the wooden ring. "I can't trust you," I uttered.

She withdrew her hand instantly and shook her head, not wanting to take it. I let it drop. The engraving "L†X" stood out from the ground as the wind blew the grass. Sunrise finally hit to signify a new dawn. Our forces were scattered, demons ran rampant throughout our world, and the one love we held onto was gone. I walked away from her, remembering Corinthians 13:13. I wanted to believe in it, but Satan's land drove us apart. I wasn't sure how we were ever going to find our way back.

To be continued...

ABOUT THE AUTHOR

REGINALD ANDAH WAS born and raised in Houston, Texas. At a young age, he had a creative mind and an interest in learning. Both attributes allowed him to obtain a bachelor of arts degree, majoring in English from Texas State University. However, his accomplishment, along with others, could not have come to fruition without faith. Growing up in a low-income household with his mother eventually landed them on the streets. Determined to take care of her only son at the time, his mother had to move from shelter to shelter as employment was difficult. Due to their unfavorable conditions, school and social life was a challenge for him. Though he excelled in academics, moving from district to district made him isolated and an easy target for being antagonized as the new student in his classes.

His teenage years were more troublesome as his mother's mental health started to decline, and he now had a brother. Though times were hard, his faith allowed him to persevere and make a life of his own. Independence was gained through adversity. He supported his family by procuring his own job while going to school. Though he always had a passion for creating, he never thought of potentially making it a career goal. It wasn't until he graduated from high school and took college courses dedicated to writing that he realized his drive for storytelling. Ever since, he has been inspired to create stories with morals centered on his faith in God.

CPSIA information can be obtained
at www.ICGtesting.com
Printed in the USA
BVHW030833251121
622255BV00024B/460/J